a self-destructing bom
drains a shitload of mana.

"It's letting off a lot of heat," said Alani with an uncomfortable frown. "I take it a physical attack is quite painful too, yes?"

"Oh, for sure," Niona confirmed. "The problem is that he moves kinda slow, but if I can make contact then yeah, it ain't pretty for the other person."

Balt said, "Maybe you could add a Speed mod to it when we get to Makanuele."

"If I go with Glom, a Speed mod is probably a necessity." She withdrew the Muggish and returned his card to its slot. "I'll file him under 'Maybe' for now. Despite your harsh words about his appearance."

"He is challenging to look at," said Balt.

"Don't be rude."

"Even if he can't move fast," Balt said, "that raining fire thing can cover a lot of ground. Seems pretty hard to dodge, too. They might be able to avoid a direct hit, but it looks nearly impossible to avoid all that collateral damage. And with all that heat, you could easily burn through a bunch of environmental cover if they try to hide."

Niona agreed with his assessment, nodding along as he spoke. She pulled out a third card and popped it into the kayet.

It was a Scrypto, the same type of Jekua Balt had to face when battling the poacher Reno. Seeing the creature brought back bad memories, and Balt's stomach twisted in knots as he gazed as the beast hovering in the air. Scryptos were strong, though, as he knew all too well.

They could move way faster than a Muggish, too. It joined Glom in the "Maybe" pile.

They went through a few more Thermal-Types. In Niona's vast collection was a Bombat, a Switchtick, a Daritine, and several other Jekuas of varying strength and usefulness. None struck anyone's fancy more than Glom or the Scrypto (whose name was, absurdly, Waistcoat; Niona offered no further elaboration). The Daritine did join the Maybes, but Balt did not think its chances were great.

Next, they moved on to the Elastics. Niona's repertoire of Elastic-Types was nowhere near as impressive as her Thermals. They immediately ruled out Armband, despite the Dullwhip's victory earlier that afternoon. Armband was good enough for some chump on the road, but the fish would be fileted in the tournament.

After summoning a string of duds (including but not limited to a Juntoo, a Yissoon, and a Lonok), she finally conjured up something that might make a decent opponent.

It was a Nuri, a Jekua that dwelled in the mountains of Hurrathsa. Much like a goat, it was covered in shaggy white hair with purple coloring on the ends of the strands. It was a quadruped with long, muscular limbs. Its body was just as bulky as its legs. The Nuri's head looked too small compared to the rest of its body. It had a wet, black snout and beady eyes in between two small, pointy ears. Protruding from its forehead were two long, sharp, spiraling horns.

"This is Garbo," said Niona.

"Lovely name," Alani said.

The Nuri clomped its hooved feet along the pathway. Its muscles visibly rippled underneath its skin with every step. Balt was both grossed out and mesmerized by the display.

Even though Nuris were not detailed in his bestiary, he was slightly more familiar with them than Muggishes. His grandmother had shown off her own Nuri a few times to him and his cousin Wasaaru. Plus, there was a Jekua that lived in Kou Tekkis's mountains called a Hyoi, and in its bestiary entry there was a handwritten note that read "Basically the same as a Nuri."

Niona proceeded to demonstrate some of the Nuri's flashier moves.

Its claim to fame were those horns. Using its Elastic magic, they could go rubbery and extend a great distance before solidifying again and being used to stab an opponent. They could also stab at close range without the magic, of course. What Balt came to learn was that, unlike a Hyoi, Nuris also possessed Electrical abilities. Garbo could do the same Static Charge that Balt had seen Pops do countless times, as well as cast lightning bolts from its horns. Niona was skilled enough with the Jekua to maintain fine control of its horns and use them like prehensile limbs, wrapping them around Balt's ankles and dragging him across the ground a couple feet, eliciting laughter from Alani.

Garbo's Electrical abilities were made a little redundant by having Pops on her team, but Niona seemed pretty adept with the Jekua and could make good use of its Elastic magic. If she was planning to go with an Elastic-Type, then Garbo was probably a good pick.

"Alright," said Niona. "Let's go with Pops and Garbo. Which Thermal, though?"

"Thermy," Alani corrected her.

"My bad, my bad. Thermy, yes."

"I don't think the Daritine," said Balt. "You've got more options terrain-wise with the Muggish or Scrypto. A Muggish is slow, but it's also fluid and hot. It can squeeze through obstacles or melt through them completely. And the Scrypto, obviously, can fly. You're more limited by the Daritine's body."

"Fair," Niona nodded. "But which one? I'm kinda leanin' Glom."

"Maybe if you pick the fourth one first, that'll help you decide," Alani suggested.

Niona's face lit up. "Good idea!" She began flipping through the pages of memory cards again.

Staring at the massive collection of Jekuas, Balt had to ask, "How do you not have a single Tidal-Type in there?" He recalled her saying during their previous conversation that she was distinctly lacking in the watery Jekuas.

"I mean, I *literally* have Tidal-Types, duh. I just don't use any and don't really want to."

"Why not?" he and Alani asked in unison.

She shrugged. "I've just never been that great with 'em," she said. "I have a few who can do some Tidal moves, or I've added a couple simple mods like with Armband, but that's about the extent of my skill with water. I don't know what it is about it, but I have some sort of mental block with it. I just can't get the hang of 'em."

Balt was taken aback hearing this. Niona seemed like such a slick Summoner, he never would've guessed there was a Type she couldn't use. He knew there were Summoners who were inherently better with certain Types, and less so with others, but the concept still felt foreign to him. His firsthand experience was still too limited to understand what it would feel like to be unable to grasp a Type of Jekua.

And he had to wonder: would such a deficiency extend to a Jekua like his Mirrorbear, which could absorb other Jekuas' powers? Or if there was a Type he couldn't master, would that be a possible workaround to using it?

So Tidal-Types were out, although Balt was curious to know which of those Jekuas she'd imprinted and tested out. But that was a question for another time.

Niona cycled through a ton of different Jekuas, but none felt right for the team. Out of all her Wind-Types, the Toryoth seemed like her best bet. Not only could it create powerful gusts, but its beak was the sharpest of any bird Jekua. Like Tidal-Types, though, Wind-Types could be tricky in tournament play if one wasn't a Master of that Type, and Niona definitely wasn't. They kept the Toryoth on the backburner, though. Before switching Types, Niona could not resist taunting Balt by having her Whif-flit flap around his head, threatening that she was going to make it defecate.

She had some good Growth-Types. A Korbir would certainly pack a wallop and intimidate other Summoners, and she had created a Hybrid of a Vossi and a Juntoo which resulted in a truly horrific creature that was horrendously dubbed a Slopape. It was a huge, lumbering ape made of mud and sticks that had no legs, but walked on its hands and stood on its springy tail. It was just as disgusting as Valentina's Vossi Hybrid, the Bogbane. And somehow, against all odds, it was even worse to look at than Glom.

"Okay," said Alani as she looked the Slopape up and down. "One thing is for certain: you cannot, under any circumstance, have this *and* the lava thing on your team." Niona burst out laughing and withdrew the Jekua.

When it came to Friction, she had even more enticing options than Growth. She had a Wallago, which was an absurdly fast wildcat sort of creature that also had some weak Wind powers, so she could at least incorporate Wind that way. But she also had a Bruiserweight, which was a compelling choice, in Balt's opinion.

She had nicknamed her Bruiserweight "Boombox," continuing her streak of giving her Jekuas the absolute stupidest names. The creature was much scarier than its name implied. It stood a good foot taller than Balt, with ropy muscles and glittering green scales. It blinked bulbous yellow eyes, staring the trio down as it stood totally still in the middle of Route 29.

"Are you any good with it?" Balt asked.

"Her."

"Are you any good with her?"

Niona made Boombox do a roundhouse kick.

Balt said, "Is that a yes?"

Boombox did another roundhouse kick.

"Can you only do roundhouse kicks?"

Boombox did a punch.

"I'm very good with her," Niona finally said. "That tip I gave you about reacting? I did a lot of my training for that with ol' Boombox here. It's been a while since I've busted her out, but it's like ridin' a bike. Which I've done a lot of this week."

Bruiserweights were strong, and their Firepunch attack was brutal. In rare cases, a Summoner could also harness their Friction magic enough to reduce an enemy's friction and slow them down. If Niona was as experienced with Boombox as she claimed, then Balt had to guess she was capable of such a feat.

Before they could debate the pros and cons of the Bruiserweight, Niona said, "Boombox makes the cut."

"You don't wanna go through the Gravity-Types first?" Balt asked her.

"Nah. It's been too long since I've hung with my girl."

All they needed to do now was pick the Thermal-Type and she'd be ready to rumble.

"I've got three pretty fast movers," said Niona. "It feels kinda redundant throwin' a fourth one on there, right?"

"You can never move too fast," Balt said.

"That's true, but it's also less fun havin' a bunch of stuff that does all the same shit, y'know? I think I'm in the mood to rain some muck down on some people. I've never used Glom in a tournament before, either. Seems like a fun challenge."

"Do you think that during the archipelago's biggest tournament is the best time to give yourself a 'fun challenge'?" Balt asked.

"Why not? I'm there to have fun too, at the end of the day," she said, echoing the sentiment shared with him by Kori, the Summoner he'd battled on Totta.

"Fair enough," he said with a shrug.

That was that. Pops, Glom, Garbo, and Boombox. A motley crew if he'd ever seen one.

Niona procured the three memory cards she needed (already having Pops's loaded up, naturally) and inserted them into her kayet with satisfying clicks.

She said, "I'm excited to get some training in tonight. We're gonna have to find a hotel with a super nice gym now that I've got the crew locked in."

The nicer the gym, the nicer the rooms. Balt was looking forward to that.

He stood up and meandered over to their bikes. "No time to waste," he said.

The two women joined him, and together they set off for Deredi City.

3

A FAVOR

FOUR DAYS WAS NOT A LOT OF TIME, BUT GETTING OFF OF Qwi Island had refreshed Alani's mind. Her experiences in the jungle and at the island's Veptilo were so miserable, it felt nice to fully remove herself from that hunk of rock and throw herself down on a different one. Or, rather, gently ride a big mechanical basket over to it.

While her mind was progressively clearing up, allowing her to finally relax and drain her stresses away, her body was lagging behind. Her left cheek still sported a nasty bruise, which she could thankfully cover up with Niona's assistance. At some point in the last few days she had searched on her linkpad for how long it took a face bruise to fade away, and unfortunately the answer was roughly two weeks. In addition to that, her arms and back still ached from the tussle with the Facet.

The night of the incident, she had gingerly laid herself down in bed, wincing with every tiny movement. Her joints were begging her to stop, to stay completely and unnaturally still until they were ready to clock in. Nearly two hours later, when she could finally fight past the soreness and fall asleep, her dreams were plagued with visions of those white-suited figures with their crystalline faces. The unnatural black streaks zig-zagging across their bodies. She had woken with a start, her body protesting the sudden motion.

Luckily, she had not dreamed of those alien figures since that night and her muscles were far less angsty, even if she had yet to make a full recovery.

She thought about the Facet often, however. How could she not? Nobody knew what they wanted with the Veptilos, but as far as she knew, they had failed in all their attempts to secure one. That was fantastic, but it meant that they were going to keep trying.

Being on a new island was all well and good, but every step brought her closer and closer to the next Veptilo. Closer and closer to another potential ambush.

Balt had pretty much not left her side since they arrived on Na Tana, which was sweet in its way, but also somewhat irritating. She appreciated the sentiment, but feared that he wasn't grasping the point she made back in that inn hallway. She did not need him to be at her beck and call every second of every day—she simply needed him to be mentally present, not letting himself get distracted by all things Jekua. And physically present, too, when it came time to visit the shrines. That was a given.

But right now, they were all separated into their own hotel rooms. Alani had put her things down and sprawled out on her bed, sinking into the fluffy comforter sitting neatly on top. With so many hours of biking every day, her muscles would've been sore regardless, so the pain was only exacerbated by the lingering effects of the Facet's attack. Pedaling that bicycle was a nightmarish exercise, but she did not want to complain. It was getting them to Makanuele faster. Once she was there, she could truly relax.

The hotel that Niona had booked them tonight was pretty nice, although it did not match the fanciness of her father's resort. Still, it was far better than any place Alani could afford on her own or even with the Church's meager funding. It was on the edge of Deredi, almost the first building they saw when entering the city. From her room, she had a beautiful view of the forest stretching out beyond the city limits.

On the top floor, six stories higher than where Alani currently sat, was a Jekua gym. She knew Niona would be wiling away the late night hours up there with her team of weird Jekuas. Four stories lower, on the first floor just past the lobby, was a restaurant called the Fork & Flame. They offered room service, according to a laminated menu situated on her bedside table. She knew Balt would be ordering from there post-haste.

Alani perused the menu and spied a few dishes that sounded pretty appealing after a long, exhausting day. She'd dipped into the bathroom shortly after settling in, and noted there was a fairly large tub in there. She could easily see herself chowing down on a meal then sliding into some warm, bubbly water.

That was what she would do. It was decided.

While there was much that appealed to her on the Fork & Flame's menu, what she ended up ordering was a simple pasta dish with mushrooms, bacon, and a creamy white sauce. No one in Tanepke, to her knowledge, could properly cook pasta. She was curious to see if the chefs on Na Tana were more adept.

The person on the phone, who for reasons unknown sounded like they had just finished crying as they spoke through a nose full of phlegm, told her the food would be at her door in about half an hour. That left her plenty of time to kill on her linkpad.

When she unlocked her linkpad, the map she'd pulled up earlier was still on her screen. If they kept up the same pace as the previous few days, they would likely arrive in Makanuele in two days' time. Aeiko, a childhood friend of her and her sister, had been living in the city for several years now, working at Lakahlo Labs. Alani had briefly texted with Aeiko the second day they were on Na Tana, mentioning that she and some friends would be in town soon, but she had yet to broach the subject of potentially staying with them. Niona's pockets seemed bottomless, so she could surely book hotel rooms for them, but Alani hated mooching off her so much. Although staying with Aeiko wasn't *not* mooching…

She wanted to see her friend, though. It had been years since she'd gotten to hang out with Aeiko. Alani could never afford to visit Makanuele, and Aeiko did not really make a habit out of visiting their family.

Alani's thumb hovered over Aeiko's contact information, over that little phone icon. She bit her lower lip and moved her thumb away.

Aeiko had always mostly been Siuv's friend, though, and Alani was the tag-along who, in all likelihood, annoyed Siuv and her other friends. All of them were too polite to ever say anything, however. While Siuv was twenty-four—six years older than her—Aeiko was only slightly older than Alani, having just turned twenty-one last season. Their birthdays were actually only a couple weeks apart. Regardless, back then they had probably thought Alani was some weird, clingy kid. Even now, they would likely think of her as just some dumb kid. Though they weren't that much older than her, they were incredibly intelligent, having skipped several grades in school. They had become friends with Siuv after meeting in one of their classes.

Alani shook her head, trying to banish those self-pitying thoughts. She and Aeiko had plenty of fun times together, right? That wasn't all in her head. And Aeiko had been perfectly pleasant in their recent chats together; they probably would enjoy seeing her, too.

She pressed that outdated phone icon and placed her linkpad to her ear. Its shrill tones rang twice before Aeiko picked up.

"Hey," they said, a touch of grogginess in their throat.

"Oh, sorry," said Alani, "did I wake you?"

Aeiko laughed. "No, it's not even eight o'clock," they said.

Alani wanted to smack herself in the head for saying something so stupid.

"I'm just tired," Aeiko went on. "Long day at the office. What's up? Can't say I was expecting a call."

Her brain leapt back to *they don't want to speak to me,* but Alani had to remind herself that nobody called anybody anymore. That was what they meant.

Probably.

"Sorry," Alani apologized again. For both calling specifically and for speaking to them at all. But then she said, "About the long day, I mean. I can't even imagine all the complicated stuff you must do on a daily basis."

"It's fine," said Aeiko. "It's challenging, but it's fun, too. Most of the time, anyway. Today was less a challenging-but-fun day and more a challenging-and-frustrating day, but those happen. It's all good. How's your trip been? Enjoying the lovely sights of the island? It's your first time on Na Tana, right?"

"Yeah, it is. It's a beautiful place." In truth, she did not think that what she'd seen of it so far was much different than Totta, but she stopped herself from saying so. Pretty was pretty, in the end.

"I'm glad you're finally getting to see the world beyond Totta," said Aeiko. From anyone else, it would probably sound condescending, but there was a lightness to their tone that conveyed the earnestness behind their words. "Who would've thought you'd turn out to be a Salt girl, though. When are you getting into town, by the way? Do I get to see all your fancy, shiny tattoos?"

Alani grinned. "That was why I called, actually. I wanted to let you know that we should be getting to Makanuele in two days, I think. If our bicycles don't break down."

Another light chuckle from Aeiko. The sound made Alani's heart skip a beat. She once more tried to shake away the nerves. Aeiko said, "You're riding bikes? All the way across the island?"

"Well, not *all* the way across," said Alani. "Your city's in the middle of the island. You're a scientist, shouldn't you know that?"

"Correction: I'm an engineer, not a scientist. And I'm not sure that falls under the purview of science anyway."

"Geography isn't science?"

"Geography is geography."

"Interesting."

Aeiko laughed again, and it brought a smile to Alani's lips. All at once she was ten years old again, hanging out with her older sister and her cool friends, utterly mesmerized by Aeiko. They were the most gorgeous person she'd ever seen, and she held on to every word they said. When it came down to it, half the reason she always wanted to hang out with Siuv and her friends was so that she could see Aeiko. Maybe more than half.

She blinked herself back to the present, years removed from her silly, unrequited childhood crush. There was no way Aeiko ever thought of her the same way, and she doubted they would now. To them, she would always be Siuv's baby sister.

"Anyway," Alani continued, "I'm calling to ask a favor, unfortunately."

"Go for it. I live to do favors for people I haven't seen in years." If they hadn't laughed at the end of that statement, Alani would've keeled over on the spot.

Still, she was reluctant to ask. It seemed foolish now, in the moment, to impose on her old friend when Niona was perfectly willing to drop her father's cash on hotel rooms.

But she pressed on. She'd already come this far. "I was wondering if it'd be possible to stay with you for a few days?" She quickly amended: "Actually, I'm not sure how long that Jekua tournament is, but we're probably going to be in town for all of that. Do you know how long it is?"

"It lasts a week," Aeiko said.

"Oh," Alani murmured.

"And actually, it doesn't start until the sixtieth." They would be rolling into Makanuele on the fifty-third.

"Oh," she squeaked again. She did not want to put them out for two whole weeks. Before she could revoke the request, Aeiko spoke.

"You, uh...how many of you are there again?"

"It's fine, really, forget I asked," said Alani.

"No, it's not that. I don't mind you staying, it's just that space is a little tight here. I've got a roommate and we also have a, uh—*houseguest*—at the moment."

"I don't want to intrude on your space."

"You're fine, I swear. I'm just not sure if we've got enough room for everyone. There's three of you, right?"

Alani nodded, then confirmed aloud because of course Aeiko could not see her.

On the other end of the line, Aeiko made some clucking noises with their tongue like they were pondering an equation. (Was that what engineers did?) After mulling it over for a few moments, they said, "I think we've got room for one or two of you, but..."

"That's alright," Alani said hurriedly. She was confident Niona wouldn't mind getting herself a hotel. In fact, she may even prefer it. Somewhere with a gym that she could train in every day for those two weeks.

"You're sure?"

"Only if you're sure," she said. "Really, I feel awkward for even asking in the first place. If we need to find somewhere else, I totally understand. I didn't realize it would be a two-week commitment."

"No, no," said Aeiko. "I think it'd be fun, honestly. It's been so long since we've seen each other. I could do with some catching up. Maybe I could even request some days off work so we could hang more. I sure as hell could do with some vacation."

"You're sure?"

"Yes."

"*Absolutely* sure?"

That laugh again. "Yes," they said.

Just hearing that one syllable sent Alani's heart aflutter. She didn't know how she'd react to seeing Aeiko in the flesh again if just their voice was stirring up these long-forgotten feelings.

She supposed she would find out in about two days.

4
THE BARRIER

GREASE DRIBBLED DOWN BALT'S FINGERS AS HE RUSHED from the polished wood table over to his bathroom, trying (and failing) to not let a single droplet hit the ground. He dirtied the sink handle turning on the faucet then washed away the remaining grease. The burger had been delicious, but it had also been an unholy mess to eat.

He dried his hands and returned to the living area, unknowingly stepping on multiple grease spots on the ground as he made his way back to the bed. He threw himself down on it, bouncing his linkpad and kayet gently into the air. They both landed and the lighter linkpad bounced again, clattering to the floor. Balt cursed.

A heavy sigh escaped the depths of his lungs, barreling past his lips, as he rolled onto his back and gazed absently at the ceiling.

It was not a good sign that boredom was already creeping in so soon after dinner. There were many hours left in the night that he would have to occupy with *some-*

thing, but at the moment he'd be damned if he knew what that something would be.

Sure, he could flip through his bestiary for the billionth time. Or browse the Jekua forums on his linkpad, see what brand of freak was posting today. What he really wanted to do was gather up his Jekuas and join Niona in the gym, but his lingering guilt held him back. He sighed again, dramatically louder this time. At the very least, he could summon his Jekuas and have them totter around the room. Probably not Pistachio, given his size, but the others. That would be the smart thing to do, the responsible thing. Pump up those mana reserves.

What he ended up doing instead was balancing his unused spoon—which he had received with his plate of burger and fries—on the edge of said plate, with a tiny chunk of red onion sitting in the bowl of the utensil. He then proceeded to whack the other end of the spoon, which acted as a small and stupid trebuchet to launch the onion piece through the air and hopefully into the nearby trash can.

This was a project that Balt resolved to complete tonight no matter how many attempts it took. He continually grabbed the bite of onion off the floor and returned it to the gleaming silver spoon, then readjusted the utensil as well as the force of his whack. After around fifty tries, he believed he had found the ideal trajectory, and now it was merely a matter of hitting the spoon's end with the perfect level of strength.

Balt could feel deep in his gut that this next one would be it. He was going to smack that spoon, and it was going to flip over the edge of the plate, and that half-inch hunk of red onion that had fallen out of his mouth as he chewed a bite of burger would careen through the air and land perfectly in that rounded blue plastic receptacle. Nothing but net.

Just as he was about to slam his hand down, there came a knock at his door. He blinked and turned to face the entryway, then there was another knock. He scurried over to the door, swearing under his breath, knowing that he would have to recalibrate his whack after he talked to whoever this was.

He pulled open the creaking door and standing on the other side was a beaming Niona.

"Hey there," she said, clasping her hands together behind her back. "Whatcha doin'?"

"Nothing," he lied hastily. "What's up?" His mind raced, seeing her standing there in the entryway. Was it possible that she reciprocated his feelings? Was she here to…?

"I'm about to head up to the gym, and I wanted to see if you would come with."

Of course she wasn't here to—well, it didn't matter. He was about to decline her offer, but she cut him off.

"I know, I know. You can't and blah blah whatever. Look, I dunno what happened with you and Alani, but I'm sure the self-flagellation ain't helpin' anything. Your whole deal is that you're escorting her, right? Don't you think it's unwise to let yourself get rusty, then?"

That was a salient point, he had to admit. Getting a little practice in would be far more productive than throwing away a piece of food via a spoon catapult. The latter would be highly satisfying if he pulled it off, though.

"Fine," he conceded. "Only for an hour, though."

"Sure, alright," Niona said with a smirk. "Just an hour. Hey, we can mod one of your dudes with that chip my dad gave you, if you want."

Balt wanted to say that he'd been so focused on Alani the past few days that he'd entirely forgotten about the Barrier mod microchip that Mr. Daneo had gifted him, but that would be a lie. He was constantly thinking about it. How could it not plague his thoughts every moment of every day? It was his very first mod chip! He was dying to use it.

He grabbed the microchip out of his bag and slid his kayet onto his wrist, securing it in place. Then he followed Niona up a few floors to the hotel's gym.

Niona swiped her room key over the electronic lock and held the door open for him. "After you," she said with a little bow.

Balt stepped inside and took a deep, contented breath. It was as if he could feel his mana stirring inside him, anxious to be released. He knew that was nonsense, but he truly was excited to train a bit.

The place was not as decked out as a full-fledged gym would be, of course, but it had a pretty solid lineup of equipment. It was too small for an obstacle course, but there were a few designated areas for sparring matches, red dummies fitted with various Type-resistant materials for target practice, and assorted weights to lift with one's Jekua. They could be used in a typical fashion—like Niona's Bruiserweight pumping some iron—or they could be used in cases such as dropping one on top of Balt's Tottaworm and trying to wriggle free, mimicking a heavier Jekua pinning it down.

"Have you given any thought to who you want to mod?" Niona asked, walking ahead of him and sitting down on a cushioned bench. She kicked her legs out in front of her, crossing one leg over the other.

Of course he had. Whether or not he'd made a firm decision, though, was another question entirely.

"I don't think Dipper should get it," he began. "I was able to do something with her that basically acts as a barrier already, so it would kinda be wasted on her." He was thinking about when he'd used her petals as a shield as they were crossing the bridge in the Qwisdeep, blocking strikes from the Wortens' tentacles. It had been effective up until he'd gotten distracted.

"The worm seems kinda silly too," said Niona. "No offense to your precious worm."

"My Tottaworm's my weakest link, though," Balt said, "as far as taking direct hits goes. A shield might be pretty useful for it, take the brunt of the damage."

"That's true, but I also feel like that's the most agile thing in your arsenal, y'know? If a big hit's comin', you could quickly slither out of the way. Or you could go all bendy and curve the body away from whatever's hitting you. It's also a smaller target in general, which helps."

Balt nodded. All of that made sense. He'd been leaning toward modding the Tottaworm, but maybe its natural abilities were good enough to avoid taking damage.

"So that would leave Milton or Pistachio," he said.

"That feels appropriate," Niona said. "Both heavy hitters, both mostly focusing on physical attacks. Gettin' up close and personal."

"Right."

He really needed to imprint more Jekuas that could blast off some magic at his opponents. Where were all the Thermal- and Electrical-Types around here? He was itching to put his remaining memory card to use.

"Pistachio's got way more reach than Milton, obviously," he went on. "He's also got the Friction advantage. Even if he needs to get in close for some reason, he could reduce the opponent's kinetic energy enough that dodging any blows should be a breeze."

"And I'd assume that Piss getting hit probably doesn't damage him as much as it does Milton, but you can correct me if I'm wrong."

"You're probably right," Balt said, ignoring her nickname for his Mosstopus. He wasn't sure if he had enough experience with the two Jekuas yet to make that call for certain, but her assessment sounded correct. "Milton doesn't have either of those advantages, so having the Barrier to fall back on if things get too hairy might be useful."

Niona jumped in with a counterpoint. "The Mirrorbear's whole thing, though, is gettin' hit. There's more to it, of course—you know what it entails better than I do—but it's worth thinking about. You don't wanna start relying too heavily on the Barrier and end up never absorbing any magic."

He'd considered that. He hoped he would be a good judge of when to block and when to absorb, though.

"Another thing is that Piss is a Growth-Type, so he's more susceptible to Thermal attacks," said Niona. "A Mirrorbear is pretty neutral."

"You could look at that two ways, though," Balt argued.

"Yeah, Pistachio has an obvious weakness I'd want to defend against, and Milton doesn't. But from another viewpoint, you could say that Milton's equally susceptible to *all* Jekua Types, while Pistachio's only susceptible to one."

She laughed. "Well, I guess that's true. You wouldn't want Glom's lava rain comin' down on him, though."

"I wouldn't want that shit comin' down on *any* of my Jekuas," Balt said.

It still seemed like Milton would be a better fit for the mod than Pistachio. He could envision himself behind the Mirrorbear's eyes, charging toward an enemy and swiping with his claws, ducking to dodge punches and putting up his Barrier to blunt kicks, then dropping the shield to absorb a stream of fire or something that he'd shove right back in the other Jekua's face.

That sounded kind of exhilarating.

Niona then said, "Also, you don't *have* to use the mod on any of these guys. You could wait until you imprint something else. I don't wanna pressure you or anything."

"Nah, not at all," he said. "I want to."

She smiled, her chubby cheeks dimpling. "So is Milton the winner, then?"

"I think he's the winner."

Niona clapped her hands on her thighs and said, "Dope! Let's do it!"

Balt walked over and sat beside her, tearing through the plastic packaging containing the Barrier microchip. He carefully plucked the chip out and popped it into a slot for mods on the side of his kayet. The device's screen lit up with the text AA-130 BARRIER MODIFICATION.

His body tingled with anticipation. This would be his first Artificial Ability, a Synaptic-Type move.

"What now?" he asked. The mod hadn't exactly come with step-by-step instructions on how to install it, which seemed like a failure on Lakahlo's part, in his opinion.

Niona explained that he needed to prime the memory card that he intended to modify, then press the button located directly next to the mod slot, and the kayet would do the rest. It would take the information stored on the microchip and alter the data on the L2 card that held his imprinted Mirrorbear. Simple as that.

It sounded *too* simple, almost. "And you're sure it'll work?" he mumbled. "It won't screw up my memory card or anything?"

"I've used tons of mods and never had any issues," Niona assured him.

Balt clicked next to Milton's card slot and proceeded to press the button by the mod. The kayet began to whir, and the screen's text was replaced by a rotating icon that evidently was meant to indicate it was working on something.

Thirty seconds passed, then a full minute, and Balt asked, "How long's it supposed to take?"

"Jeez, the impatience," Niona chortled, elbowing him. "It's not some instant thing. It's rewriting parts of the data you imprinted, letting this magical creature thing do some magic it wasn't capable of doing before. It takes a little time!"

Balt let out an exaggerated groan, as if this were the most inconvenienced he'd ever been in his life. They both laughed. Then he said, "I'm guessing I can't summon anything while this is doing its business?"

"Correct."

"Lame."

"I can summon stuff, though," Niona said, rising from the bench. She pressed a button on her kayet and began to channel her mana into it.

He said, "I'm shocked you still have any mana left over after that grueling battle today."

"Oh, totally. I had to chug sixteen Thunderjolts to rejuvenate myself. As a result, I'm wearing a diaper right now, just in case."

Balt guffawed and she grinned as her soulclay hit the ground and started taking the form of Garbo, her Nuri. It was then Balt realized what a sense of relief he felt, a sense of pure ease. It was like he was finally relaxing after tensing his muscles for the past four days. Some time with Niona and their Jekuas was exactly what he needed.

While his kayet cycled through its modification processes, he watched Niona fire off some of Garbo's moves at a dummy that was vaguely shaped like a monkey Jekua. She pierced its plush material with the Nuri's spiral horns, headbutting it and slamming its musclebound sides into it, nearly tipping the thing over. Balt then learned that she had modded Garbo with some Thermal powers, mostly of the *sub*thermal variety. The goat-esque creature blasted the dummy with an icebeam, freezing it in a block of ice, then immediately fired a lightning bolt at it, shattering it to pieces.

"Shit," Niona muttered, withdrawing Garbo. "Well… hmph. Shit. I was really hoping that thing was resistant to ice. Or Electrical resistant. Whichever one it needed to be resistant to for that to not happen. Gonna have to pay for that, I guess." A deep frown etched across her face. Balt was honestly a little surprised to detect some genuine dismay in her tone.

Moments later, his kayet dinged and the screen informed him that the modification process was complete. A painless procedure. The mod chip popped out of its slot on the side of the device, now unusable. It was a classic Lakahlo move, making one-time use items so that a person continued lining the company's pockets for eternity.

"Let's try this puppy out," he said, removing the microchip. The ridiculous, sentimental side of him almost wanted to keep it since it was his first mod, but logic won out and he tossed it into a trash can. But then he internally cursed himself, realizing the chip would've been a viable candidate for his spoon catapult downstairs. Slightly more sanitary, too.

Since Milton's card was already primed, all he had to do was push his mana into the kayet. His soulclay poured out of the device and a few seconds later, his trusty Mirrorbear stood on all fours before him. The Jekua stared blankly with those tiny blue eyes.

Balt looked to Niona, who still seemed stressed out about the dummy she'd demolished. When she withdrew Garbo, the ice encasing the dummy pieces had dematerialized, leaving behind chunks of red scattered all over the floor.

"Who you pittin' against Milton?" he asked, drawing her attention away from her mishap.

She answered without missing a beat. "Pops." Then she promptly loaded the Toolu's card and summoned the little scamp.

Pops's new appearance was remarkably less adorable than his previous Suelu form, now sporting his black carapace and gaggle of legs and ear-tendrils. Coupled with Glom, half of Niona's tournament team was truly nasty to behold. Not to mention Garbo's horns stretching out wasn't the loveliest sight.

Together with their Jekuas, they walked over to one of the sparring areas. Balt stood on the far end, while Niona positioned herself and Pops on the other. "You ready?" she asked him as he turned Milton to face her Toolu.

He wasn't sure how to answer. In addition to lacking any instruction on how to install the mod, the packaging also did not state how to actually use the move. Much like the other abilities his Jekuas possessed, Balt could innately feel the power within his soulclay. It was strange, feeling something there that wasn't there before. It was like suddenly having a third arm with which to pick stuff up. He could access the power easily, but using it effectively was another matter entirely. Not only using it with the correct timing, but also making the Barrier cover Milton's whole body and not just his foot or some other limb.

So his response was simply a shrug. "Guess so," he said.

As was her nature, Niona did not hesitate to fire a lightning bolt straight at Milton before Balt had even tapered off the "oh" of his second syllable.

He grinned.

The bolt cut through the air, shimmering and crackling with electrical energy. Balt tensed, and Milton's body mirrored his own. He remained out of the Jekua's perspective, but reached into his soulclay to conjure the Barrier.

There was too much delay. The bolt struck Milton in the shoulder, sending a jab of pain shuddering through Balt's own shoulder. He grimaced and swore under his breath. The Barrier hadn't even appeared, he'd been too debilitated by the bolt to finish conjuring it.

"Gotta go faster," said Niona.

"I appreciate your wisdom."

"Any time. Ready for another?"

She fired off another bolt before he could reply. He liked that she kept him on his toes, since his opponents would not be asking if he was ready for their next move, but it was frustrating at the same time, never being able to moor himself. In the end, he knew it made for better practice.

Again, he failed to summon the shield in time. He was caught too off-guard. "Go again," he told her.

Another bolt shot from Pops's disgusting half-bug half-rodent body, and this time Balt was prepared for it. He keyed into the Mirrorbear's mind, envisioning the Barrier engulfing his body. A split second later, a wavering purple bubble appeared, with Milton safe inside.

The lightning bolt hit the Barrier, dissipating upon impact and sending a visible ripple coursing across the Barrier's surface, like glass cracking. The lines swiftly disappeared after a couple moments, and then Balt dropped the shield.

"Nice!" said Niona. "One outta three ain't the best rate, but…"

"Shut up," he told her. "Let's keep going."

They continued on that way for another fifteen or twenty minutes, with Balt successfully blocking at least half of Pops's lightning strikes, if not more. Near the end, Niona started targeting specific parts of Milton's body to see if Balt could isolate the Barrier on his arm, his neck, and so forth. It worked a couple times, but Balt deemed the extra effort required not worthwhile; it was much easier and probably more effective to just throw a shield up over the entire body. He enjoyed the experimentation, though.

When Niona called Pops back to his memory card, Balt did the same with Milton to give himself a temporary break. No use expending mana while he waited, even if it was only for a minute or so. She loaded up a different card, taking a step toward him, and asked, "Wanna get close?"

Balt's face flushed red, heat filling his cheeks, burning like coals. "I—uh, I, what?" he stuttered.

Pink soulclay slithered out of her kayet and faded into the form of her Bruiserweight.

"You're doin' well with the long-range shots—still need a ton of practice, of course, but you're off to a good start. Wanna see how you do in close quarters?"

Balt blinked rapidly, his heart still racing and warmth still flooding his face. Of course that's what she meant. *Idiot*, he chastised himself.

"Yeah," he said. "Totally."

He gave himself another few moments to recover from the embarrassment he now felt, praying to the Veptists that Niona hadn't noticed. Then he summoned Milton again, and Niona walked backwards, returning to her side of the small ring.

Boombox remained in the center, with Milton standing before him. The two Jekuas appeared as if they were sizing each other up, if only they possessed any sentience of their own.

Niona inhaled deeply, then exhaled loudly. Balt did the same.

She said, "You ready to go?"

He opened his mouth to speak, but of course he could barely get a sound out before Boombox swung.

5
MAKANUELE CITY

TRUE TO WHAT ALANI HAD TOLD AEIKO, THEY RODE INTO Makanuele's city limits two days later. Their hotel stay the previous night was not as fancy as that in Deredi, but Alani was still able to rest enough to push through one last bike ride.

After their stay in Deredi, she had noticed a subtle change in Balt's demeanor. He seemed much more like himself. He still wasn't as boisterous or easygoing as usual, but he definitely seemed more at ease. Less reserved, less anxious. Her first assumption was that he'd done some training with Niona at the hotel, which was fine by her. She despised the tension that had grown between them this past week. Maybe she was partially to blame, given how she'd unloaded on him. It took the continued aching of her joints to remind herself that she was entitled to feeling hurt by his actions, both physically and emotionally.

The trio brought their bikes to a rolling stop on one of

the less-populated sidewalks and hopped off before pushing the bikes further out of the way. Makanuele was much like Himony, but lacking all the gigantic resorts. It was a typical city, with towering skyscrapers and buildings crammed together, packed so tight they almost converged into one huge megabuilding. They couldn't spy even a glimpse of it from here, but apparently the city's stadium was located at the center, embedded in a large, shallow-inclined crater that the rest of the city surrounded. Cars lined the streets, honking at each other despite sitting idle at red traffic lights. It was not really a tourist destination like Himony, but people from all over the world wandered the city; it was a diverse place in general, but there were more visitors than usual due to the upcoming Jekua tournament. The Makanuele Rumble was set to commence in exactly one week.

"Should we go straight to the stadium?" she asked, her question pointed at Niona. Competitors needed to sign in upon arrival in the city. The other woman stood beside her light green bike, tapping her fingers on the seat as she leaned against it.

"First we should probably return these," she said, jiggling the bike. "Unless y'all are wanting to bike around the city. It's pretty big."

Balt didn't say anything, waiting for Alani's input. She said, "We can return them, sure. I don't mind walking." Doing so would probably make her body ache less, bouncing up and down on that uncomfortable seat and pumping her legs. It'd save them a bit of money, too. Walking around Himony hadn't been so bad.

With that, Niona tracked down the rental shop's location on her linkpad and they walked their bikes in that direction.

The city was teeming with life. Every which way, Alani's senses were assaulted by sounds, by sights, by smells. Some sort of meat was sizzling on an unseen grill nearby; she could hear it and smell it, the aroma intoxicating, but she had no idea where it was. As they passed a narrow alley, she spotted a tiny food stall set up in the building's shadows with a line ten people deep waiting for whatever the man was grilling. The stall bore no sign or menu.

Eventually, the buildings on their right gave way to a large park, filled with enormous, hunched trees and flowering bushes that encroached on winding paved paths. Butterflies fluttered amongst the foliage and Dewrats scampered across the grass, scrambling up trees and bothering the squirrels and birds above. There was nothing like it in Tanepke; the small town had stunning white sand beaches, but there simply wasn't ample space for a large park such as this. If there was, Alani would've found herself spending most of her free time there rather than on the Church's manicured grounds.

"Looks like we could cut through here," said Niona, nodding toward the park. "Want to? Prettier than a bunch of concrete."

"Absolutely," said Alani with a smile.

They veered into the park, sending a skittish Dewrat scurrying into a bush. Alani giggled seeing it poke its head out through the leaves, sniffing the air as if to determine whether or not they were a threat. It decided they were and vanished into the shrubbery.

The air in the park smelled noticeably fresher than that in the city streets. Its lack of delicious food smells was an unfortunate loss, but it more than made up for it with the abundance of flowers. Alani breathed in deep lungfuls of it, letting it out in loud sighs.

"Something wrong?" Balt asked by her side, pushing his bike through the grass. The three of them were walking just off the path so that they didn't get in other people's way, with their leisurely pace and bulky bicycles.

Alani shook her head, her face scrunched up in confusion.

"Just seemed like it, with the big sigh and all," he clarified.

"Oh," she murmured. "No, that was a…relaxed sigh. Not a distressed sigh." She offered him a kind smile to assure him that she felt completely fine.

They were halfway across the park when Niona said, "Oh! By the way, I was able to book a room at a place pretty close to your friend's apartment. There's no gym in it, but there's a gym that's basically between the two. So your girl is gonna be able to get some good training in every night and not be too far away."

"Oh, nice," said Alani.

She had broken the news to Niona the day before that there wouldn't be space for all of them at Aeiko's, and as she expected, Niona was not heartbroken about it. In all likelihood, she'd probably be spending most of her time here either at the stadium or in the gym, anyway. It didn't matter much to her where she passed out after.

Alani then said, "Should we go to the stadium next, so you can sign in?" She didn't want to delay too much and have something go wrong. Ambling around the park was nice, but with this apparently being a two-week venture, she would have plenty of time for that.

"Sure, that's fine," Niona said.

Then Balt cut in. "Well," he started, his voice whiny, "I think we should go to the Church next. That's the main reason we're here. The main reason *we're* here, anyway," he said, the emphasis meaning himself and Alani.

"Alright," Niona said, unbothered.

"The Church could wait," Alani said. After how wrong things went in Mé Lutako, she wasn't exactly overeager to visit the next shrine.

"No, no—I mean, yeah, technically it maybe can, but it shouldn't. It's what we're here for. We really shouldn't dally." His words were tripping over each other, tumbling out of his mouth faster than he could enunciate them. "If Niona wants to head on over there without us, that's cool, but we should get to the Church as soon as possible. We can meet her after. The Church stuff is more important." Clearly overcompensating for his lackadaisical approach to the pilgrimage on the previous island.

His insistence was irksome, but before Alani could refute anything, Niona spoke. "That's fine, honestly. It can wait. Tomorrow's the last day people can sign in before they're dropped from the roster. I'm not that worried about it. If we get to it today, that's great, but if we gotta wait 'til tomorrow, it won't be a problem."

"That settles it, then," said Balt. "The Church is next up on the docket."

Alani almost rolled her eyes, but she didn't say anything. It would feel hypocritical if she'd made such a fuss over his lack of focus on the Church, only to complain when he actually exhibited any, no matter how annoying his method of doing so happened to be. When it came down to it, nothing he said was false. Regardless of her inhibitions, the right thing to do was go see the local Elders as soon as she could. And, on the bright side, if they got the Veptilo business out of the way, that would leave her with almost two weeks to spend with Aeiko without that lingering task hanging over her head the entire time.

They continued on toward the bike rental shop, walking through the park's soft grass. A minute later, Balt told them to circle around, far away from a lone red flower that was sticking up out of the grass. Alani did not understand why—it wasn't as if they were going to trample the thing anyway—until the earth started to lightly rumble around the flower. It was then the ground shifted, and the patch of grass where the flower rested rose up, revealing a Jekua's large, round head. The creature's body followed as it clambered out of the ground. It was a tall, hulking thing, with a shapely body and a flat face. Its head was covered in grass, with the red flower poking out from the direct center of it, and its body seemed to be made of hardened red clay. It stood on two tiny legs that did not look strong enough to support the rest of its wide body, but evidently looks were deceiving. Or maybe there was some sort of Gravity magic at play, Alani had no clue. The Jekua's emergence left behind a sizeable hole, which was magically refilled with dirt and grass. It then sauntered away in the direction from which they had come, dragging its meaty knuckles on the ground.

Balt explained that the Jekua was called a Staman. It was a Growth-Type, of course, and he'd identified its presence by that vibrant flower sprouting out from the ground. While it looked like a natural flower, in actuality the stamen were extra sets of eyes. Balt had somehow noticed the tiny things blinking as they approached.

Shortly after, they exited the charming park and came upon the rental shop. It was squished between a tai dair joint and a trading card store. The three of them ducked inside with the bikes, paid what they owed, and were back on the street in less than five minutes.

Alani wished they could walk through the park again (and part of her was curious to know where the Staman had gone), but according to their map apps, the local Church of Salt and Sanction was located in the opposite direction. A tragedy.

Balt led the way, following the route on his linkpad. He was more invested in getting to the Church today than she was. She felt guilty for being so annoyed by his enthusiasm, but it just seemed so…wrong.

This wasn't Balt. This wasn't her friend. She'd been angry with him, justifiably so, but she didn't want him closing himself off and wrapping his whole life up in her stuff. That wasn't fair to him.

It was an issue for another time, though. Not something to discuss in the crowded streets of an unknown city, accompanied by a third party.

Soon they were at the Church's doorstep. So to speak. They stood before an entry arch, carved from a glittering, translucent blue substance, much like the arch at the entrance to Tanepke. The Church grounds were surrounded by a tall brick wall, with similar blue rocks stationed at each of the wall's four corners. Two coral golems were stationed underneath the archway, which the group slipped past to enter.

The grounds were larger than that of Tanepke's Church, but clearly not so studiously maintained. There were overgrown hedges, errant weeds, and a handful of fountains that were turned off, filled with stagnant water. Besides the two golems at the entrance, Alani did not see any others wandering around, which was unexpected for a facility so large. All the buildings within the grounds were much larger than the ones in Tanepke too, with far more extravagant architecture, though a fair amount of it seemed to have fallen into disrepair. They walked past the chapel and headed toward the back half of the grounds, where she knew the offices would be located. Being covered in manastreams, she should have no trouble getting in. This way, they wouldn't accidentally stumble in on an ongoing sermon or other community activity in the chapel.

The offices were dimly lit, with no overhead lights; they relied on lamps and natural light that eked in through the windows. A few people milled about, shuffling past desks overrun with stacks of papers and half-drunk mugs of cold coffee. It was a reflection of the grounds as a whole: technically functional, but in need of some upkeep. Not that Alani was one to judge, with the state that her childhood home was usually in.

It took half a minute before someone greeted them. A young woman hurried over after she rounded a corner and spotted them, her hair pulled up in a high, tight ponytail. Her skin was unmarred by manastreams, indicating she had to be a pretty fresh initiate.

"Hi, hi, hello," she said, her voice tinny. "Welcome. My name is Eila. What can I help for—what can I do for you today?" Her tan cheeks showed the barest hint of a blush after her minor slipup. Alani genuinely could not recall if she'd been this nervous as an initiate.

She smiled wide, trying to imbue the girl with a sense of calm. The shineink on her arms and cheeks pulsed, faintly illuminating the other girl's features in the low light. "My name is Alani Temel. I've traveled from Totta Island on a pilgrimage," she explained. "Is there an Elder available who I could speak to?"

Eila nodded without a word and disappeared into the back room, hopefully to procure an Elder, though it was impossible to know for sure what she was doing. But a minute later she returned with a wrinkled, gray-haired man who certainly fit the descriptor of *elder*.

"Good afternoon," said the man with a smile. There were numerous black gaps where he was missing teeth. "I am Elder Jola. I hear you are joining us on a pilgrimage? From Totta?"

"Yes," Alani nodded.

"It has been years since I visited Totta," said Elder Jola. "It is not the easiest thing, lugging these old bones around, you understand. From where do you hail?"

"Tanepke."

"Ahh. I cannot say I have had the pleasure of visiting," the man said, rubbing his stubbly chin. "Where is it?"

"On the southern shore."

"That explains it. Most of my time was spent on the western coast. But anyway," he said, waving his hand, "that is neither here nor there. You did not come all this way to discuss the exploits of a youthful Elder Jola." He chuckled, and Alani did too. Balt and Niona shifted awkwardly behind her. "May I see your documents?" Elder Jola then asked.

Balt grabbed the official Church documents explaining her pilgrimage out of his pack and handed them over to her. She then gave them to Elder Jola, who had to hold the paper a mere inch from his face, eyes squinted, in order to read the text. After an excruciatingly long wait, he finally finished reading the page and returned it to Alani's possession.

"Everything appears to be in order," he said. "When would you like to visit the shrine?"

"Whenever is convenient for your guide," Alani replied.

Elder Jola nodded. "The thing is," he said, "the Veptilo is located at the center of the stadium, and there is a big Jekua tournament taking place soon. I do not recall exactly when, but it is in the next few days. So if you do not wish to wait until that is over, then time is of the essence."

This news struck her as odd. "The Veptilo is inside the stadium?" she said.

The Elder nodded. "Indeed. It is at the heart of the crater that our beautiful city surrounds."

His explanation did not do much to satisfy Alani's curiosity. She said, "Why was a stadium built around it? Does the Church not own the land? My apologies, it is just surprising to me, after visiting the shrines on Totta and Qwi."

"Yes, yes, it is a peculiar situation indeed," said Elder Jola. "The land was previously undeveloped, and the Church did own it. But, well, sometimes people fall on hard times. The Church needed to raise some money, and the best offer came from a company that wanted to build a state of the art stadium."

Alani could hardly believe what she was hearing. Why had this branch of the Church gone broke? Who was mismanaging their money to such an extreme degree that they felt their only option was to sell the land containing the island's Veptilo? If the current status of the grounds was anything to go by, that same person was probably still in charge of the accounting. The land must have been so beautiful, before the developers came in and built a gaudy stadium on top of it.

But that was in the past. The point was, she would need to visit the stadium to perform the ritual. It was probably wiser to get in there before it was completely overrun by the tournament; there was no telling when it would be cleaned up and reopened after the tournament's conclusion.

"As soon as your guide is available would be great," she said.

Elder Jola smiled. "Let us ask Eila, then," he said.

That girl is the shrine guide? Alani thought incredulously. They had trusted an initiate with that duty?

Eila came hurrying back over to them at the sound of her name. "Hi, hi," she said again. "Yes?"

"When might be the soonest you and Elder Neiata

would be free to take our guests here down to the Veptilo?" He turned to Alani and said, "Eila here is in training to eventually take over from Elder Neiata, once she receives her manastreams."

The young girl pondered that for a few seconds before answering. "Tomorrow, I think?" She blinked rapidly, looking Alani up and down. Alani could not figure out what about her made the poor girl so nervous. She could only be three years older than Eila. Maybe it was the Elder tattoos on her face.

"How's tomorrow?" Elder Jola asked.

Alani turned to face her friends. She might be the "leader" according to Balt despite how little she felt she was, but she wanted their opinions. "How's that sound?" she asked them.

"Perfect," Balt said almost before she was done asking.

Niona shrugged. "Works for me," she said. "We can scoot on down there to do whatever and get all signed in then, too." Alani enjoyed the woman's company, but she had to confess she hadn't expected her to spend all her time with them once they reached Makanuele. She figured Niona would branch off to do her own thing, not wanting to be dragged down by Alani's Church obligations.

Alani turned back to Elder Jola. "Tomorrow is great," she said.

The Elder smiled, while Eila looked terrified at the notion of being responsible in any capacity for Alani's pilgrimage. But the girl said, "I'll tell Elder Neiata straight away," and hurried away into the depths of the office building.

Elder Jola offered them a warm meal, which they gladly accepted after several hours of biking and working up an appetite. A late lunch was just what they needed. While they sat around the table, making stilted conversation with the Elder, Alani texted Aeiko to make sure it was okay they showed up on their doorstep soon.

Totally! their reply said. *Can't wait to see you!*

Alani smiled. Then she typed: *Same here.*

6
NOT AWKWARD

THE CITY'S STADIUM, WHICH WAS CALLED XATETU FIELD (named after the crater in which it was built), was located at the center of Makanuele. The Church's compound was in the southeast, and Aeiko's apartment was on the direct opposite side of the city, northwest of the crater. Alani said that they could stop by the stadium on their way so they could sort out signing in for the tournament, but she assured her it would be fine to wait a day. So, after making their arrangements with the Church Elders, they headed straight to Aeiko's place.

As a concession, they decided to walk along the sidewalk at the edge of the crater. All around the crater's perimeter, the innermost part of the city, was a low brick wall painted green. Over the years, graffiti artists had decorated the entirety of the wall, covering it in tags, portraits, landscapes, vulgarity, and everything else under the sun. The wall was periodically broken up by staircases that descended into the crater, and the vantage point offered a clear view of all that lay within.

At the very bottom was, of course, Xatetu Field. The stadium was enormous, dwarfing Tanepke's pitiful (in comparison) Zampano Stadium. From this distance, it looked a fair bit bigger than Himony's Energy Park as well, but Alani's eyes might have been playing tricks on her. All around the stadium were beautifully kept grounds, filled with gently swaying trees and vibrant flower patches running along lengths of handcrafted stone walkways. There were several different courtyards, picnic areas, gazebos, and other spots scattered around the crater, but the focal point was the stadium. It was a shame the crater had been overtaken by some company's desire to turn a profit, but at least they'd maintained a modicum of its natural beauty.

The crater was filled with people enjoying the warm sunshine and clear skies. Alani spied a few couples walking around hand in hand, some teens lounging on blankets playing video games or reading books, a handful of Summoners training Jekuas…so many people simply enjoying their day. Not stressing about Church business, like she was. Though maybe those Summoners were preparing for the tournament and were riddled with anxiety, she didn't know. A small flock of birds suddenly shot out from a tall, crooked tree and disappeared into the maze of skyscrapers.

They passed by one of the wall's many staircase entrances, and sprayed onto the green brick was the phrase "Fe nestwe Xatetu." Alani recognized that it was Volukhan, and obviously something about the crater. "Fe" meant "you," but she wasn't sure about "nestwe." She asked Balt and Niona if they knew what it said, but the most either of them could offer was a weak shrug.

"So, who is this person we're goin' to see? How do you know them?" Niona asked as they continued around the curve of the green wall.

"Aeiko Fentao," said Alani. "They grew up in our hometown, actually. I guess they were mainly my older sister's friend, but I hung out with her and her friends all the time."

"Wait," said Balt, "are they Tin Fentao's kid?"

"Yeah."

"Man, I did *not* get along with their dad."

Niona chuckled. "Why were you regularly interacting with someone's dad?"

Balt said, "He ran that corner store at the edge of the Undertow, right? The one with the big cardboard standee of a Flarrow by the door that said 'Our prices are flaming hot' or something? All half-bent and ripped and nasty from getting rained on all the time."

"Yep," Alani confirmed again.

"That thing was *so old*. When's the last time anyone saw a Flarrow outside of Yuluhu? Anyway, not the point. When we were kids, he caught me and Wasaaru throwing rocks at that wall in the lot across from his shop. He came running outside, waving his arms in the air and screaming at us to stop making such a racket."

Niona laughed. "How were little rocks hitting a wall making enough of a racket for him to hear across the street and inside a building?" she asked.

"Well, they were pretty big rocks," Balt admitted, "and

we were screaming at the top of our lungs every time we threw one."

"Ahh."

"Why were you throwing rocks at a wall?" Alani wanted to know.

"I dunno," said Balt. "Seemed fun at the time."

"You're an idiot," she giggled.

He went on. "He was super pissed. Scared us right off. Took us forever to find another good wall to throw our rocks at."

"I am dying to know what constitutes a 'good wall' to throw rocks at, but that's a conversation for another time," said Niona.

"Trust me, there's a lot to consider. Anyway, after that, any time either of us went in that store, he would call us the 'Rockboys.'"

"That…does not sound very bad," said Alani. "Sounds mostly like a harmless little tease."

"I could think of worse insults for you right now," Niona said.

"Believe me, there was venom in that word! He meant it as the worst insult imaginable. You could just tell by his tone and the glare on his face that, to him, being a Rockboy was the lowest of the low."

"Poor you," said Alani jokingly.

"We were seven!" Balt exclaimed. "Throwing rocks was cool! An adult calling us Rockboys was scarring!"

"Yeah, it seems like it really messed you up," Niona said. Alani laughed.

"Whatever. I hope your friend's more tolerant than their dad is."

Alani clucked her tongue. "Actually," she said, "now that you mention it, when I talked to them the other night, they *did* ask me if there were any Rockboys in our group…I told them no, because I hadn't heard this story before…"

Balt was silent for a beat. Then, "I don't know if you're joking. I genuinely don't."

Alani and Niona cackled at him.

They soon veered away from the crater's perimeter wall and started down the busy city streets. Car horns blared at them as they navigated crosswalks (which was baffling, since the traffic signals indicated they could walk), and numerous unseemly smells intermingled and assaulted their nostrils. There were gutters nearby, of course, but the scents were not just sewage. Something dastardly was afoot. If this was what it was always like traipsing around a city, Alani would be happy to remain in a small town. For all its faults, at least Tanepke was still quiet and stench-free. Mostly.

While Alani used her linkpad to navigate them toward Aeiko's apartment building, Balt was using his to write down the names of various restaurants they passed that he wanted to try. If he insisted on not participating in the tournament, then it seemed he would otherwise occupy his time gorging himself. If he had enough money, anyway. Some of the places they passed seemed far out of his and Alani's budget.

The walk from the crater to Aeiko's apartment—a building called Corsseo Court—took about twenty minutes. Corsseo Court was a huge, U-shaped building standing five stories tall. Nestled within the U was a pretty courtyard, with a massive pergola in the middle and plentiful seating and outdoor cooking implements. The greenery was nowhere near as impressive as that around Xatetu Field, but it looked like an exceedingly pleasant area in which to hang out.

They entered the building, strolling through the lobby and heading for the elevators. Outside it looked like a quaint little place, but inside it had the slight feel of a hotel. It was jarring. The interior did not feel very homey to Alani, but she was sure the individual apartments made up for that. Giant metal block letters hung on the wall saying WELCOME TO THE COURT did not particularly help in that regard, though.

She jabbed the button for the fourth floor, and the elevator doors slid shut with an electronic ding. The dings continued with each floor they passed, until finally they came to a halt. The doors smoothly slid back open, revealing a blue-carpeted hallway lined with gauche watercolor paintings in between every green doorway. Lamps dangled from the ceiling to illuminate the hall, but at this hour they were turned off, letting natural light bleeding through the windows do the work for them.

"What number we lookin' for?" Niona asked as the three of them stepped out into the hall.

"412," Alani replied. She eyed one of the paintings, a depiction of some gigantic yet elegant beast bursting forth from the sea. Or at least that's what she assumed it was, since the quality of the brushstrokes made it hard to tell for sure.

The apartment in question was at the end of the hall, near a wide window that overlooked the courtyard below.

There was a small group of friends setting up by one of the outdoor grills with an overflowing bag of groceries.

Alani sharply inhaled, hoping the others didn't notice. She was suddenly flooded with nervousness at the prospect of seeing Aeiko again. But it was just her dumb childhood crush rearing its head, it was fine. Everything was going to be normal and not awkward. Not awkward. Not awkward. Not awkward.

If she repeated it enough times, it had to be true.

She reached forward and rapped her knuckles on the door. The plaque sporting the apartment number, covered in fake gold plating, rattled with each knock. She took a step back, stumbling into Balt, who jokingly chastised her. She was too anxious to bite back.

Get ahold of yourself, she said in her mind. *Don't be weird. Be normal.*

The door opened.

Aeiko was the one who opened it.

Obviously.

Get ahold of yourself, Alani thought again.

But it was hard.

She felt that rush again immediately. That naïve, youthful flutter in one's stomach when they sighted their crush rounding a corner. Coming closer. Their features seemingly lighting up whatever room they were in. So bright that it was blinding, but impossible to turn away from. Seeing Aeiko again after so many years brought all of that back. Alani felt like she was ten years old.

Aeiko stood beyond the threshold, their hair long and flowing down to their shoulders. That was considered long for them, anyway. Their big, gorgeous eyes were a deep, dark brown, obscured by long, curled lashes as they blinked. They were wearing an orange cropped tanktop and tight-fitting jeans with pockets so small surely not even their linkpad could fit in them. A white earbud was lodged in their left ear, just barely visible amongst the black forest of their hair.

They smiled.

Alani smiled.

Was it an awkward smile? She couldn't tell. Was she showing too many teeth? Or not enough teeth? Were her cheeks dimpling? Suddenly she had no idea whether or not she had dimples. If she did, was that good or bad? Or was it bad to not have dimples? She needed to brush up on whether dimples were good or not. It was not something she could ask Aeiko directly, that would be insane. And did her lips look weird? She was worried her lips were curled up in a snarl. She did not want to look like a freak the first time she saw Aeiko in however many years. If she had been smart, she would've practiced this smile when she was alone in her various hotel rooms. She'd known for days she was coming here, she had absolutely no excuse to have not practiced. Foolish. Positively foolish.

"Hey," said Aeiko. Then, "Wow, it's so wild seeing you after so long. You look so much older!" They leaned in and wrapped Alani in a tight hug, holding her close.

Alani was going to die. She said, "Thanks! I think?"

Aeiko chuckled as they pulled back and said, "It's definitely not a bad thing. Come on in. I'm Aeiko," they said to Balt and Niona, who stood silently behind Alani. The two greeted them in turn, and then they all entered the apartment.

The apartment was certainly homier than the complex's lobby, but not by a whole lot. The walls were a neutral tan color, and the floors were dark brown hardwood. Not a single inch of plush, warm carpet. All the furniture was gray or black, and there were no real decorations to speak of. The only pop of color was a gray blanket that happened to have a blue logo in the bottom corner, folded up on the gray couch. There were a few books piled up on the shelves, but aside from that, the living area was pretty bare. In truth, it totally fit the stereotype of how a Lakahlo engineer's living space might look.

"Welcome to the pad," said Aeiko. "I know it's kind of cold," they then said, as if they could peer straight into Alani's brain. "I let my roommate take the lead with the decorating when we moved in, and I, uh...just did not care enough to add anything to it, I guess."

"Are you talking trash in there?" came a light, airy voice from somewhere deeper in the apartment. From one of the doorways emerged a blonde woman, her hair shaved down to stubble. Her eyes were rimmed with blue eyeliner and she wore a loose green jacket over a white shirt and pink shorts. She beamed as she approached the group standing in her living room.

"Only a little," said Aeiko, suddenly blushing as the woman grew nearer. "This is Holly," they said.

Holly held her hand out as she came to a stop, and Alani shook it. Balt and Niona followed. Then Holly took a few steps back, her arm brushing against Aeiko's. It was slight, and it was hardly a moment, but Alani noticed it. She felt like an idiot for noticing it.

Get ahold of yourself.

"I happen to think my sense of style is quite nice," Holly said, smirking. "It's slick. It's cool. Anyway, nice to meet you. You and Aeiko grew up together?"

Alani nodded. Aeiko said, "We both came up in the Undertow." Then their eyebrows lifted, like a lightbulb went off in their head. "Wait—you said your name's Balt?"

"...yeah," Balt said dubiously.

"Are you *the* Balt? The kid my dad complained about all the time? The Rockboy?"

Niona howled with laughter. Alani chuckled, too nervous to laugh as boisterously as she wanted to. Balt's jaw hung slack.

"That was *one time*!" he said. "Why was he so hung up on it?"

Aeiko laughed. "I don't know," they said. "You really made an impression, though."

"Yeah, apparently..."

Niona said, "Your dad might have some advice on how to handle a Rockboy staying in your apartment. Might wanna hit him up."

"Stop," Balt told her. She laughed at him again.

The name *Holly* was stuck in Alani's mind, like a popcorn kernel in her teeth. She'd definitely heard of this woman before, though they'd never met. Where had she seen her?

Then it hit her: Aeiko had posted about Holly online before. Of course they had, she was their roommate. But the reason they'd posted about Holly before was because they had dated.

That was why they'd moved in together. They weren't

simply roommates. Not at first, in any case. Alani had read that they'd broken up a long while ago, sometime in mid-Spring, if she recalled correctly. That explained why Aeiko looked so embarrassed when Holly came bursting out of her bedroom.

This realization brought heat to Alani's (possibly dimpled?) cheeks as well. She stared at Holly, imagining her and Aeiko kissing. Her stomach did a flip.

Why were they still living together? Was that not incredibly awkward for the both of them? It seemed to be for Aeiko, at least, if Alani was reading them right.

"The couch folds out," Aeiko said, moving away from their ex and walking over to the aforementioned couch. "Not sure if you two want to share it, but if not, we've got plenty of blankets and pillows in the closet to make a pallet or something on the floor. Sorry we don't have much more space."

"No, it's totally fine," Alani assured them. "We appreciate you opening your doors to us at all. Really, if it's too much trouble, just say so and we can go find a room somewhere."

"It's cool!" said Aeiko. "It'll be fun having you around."

"And I am fine with the floor," Balt chimed in.

"You're not staying with us?" Holly asked Niona, looking her up and down with flirty eyes.

Niona either did not notice the flirtatious look or decided to ignore it. "Nope," she responded flatly.

"Shame."

Moving right past that, Aeiko said, "Feel free to help yourselves to anything in the kitchen."

"Unless it's mine," Holly cut in.

"...right. Uh...yeah, so, pretty much anything in the kitchen. But if you want to eat out, there are tons of good places nearby. We always talk about how we're at the center of all the best restaurants in the city. Any type of cuisine you'd want is basically a ten-minute walk away, at most. I still have to go to work for the next few days, but once I'm on vacation, I'd be happy to show you around. There's a ton to do around here, as you can probably guess."

Did that mean they were going to be left here alone with Holly? Or would she be gone too, squirreled away in some office building? Alani wasn't super comfortable with the notion of hanging around the woman alone for extended periods of time. Largely due to her being a stranger, but being Aeiko's ex was a factor, too.

"When are you checking out the Church, by the way?" Aeiko asked.

Alani told them about their brief visit on the way over, and their plan to visit Xatetu Field in the morning. While she spoke, it was clear from Aeiko's expression that they were still greatly confused by Alani's dip into the religious life. Holly listened with a blank stare, probably not caring about or processing any of it.

There came a clomping from the other bedroom, and Alani nearly fell over at the sight of a coral golem stooping under the doorframe to enter the living room. It stood a couple feet taller than any of them, and its body was mostly purple with speckling of blue and orange. Its right hand was yellow, which it used to wave to all the newcomers.

Alani couldn't think of a time she'd ever seen a coral

golem wave. She raised her hand, quirking an eyebrow, and waved back. It was only polite.

"Oh," Aeiko muttered, "this is our other houseguest. We've taken to calling him Brine."

Alani wasn't sure what to make of this. Neither were Balt or Niona, apparently. None of them had ever seen a coral golem in someone's home. They were always bought and used by companies or the Church, not kept as pets or whatever was happening here.

"Hi, Brine," she said. The golem waved once more.

"He gets in the way a lot. Get used to that," Holly said dryly, tearing away from the group and walking to the fridge. She grabbed a bottle from it and popped the cap off. "He's pretty, though, I'll give him that." She took a swig from the green glass bottle.

Brine, seemingly unaffected by Holly's complaint, stomped over to the couch and sat down, staring ahead at the blank television screen. The golem sat completely motionless.

"Why do you have a coral golem?" Balt asked on everyone's behalf.

Aeiko grinned. "Yeah, it's weird, I know. My project team at work is developing a new version of the tech that absorbs mana and gives the golems life. Brine comes home with me so I can monitor the device."

"Kinda like a class pet," said Niona.

"Not far off, really," said Aeiko. "At first, I was annoyed being the one saddled with him, but I've grown fond of the big lug. Isn't that right, Brine?"

Brine turned his craggy, featureless head in their

direction, staying still for three full seconds, then turned back to the television.

"Holly isn't wrong, though, he *does* take up quite a bit of space," Aeiko sighed. "Sorry in advance."

"I dunno, I think it's kinda cool," said Balt, crossing his arms. "What's different about the version you're working on? What's it do differently than the devices golems already use?"

Aeiko's cheeks flushed again. They said, "I mean, essentially nothing. But that's the point. It does what the current devices do, but much more efficiently, and hopefully self-sufficiently. The ones that we use now last for a really long time, like almost half a season at a time, but at some point you always have to power down the golem and recharge the device, which can take a full day. The goal with this one is for it to absorb just as much mana and distribute it accordingly throughout the golem, but also divert some of that to continually recharge the device. So, ideally, you would never need to charge it up again. The golem would be able to just operate indefinitely, until you decide to manually shut it off, for whatever reason."

That sounded convenient. There had been more than a few occasions at the Church when Alani was given the duty of gathering their golems' chips and charging them up. It was a mild hassle retrieving the devices, given how much bigger the golems were than her. One less chore to do sounded pretty good in her book.

Balt asked a few more technical questions about Aeiko's work, which they answered in as much detail as they could without totally confusing everybody. While they chatted, Holly gulped down her beverage then threw the bottle away with a clatter. She then disappeared back into her room.

Aeiko glanced at the closed door before turning back around. "Don't worry," they said. "She's just kind of busy right now. She will definitely be making her presence known later."

Ahh, Alani thought. *Perfect.*

"Anyway, do you two want to get settled in? Unload your stuff or whatever?" They gestured toward the living area, then told Brine to get up and move. The coral golem stood obediently and wandered into the kitchen, where he proceeded to stand and stare at the four of them.

Balt surged forward, tossing his bag onto the ground and pointing at a nearby door. "That the closet?" he asked. When Aeiko confirmed, he popped the door open and started gathering the pillows and blankets that would comprise his bed for the next two weeks.

As Alani walked toward the couch, passing Aeiko, their arms brushed against each other.

It was subtle, and it was slight, but Alani noticed it.

She was going to die.

7
PUKE AND PAWS

AFTER SEEING THE PLACE, NIONA WAS SOMEWHAT GLAD she'd gotten her own hotel room. Not that Alani's friend's apartment was bad or anything, but it would undeniably be pretty cramped in there. She needed to keep herself loose for the tournament. Plus, she didn't want to worry herself about disturbing people by coming back at absurd hours of the night or tiptoe around dozing Balts if she wanted to hit the gym before sunrise. It would be easier this way.

Also, having a coral golem walking around creeped her out. Brine was probably a perfectly pleasant fellow, but something about the golems had always unsettled her. And why was just his hand yellow?

They'd hung out for a while, with Aeiko preparing the lot of them an early dinner which they gobbled down gratefully. Their roommate Holly was a bit of a kook, with a sort of crazed glint in her eyes, but it was in a way that amused Niona. For the moment, anyhow. She knew from experience that such a personality could get old fast. She didn't think she had it in her to live with somebody like that, but it was funny to observe them for a couple hours.

When they finished eating, Niona chilled a short while longer to let the food digest and then got up to excuse herself. She needed to check in to the hotel, and she also wanted to track down the gym.

As per usual, when she asked Balt if he wanted to accompany her, he clammed up. Niona had pulled him over into the kitchen, away from the others. Alani looked shellshocked sitting on the couch beside Aeiko and Holly, eating some dessert Holly had bought at a nearby convenience store. Brine was standing idle in the doorway to the bathroom. When she asked if he wanted to come train at the gym, get a few more sessions with that Barrier under his belt, she caught his eyes shifting in Alani's direction.

"Uh…I don't think so," he mumbled, tearing his gaze from Alani to look down at the floor. When he looked back up at Niona, it was with guilt in his eyes.

She rolled her eyes and snorted. She didn't know what had transpired between them, but this weird tension was beginning to grate on her. "Seriously?" she said with a huff.

Balt smiled weakly, with no warmth in the expression, then shrugged. "Sorry." After a pause and a sigh, he said, "I just can't abandon her."

Niona cocked an eyebrow. "Abandon?" she said. "That sounds a bit dramatic. She's hangin' out with a childhood friend and eatin' little mini chocolate cakes. You aren't leavin' her on a sinking ship in the middle of the ocean. C'mon."

"I know, but it's just—look, she got hurt while we were watching the Korjes, and I could've stopped it. I should've been there. I agreed to come on her pilgrimage and protect her, but I messed up. I just wanna make up for it."

That was the end of the conversation, as he then returned to the living room to plop himself down in the plush armchair. Brine waved to him on his way over.

Oh well, Niona thought. *His loss, I guess.* She could kind of understand his reasoning, but still thought he was missing a great opportunity here. She hoped he would come around before it was too late, but it wasn't her place to get in the middle of their business.

She bade the group farewell (taking care to wave to Brine near the bathroom), then shuffled out of the apartment.

Out in the courtyard, a group of friends were eating burgers and drinking beers, laughing heartily at some joke or story one of them told. It was a much livelier affair than the one up in apartment 412. With the tension between Balt and Alani and whatever was going through Alani's head when she sat near Aeiko and Holly, the air in that apartment was stifling. Niona took in a deep breath, but gagged on some rank stench emanating from the city streets.

She wound her way through the streets, heading even further northwest. The hotel was nearly at the edge of the city limits. It'd be slightly annoying having to walk all the way over to the stadium from there, but part of her thought it'd do her some good to put a bit of distance between herself and the festivities. She could always call up a car to drive her over, but the walk would help clear her head before and after matches.

The route from Corsseo Court to the Halwell Hotel took her past the gym she'd planned on using. It looked like a decent setup, and through the windows she could see a ton of Summoners inside. Not all of them would be practicing for the tournament, but she expected a fair amount were.

It wasn't long before she reached the Halwell and checked herself in at the front desk. The hotel wasn't as glamorous as the places she typically stayed at, but she'd prioritized something close to both Aeiko's apartment and a gym. She trundled upstairs to her room on the second floor and only stayed long enough to drop off her bag and use the restroom. The urge to pee had presented itself to her back at the apartment, but she couldn't bring herself to move Brine out of the way.

The moon hung bright in the sky by the time her shoes hit the pavement again. With the city's abundance of lights, everything from the traffic signals to late-night office buildings to neon bar signs, it was hard to see any stars twinkling above. It was the same in Himony, but at least there she could walk down to the beach and watch the stars shining over the lavender sea, unobstructed by the city.

She made her way back to the gym, narrowly avoiding a puddle of some unidentified liquid that was not present earlier but now covered the sidewalk, with a couple roaches skittering around its edges.

Inside, a large, sweaty man with rectangular glasses greeted her from behind a counter. The man patted his forehead with a hand towel before he spoke. "Evening," he said, nodding his head. There was a gap in his smile where he was missing a tooth. "Have you visited us before?"

"Nope. First timer."

"Exciting! Are you interested in a membership? We offer thirty-day and annual plans. You save a bit with the annual, of course. Or are you just in for the night?"

Niona pondered that for a moment, then asked about the session rate versus a single month's membership. Given how often she planned to be in there over the next two weeks, it actually turned out to be cheaper to just buy a membership for a single thirty-day period. Doing so also gave her the benefit of a guest pass, should Balt ever pluck his head from his ass and decide to join her.

She grew antsy as the man drew up the paperwork, but the extra time spent would be worthwhile in the end. As she finished signing everything, she eyed him and said, "You have it set to cancel after the thirty days, right? No renewal?"

The man nodded. "Yes, yes, of course." He blinked rapidly as he answered, offering absolutely no trustworthiness in his expression. Niona made a mental note to check her bank statement at the start of Fall.

Beyond the front desk was another counter where Summoners could purchase water, Thunderjolt, mod chips, and assorted snacks. She hadn't thought to stop by a Jekua shop before coming, so she walked over to the counter to see what mods they had for sale.

Surprisingly, they didn't have any Ability chips. Niona

wondered if the gym didn't sell them at all, or if they'd all been bought up in anticipation of the Makanuele Rumble. That wasn't what she was looking for anyway, though. She was hunting for at least a Speed++ microchip with which to alter her Muggish, Glom. A Speed+ would be okay too, but she needed as much extra *oomph* as she could get. If there happened to be a Speed+++, that would be even better.

As it turned out, they only had Speed+ chips in stock. There was a space for Speed++ and Speed+++, but they were both sadly empty. She asked if there were any more hidden away in the back, but the pimply teen running the counter shook his head.

"I'll just take that one, then," she said, pointing at the Speed+ mod.

There were multiple in stock, but it wasn't possible to stack the same type of mod on a single Jekua. Her kayet would accept her trying to install two Speed+ chips on Glom's memory card, but the effects wouldn't double. Since it was essentially adding "code" (for lack of a better term) to preexisting data, it wasn't as if inserting a second one would add even more to it. It was a predetermined bit of data written by some engineer at Lakahlo that slotted in to Jekua data, so it would always be the same.

She paid, then made her way over to a bench and slid the microchip into her kayet. While she waited for it to install on Glom's card, she watched some of the other Summoners train, trying to guess who might pop up as her opponents in the tournament.

Two young women were sparring twin Bombats against each other. It seemed they'd probably imprinted the same one and were now just messing around with the fuzzy little firestarters. They had the air of casual Summoners, not likely to be competing. Both women repeatedly made their Bombats start to heat up, the slick black fur starting to turn bright orange, but neither followed through with the Jekua's full-blown explosion technique. Whether that was because they were scared to or because they simply couldn't achieve it, Niona didn't know, but the girls looked like they were having a fun time.

Hanging from the ceiling were bars for Jekuas to swing from and hoops for them to jump through. It was an uncommon sort of obstacle course, but Niona had seen something similar a few times before. The gym's full course was located in the next room. An old, grizzled man was currently making his Whirlcruel swing from bar to bar. Niona had never seen such a thing, and she had to think it was an incredibly tough task. Whirlcruels were Tidal-Type Jekuas with long, squid-like bodies. Their skin was a pale white, and they had large, red beaks. They lacked any tentacles like a normal squid, though, pushing themselves through the water with Sonic magic. When they breached the ocean's surface, they used Tidal magic to create four tentacles out of water. The Summoner was using these watery tentacles to somehow grasp the bars and swing the huge Jekua along the ceiling. Niona didn't know how he was doing it; he had to have extraordinary control over the beast's tentacles, or perhaps he'd modded it with some sort of Thermal-based chip that allowed him to discreetly solidify the tentacles to give himself a better grip. Whichever the case, it was impressive, and it spoke to the man's experience and skill. A piece of Niona hoped he wasn't in the tournament, but another piece welcomed the challenge.

Below the dangling squid, in the target practice area, every rubber mat was occupied by a Summoner pummeling a Jekua-shaped dummy. The person who caught Niona's eye in particular was a woman around her age using a Hiss. The Jekua was human-sized, but with a thick snake's body covered in yellowish-orange fur. Its torso was striped with black, and it had two muscular arms with sharp, curved claws. Its head was angular and pointed like that of a cat, but with flappy ears that looked more like fish fins. Niona knew that Hisses were Radiant-Types, but she couldn't remember if they possessed a secondary Type.

This woman's Hiss was stunningly fast. It might have been a trick of the eye, though. She was using its Radiant magic to create a flash of blinding light, during which time the Hiss would dart forward to viciously attack with its claws. It would then flash again and suddenly be on the other side of the mat, far from the dummy. It was a neat idea, but not one that was really worth practicing with an immobile target.

Niona's kayet alerted her that it was finished modifying Glom's memory card, so she promptly discarded the Speed+ chip in the trash. She then marched over to the Summoner with the Hiss.

"Hey there," she said from the sidelines. When the woman turned to face her, she waved amiably. The woman returned the gesture.

"I'll be done in a couple minutes," the woman said.

She was about to turn away again when Niona said, "Nah, it ain't that. I wanted to see if you were up for some sparring. Seems to me like your technique might be better suited for a real opponent, and I just installed a speed mod that I wanna try out. That fast-ass Hiss of yours looks perfect for that."

The woman scrunched her face up in thought, then the Hiss idling behind her melted into soulclay and returned to the kayet on her wrist. "Sure," she said, stepping off the mat. "Name's Elodie, by the way."

"Niona." Together they ambled over to one of the few available sparring rings. "You entering the tournament next week?"

Elodie grimaced and shook her head. "Unfortunately, all I've got is this Hiss and a Toryoth I just imprinted the other day. Some pipe burst a few weeks ago and my damn house flooded. Ruined all my memory cards, fried every Jekua I had."

Niona's stomach dropped. "Oh, wow," she muttered. "I'm so, so sorry. That's awful." Losing her Jekua collection would be a more devastating blow than even losing a house.

"Mhmm," Elodie grumbled. "I was actually here when it happened. Had my kayet and my Hiss's memory card with me at the time, so it was the only one left unscathed."

"Sorry," Niona said once more. "That really sucks. How's your house?"

From the discontent in Elodie's tone as she summarized the ordeal of getting the pipes, carpet, furniture, and other belongings replaced, Niona felt immense joy about not being responsible for a house.

The two entered the ring and stood at opposite ends. Before they summoned their Jekuas, Elodie asked, "What am I going up against, exactly?"

"A Muggish."

Elodie frowned ever so slightly. "I don't even know what that is," she admitted.

When Niona summoned Glom, Elodie looked just as disgusted by the Jekua as Balt and Alani had been a couple days prior. She chuckled at the other woman's dismayed expression.

A few moments later, Niona and Glom stood face to face with Elodie's Hiss. At this angle, the cat-snake-monster looked way more intimidating. Niona hadn't battled a Hiss before, and she wasn't totally sure what they were capable of, but she didn't anticipate Elodie doing much besides practicing her illuminating dash move.

The Hiss started forward.

Let's see what you've got, Glom.

Naturally, the battlefield lit up, completely obscuring Niona's vision. She shifted Glom to the left, but when the light faded, Elodie's Hiss was right there to greet him. It swiped at Glom, tearing through one of his soupy arms. Then there was another flash, and the Hiss had put twenty or thirty feet between them.

There was only a split second between her vision returning and the Hiss attacking. She didn't know if a first-level Speed upgrade would be enough of a boost for something as inherently slow as a Muggish to dodge that, but she had to try.

Across the way, Elodie was grinning smugly. Niona

pitied the woman for losing all of her Jekuas, but she still wanted to beat her ass.

She had to take the initiative, land a blow on the other Jekua. Glom glided forward, looking like a sentient pile of vomit bubbling across the floor. Niona frowned, not super pleased with the Jekua's speed, but it was at least a *little bit* faster than before.

The Hiss lunged forward, claws outstretched. No flashbang this time, but much less space between the two Jekuas. Glom still didn't have ample time to avoid the attack, enduring another swipe from the creature's claws. They tore straight through the Muggish's mucky chest, eliciting another scowl from Niona.

She slid Glom away from the Hiss, but Elodie wasn't going to let up. The beast surged forward again, and Niona saw it arch its back, readying itself to pounce again.

This time, she was ready. When the Hiss leapt into the air, she flattened Glom's viscous body against the mat. The Hiss soared through the spot where Glom's head had previously been, landing on the other side. When Glom rose up again, he was already facing the Hiss, and he spewed a ball of magma at it.

The ball splashed against the Hiss, burning off some of its fur to expose the pale skin beneath. It sizzled and crackled like grilling meat. Elodie looked pissed, the smug expression wiped clean off her face.

While the Hiss's skin was burning, with fur sizzling into nothingness, Glom whipped around the creature, blasting its chest with another magma ball as he slid across the ring. More fur dissipated, and the skin beneath darkened and scarred.

The Jekua swung at Glom again, but this time Niona was able to avoid the attack by splitting Glom's head in two. The Hiss's claw swatted at the empty air between the two head halves, though it connected with the Muggish's chest just below. Striking that area drained less mana than it would've if Glom's head had been hit, but with the extra mana it took to split apart the head in the first place, it was basically net zero.

Niona was starting to understand how to use Glom's added speed to her advantage, though. On the whole, the Muggish was still much slower than a lot of other Jekuas. Moving across the battlefield was not his strong suit. She could distinctly feel herself moving his body faster, though, like when she needed to separate the head or completely flatten the body. Morphing Glom's body could be done fairly quickly, even if moving the entire thing still took a bit of time.

So for the next few minutes she practiced that, focusing more on using the advantages of Glom's liquidy state to curve his body in unexpected ways to dodge attacks. When Elodie slithered her Hiss away and came in for another illuminated dash, Glom always got hit (except for one instance that Niona had to chalk up to luck rather than skill). If they engaged in close quarters combat, though, they were more evenly matched despite the Hiss's agility. Niona was frequently able to anticipate Elodie's moves, shifting Glom's body in wild ways so that the Hiss pawed at nothing but air.

At one point, she once again went for the head-splitting maneuver, but this time hastily closed up the gap just as the Hiss's claw filled it, encasing its entire hand in molten hot magma.

"Dammit!" Elodie shrieked, yanking the Hiss's hand away from Glom's body with a wet *splot*! It emerged hairless and dark, dripping with globules of Glom's body. They fizzled and smoked when they hit the floor.

They traded a few more blows, and by the end of it the Hiss's remaining fur was no more than a handful of patches on its back. Not to say that Elodie hadn't done her fair share of damage; given Glom's liquid body, it was impossible to see where an opponent had struck him, but Niona was certainly feeling it in her mana reserves.

She was going to need a break soon, but she wanted to land one more good hit.

The Hiss was on the other side of the sparring ring, preparing for its light-up dash assault. Once again, Niona wanted to cut the distance between them so that its advantage was lessened. It could still perform the move, of course, but with less space for it to move around in while the Summoner's vision was obscured, the easier it would be to predict its trajectory and dodge.

Glom raced across the ring—or what counted for "racing" in the Muggish's case. He scrambled across the mat, and he was a quarter of the way to where the Hiss sat before another of its flashbangs went off.

There was plenty of space in which the Hiss could maneuver, and Niona wasn't going to bother trying to move out of the way. Glom stopped in his tracks so that she wouldn't use up any more mana than necessary. She could distantly hear the Hiss sliding along the mat, and she knew it was getting close to her Jekua.

The blinding light had barely faded when the Hiss leapt forward. Part of the magic had to be that Elodie could still see clearly; it would be less useful otherwise. But Niona could make out the Jekua's vibrant yellow fur (what was left of it, anyway), and she acted accordingly.

She flattened Glom's body again, but this time began to stretch it out lengthwise, making the Muggish's body into a long, red stripe across the floor. With his increased speed, Niona was able to stretch Glom's body out before the Hiss could hit the ground. Assuming Elodie had always maintained a clear look at Glom, it wasn't something Niona could have done beforehand, or else Elodie would have reacted differently. The speed was vital.

Niona grinned, imagining Balt naming the move something weird like *Skidmark*.

Elodie's Hiss crashed onto the ground, rolling its body through the streak of magical magma, covering itself in excruciating burns. The woman stomped her foot in frustration and withdrew her charred Hiss. Niona did the same with Glom, trying her very best to not sport a self-satisfied expression and utterly failing.

She thanked Elodie for the quick match and wished her luck rebuilding her Jekua collection, along with whatever household repairs there were still to be done. They both retreated back to the counter to buy some Thunderjolts, and they chatted a bit while drinking and replenishing their mana. Eventually, they parted ways, with Elodie returning to the target practice area and summoning her freshly-imprinted Toryoth.

Niona, meanwhile, headed toward the obstacle course room. She wanted to keep working on Glom's overall speed as well as specifically shifting his body to move around obstacles.

When she entered, she spotted the Whirlcruel guy in there, having presumably tuckered himself out with the ceiling bars.

She offered him a kind smile, which he reciprocated. Maybe he'd be up for a race.

8

IN THE LIVING ROOM

SOMEWHERE AROUND EIGHT YEARS AGO, MANY YEARS before her sister gathered up her belongings and stormed out of Ti House, bound for greener pastures in Hurrathsa, Alani and Siuv were inseparable.

They would spend time together in their shared bedroom, doing all they could to dissociate themselves from their parents. Drunken arguments filled the halls of Ti House, from almost all the families living therein, but many of them originated from the Temel apartment.

Siuv would lay on her bed, its sheets messy and the pillows stacked against the wall for her to lean against. The girls' parents—who were perhaps the messiest individuals Alani had ever laid eyes on, even to this day—incessantly droned on about how the girls needed to keep their room clean. Foremost on the checklist of cleanliness was making their beds every morning before school, and so ignoring that request was one of Siuv's small acts of rebellion.

Alani could never bring herself to disobey her parents, no matter how much she wanted to. Her bed was pristinely made up every single morning, without fail. There was always that part of her ten-year-old brain that thought maybe, just maybe, if she was a good enough daughter, it would inspire them to clean up their own act. If she did as she was told, they would be proud of her, and the lack of disappointment would prevent them from turning to their drinks every day. Now that she was older and wiser, she realized how pitiful that line of thinking was. Torturing herself, placing her parents' behavior solely on her shoulders.

While Siuv would lay against her pillows, kicking her feet around to make her bed even more disheveled than it already was, Alani would sit cross-legged on the floor with her toys. Her toy collection was small, and she only owned a few "real" toys, most of those being hand-me-downs from Siuv once she'd grown out of them. Along with her couple of princess and animal and Jekua toys, she would play with colored erasers and uniquely-shaped rocks she'd found outside in the Undertow's sandy streets.

Her parents couldn't afford to buy her any of the cool playsets she heard kids at school talking about—big plastic houses, shaved ice shops, extravagant treehouses, and so on. So instead, she would take pieces of paper and crudely draw what were essentially blueprints to different locales. What she ended up with were merely bird's eye views of the places she wanted to play with her toys in, but the few occasions when she'd attempted to construct something with three dimensions out of cardboard or thicker cardstock, it had ended in catastrophe.

She was content with her flat, handmade homes and shops.

She and her sister spent countless nights like this: Alani on the floor, playing with her toys on her pieces of paper, while Siuv clacked away on her linkpad in bed. Alani was unbelievably jealous of her sister's linkpad, but her parents insisted that she was too young to own one. Not that they could afford another yet, anyway, but they leaned heavily on the "too young" excuse.

Every so often, Alani would squeakily ask her sister for a suggestion as to what her characters should do, and her sister's answer was always dependent on her current mood. Most of the time, Siuv would gladly offer up a scenario for little bright-eyed Alani. But there were times when, after a long day of schoolwork or dealing with their parents (or both), Siuv was too frustrated to humor her sister and would blurt out ridiculous, not at all age-appropriate situations for her toys that would make Alani balk, just to shut her up.

What young, foolish Alani did not know was that oftentimes her sister was messaging Aeiko on her linkpad. Since Aeiko had skipped several grades and was therefore the youngest person in their class, Siuv had noticed how nervous and lonely they seemed. She had decided quickly to become friends with them and take them under her wing, in a way.

Alani only became aware of the times Siuv was texting Aeiko when their bedroom door would swing open wildly to reveal Aeiko standing there, looking positively radiant. Alani's head would turn to the doorway, her neck nearly snapping with the motion, her eyes bulging out of their sockets. Her heart would beat madly, trying to break free of her chest so that it could go to Aeiko.

Without thinking, she'd sweep away her mass of toys and papers under her sister's bed, praying to any higher power who would listen that the older girl had not seen any of it. But of course, with Siuv refusing to make her bed, her sheets and comforter would be hanging off the side and all of Alani's stuff would just slam into the blankets, remaining completely visible to Aeiko.

All this to say that now, eight years later, Alani once more felt exactly like that nervous child itching in her skin on her bedroom floor as she sat in the presence of Aeiko. This time around, at least she didn't have a collection of toys to deepen her embarrassment and make her feel even more like a baby.

Even though there weren't many years between them, she still felt like a child in Aeiko's eyes. Nothing they had said or done indicated that it was how Aeiko actually saw her, but the feeling remained. She knew it was her own warped perception of herself, comparing herself to her older sister like she always did, but she failed to suppress it.

Holly latching onto them like a barnacle on the underside of a boat was not helping matters either. By the way Holly acted, Alani was starting to doubt herself about whether she'd truly read that they had broken up. Or maybe they had, but got back together in the interim? It was impossible to tell. Aeiko wasn't initiating anything with Holly, but they also weren't pushing her away when she got clingy or touchy-feely. Maybe they were just too embarrassed to make a big deal out of it in front of people.

"It's the absolute *best*," Holly said, her hand resting on Aeiko's shoulder, pressing her weight into them. "Really, you'd love it. You *have* to try it."

"Definitely," Alani said, nodding mindlessly. She'd been too distracted by Aeiko's cheekbones to pay attention to whatever it was Holly was saying. Something about a restaurant? Or some sort of activity? She shot a glance at Balt, hoping he'd step in and clarify.

"I've never been somewhere like that," he said. "Does the table get hot with that little grill in the middle of it? And how do you know when the meat's done cooking? I'm no chef, I dunno if I'd trust myself to cook my own food."

Alani ascertained they were discussing a restaurant where the servers brought raw meat to the table and the patrons cooked it themselves on a small grill. So kind of a restaurant *and* an activity.

"Oh, it's a breeze," Holly assured him. "The meat is cut super thin so it cooks super fast. You'd definitely be able to tell. They even have an all-you-can-eat special where you can just pay to have them bring you refills every time you run out."

"Meat refills," Alani murmured. "Not a phrase I ever thought I'd hear."

She thought she'd only spoken loud enough for herself or maybe Balt to hear next to her, but she caught Aeiko smirking at the comment.

Holly moved her hand from Aeiko's shoulder down to their leg, patting them on the thigh. "We should all go!" she said brightly. "It'd be fun, don't you think?" She turned her face toward Aeiko's, and with how far she was leaning over, it wouldn't take much more to plant a kiss on their cheek. Alani shuddered.

"Yeah, sure," Aeiko said dismissively.

"I'm down for anything y'all wanna do," said Balt. "My schedule is wide open."

Aeiko stood, sending Holly's hand flying off their leg. They said, "Well, for now, I think it's time to get to bed. I've still got work in the morning, unfortunately." The statement was followed by a disgusted sigh.

Holly followed suit, jumping up from the sofa. "That's true. Early morning at the lab tomorrow!"

"You work at Lakahlo too?" Alani asked.

She nodded and said, "Yup. That's where we met, actually." Aeiko moved around to the other side of the couch before Holly could wrap her arm around them or jump on their back or whatever it was she was clearly compelled to do.

"Ahh, cool." Alani had trouble picturing someone with Holly's disposition working in a quiet, stuffy office environment. She probably livened up the holiday parties, though.

"Yup. Well, goodnight everyone! Great meeting the both of you. And your other friend too." A slight smile etched onto Holly's face, once again making Alani question whether she and Aeiko were an item if she was so intrigued by Niona.

Alani and Balt both told her goodnight, and she disappeared into her room, closing the door with a soft click. Aeiko still stood behind the couch, lightly smacking their palms on the cushions.

"So," they said, "anything else you need to get comfortable?"

They both thought for a moment, then shook their heads. "I think we're fine," Alani said. "And again, thank you so much for hosting us. We really appreciate it."

Aeiko smiled, and it seemed to Alani that it was their first genuine smile of the evening now that Holly had wandered off. "It's really not a problem, don't worry about it." Then they turned to the coral golem, who had recently migrated from the bathroom to the kitchen, and said, "Come on, Brine."

The golem began its slow march into Aeiko's room. Balt said, "He sleeps in there with you?"

"Not really *sleeps,* but stands around while I sleep, I guess. Typically, he chills out here in the living room, but he can stay with me while you're here."

Alani was grateful for that concession. She didn't mind Brine's presence at all, but given how much he enjoyed changing his position at random, she feared waking up in the dark to use the restroom and crashing into his bulky, craggy body.

As Brine shuffled into Aeiko's bedroom, they said, "There's a spare key over on the counter so you can go explore the city and stuff tomorrow. I'll try to keep quiet when I leave in the morning, but I can't promise the same for Holly…I'll text her in a minute to remind her, but…" They trailed off, leaving the unnecessary unsaid.

They thanked Aeiko profusely again before they excused themselves to bed, leaving Alani and Balt alone in the living room.

"I like them," Balt said after a few seconds of silence.

"I'm glad," said Alani. She began removing cushions from the couch so that she could fold it out. She felt awkward doing so, for some reason, and almost wanted to simply sleep on the couch so that she didn't have to go through the whole process.

"Holly's a bit much," Balt said, whispering. "Aeiko's cool, though. And Holly's not that bad, just kinda…" He looked to the ceiling, pushing his tongue against the inside of his cheek, searching for the right word.

Alani provided one for him. "Loud?"

"I was gonna say *outspoken*, but yes, that works too."

She grinned. "I think you were going to say *shrill*."

"That's a terrible accusation!"

"What? That you think she's shrill, or that she *is* shrill?"

"Both, honestly."

"You didn't deny either one, though."

"I said it was terrible."

"Terrible doesn't mean untrue. There are plenty of terrible true things in the world."

He laughed, having no other rebuttal. Alani was glad that they were starting to settle back into their normal groove after the events on Qwi. It had been hardly a week, but she missed joking around with him. It was helping her feel less on edge being in Aeiko's apartment, too.

They shared a comfortable silence while they both arranged their sleeping areas. Balt had to help her yank the bed out from the couch, then he laid out his blankets and pillows on the floor by the wall while she made her bed. She once again offered to share the bed with him, but he insisted he was looking forward to sleeping on his pallet. He even dubbed his comfy arrangement on the ground his little Pallet Town, and called himself the mayor. Less than ten minutes later, they were both snug under their covers with the lights turned off. Alani wasn't even sure what time it was, but she was getting sleepy.

After another minute of silence, Balt's voice cut through the darkened room. "What should we do tomorrow?" he asked. "After we're done at the stadium, I mean. Anything on your bucket list?"

"Am I dying?" she huffed amusedly.

"Your Makanuele bucket list, I mean. That barbecue joint Holly was shrilly talking about sounds pretty cool, but that might be better as a big group activity or something. Anything you wanna do, though, I'm game."

She breathed in deep, then let it out slow. Not even thinking about what places she might want to visit or foods she might want to try. There was only one thing on her mind, though she had not been planning to say it right this moment, necessarily. It just spewed from her, needing to release itself.

"I'll be fine on my own," she said first. Before Balt could interject, she said, "I know what I said before, and honestly I don't think I was overreacting, but..." She took a second to ponder how to phrase the next part. "Look, I appreciate what you've been trying to do this past week. I do. But it's not what I wanted, not exactly. I just wanted you to realize that you were putting your wants over my needs *every time*. I never meant that you should just throw away everything that's important to you for my sake. I just wanted to stop fading into the background."

She barely knew what she was saying, the words were

just spilling out. Balt remained silent, bundled up in his pallet on the hardwood floor.

"I wanted you to stop thinking of my pilgrimage as secondary to your Summoner career. That's all. I didn't want you to stop pursuing your dreams *entirely*. I mean, the whole reason you agreed to come with me in the first place was so that you could compete in this tournament. I never asked you to bow out of it, and I don't feel good about you making that decision on my behalf. I know how important it is to you."

Alani paused then, giving Balt an opportunity to say something. Her mouth was dry and her body was buzzing. She loathed having conversations like this. It was so much easier to just keep all these feelings bottled up inside.

"Are you saying you want me to compete?" he said meekly.

"Yes, you dolt."

That garnered a chuckle from him. Then, gravely, he said, "I don't know if I can."

"You can."

"I don't want to abandon you again."

His words struck her. It took her a moment before she pressed on. "You aren't abandoning me," she said. "I'll have Aeiko. We'll have plenty of fun together while you're off screwing around with Niona."

"But—"

"I forgive you, Balt. I do. I'm not gonna lie and say you didn't hurt me back there, but it's okay. Honestly."

Silence permeated the room as they both mulled over her words. She waited for Balt to say something, but after a minute, she wasn't sure he was going to.

"You haven't been yourself this past week," she said. "I know you're trying to do what you feel is right, but I miss the real you. I miss the you who doesn't feel like he has to walk on eggshells around me. For as long as I've known you, all you've ever blathered on about all day every day was Jekuas, and now it's like you're facing down the barrel of a gun every time you even mention the word. I don't want that. I don't want to be the cause of your unhappiness. It's hard for me to imagine anything worse than being the reason my best friend is unhappy."

After a beat, he whispered, "…you're sure?"

"Sure I don't want my friend to be unhappy? Yes."

"You know what I mean." His tone was serious.

Alani said, "Of course I'm sure. I want you to accomplish your goals, you idiot. I want you to do what you've always dreamed of. I'll say it bluntly: you were being selfish in the VWC. But it'd be selfish of me now to deny you the opportunity to do this. You should do it." Then, for added emphasis she said, "I want you to do it."

"Really?"

"Stop asking if I'm sure and trying to talk me out of it. Yes, really."

"Okay." After a beat, he said, "I…actually, I don't know if I *can* compete. Sign-ups are already closed, I think."

Alani was eager to surprise him. "I asked Niona to sign you up the other day, when we were in Deredi," she said.

"For real?" Balt said. She could hear him sitting up, presumably looking over at her.

She grinned, though he couldn't see it. "Yes."

He breathed out. "Wow. Thank you for that."

"I wanted to see you in that arena, battling it out with Dipper and winning the whole thing."

Balt laughed. "I mean, I'm not gonna win the whole thing. That's ridiculous." She heard him lay back down.

"Well, you'd at least better try."

There were a few more moments of silence between them, but they were not as tense as before.

"Alright," he said. "I'll try. For you."

She could practically hear the smile in his voice.

9
THE THIRD VEPTILO

SLEEPING ON THE FLOOR WAS NOT AS BAD AS BALT THOUGHT it might be. Since she was a nice person and a good friend, Alani had of course told him that they could share the sofa bed, but he had declined in lieu of her comfort. He was glad the hard floor had not totally destroyed his body, although he might need to grab an extra blanket tonight.

By the time they rolled out of bed, Balt and Alani were the only two left in the apartment. Aeiko and Holly had snuck out at some point to head to Lakahlo's Makanuele office, and evidently they had even taken Brine with them. Balt was befuddled as to how he had slept through the massive coral golem stomping around the living room.

Now they sat at the kitchen table, drinking cups of coffee poured from a pitcher that had been brewed and waiting on the warmer when they awoke. Another thing Balt was surprised they'd slept through. They were chatting amiably about nothing in particular while Balt made

Milton walk circles around the couch. The thick Mirror-bear kept scraping up against the wall and jostling some side tables, but Balt was going to put everything back in its place when he withdrew him. Milton was just slightly too bulky to navigate a lot of the apartment's spaces, but he was nothing compared to Brine's hulk.

Now that the two of them had cleared the air and Alani had given him the go-ahead to compete in the tournament, a weight had lifted off Balt's shoulders. He felt like he could finally be himself again, summoning his Jekuas and speaking openly with his friend. He knew he still needed to put forth a strong effort to make things up to her for how their entire Qwisdeep trip had gone, though.

Maybe if he earned some winnings from the tournament, he could use some to buy her a nice gift. As that thought crossed his mind, he realized he wasn't sure what the actual prize for winning the tournament was; there was no chance at all he would win the top prize, but maybe a lesser one was in the cards. That'd be something to ask Niona about once she arrived and he told her the good news.

Another thing he would need to ask her about was the entry fee. He was running significantly low on funds, so that aspect was worrisome. He had left home without a ton of savings in his bank account, assuming that they'd be able to get by just fine with the Church's contributions. His parents had actually transferred a small sum of money a couple days earlier, along with a text message explaining they'd send him some every few weeks. That was nice of them, considering he'd never requested such a thing and also because they had been against him embarking on the pilgrimage to begin with. He appreciated this unexpected allowance, but he wasn't sure it would be enough to buy his way into the Rumble.

Alani finished gulping down her coffee and disappeared into the bathroom with her bag to get ready. They would need to leave in half an hour or so to make it to the Church in time for their meeting with Elder Neiata and that weird trainee girl Eila. Balt had walked Milton over to the front door to see if he had enough control over the bear's paws to maneuver the small lock when there came a loud pounding on the other side.

It would be a great bit to make Milton answer the door, but he failed to get a good grip on the lock. He'd have to try it later. Pulling off dumb bits would be a good motivator for his training. In the meantime, he withdrew the Jekua and hurried over to let Niona inside.

"Yo," Niona said, strutting into the apartment. "You ready to tumble down into that crater?"

"Yep," Balt replied, which was a blatant lie. He still needed to slip into the bathroom after Alani to get dressed and brush his teeth. He pointedly turned his head away from Niona as he spoke so that his morning breath wouldn't hit her.

Niona glanced around the room for a second, noticing that it was just them. "Our gracious hosts head to work already?" Balt nodded, keeping his mouth shut, and she said, "They took the big guy with 'em too?"

"He's technically a work project, I guess, so yeah."

"True. Why are you smiling like that?"

"Like what?" Balt had not realized it, but a wide grin split his face. His cheeks flushed as he returned to the kitchen table and sat down, the chair scraping loudly against the floor. Still grinning stupidly, he put his mug to his lips.

Niona followed him to the table and sat in the chair previously occupied by Alani. "Like you've got somethin' up your sleeve. C'mon, let's see it, take that shirt off."

Balt almost spit out his coffee before he connected her shirt sleeve metaphor. His cheeks flushed even more, if that was possible. Yet another reason for him to turn his head away from her. If only it wouldn't be absolutely insane for him to sit facing the other direction while they conversed.

But since that was not an option, he looked her in the eye like a normal person does during a conversation and said, "I'm gonna be competing after all."

Niona's eyebrows shot up and a toothy smile spread across her face. "For real?" she said, leaning forward eagerly.

Balt nodded.

"Dope. So y'all finally made up? I figured you would at some point when she asked me to register you. That's why I kept buggin' you to come to the gym with me! I thought y'all should hash things out, though, and let her break the news to you instead of me."

"Yeah, we had a nice talk last night," he responded. "Honestly, I do still feel a little weird about it still, but I think it'll be alright."

That was good enough for her. She drummed her hands on the table and said, "We've gotta get you up to speed! You've missed out on a week of good, solid training."

"You think a week would really make all the difference?" Balt said amusedly.

"Oh, hell no," said Niona. "You're probably gonna get squashed no matter what. But that week *might* have made all the difference between you makin' a fool of yourself and not..."

"Wow," he muttered.

Alani then emerged from the bathroom wearing her pink and yellow formal Church robes, with the three thin gold bracelets clinking together on her wrist. They were like her own little version of a kayet, Balt realized. He was blanking on what they were called, though. It struck him with a pang of guilt, not remembering such a simple detail that was so crucial to Alani's ritual.

She brightly greeted Niona and set her bag down. "All yours," she then said to Balt, gesturing to the bathroom.

Balt hastily made himself presentable while the two women chatted at the table, then the three of them headed out to the Church grounds in the southeast corner of the city. It felt silly trekking straight past Xatetu Field, their ultimate destination, but Balt didn't object. It was a nice summer's day, with plenty of sunshine warming their skin. He loved this season on the islands.

This early in the day, there were far less people present within the crater than they'd seen before. Nobody was near the stadium, and Balt wasn't sure if the place was even officially open to the public yet. He saw a few people walking dogs, and another handful training with Jekuas, though from this distance they were no more than indistinct colorful blobs.

When they reached the Church, Eila was standing outside awaiting them. She was still a bundle of nerves just like the day before, her eyes flickering back and forth anxiously while she shifted her weight from foot to foot. After welcoming them, she scampered away to find Elder Neiata so they could depart.

The Elder was a woman in her early fifties, with thick black hair hanging in a long braid down to her waist and a lithe yet muscular frame. She was wearing robes that matched Alani's, though hers were sleeveless. The manastreams on her face glowed as she smiled pleasantly at them, the shineink dipping into shallow wrinkles on her face.

"Blessed morning to you all," said Elder Neiata, bowing her head slightly. "I am honored to join you on your pilgrimage on such a fine morning as this."

"Blessed morning to you, Elder," said Alani, tilting her head in reverence. "I hope Nuritayhu is smiling upon you this day."

"I woke up with a crick in my neck, but I think I'll live," the older woman joked. Eila tittered nervously at her side. The young girl's behavior made Balt wonder if this was going to be her first real expedition to the island's shrine.

Offering Elder Neiata some solidarity, Balt said, "I slept on a floor." He thought that maybe the dumb little comment would somehow help to put Eila at ease. When everyone turned to blankly stare at him, though, he could not fathom why he had thought that for even a mere second. At the rear of the pack, he faintly heard Niona laughing at him.

Moving right along, Elder Neiata led them away from the compound and they walked back toward Xatetu Field. Alani walked alongside the Elder, discussing how her previous shrine visits went. Eila was behind them, scrolling through lengthy documents on her linkpad that looked exceptionally complex. Maybe that was the source of her stress this morning. Balt and Niona walked together behind her.

"How was the floor?" Niona asked him, sporting her classic shit-eating grin.

"Don't start."

They came to one of the crater's many entrances and started down the stone steps. The lack of railing made Balt nervous, but the way into the crater was a pretty shallow incline, so if he fell it likely wouldn't hurt that badly. He would just look like an unbelievable idiot taking a tumble all the way down.

Luckily, the entire group made it to the bottom of the stairs without anyone taking a tumble. Elder Neiata continued leading them across the rocky pathway, navigating past beautifully ornate water fountains and hedge sculptures depicting large, powerful Jekuas. There was even one of a Mosstopus, which Balt found amusing since the creature already looked so much like a giant plant. The Romproar hedge was especially impressive, with the beast reared up on its hind legs and swatting its claws at an imaginary foe.

At the stadium's entrance stood two guards (flanked by

two statuesque coral golems) who were chattering away as the group approached. One was showing the other something on his linkpad, which he hurriedly stuffed in his pocket at the sight of the Church Elder. "Morning, ma'am," he said, attempting to bow deeply but being stopped by his protruding gut.

"Blessed morning to you, gentlemen," said Elder Neiata.

A few more pleasantries were exchanged, then the men opened the doors to allow them entry. Elder Neiata had surely contacted the stadium officials yesterday to inform them they'd be visiting the Veptilo, wherever it was stored inside. They entered, following the other guard while the large-gutted one remained stationed outside.

The stadium's interior was about what Balt had expected. In his experience, once you'd seen one stadium, you'd seen them all. This one's walls were painted a metallic blue with purple trim, and there were floor-to-ceiling paintings adorning them every couple hundred feet. The art ranged from portraits of Summoners to cometball champions to logos for brands that sponsored the stadium. Balt wouldn't have been shocked to stumble upon a portrait of his grandmother in one of those halls, but right now he couldn't spot her.

They strolled past shuttered stalls, behind which they could hear people clattering away in the kitchens, probably preparing for the festivities to begin in about a week. Once the tournament commenced, lines would stretch from every one of the counters across the whole width of the hallway. Trying to pass through would be a headache and a half, but the aroma of all the fresh rice and fried foods and greasy pizzas would be intoxicating. Some might be put off by all those smells intermingling, but Balt did not count himself among them.

He had never been inside an empty stadium. It was somewhat creepy, in all honesty. Something about it felt very dystopian. Seeing a place that was meant to be filled with such energy, such vibrancy, completely devoid of any life.

"It's strange, huh?" Niona whispered at his side. "Knowing that in a few days, this place is gonna be jam-packed with people comin' in from all over the islands to watch us fight."

Balt nodded, and his stomach dropped a little. Gathering a small audience on the beach or in the jungle watching him battle was one thing, but it was an entirely different story being observed and judged by thousands of people. The tournament was going to be televised, too, so there was no telling how many more thousands of people would tune in.

Once again, Balt's thoughts were invaded by Niona's remark about him making a fool of himself on the battlefield.

They ventured deeper into the stadium, and the further they went, the more guard and golem presence they found. Humans and golems alike patrolled the halls, keeping a lookout for any trespassers. It was the most coral golems Balt had ever seen in one place before, and all of the guards were armed with tasers, while a select few also possessed firearms.

Whatever company it was that owned Xatetu Field, they were not skimping on the security. No one was getting this deep into the stadium that they did not want to be there. And if they did, they wouldn't last long.

It was then that Balt recalled the weird tingling he felt in his mana reserves when they'd visited the first shrine on the coast of Totta. He wasn't getting even an inkling of that right now, but they had to be close to the center of the stadium. The battlefield wasn't far off. Surely they should have been able to feel the Veptilo's resonance by this point, right?

His poorly-received floor comment from earlier prevented Balt from piping up to ask about the resonance. He kept quiet, the group's footsteps echoing down the hall as they clacked along the tile floor.

Eventually, the guard brought them to a locked doorway at the end of a hall. He swiped a keycard and a tiny light on the door changed from red to green, emitting a short, high-pitched buzz. Inside, they were greeted by a different guard, an older man around Elder Neiata's age who thanked the other man for his assistance.

"I'll be taking you the rest of the way," the man then said. "My name's Chief Guapora. How're y'all doin' this mornin'?" Despite his Volukhan features, he spoke with a heavy twang in his accent.

"We are excellent," said Elder Neiata. Everyone else mumbled in concurrence.

Chief Guapora led them further yet into the stadium's center, and still there was no resonance. It was only a minute before they came to a halt in front of a wide elevator, which they filed into. Guapora hit a button marked V, which for all Balt knew stood for "Veptilo." He smirked with amusement at that.

The elevator rumbled to a start, heading downward into the earth. Balt would have of course assumed there was a basement and probably loading docks and such beneath the stadium, but the elevator seemed to be going farther down than he anticipated.

As they descended, that familiar feeling crept up in his stomach. Slowly, it began to feel as if his entire body was shifting, like his organs themselves were vibrating. It was intense, and not wholly pleasant. There was a mild satisfaction to the feeling, knowing that it was his inner mana reacting to the Veptilo's presence, but he would be lying if he said it was *comfortable*.

Looking to Alani, she appeared just as perturbed by the sensation as she was the first time. Balt frowned, hoping that her reaction at the shrine itself would not be so extreme this time around. He then glanced at Niona, whose face was scrunched up in concern.

"Do you feel that?" she whispered to him, leaning closer to his ear.

He nodded. "It's normal."

She did not look especially satisfied by that reply, but she said, "Okay."

The elevator came to an abrupt halt, and its metal doors slid open to reveal a dark hallway. Chief Guapora stepped out and flicked on a light switch, illuminating a barren hall that stretched out far before them.

Well, not totally barren. While the hall lacked any decoration of any sort, and there were no doors on either side, the hall was lined on both walls with coral golems.

Golems in a multitude of colors stood sentry along the stretch of hall, apparently having been previously standing there in the pitch black darkness.

"Creepy," Niona muttered. She rubbed her arms, still obviously disturbed by the Veptilo's resonance.

Their group started down the hall.

Clearly they were not the first people on a pilgrimage to be confused by this whole venture, as Elder Neiata dove into an explanation completely unprompted: "The Veptilo used to be on the surface, jutting out from the earth, as I'm sure you noticed at the other shrines. When they began to build the stadium, however, the Veptilo was located in the spot where they hoped to construct the building."

"They couldn't just…build it in another part of the crater?" asked Alani.

"That would have been ideal, but alas," Elder Neiata sighed. "In any case, what they did was excise a small plot of land that contained the Veptilo, removing it and the earth around it so as to not disturb or damage it. At the Church's request, they were to keep it in roughly the same area that it was found, so as to not anger the Veptists or disrupt its connection to the Vept. As you can imagine, however, they were none too keen on having their guests feeling the Veptilo's power while they were trying to enjoy their sports for hours at a time."

"No kidding," Niona huffed under her breath. The Elder did not hear her, but Balt grinned.

Elder Neiata continued. "So, they constructed this level far below the stadium, where the Veptilo could rest undisturbed."

"Sounds like a lot of work," Balt said.

"It was," the Elder agreed, "but part of the contract for selling the land included stipulations about the Veptilo. The Church could not allow such a sacred thing to be destroyed. It had to be handled with the utmost care and attention."

Maybe they should not have sold it off, then, thought Balt. Given his own monetary woes, though, perhaps he had no room to talk.

As they passed the lines of coral golems, Balt couldn't help but marvel at the intense level of security for this thing that the stadium's owners clearly did not actually care about. It was possible that might have also been part of the Church's agreement to sell the land, he figured.

The plus side was that the group who was after the thing—the Facet, or whatever they were called—would have a hell of a time reaching this Veptilo. They might as well not even try.

At the end of the long hallway was a single purple door that matched the accent colors throughout the stadium. On it was another electronic lock, as well as one more coral golem positioned in front of the door.

"Only three people have access to this door, including me," said Chief Guapora before commanding the golem to move. It stepped to the side, its featureless head still pointed forward. "The other two are not currently on the island, so it's just me for now."

"Lucky it wasn't his day off," Niona said to Balt.

Chief Guapora opened the door to a black room. When he flipped the lights on, Balt could see the glimmering Veptilo just past the man's shoulder.

They entered.

The Veptilo's resonance was stronger than ever. Niona seemed more bothered by it than Balt was, which he wasn't expecting. He would have guessed that his extra sensitive soulclay would also make him more susceptible to the Veptilo's effects, but maybe not.

It was strange seeing the shrine here, so far underground. It was exactly the same as on the islet near Totta, but transposed to this random, tiny, dark room underneath a massive sports arena. Just as Elder Neiata had said, the crystal (or whatever it actually was) jutted out from a mound of earth in the middle of the room. It was taller than the first one Balt had seen, and skinnier, too. The matte pink spike stretched halfway to the ceiling, all jagged edges. Like the first one, it had a few Churchly things which Balt assumed were prayers carved near its base. A few stone tablets sat propped against each other on the floor at the base of the dirt pile, sporting even more etched words.

Elder Neiata gestured toward the shrine, making room for Alani to approach. Chief Guapora knew the drill and stepped back, making himself flat against the wall, out of the way.

Alani knelt down at the shrine while everyone watched her.

Balt noticed then that the mound of dirt wasn't actually sitting on the floor like the tablets, but rather it was on a platform just barely raised up off the ground. His eyes wandered and he saw some sort of mechanical structure going from the floor to the ceiling, with a huge rectangle outlined in the ceiling above the shrine.

Was that some sort of opening? Maybe the platform was what they'd used to lower the shrine down into the room all those years ago. That made some sort of sense—as much as any of the situation made sense—but it was odd that it remained on the platform still.

Alani began reciting the requisite prayers, her voice too soft for anyone to make out the words. Balt watched her, waiting for the same reaction she'd had at the first shrine.

Only a second or two after she ceased speaking, Alani gasped and fell forward, banging her elbows on the ground and nearly smacking her head on the stone tablets. Balt rushed forward, shoving past Elder Neiata and Eila, who let out a shrill yip.

He crouched beside Alani, placing a comforting hand on her back. "You okay?" he asked her.

She nodded. "Nothing to worry about," she said, mirroring Lamat's words at the first shrine.

Despite her assurances, Balt did not like this. He remained at her side until she had recovered enough to stand on her own.

"I know it can be a shock," said Elder Neiata. "You have done well, Alani Temel. You can rest easy tonight knowing that the Veptists have seen you."

Balt wasn't confident that the woman's words were as comforting to Alani as she thought they were, but he didn't say so.

Alani took a deep breath and let it out slowly. She was still staring down at the ground, her palms stretched out on the cold floor to hold herself up. She tilted her head and gazed upward at the Veptilo.

"You sure you're alright?" Balt asked again.

It took her a moment, but she tore her focus from the Veptilo and looked at him. She nodded curtly. "I'm just glad it's done with," she said. Then, "Let's get out of here and go get you two signed in."

10
FAMILY NAMES

ONCE ALANI FINALLY CAUGHT HER BREATH, BALT HELPED her to her feet and they rejoined the group. Elder Neiata smiled serenely and placed a hand on her shoulder, squeezing then letting go. She didn't say anything.

"All good to go?" asked Chief Guapora before taking a big, mucus-y sniff. He wiped at his nose as the Elder nodded, then held the door open so they could step out one by one.

They marched down the seemingly neverending hallway, past the silent and hollow gazes of the coral golems. There had to be at least forty of them in the otherwise empty hallway. Niona found it uncomfortable enough hanging around just one golem at Aeiko's apartment, so this was not her favorite hallway she'd ever been in.

The entire ritual had made her deeply uncomfortable, really. The literal discomfort in her body as it reacted to the big pink rock's presence was one thing, but also how oddly Alani was affected by it. Listening to her whisper the Church's little prayers, feeling the mana buzzing inside her, watching Alani collapse to the ground.

No good.

Niona's mother had been a devout follower of the Church of Salt and Sanction, dragging her husband and daughter to services every week. As a child who blindly listened to everything her parents said and didn't think for herself, Niona had decided she was a follower too. This was in spite of the fact that she found Church services to be dreadfully boring and also stupid. The older she got, the more obvious it was to her that her father did not particularly care about the Vept or the precious Veptists either, and merely tagged along to make his wife happy. As a teen, Niona asked him why he bothered when there were so many better ways to spend his time. He shrugged and said, "It makes her happy. Why wouldn't I come with her?"

After that, she adopted the same mindset. It didn't hurt her any to join her mother each week, aside from the loss of a few hours. Even though she was not enthusiastic about what the Elders were saying, or participating in any community activities, she still thought of herself as a follower of the Church. How could she not be, after attending for so many years? It was in the fabric of her being.

That changed when her mother passed away, however. Niona was fifteen years old at the time, finally at an age where she was starting to question the beliefs that her parents had instilled in her when she was young and decide whether or not they truly were her beliefs as well.

The funeral service was held at a Church in Himony,

of course. Half the hotel staff was in attendance. They had adored her mother; especially the dancers who she'd worked with for the various performances that the resort showcased. Fuo Taret was so severely broken up about it, it was as if she was part of the Daneo family too.

Niona and her father stopped going to Church services after that. At first, Niona told herself it was just because she was depressed about her mom, but even when she was pulling herself together and getting back out in the world, she felt no compulsion to go. Her father was busy running the resort, and she preferred spending that time with her friends, so she didn't return.

A distant part of her also knew that stepping foot in that chapel would remind her of her mother. She wouldn't be able to think about anything else if she sat in one of those pews, the Elder's words droning in her ears. The Church had never meant much to her, so she didn't want her memories of her mother wrapped up solely in the Church. She wanted to remember her mother as the woman who read her stories, the two of them nestled together on the living room sofa. Or as the wild, fiery dancer brandishing her flower petal skirt.

Somehow, in the span of ten years, Niona had never found any reason to enter a Church since that funeral. Until yesterday, when she'd gone with Balt and Alani.

Between that short visit and today's bizarre ritual, she was ready to put the Church and its Elders behind her for another ten years at least.

Elder Neiata and that mousy girl Eila trailed shortly behind Chief Guapora, while Niona hung back to see how

Alani fared. "I'm okay," she told her. "This happens every time."

"It does?" said Niona. "That seems…" She wanted to say *weird* or *shitty* or *screwed up* or any number of negative things, but she refrained. "I dunno," she said.

Neither Balt nor Alani said anything, so Niona dropped it.

The six of them rode the elevator the long way back up to ground level in silence. Near-silence, anyway. Chief Guapora continually sniffled the entire time. The man was in desperate need of a tissue.

Niona was relieved to feel the shrine's resonance draining from her body as the elevator climbed higher and higher. That wasn't a sensation she was eager to experience again any time soon. If she happened to stick around with these two, she would maybe opt to not participate in the whole ritual side of things. Honestly, she probably would've skipped it today in lieu of training if not for the fact she needed to sign in for the tournament there anyway.

A couple minutes later, they reached the chief's office, where he bade them farewell.

"Thank you for accompanying us," said Elder Neiata. "Perhaps next time, Eila here will be handling things without me."

It was said mostly in jest, but still the young girl anxiously uttered something inaudible. To Niona, it seemed a pretty simple task to escort someone to an office and then to a basement, not something worth feeling even the slightest bit nervous about, but who was she to judge?

They left Chief Guapora to the rest of his day's tasks,

which hopefully included clearing his nasal passages. The closer they came to the front halls of the stadium, the more Alani seemed like herself. Whatever unsettling effect that rock had on her must have been wearing off.

Near the entrance to the stadium, the halls were now occupied with people other than themselves. There was no sense of time in the darkened hallways underneath the stadium, so Niona had no idea how long they'd been subterranean, but at some point the stadium had opened its doors to the public. A few (though not very many) of the food stalls were now open for business too, as Niona knew they were every day. Even when there were no sporting events taking place, a vendor could make a good chunk of change selling to people who were spending their day around the crater's courtyard. There were some people waiting to buy breakfast tai dair, others grabbing what appeared to be some sort of pancake on a stick, and some who were searching for the tournament sign-in counter.

Niona and Balt stayed behind while Alani spoke to Elder Neiata near the exit. Eila stood near them, nodding along to everything both women were saying.

"Is she actually okay?" Niona asked.

Balt shrugged. "She says she is," he said. "I dunno what I can go on besides that. The ritual does rub me the wrong way, though. If the Elders know how much it affects people, I don't know why they don't, like…warn them? Or do anything at all to assist them?"

"Yeah, the old lady did kinda just stand there and watch."

"So did the guy we visited the first shrine with. It was

like she got whacked in the back of the head and the dude was just all, 'This is normal, don't worry.'"

Soon, Elder Neiata and Eila exited out into the bright sunlight and Alani walked over with a concerned expression.

"What's up?" Balt asked her.

She sighed. "The next shrine is on Yuluhu," she said.

Niona's brow furrowed. "They're makin' you go to Yuluhu for this shit?" she blurted out.

"Mhmm. It's in a town called Lopatowk, on the northeastern coast."

Outsiders couldn't navigate the island without immense hassle, and even then there was always the slight risk of being infected by the disease that plagued its population. Was visiting some shrine genuinely worth all that trouble?

Maybe she would not be joining them on the remainder of this pilgrimage after all.

"Anyway," Alani muttered, "shall we get you two into the tournament?"

That sounded like a plan to Niona. She was getting sick of all the Church talk. It was icky, made her skin crawl.

Being the most experienced with this sort of thing, Niona took the lead as they sought out the sign-in table. They followed the curving hallway down lines of food stalls and merchandise booths until they eventually came upon a counter with vibrant signage designating it as the place to complete their registration for the Makanuele Rumble.

There were only two people ahead of them in line. It

was likely that most of the other competitors had already signed in; they were cutting it pretty close to the deadline. That was what happened when your father took you on a surprise trip with an undetermined end date. It was hard to plan your life around such things.

A plump, red-haired woman greeted them as they stepped up to the counter. "Good morning," she said. "Welcome to Xatetu Field. Are you registered for the tournament?"

Niona saw no other reason why they would be standing at this counter and speaking to this woman, but she humored her. "Yep," she replied with a smile.

The woman peeked over Niona's shoulder and saw Balt standing there with a kayet on his wrist. "You too, dear?"

"Yeah," said Balt. Niona stifled a laugh at the woman's *dear*.

They told her their names, and she looked them up in her system. "Perfect," she said sweetly. "Got you both right here. Just a little bit more information we'll need from you." The woman handed each of them a short form to fill out. Balt stepped up to the counter next to Niona while the woman fetched them some pens.

"I'm sure you two know this already," the woman said, "but the Makanuele Rumble has sixty-four participants and it is single elimination. The opening ceremony and first round matches will be on the sixtieth of Summer, with the finals concluding on the sixty-sixth followed by the closing ceremony."

The form went into more detail about the competition itself. As was the case with most large-sized Jekua tournaments, considerably more people were able to sign up than would ultimately be competing. The Makanuele Rumble accepted four-hundred Summoners during sign-ups, and then there would be a special elimination round thinning the herd to the sixty-four who would actually be competing. The way it worked was that the group would be divided into smaller groups, and each division would face a unique non-combative challenge. The last people standing in each group would be the lucky few who moved on to the actual tournament. Each year the challenges were randomized, so there was no way for a Summoner to plan for a certain challenge.

Also like most tournaments, there would not be one single battlefield. The arena's environment would be changed for each of the six rounds, but the form did not specify what those six environments would be. Part of the challenge was adapting to the new terrain, although Summoners who competed later in the day would have the advantage of already knowing what the arena looked like.

A four-Jekua team was required to compete, and the form laid out the rules for swapping in each round. For the odd rounds, it was required that Summoners swap Jekuas when their opponent did, with no repeats. Niona smirked at that, since she had personally taken advantage of a loophole in a previous tournament where the rules said you had to switch, but not that it had to be a different Jekua, so she'd busted out her first Jekua again late in the battle and won. During even rounds, Summoners could swap Jekuas whenever they wanted. They could even use a single Jekua the entire match while their opponent used all four of theirs, if that was what their strategy entailed. It was all pretty standard stuff, nothing that she hadn't seen before in her years of competitive battling.

Balt suddenly asked, "Is there somewhere we can see the list of people who're signed up?"

"Not at the moment," the woman answered. "We will not be compiling a public list of competitors until after the elimination round this afternoon. You'll be able to see the full list of Summoners when the bracket is posted on the fifty-ninth."

Niona finished filling out her form quickly, while Balt took his time, meticulously reading over every word. It was kind of cute, in a little kid way. Baby's first tournament.

He finished reading things over and writing in the pertinent information, then slid the form back over to the woman behind the counter. Niona did the same.

"Great! Thank you, Ms. Daneo; Mr. Vana."

Something about that name rang familiar in Niona's mind. But before she could think too hard about it, the woman asked them for the entry fee.

Niona handed the woman her credit card without hesitation, while Balt stared blankly across the counter.

"Uh…" he mumbled, slowly reaching for his form.

"Wait, what?" Niona asked, watching his fingertips inch toward the paper.

He looked sheepish as he said, "That's…more than I expected it to be." He started to pull the paper away from the woman, but Niona stopped him and handed it back.

"I'll pay for his too," she said.

"No, wait," said Balt.

"Nah, it's cool," Niona told him.

"No, you don't have to—"

"I want to! Come on, it's your first tournament. I'm not gonna let you sit on the sidelines. It's fine, honestly. Don't even think about it."

Balt still looked distressed by the turn of events, but he relented. "Fine," he said. "I owe you one, though."

"That's true, you do."

The woman gladly took her payment and offered them both a wide smile. Then she said, "Now I just need to know what Jekua you intend to use in the elimination round. Choose wisely, because you cannot change your mind later."

There was no way of knowing what the challenge she faced might be, so Niona figured there was no point in belaboring over the decision too much. She'd be slotted into a challenge befitting whichever Jekua she picked. "A Muggish," she said without any more thought.

Balt seemed to be overthinking his choice, so Niona gave him a nudge. "Tottaworm," he blurted out.

Niona chortled. "Really?"

He shrugged. "It's not the strongest, but it's versatile. Sort of." She could already tell he was second-guessing himself.

But it was too late to go back on the decision. The woman input their choices on her computer then said, "That's it! You're ready to go. You'll receive periodic updates about the tournament on your linkpads, including information about where to meet this afternoon for the elimination round." Beside her, Niona heard Balt gulp. Then the woman said, "Best of luck today! No matter how you do, be sure to come down for the opening ceremony! You won't want to miss our surprise guest." She winked cheekily.

Niona couldn't even conjure a guess as to who the surprise guest at a Jekua tournament might be. Some old, croaky retiree who used to run the circuit? Some spokesperson from Lakahlo talking about a flashy new mod chip they created? The mindnumbingly dull possibilities were endless.

She pulled Balt away from the counter. He still looked ashamed by the fact he had to borrow money, but he thanked her again and she assured him it was no trouble. It was her father's money, technically speaking, but he wouldn't give a shit either.

Alani was leaning against the wall, typing on her linkpad. Before they went over there, though, Niona wanted to ask Balt something. While the red-haired woman was taking her payment, she'd realized where she had heard the name *Vana* before.

She looked him in the eye, then broke into a grin seeing his expression. It was a mixture of confusion, fear, and shame. "What?" he said.

"I wanna ask you somethin'."

"...what?" he repeated.

She pursed her lips, then said, "Are you related to Remisti Vana?"

He hesitated, but said, "Yeah. She's my grandmother."

Niona shoved his shoulder, sending him stumbling back a step. "How could you not tell me that!" she exclaimed.

Remisti Vana hadn't been one of Niona's favorite

Summoners, but she'd seen more than a few of the woman's battles on television. In her youth she might have even seen one in person, but she couldn't remember for sure; if so, she would've been extremely young and it would've had to be the tail end of the woman's career. She did remember that Remisti Vana was one hell of a Summoner, though, and that she had plenty of fans. Vana had won a frankly absurd number of tournaments.

Balt shrugged. "It just never came up, I guess," he said.

Niona wasn't buying it. "But all we ever talk about is summoning, and your grandma is a worldwide champion! It has been relevant to literally every conversation we've ever had."

"I dunno," Balt said meekly. Then, "It's just kinda weird being related to someone so famous and trying to follow in their footsteps. It's not like I'm ashamed of it or anything, obviously, I'm super proud of what she accomplished and that she's my family. But there's, like…if I told you I was related to Remisti Vana when we first met, don't you think you would've had different expectations about me?"

"Like what?"

"Like that I'd be some super strong Summoner, or something? Not just some idiot who found you on the beach."

She hadn't thought of that. "Maybe," she conceded. Then, jokingly, "I maybe woulda asked you to give me pointers, instead of the other way around."

"Exactly," he said, not taking it as the joke she intended. "It's just a lot of pressure that, uh…I dunno. There's just a lot of weight behind that name, and I guess now that it's gonna be broadcast in a Jekua tournament, all this is just starting to feel a lot more real. I feel like this is a chance to prove myself."

When he put it that way, Niona could relate. There was a lot of weight behind her family name as well. In Himony, everyone knew who the Daneos were. The entire Church community knew her mom, and the entertainment and hospitality industries knew her dad. Pretty much anywhere she went, her father had a connection, and if he didn't have a connection then his money could cover it.

Being able to pay her way through life without a care in the world was obviously a luxury that not many had, and one that Niona was endlessly thankful for. She loved her father and appreciated his endless generosity but, much like Balt with his grandmother, she did not want to spend her whole life living in his shadow. Relying on his name to get by. She wanted to build herself up, make a name for herself.

She wanted to become more independent, and this tournament was the first step on that path. Just like it was the first step for Balt to make a name for himself, show the world that he was fully capable on his own merits. This was the biggest tournament she had competed in, and if she attracted the eyes of a sponsor, that could be her ticket to a real career as a Summoner. That would be how she could start to separate herself from her father. Let her own skill and experience be the source of her worth, both in the sense of her finances as well as her self-esteem.

She shot him another mischievous smirk. "Well, if you

wanna win," she said, "you're gonna have to make it through the elimination round first."

"That is true," he said, sounding terrified.

"We're also gonna need to get some training in. You've already missed a lot of good days."

"That's definitely true too. You're way more experienced with competitions than me, so I'll take any advice I can get."

"And get you shall. Although, I'm gonna need some good Remisti Vana stories. Plus any tips or tricks she gave you over the years. You owe me, you said it yourself."

"Deal."

11

ELIMINATION ROUND

THE HOPEFUL COMPETITORS, ALL FOUR-HUNDRED OF THEM, met in a sizeable parking lot near the stadium and were loaded onto shuttles before being whisked away to some unknown location on the other side of the city.

They had gotten a notification on their linkpads about where to meet not long after signing in at the registration desk, so Balt and Niona had set off while Alani made her way back to Aeiko's apartment on her own. Balt hadn't wanted to send her away, but there were no spectators allowed during the elimination round.

He stared out the shuttle window, watching the bustling streets of Makanuele roll by. When he asked Niona where it was they were going, all she offered him was a slight shrug.

Twenty minutes later, he got his answer. It was a looming ovular building constructed from a pitch-black material that radiated heat on this hot Summer day. It took a while to unload all the shuttles, but finally the huge group of Summoners congregated around the entrance to the strange building, with four tournament officials stationed at the front. Each of them was wearing a differently-colored, perfectly-tailored suit; one was in red, one in blue, one in purple, and one in orange.

The person in orange, a tall, bald man with small round glasses, spoke into a microphone. "Greetings, everyone," he said, flashing a toothy smile. "Welcome to the elimination round. As you well know, there are four-hundred of you hoping to compete in the Makanuele Rumble today, but there are only sixty-four slots available. That means that for a whopping three-hundred thirty-six of you, your tournament journey will end in a few short hours."

Balt gulped. How humiliating would it be if he didn't even make it past the elimination round? Remisti Vana's grandson, kicked out of the tournament before it even really started. On top of that, Niona would undoubtedly give him endless shit for it.

Next to him, Niona did not look worried at all. She never did. She stood there with her arms crossed and an eager smile plastered on her face, clearly ready to go inside and get this whole thing over with.

The bald man continued. "If you check your linkpads, you will see you've been assigned a color based on which Jekua you chose for this round. Your color will determine which of us you will follow through the facility to face your challenge. Please check your apps now, and then follow us."

Balt leaned over to Niona and whispered, "Wait, so

we're all doin' this at the same time? We don't get to watch each other's challenges?"

"Nah," she said, shaking her head. "The way the challenges work, the amount of time they take can vary a lot, so it's easiest to do 'em all instead of waitin' for each one to finish. They wanna get through this fast. All at once, baby."

That was disappointing. He knew that no two challenges would be the same, but he'd been hoping he could watch another one and perhaps try to salvage some sort of strategy from it. He also wanted to see how Niona fared, if she ended up in a different challenge than him.

He pulled out his linkpad to check the tournament app, as did Niona. Next to his name, up at the top of the screen, was a red banner.

"Whatcha got?" Niona asked him. "I'm a purple girly."

"Red," he replied, raising his linkpad to show her.

"Guess this is where we say goodbye. Good luck, pal."

"Same to you."

The competitors filed into the black building, splitting apart to follow their color's representative through the halls. Balt glanced around at the other people in the crowded hall as they marched through, wondering if he would recognize any of the other ninety-nine Summoners he was up against. There was nobody he knew within his immediate vicinity, which was probably for the best. He didn't need the extra pressure of performing well in front of somebody who knew him.

After a couple minutes, the throng of people came to a halt behind their red-suited leader, a stout woman with a buzzcut that was dyed pink. "Alright," the woman said, clapping her hands together, "who's ready for this?"

The crowd cheered, Balt included. Internally, however, he was more nervous than he'd ever been in his life. His stomach did somersaults.

"Here's how it'll go down, so listen carefully. When we walk inside, there'll be a staircase on either side of you. Go up whichever one's closest, doesn't matter. You'll be performing your challenge from the walkway up there. In the middle of the room will be a raised platform, and that's where you'll summon your Jekuas. Got it?"

There was an affirmative murmur from the crowd, but then someone asked, "What is it we're actually *doing*?"

The pink-haired woman grinned. "Finding out is part of the fun," she said cheekily. "There's only one rule here: under no circumstance are you allowed to attack a fellow competitor. Use whatever abilities you want, but if you cause intentional harm to another Summoner's Jekua, you're out." Then she added, "Sabotage *is* allowed, however. But if there aren't any other questions, let's get to it!"

She swung open the doors and the lot of them rushed inside.

Balt took the left-side staircase, his shoes clanging on the metal with his ascent. The person behind him was over-eager and practically shoved him forward, nearly tripping him. He wanted to say something, tell the guy to chill out, but anxiousness held his tongue.

The metal walkway snaked around the entire perimeter of the rectangular room, which was far larger than Balt had anticipated. It made sense, though, considering it needed to accommodate one-hundred Summoners and their Jekuas. As the woman described, floating in the center of the room was a red platform that looked to actually be a collection of connected tiles. There was a huge gap of empty space between the platform and the floor below. The Summoners had a good view of the platform from where they stood on the walkway, which was slightly higher than the platform. Balt could just barely see the seams in between each square tile, and he suspected he was starting to understand what the challenge would be. Hanging from the ceiling was an enormous LED screen that simply read "100" in bright, yellow text.

While the four events were randomized every year, the tournament officials typically chose them from a larger pool of twenty-five or thirty different challenges. Based on what little Balt knew about the potential elimination round challenges from past years, he suspected this was probably the one where the goal would be for the Summoner to keep their Jekua on the platform for as long as possible. Tiles would be periodically disappearing, sending Jekuas plummeting to the floor, at which point they were eliminated. With the platform gradually introducing more and more holes, the available space was going to get crowded awfully fast.

Shit, Balt thought to himself, realizing that he would have to do this with his Tottaworm. How the hell was he going to pull this off? Nimble movements were not exactly in the worm's wheelhouse. What a stupid impulse decision. He wished he'd chosen Dipper.

The pink-haired woman had remained on the lower

floor, where their poor Jekuas would be falling, and was now speaking into a microphone. "Let's not waste time here, folks. Summon your pre-chosen Jekuas now!"

"Shit," Balt muttered aloud this time. He clicked on his kayet to prime the Tottaworm's memory card and funneled mana into the device.

A rainbow sea of soulclay poured out from all corners of the room, converging on the red platform. Balt felt a pang of embarrassment as his own faded into the form of his Tottaworm, which stood next to much more impressive Jekuas such as a Korbir and a Bruiserweight.

I am so screwed, he thought.

He then took a moment to inspect the rest of his competition. All the Summoners had been placed into their respective groups based on the Jekua they'd chosen. At a glance, there were no flying Jekuas among the hundred in their group, which made complete sense. They would've had an obvious advantage in this particular challenge. Balt couldn't immediately make out any Gravity-Types either, who could theoretically alter their gravity to float above the platform and breeze through to the final competition.

"Here we go!" the tournament official shouted into her microphone. Seconds later, a shrill buzzer blared in their ears, making Balt jump. The guy next to him laughed at his twitchiness.

Balt immediately shifted into his Jekua's perspective. Since the Tottaworm wasn't the fastest mover on its own, even the tiniest advantage to his reaction time would be beneficial.

He looked around at the other Jekuas, who all stood

inert on the platform, waiting for something to happen. Some of them probably had no idea what they were in for, confused as to why everyone was standing around without being able to attack each other.

It wasn't long before things kicked off.

There was no telling how many tiles in total comprised the platform, but a few seconds after the buzzer, some of them suddenly vanished. Thankfully it wasn't one that Balt's Tottaworm was on, because he had not seen it coming at all. Howls of frustration echoed through the room as several Jekuas tumbled through the air, crashing onto the floor below. Mere seconds into the challenge, they were already out of the running.

"What the hell?" the guy next to Balt mumbled to himself. He was pleased to hear that the jerk was befuddled. Hopefully he'd be gone shortly.

Now that everyone was aware of what the challenge was, Jekuas scrambled wildly all over the platform. Balt remained still, not sure what the others gained by constantly moving. He planned to wait and see which platforms would be disappearing and only move if absolutely necessary.

Suddenly, he felt a minute vibration deep within his Tottaworm's body. It was so slight, he almost didn't notice it. Without his Jekua's Sonic prowess, he might not have.

On a hunch, he slithered over to a different tile, narrowly avoiding being flattened by a massive Sleethog bounding past. But he still felt the vibrations on the new tile, so he continued onward to a third one, which felt normal. He curved the Tottaworm's body around to look at the two previous tiles, then saw them disappear in a flash.

They blinked out of existence just as the Sleethog barreled back over one, its girthy front hooves coming down on nothing but air. The enormous Thermal-Type hippo smashed its fat snout on the tile in front of it, blood gushing out, and then it plunged through the newly-formed hole in the platform.

Jumping back into his own perspective for just a second, Balt checked the LED screen up above. The number on it was now "72."

All he had to do was wait it out until only sixteen of them were left. If twenty-eight Jekuas had fallen in the half a minute that had passed since the challenge started, then surely it wouldn't take long for another fifty-six to bite the dust. This whole thing might be over in another minute or two.

And, on the plus side, he now had a valid strategy. He could keep his Tottaworm still until he felt the tile underneath it begin to vibrate, then move aside. Simple as that.

Maybe using his Tottaworm wasn't as big of a handicap as he'd originally thought.

His stomach began to settle, and the anxiety he felt loosened its grip. He was still nowhere near Niona's level of confidence, but he was feeling better about everything now. Somewhat, anyway.

As it turned out, the challenge was not over in a minute or two. Balt continued sliding his Jekua around while others rampaged around him, and he only had one close call when he'd had to spring out of the way of the Korbir, nearly landing on a disappearing tile.

But the other Summoners were getting the hang of things now, and the count had only decreased to "57" in the past five minutes. Balt wanted to speed along the proceedings a bit.

The pink-haired woman *did* say that sabotage was allowed, after all.

He positioned his Tottaworm on the edge of a tile, and across a stretch of empty space there was an Eclipse Jackal pacing back and forth, awaiting the next wave of disappearances.

Balt would be lying if he said that part of the reason he targeted the Jackal wasn't because it might potentially be his cousin's Jekua. Either way, it would be one less Summoner in the fray.

He elasticized the Tottaworm's body and stretched it out far, bridging the gap between himself and the Eclipse Jackal, then wrapped the worm's head around its furry black leg. Then he un-elasticized the worm's body so that it shot backward across the gap, yanking the Jackal along with it. The other Jekua smacked its chin on a tile as it was knocked off its feet then pulled backward. Halfway across the empty expanse, Balt unfurled the Tottaworm from the Jackal's leg and watched it careen to the floor.

Seeing the Jackal below morph back into soulclay and return to some stranger's kayet filled Balt with a touch of guilt, but he quickly dismissed the feeling. He needed to be in the top sixteen.

The tile beneath his Tottaworm began vibrating, so he slid to the one on his left, but it was about to go as well.

So was the one next to that.

And then there were several empty spaces beyond that.

He was rapidly running out of time.

The vibrations were increasing in intensity.

Balt coiled the Tottaworm's body, increased its elasticity, then sprang forward. The tile disappeared just as the Tottaworm flung itself through the air, coming down hard on a tile across the gap. He was beyond grateful that the one he aimed for hadn't vanished too.

The impact took out a small chunk of his mana, but Balt wasn't particularly worried about his levels during the challenge. He didn't expect any movement or technique he implemented to drain himself enough to even remotely worry about soulsickness, and the Tottaworm expended less mana in general anyway.

Since there would probably be a bit of time before more tiles disappeared, Balt took the opportunity to jump back to his own perspective up on the metal walkway so he could assess the playing field.

Roughly half the platform was gone now, with tons of large, random gaps. He tried to ascertain whether there was a pattern to the tiles that were going away, but if there was, he wasn't smart enough to see it.

Forty-nine Summoners remained, and Balt watched as they started to revel in their sabotage of each other. He saw a Voltmare charging after a Dewrat, trying to chase it off the edge of the platform, but the Tidal-Type was able to conjure a series of watery platforms that it then froze with Thermal magic and raced across them. The Voltmare followed, but the blocks of ice melted as soon as the horse touched them, sending it to the ground. Elsewhere, a Conuto was scuttling around, using its Radiant magic to create a burst of blinding light from its exoskeleton, obscuring the area around it so that Summoners couldn't see whether their Jekuas were safe or not. In the middle of the platform, a pair of Juntoos carelessly ran into each other and were still tangled in one another's elastic limbs as the tile they were standing on blinked into nothingness.

Balt took a deep breath, then returned to his Tottaworm's body.

That Dewrat he'd seen was still running around frantically, using its magically-conjured ice blocks to cross gaps in the platform. It would probably make it to the end, unless Balt took it out.

He sprang in the direction of the Dewrat, then stretched out the Tottaworm's body as it slithered toward the other Jekua. It took no more than a few seconds for the worm's front half to reach the Dewrat. The creature was so small that Balt could barely wrap his Tottaworm's girthy body around it, but he managed to do so then made his Jekua go rigid. The rat was going nowhere.

It was only then that Balt realized the platform beneath the two Jekuas was vibrating, and given its level of intensity, it would be gone in a few moments. He'd been too caught up in snatching the Dewrat to notice. A foolish, avoidable mistake.

He thought he might be able to flip the mistake in his favor. He could feel the Dewrat struggling in his grasp, trying to break free and flee the soon-to-be-gone tile. Meanwhile, he stretched the back half of his Tottaworm toward the next tile while keeping the front half rigid, sort of using the same concept as when he performed the Jekua's Spearshot technique.

When the worm's back half touched the adjacent tile, Balt felt no vibrations. That was good.

He braced himself.

A second later, the other tile disappeared and Balt instantly elasticized the Tottaworm's front half, letting go of the Dewrat.

He didn't get the chance to relish in the Dewrat's demise, because his own Jekua's body instantly and violently retracted like a tape measure. Its front half slammed into the back half, propelling it across three or four tiles before hitting the backside of a Nonnim. The larger Jekua turned to face him, baring its yellowed fangs.

A Nonnim was a Thermal-Type creature that closely resembled a sloth, although it possessed far more agility and grace. But it had the same general body type, with an impressive paunch and long, curved claws at the end of its paws. It walked on its hind legs, standing as tall as a typical man, and its wiry fur was a sooty black with streaks of red, orange, and yellow, like it was on fire.

Despite their visual similarity to sloths, Nonnims were actually formidable opponents. Not only was their Thermal magic extremely powerful, but their sharp claws could do some serious damage on even the most durable Jekuas. Balt had once seen one tear straight through a Menguwist's shell like it was paper.

In short, he was glad that they weren't allowed to attack each other during the challenge, because his Tottaworm would be absolutely annihilated by a Nonnim.

He looked around the platform and his stomach dropped seeing how big the gaps were getting, how few tiles were actually left. In addition, it seemed that tiles were disappearing with more frequency.

At a certain point—one that was not terribly far off—his Tottaworm's agility would not be able to keep up with how quickly tiles were disappearing. Not only that, but he could only fling it so far. Some of these gaps were getting too big for his Jekua to cross comfortably.

His tricks had worked at first, but they wouldn't last for much longer. He needed to change up his strategy, but he wasn't quite sure how. Without being able to switch Jekuas, his options were severely limited.

Then Balt got to thinking. In that same tournament where he'd watched the Nonnim obliterate a Menguwist, he'd also seen how fast it could move around the battlefield when it ran on all fours. The bastard could jump pretty far, too, crossing at least a quarter of the battlefield in one leap.

A Nonnim could get around a hell of a lot faster and easier than a Tottaworm.

Before it had a chance to move, Balt stretched his Tottaworm's body up and around the Nonnim's waist like a belt. He then solidified its body so that it would stay in place.

The pink-haired woman had explicitly stated that the *only* rule was that none of them hurt each other. Nothing said he couldn't ride another Jekua.

He wished he could see the Nonnim's Summoner react to what he'd done.

Even through the Nonnim's body, Balt could sense the subtle vibrations of the tile at their feet. He knew that Nonnims didn't possess any other Type besides Thermal

—unless this Summoner had modded theirs with some Sonic powers—but somehow the Nonnim knew it was time to move. It could worry about the pathetic grub wrapped around its stomach later.

It leaned forward and took off running on all fours.

Balt switched to his own point of view, maintaining his firm grip on the Nonnim's waist as it bounded across the tiles, vaulting over gaps and skidding around other Jekuas.

Up on the LED screen, the yellow number had changed to "35." That last wave of tiles had caught a lot of Summoners off-guard, it seemed.

Getting close now, Balt thought excitedly. He might just pull this off. Some might say he was cheating by hitching himself to another Jekua, but as far as he was concerned, it wasn't technically cheating if it didn't go against the rules.

Although if they called it *cheap*, he'd give them that.

He returned to the Tottaworm's perspective, being jostled around by the Nonnim's jerky movements. If he had to guess, the other Summoner might have been trying to buck him off, but the Tottaworm's Elastic magic stayed strong.

Tiles were vanishing every couple seconds now, and they were no longer doing so in distinct waves of multiple tiles at once with pauses in between. A couple tiles in the middle would disappear, followed by one or two in the top corner mere seconds later, then a great mass of them in the center again, and so on.

Through his own eyes, Balt watched the LED screen's number slowly ticking down. They were in the twenties now.

The Nonnim continued dashing across the platform, pausing to inspect certain tiles before making its next move. Balt still didn't know how its Summoner was choosing where to go, but he also didn't care. Whatever their method was, it worked.

A few more Jekuas fell through the holes, and now only six more would need to be eliminated before the challenge was over.

Down on the platform, the Nonnim screeched to a halt on a set of two adjacent platforms which also held a Wallago, a lithe wildcat. The tile behind it suddenly disappeared, and now all around them was empty space, with the Nonnim and Wallago standing on a red island floating in the air.

Balt tightened his Tottaworm's grip, suddenly feeling very vulnerable.

Then the tile the Nonnim was standing on began vibrating, as did the one holding the Wallago.

"Shit," Balt swore, not sure what he or the Nonnim would do. Even if the Nonnim didn't make it, he had to do *something*. He did not intend to be one of the last six who were cut.

Only two or three seconds now until the two tiles were gone.

The Wallago surged ahead, setting itself up for a head-on collision with the unmoving Nonnim.

Come on, do something, Balt mentally urged the other Summoner. If they didn't act fast, he'd have to improvise, and he didn't think he would be getting out of this situation on his own.

Then the Nonnim moved aside, letting the Wallago dart past but rotating to face it.

Abruptly, the Nonnim burst forward, claws scraping on the red tile, leaving deep scratch marks.

The Wallago was already in the air, attempting to leap across the large gap to the nearest tile it could reach.

Then the Nonnim jumped, landing atop the Wallago.

The next moment, the two tiles were gone and the Nonnim was pushing off the Wallago's back, using the other Jekua as a stepping stone across the empty air. Its claws embedded in the cat's flesh for a split second, but that was purely due to anatomy and was not technically an attack.

Balt couldn't help but laugh as the Wallago was shoved downward, lashing out with its claws in a fruitless effort to grab hold of a tile. The Nonnim, meanwhile, was able to land safely on another tile, with Balt's Tottaworm safely strapped to its belly.

He checked the screen once more, his stomach dropping to his ass.

It read "17."

One more elimination.

Balt sucked in a deep breath, mentally preparing himself for this last minute or two, and then all of a sudden the seven transformed into a six. A Giggit accidentally hopped left instead of right and careened to the floor.

The multitude of vibrations Balt could feel around his Tottaworm and the Nonnim immediately ceased, and the tournament official's voice rang out through the cavernous room.

"We have our sixteen!" she cheered. "If you are one of the remaining Summoners, please join your Jekua on the platform."

Several walkways emerged from the overlook on which they stood, granting them access to the large red platform. As Balt began to cross over, he was relieved to find that the missing tiles were starting to reappear so that the route to their Jekuas wasn't so treacherous.

While he walked, he unwrapped his Tottaworm from the Nonnim's waist and coiled it in on itself beside the other creature. When he reached the two of them, the Nonnim's Summoner was already there.

The guy was a few inches taller than Balt, with wavy brown hair and a scar on his chin. He looked Balt up and down as he approached.

"Uh…thanks for the help," Balt said timidly as he came to a stop aside his Jekua.

The other Summoner narrowed his eyes and pursed his lips, but then he broke into a peal of laughter. "That was funny," he said, extending his hand. "Name's Toby. Good job out there."

Relieved, Balt took the guy's hand and introduced himself. "Thanks," he said.

He took one more deep breath, his heart swelling with pride. He'd made it through the elimination round.

It was official now.

He was competing in the Makanuele Rumble.

12

REMISTI VANA'S BIG BOY

NOW THAT BALT WAS OFFICIALLY LOCKED IN FOR THE Makanuele Rumble, there was no turning back. His name was going to be plastered on that bracket alongside sixty-four other Summoners, all duking it out to reach the top spot.

When he'd asked earlier about the competitor list, it was because he wanted to see if Wasaaru's name was on there. He knew Wasaaru was making his way across the islands to compete, but they hadn't encountered him at all on Qwi or during the week they'd already been on Na Tana, so Balt had no clue if his cousin had made it to the city in time.

If he had, what was his Jekua team going to consist of? The Eclipse Jackal was an easy guess, seeing as he was pretty skilled with the Radiant Jekua so soon after imprinting it. Balt wasn't sure he'd want to use his Suelu, though, considering how common they were. If he knew

Wasaaru, he suspected the guy might want to show off some flashier Jekuas. Rare stuff that he had imprinted in the Volukho Wildlife Center.

As for Balt, his team was predetermined. Participants had to have four, and he only had four Jekuas to his name. There were wild Jekuas on the outskirts of the city that he could go scout for and imprint, but this close to the tournament, it was probably smarter to work with the team with which he was already comfortable. He was going up against people with a lot more summoning experience than him, and it was even possible that there were some Masters among them. Now wasn't the time to introduce new variables to the mix.

He really hoped he wouldn't be going up against Niona in any of the first few matches. There wasn't any doubt in his mind that she'd wipe the floor with him using any one of her Jekuas, regardless of how rusty she was with most of them.

The reason he thought that was because she was currently wiping the floor with him with *all* of her Jekuas, regardless of how rusty she was with most of them. After the elimination round concluded, they had met back up with Alani and grabbed a bite to eat.

While they ate, Balt and Niona regaled each other with stories of how their challenge went. She was highly amused by his strategy of mooching off a stronger competitor, but he claimed that anything was fair game. He'd made it to the end, after all. She had to give him that.

Apparently her challenge had involved shoving everyone's Jekuas into a long, straight tunnel, at which point they were pummeled by an extraordinary blast of wind. The goal was to maintain their Jekua's grip on the ground as the wind funnel grew more and more powerful with each passing minute. If they were knocked off their feet and hit the back wall, they were out. Her Muggish's sticky gloppiness had been a nice asset.

On their way out of the big black building, they heard that the third challenge had been made for flying Jekuas. Summoners had to make them fly around a huge, empty room while projectiles whizzed through the air. If a Jekua got hit, it was out. Unfortunately, they hadn't encountered anyone who competed in the fourth challenge, so they never found out what it was.

After their meal, the trio explored the city for just a bit, then Niona brought Balt to the gym near her hotel once they dropped Alani off at Corsseo Court. Aeiko's work day was almost over and she wanted to see them.

The two were now standing on one of the gym's sparring mats. Balt's forehead had a sheen of sweat that he wiped on the back of his arm, but that still felt gross, so he subsequently wiped it on his pant leg. That didn't feel not-gross either, but oh well. Niona's Bruiserweight, Boombox, stood a few feet away, bobbing and weaving like a professional boxer. Behind her, Niona stood with her arms crossed and a maniacal grin stretched across her face.

Balt was channeling his swiftly-depleting mana into Dipper's memory card. He felt he needed more practice with Milton, but Boombox was not an ideal opponent for the Mirrorbear, given that both of the Jekuas relied primarily on physical attacks and Boombox had a huge advantage in the speed department. He'd thought that Dipper's ranged attacks would work better against the Bruiserweight, but Boombox was still proving to be a tricky opponent. When Dipper fired a wide enough spread of petals, she could hit her, but so far all of her Seed Shots and Vine Whips had failed to land.

"Can I switch?" he asked.

Niona balked. "You sure?" she asked. "If this was round one, that'd mean I have to switch too."

That was true. And it was something to keep in mind, he realized. If he was fighting in one of the odd-numbered matches and he truly could not land a hit on a Jekua, he *could* just switch his own out to force his opponent to do the same and get it off the field…

It would be a coward's move, but it would work. If it secured him a win, then it was a viable option. Much like how he'd gotten through the elimination round.

But he didn't want to do that right now. "Let's pretend it's round two, then," he said.

"Oooh, awful sure of yourself, eh? Big boy is sure he's gonna make it to round two! That's that Vana blood runnin' through his veins, I bet."

"Ha ha," he mumbled sarcastically. Ever since they got to the gym, she'd been giving him shit about his hidden relation to Remisti Vana. The amount of times he'd heard the phrase "big boy" in the past hour was verging on ridiculous.

"Go ahead. We're in round two. I'm whoopin' you, though, so don't get starry-eyed about seein' round three."

Her assaults had indeed been relentless. She wasn't going easy on him at all.

Balt withdrew Dipper, watching the adorable flower-covered Puffolin morph into yellow soulclay before she was sucked back up into his kayet. Then he clicked to prime Pistachio's memory card and began summoning his Mosstopus.

The green terror loomed high over Boombox, who had stopped shifting from foot to foot while Niona waited on Balt. He made the Mosstopus raise his tentacles into the air in an act of intimidation. It made Niona laugh.

He struck out with one of Pistachio's tentacles, slapping Boombox in the face. The lizard's head reared back and she was almost knocked off her feet.

Niona recovered quickly. Boombox ducked out of the way of another swing, grasping the tentacle as it arced overhead. The Bruiserweight held on tight, being lifted into the air, and moving with the added mass made Balt's mana drain slightly faster.

Boombox's Friction decreased and she slid down Pistachio's arm with immense speed, landing a harsh kick on the Mosstopus's side before propelling herself away and landing in a tucked roll. Across the way, Niona looked mighty proud of herself with that maneuver.

That was what Balt had been expecting, however. Not that exact move, of course, but he had bet on Niona moving in closer since that was a Bruiserweight's specialty. While the bipedal lizard clung to Pistachio's arm, he'd emitted a light fog from Pistachio's gaping mouth. It hadn't been much, but still, Niona was too distracted pulling off her fancy move to notice it at all.

She noticed the newfound resistance in her Jekua's

movements, though. For a second she frowned, then she chuckled. "Fair enough," she said.

Boombox leapt forward, but Pistachio was able to scramble out of the way with the additional kinetic energy he'd absorbed from her. He continued swinging tentacles at the Bruiserweight, but only a couple hits connected. The last one hit hard, though, and sent Boombox flying backward to the edge of the ring.

Before the lizard could stand up, Balt started hocking a massive loogie in the Mosstopus's throat. He could feel slime tickling in his own throat, which was a truly vile sensation. Pistachio spit a gigantic slimeball that splashed all over Boombox, effectively sticking the creature to the ground.

Between his efforts with Dipper and now with Pistachio, Balt's mana reserves were nearing the halfway mark. He'd taken too many hits and fired off too many missed shots when Dipper was summoned. Controlling Pistachio required more mana per second, but the Mosstopus had already been more effective in combating Boombox than Dipper was. It was a good trade-off.

Boombox's arm unstuck itself from the ground with a wet *shlup*! as she tugged against Pistachio's yellowish-green slime. There was even a splash of purple mixed in there.

"You are so nasty," Niona said.

While her Bruiserweight struggled to free herself from the slime, Pistachio loosed another kinetic energy-draining fog. It roiled on the surface of the battlefield, reaching across to envelop Boombox. The green lizard writhed furiously, but each pump and kick grew more and more languid, like she was trapped underwater.

"That's fine," said Niona. A second later, Boombox slid out from the slime with ease. She still moved slowly, but Niona had been able to decrease her friction against the slime enough to slip out of her viscous bonds.

Boombox started running toward Pistachio in the middle of the ring. Niona had been able to increase her speed a little bit, but she was still sluggish. It granted Balt plenty of time to prepare an attack.

But then in a flash, Boombox was nothing more than bright pink soulclay swimming through the air into Niona's kayet. Almost instantly, more soulclay spurted out on the other side of Pistachio, behind his back. It took the form of her Nuri, Garbo.

Garbo's spiral horns immediately extended outward as the Jekua charged forward. They pierced Pistachio's backside, sending sharp pain cutting through Balt's own back. He had to stop himself from yelping.

If he could merge his perspective with Pistachio's, he'd be able to react quicker, but the Mosstopus's lack of eyes made the experience nearly debilitating. As it was, he had to rely on controlling his summon the old fashioned way.

For now, though, he withdrew Pistachio. His back was killing him. "Alright, alright, I give up," he said.

"Ooooh, so sad," Niona teased him. "I warned you not to get too excited about round three, big boy."

"Yeah, yeah."

Garbo returned to Niona's kayet as she sauntered across the mat to where Balt stood. "You see what I did there?" she asked.

"You stabbed me with your goat's horns."

"Yes. Because I was fast. When you summoned Piss, I was laughin' 'cause you moved so slow!"

"I had to load the right card," Balt said, defending himself. What more was he supposed to do?

"But so *slowly*! Some people's childbirth takes less time than it took for you to swap cards. You gotta be quick on the draw when you're in tournament mode, or else you're gonna look like an idiot like you did just now."

"You thought I looked like an idiot?"

"You're missing the point. I was able to get the upper hand on you 'cause you were readyin' yourself to whack Boombox. Before you could adjust your plan, I already had Garbo out on the offensive. If you take too long to switch Jekuas, your opponent is gonna have all that time to plan their new next move. You feel me?"

"I feel you," he said.

They continued their conversation as they popped open some cans of Thunderjolt. Balt had gone for a blueberry, while Niona bought herself a raspberry lemonade one. As she took a sip, Balt was a little jealous of her choice.

"So what am I doing wrong?" he asked, wiping some of the energy drink off his upper lip. Much like the sweat, he then proceeded to wipe it on his pants, feeling very much like a child.

"Going slow."

"Right, but how do I remedy that?"

"Go faster?"

"This is a very illuminating conversation."

"Sorry, I'm just messin' with you. Alright, so what your

problem is is that you're waiting until each step of the process is done before you move on to the next."

That didn't make any sense. "I can't load a different card before the soulclay is back in the kayet," he said. "It has to be loaded back onto its memory card."

"You're right. But when you summon a Jekua, you push your inner mana out into the kayet and into a specific card, right?"

"Right."

Summoning involved channeling mana into the kayet, and from there, into one of its four specific slots containing a memory card. When he'd only had one memory card, he could just shove his mana in there without another thought, but it took a bit more concentration when all four slots were loaded. Not much, though; it was still a very basic skill, and one that didn't take much practice. He'd never once felt out of his depth doing it.

Niona went on. "So what you can do is this: when you know you want to switch Jekuas soon, start channeling inner mana into whichever slot you're gonna hit next. Have that mana ready to go, so that as soon as your soulclay is back, you can slap that button and immediately start summoning again."

In theory, that sounded possible. Balt said, "But isn't that a huge drain on your mana? Having it already summoned but also using even more to get another Jekua ready?"

"It is," Niona nodded, before taking another swig. Then she said, "There's no difference between that and waiting, though. It's the same amount of mana being used. All that's different is *when* exactly it's being used."

"So that's only a good strategy if you're absolutely certain you want to switch," said Balt. "Otherwise, if you channel extra mana into the kayet but never end up switching, that's just a ton of mana wasted that you could've otherwise battled with."

Niona smiled. "Very astute," she said. "Yeah, you don't really wanna do it unless you know for sure you're gonna use it. When you're in an even-numbered match next week, it's really only something you wanna do when you're getting ready to change. In one of the odd-numbered rounds, though, I'd say it's probably a fair bet that you'll end up switching, and you never know when your opponent's gonna make you, so it *could* be to your advantage that you have it ready to go. You could swap out and be on the move before your opponent has a chance to get their new Jekua out there."

"But then that's mana I'm spending waiting on them to summon," Balt countered.

"True. It depends on whether you want to save that mana or buy those extra few seconds to position yourself on the field."

"Waiting could also mean I can see how they position themselves, and then I can act accordingly."

"Also true. That's essentially what I did summoning Garbo behind Piss. It's always a gamble, and you always gotta weigh whether your mana can take the hit."

That was another thing that had come to mind. "If I'm splitting up my mana, then that leaves me even more vulnerable to attacks," Balt said, thinking through things aloud. "A hit that might just knock me down a peg under normal circumstances could throw me into full-blown soulsickness if I've channeled a bunch of my reserved mana into the kayet and it's just sitting there uselessly."

Niona nodded again. "You're not wrong."

"So theoretically, I could've hit Boombox with a strong enough move while she was stuck in the slime that it would've cost you the match."

She chortled. "Nah. Your ass don't got any strong enough moves to knock that much mana out of me."

"I said *theoretically*."

"Not even in your harebrained theories, pal."

"You're insufferable."

"Fine," she relented. "Yeah. Some other, more powerful Summoner could've done that, yes. Not you, though."

"This whole session has been a lovely confidence boost, thank you. Glad I signed up for this tournament."

"Hey, you're learning!" Niona grinned. "Even Remisti Vana's big boy has gotta start somewhere, huh? And technically, *I* signed you up."

"I think I need a new teacher…"

"Whoa, now! I'm the best teacher you'll ever have."

She definitely wasn't a *bad* teacher. She'd given him a lot to think about. There were a lot of risks associated with the swapping technique she'd laid out, but some potential advantages, too. One thing he wasn't sure of was what intricacies were involved with splitting his mana up, trying to control a Jekua while also storing some in his kayet. He'd have to keep a mental handle on both simultaneously.

When he voiced this concern, Niona confirmed his worries. "It does take some practice," she said.

Balt sighed, swallowing a huge gulp of Thunderjolt. He could feel the mana trickling back into his reserves, filling up his body with magical energy.

He said, "Then I guess I'd better get to practicing."

13
STRINGS OF LIGHT

HOURS LATER, ALANI WAS FINALLY FEELING LIKE HER normal self again. The effects of the Veptilo had lasted longer this time than the previous two encounters. She wracked her brain, trying to remember if the effects had lingered longer the second time as well, but she couldn't be sure. With that instance, she had been contending with soreness from the attack too, so it had all mixed together. Pain was pain was pain.

But she felt better now.

Balt and Niona had scampered off to train for their tournament (after much deliberation between herself and Balt, during which she had to continually convince him he didn't need to feel guilty), while Alani went back to the apartment. She'd been waiting around for Aeiko to return for a while now, attempting to entertain herself on her linkpad.

Suddenly a text came in from Laowa, one of her friends at the Church in Tanepke. They'd texted a little bit when Alani had first left town on her pilgrimage almost four weeks ago, but that habit had died off quickly. Alani had been busy traveling, and she just assumed Laowa was busy either with studying her Veptlore or lusting after Usuel. This was the first time either of them had spoken to the other in weeks.

Are you okay? Laowa's message read.

Alani blinked and reread the message. It was a strange way to initiate a conversation. Or maybe it was not totally off the mark, but at the very least it was phrased weirdly.

She typed: *Yes. How are you?*

Laowa responded immediately, ignoring her polite reciprocation and instead just asking: *Where are you?*

So she was definitely acting weird. It wasn't just poor wording.

Why? she asked.

Are you safe? came Laowa's reply.

The obtuseness was grating on her. She asked, *What is going on??*

Where are you? Laowa asked again.

Alani was going to throw her linkpad at the wall. *Makanuele City,* she typed.

There was a delay before Laowa said anything else. Alani imagined the young girl setting her linkpad down and breathing a huge sigh of relief, although she still did not know why.

Oh thank the Veptists. Praise Nuritayhu.

What is going on? Why are you acting weird?

You haven't heard what happened? asked Laowa.

Alani thought it was abundantly clear based on the rest

of the conversation that no, she had not heard what happened. She told Laowa so.

She awaited Laowa's response. When it came in, Alani scanned over it, her eyes widening as she absorbed everything.

Maybe the news hasn't broken anywhere. I bet the Elders are trying to keep it quiet. But I overheard Elder Poul and Elder Fanareot talking about it an hour ago. They're freaking out. I've never heard them sound so nervous. It was weird. They said that the shrine on Qwi Island was attacked by that group, whatever they're called, and they stole it. They stole the shrine somehow. It's gone. The Church doesn't know what to do or where it is or how to get it back or anything. The Elders on that island are going to talk to the authorities, but Elder Poul doesn't seem confident that they're going to be able to do anything. I wasn't sure where you were in your pilgrimage, if you had already been to Qwi or if you were on your way or if you were there when it happened...

The Facet had done it?

They had successfully stolen Qwi's Veptilo?

She couldn't believe it. She refused to believe it. After the close call they'd had merely a week ago, did the Church not buff up their security? They should have flooded the area with coral golems, hired Summoners to stand guard 24/7.

Or had they done so, and it still wasn't enough? Those crystalline monsters the Facet fought with were powerful, and if they had come back with even more or even stronger ones, then perhaps all the security the Church could muster wasn't enough to stop them.

Still, it was impossible to imagine the shrine at Mé

Lutako without its Veptilo. What did it mean for the Veptilo to be removed from the earth? Did it lose its connection to the Vept?

She shuddered.

Alani read the message four times before composing a reply. It was hard to find the right words to say.

That's crazy, she started. It felt childish, but in that moment, she felt like a lost child. Completely out of her depth. *I'm safe, though. I visited the shrine on the forty-sixth.*

She started writing about her encounter with the Facet there, but quickly backspaced it all away. There was no reason to upset or worry Laowa even more.

I just went to the shrine here on Na Tana today, too, she continued. *So I'm good here as well. They have extremely heavy security around it here, far more than they had at the Qwi and Totta shrines. I don't see how the Facet could realistically ever reach it.*

If they somehow made it all the way underground, which was a tall order, then that long hallway lined with coral golems would surely put a stop to them, regardless of their fancy crystal beasts.

It also begged the question of whether the Facet would stop their attacks now. Did they only need a single Veptilo for whatever the hell it was they were doing? Or would they continue until they acquired all of them?

The Elders still have no idea what they want with the Veptilos? she asked Laowa. She realized that Laowa probably didn't even know what a "Veptilo" was, but she assumed the girl could piece it together with context clues.

Nope, said Laowa.

There came the sound of a key in a lock, and Alani's

head swiveled to look at the door. It swung open and Aeiko stepped inside, stuffing the key back into their pocket, followed by Brine. The coral golem had to stoop down to fit through the doorway.

Aeiko gave her an exhausted smile and a tiny wave. Alani reciprocated. She then peeked behind Brine, looking for Holly, but she wasn't there.

Apparently she had not been subtle, because Aeiko said, "Holly's still at the office. She usually works a little later than me." They threw themselves down on the couch near Alani, while Brine stood in the kitchen.

Alani glanced down at her linkpad, but didn't know how to conclude the disturbing conversation with Laowa. She looked back up at Aeiko and said, "Want to go get something to eat?"

She was angling to duck out without having to invite Holly, and hopefully the ploy was subtle enough for Aeiko to not realize it.

They nodded, letting out a sigh. "Yeah, just let me get changed real quick." They were wearing a green striped button-up shirt tucked into some tight-fitting pants. Alani thought it was a cute outfit, but it definitely still said "office job" loud and clear.

Aeiko disappeared into their room, while Alani wrote a quick thank you to Laowa and wished her well. Then she slid her linkpad into her pocket and tried to put the whole incident out of her mind. She looked over at Brine, who waved to her with his yellow hand. She waved back, and then Brine held up two fingers. Alani laughed and mirrored him.

A couple minutes later, Aeiko emerged wearing a

flowy green shirt and pink shorts. "I am too tired to put together a good look," they said with another sigh.

"That looks fine to me," said Alani. "Long day at work?"

"Very long. Not worth conversing about either, really."

"Got it. Where do you want to go?"

Aeiko considered where they should eat. Their face lit up as they said, "There's this cool, sort of new place a few blocks away. It's kind of near the crater. It's got a rooftop patio and they serve, like…not full entrees, but more like smaller dishes that you're supposed to share."

The rooftop patio sounded super appealing to Alani, assuming it wasn't going to get too cold as the evening wore on. They agreed on the plan.

They left Brine behind in the apartment to greet Holly upon her return. Alani had the brief thought that if no one was home when Balt finished up at the gym, he would not be able to get in since he lacked a key, but that was a problem for later. In all likelihood he'd be out late anyway, not returning until long after everyone else was home. When he and Niona got on a roll, they could be sucked into their summoning for hours.

The restaurant was close enough that they didn't need to hire a car to get there, they simply walked. As they did, Aeiko asked Alani about her day. She talked about how unsettling it was being inside the big, empty stadium, and she described the tasty lunch she'd eaten. She didn't find it necessary delving into the dirty details of the ritual. Aeiko had never been a Church follower, and it was not something Alani was eager to discuss anyway. She wanted to keep conversation light.

They had to wait fifteen minutes for a table on the patio, which was less of a wait than Alani had expected. The restaurant was abuzz with activity, their own conversation barely audible over the crowd's din. Makanuele was packed with people between its residents, Summoners competing in the tournament, people in town to spectate, and then the regular non-Jekua enthusiasts visiting on top of it all.

The person manning the host counter soon led them upstairs onto the rooftop patio, which was lit up with great gorgeous bulbs of light strung up all across it, held aloft by pillars of craggy multicolored rock. They were brought to a small, two-person table near the patio's edge that overlooked the massive crater nearby. It too was lit up, and Alani could make out tons of people milling about within it.

Aeiko ordered themselves a gin and tonic, while Alani stuck with a plain water. They perused the menu, and by the time the waitress returned with their drinks, they were ready to order.

They made idle conversation for about twenty minutes while they waited for the food, and when it was brought to the table, Alani was nearly bowled over by the intoxicating scents rising from each plate.

It was surprisingly easy to agree on dishes to split. The simplest was a large bowl filled with guacamole, accompanied by a hefty platter of vegetables and thick chips to dip into it. Then there was a bowl of ceviche, bursting with freshly diced vegetables and raw fish and shrimp, all lightly tossed in citrus juices. Alani had been skeptical about that one, but she ended up enjoying it. Not as much as she enjoyed the roasted potatoes, though, which came with a thick, luscious herb aioli. None of it came close to topping the rice bowl, though. In addition to gorgeous steamed yellow rice, it contained pork belly, cubed pork ribs, and mushrooms. The dish was tossed with some kind of mildly spicy sauce too, but Alani wasn't quite sure what it was. All she knew was that it left a satisfying tingle on her tongue that left her wanting to scarf down spoonful after spoonful. It was possible they would need to order one more bowl of that.

While they feasted, Alani asked how long Aeiko was expecting Brine to stay with them.

"I don't really know," they replied, their long hair waving in a gentle breeze. "The whole thing is up in the air, really. I might hand him over to someone else on a different team at some point, but not until my team gets a handle on what we're trying to do."

"The self-sustaining battery thing?"

"Right."

"How does that work, exactly? The whole thing, I mean. I've never understood coral golems."

"It's pretty complicated," Aeiko said with a grin. "At its essence, the chip attached to the coral is absorbing mana from the air or whatever. It then basically goes through a conversion process, where it transforms mana from...I guess it's not technically a *gas*, I dunno how to explain it, but it transforms it into a liquid. Something more tangible. Then it injects it into the coral, and that magical gunk gives it life. Obviously it's all a lot more technical than that, and it took years and years to perfect the technology, but that's the gist of it. Our version would be a slightly bigger device that would basically absorb mana, but only use a portion of it in the conversion process and use the other part as an energy source to continually power the device."

Alani said, "So it's kind of like a blood transfusion, but it's magical lifeforce stuff."

Aeiko laughed. "Look at you with the scientific terminology! 'Magical lifeforce stuff.'"

Alani laughed too. She was glad that the anxiousness she initially felt around Aeiko was slowly melting away, leaving them with casual and comfortable banter. Although, she was still acutely aware of the fact that one look from Aeiko, the flutter of their eyelashes, could send her spiraling again. But she was glad that they had resettled into the familiar groove they'd shared in their younger years.

Aeiko went on. They said, "Yeah, it is kind of like a blood transfusion, I guess."

"Does it only work with previously living things?" Alani asked. "Like coral, I mean. If I strapped it to a door, would the door come to life?"

Again, Aeiko laughed at that. "Uh...well, yeah, so the version that coral golems currently use and what I've got on Brine would only work with living stuff. There are teams experimenting with versions that could affect nonliving items, and it seems to be going well."

"What's the point of that?" Alani crunched down on a chip piled high with creamy guacamole.

"There are lots of different, weird applications for it," Aeiko said. "I know some groups are working on doors that automatically open when people approach, but, uh...I mean, we already have those that just use electricity and sensors and stuff rather than magical sentience. Another, though, is based on security. Like buying a safe or whatever that uses the tech, and it has enough awareness to only unlock for its owner, or something. They're still working out a bunch of kinks, but tests seem to be going fairly well so far, last time I heard. Those are totally different teams, though. Again, not *especially* useful, if you want my opinion, but Lakahlo is always experimenting with new stuff."

"Do you like it there?" Alani asked. She didn't know how Aeiko felt about their work. They hadn't really ever talked about it since they moved to Na Tana to work for Lakahlo Labs. Aeiko had always been the smartest person Alani knew, so it was no surprise to her when they announced they'd gotten hired at such a prestigious, groundbreaking tech company, and at such a young age.

"I do," Aeiko said. "I like working with my hands to actually design and build this stuff, and I love the challenges new ideas present. It's like getting paid to solve a puzzle."

"That does not sound like the job for me," said Alani. She had never been the type of person who found pleasure in a challenge. Who wouldn't want their life to be simple? Who wanted conflict? She got enough of that at home. She didn't need it in a workplace too.

"It's funny how different our jobs are despite both working with the Vept," Aeiko said. "How are you liking the Church stuff, anyway?" they then asked. "I must admit, when I found out you were becoming an initiate, it caught me by surprise."

That made sense. Aeiko had already moved away by the time Alani joined the Church, and not once in her childhood had she ever expressed any interest in joining.

"It's good," she said, her voice soft.

"You don't sound super enthusiastic," Aeiko said lightly. They spooned some of the ceviche onto a chip and took a big bite.

Alani shrugged. "I guess it's complicated, too," she said, echoing Aeiko's earlier words.

"The tattoos are cool, at least," said Aeiko with a cheeky grin. "I've always wanted a tattoo, but I still can't decide what I'd want."

"They all represent something in the Church," Alani explained. She pointed to the glowing manastreams on her face, tracing over the swirling lines. She knew exactly where each and every one of them was. "These mean that I'm supposed to become an Elder someday."

Aeiko's eyes widened and they had to put a hand to their mouth so they didn't drop their food. "Really?" they said. Alani nodded. "That's wild. So you're going to be, like, a bigshot in the Church someday?"

"I suppose so."

"That's cool. I've always seen Church people with the tattoos, obviously, but I didn't know they meant anything specific. That's kind of neat. I don't know if there is any sort of meaning or message I could commit to putting on my body. I think I'd need to just do some dumb little picture that I think is cute."

"Have you had any ideas over the years?"

"A few," said Aeiko. "I thought about getting a little

Suelu eating a berry or something. Or one of those little takeout cartons of noodles with a face on it."

"Ahh, to tie in with your company's intrepid research making inanimate objects not be inanimate anymore," Alani joked.

"Oh, yes, that's exactly why," Aeiko laughed.

"The next question is: regular ink, or shineink?"

Aeiko grinned. "I've always liked shineink. I think it's super cool. Yours looks great."

"Thank you. If I had to pick between those two, I would say the takeout container."

"Why's that?"

"With a Suelu, people might assume you're a Summoner."

"Is that bad?"

"In my experience, Summoners are huge dweebs," Alani smirked.

"That's true," said Aeiko. "I'm a huge dweeb too, but not *that* kind of dweeb..."

They both laughed at that.

Then Aeiko said, "Your sister has a tattoo now, you know."

"Does she really?" Siuv had never told her that. When did she get it? "What is it? Where is it?" she asked. Wherever her sister was tattooed, it was not immediately visible in any of the photos she'd posted recently.

"It's a Jekua, actually!"

"Dweeb."

"I know. It's a, uh...what's the thing called...I don't know. There are too many of the damn things to remember all their names. It's some type of bird one. It's on her ribcage, and there's a lyric from a song she likes next to it."

"Oh, gosh," said Alani, stopping herself from saying more.

"Gross, right?" Aeiko grinned.

Alani barked out a laugh. "I didn't want to say it, but..." She trailed off, letting Aeiko finish the thought.

"It's even more dweebish than a Summoner getting a Jekua tattoo! Don't worry, I made fun of her for it when she showed me. She called me a hater. She's not wrong."

They shared another laugh. A piece of Alani was disappointed, though, hearing that there was something about her sister she hadn't known. Something that was kept from her. She was sure it wasn't malicious or intentional, simply a result of them not speaking much. That was on her as much as it was on Siuv.

"How often do you two talk?" Alani asked Aeiko.

They shrugged. "I dunno. Uh...I dunno, every few days, I guess? At least once a week. We just text and stuff when something comes to mind." They must have noticed the dour expression on Alani's face, because they said, "Do you not talk much?"

"Not really. We do every once in a while, but...we kind of fell out of touch when she moved away."

"Ahh," Aeiko mumbled. "Yeah, it's hard maintaining a relationship when you're so far apart. The time difference can be a killer."

Alani nodded absently. She could tell just by looking at Aeiko that they knew there was more to the story than that. They were best friends with Siuv; there was no way

Siuv hadn't vented to them about their parents at some point over the years.

There were a few seconds of silence where they each ate some bites of food from the fantastic spread laid out on their table. The strings of light glimmered above their heads, twinkling like stars. Making up for not being able to see the real ones in the night sky.

Aeiko said, "Wanna call her up? I dunno what time it is in Hurrathsa, but maybe we can get her to show you that tattoo."

That sounded fun, actually. Alani smiled and nodded.

Aeiko pulled out their linkpad and placed it on the table, propping it up against the chip basket. They angled it so that both of them were within the camera's frame, then initiated a video call with Siuv.

Her sister answered after only a few rings. The room she was in was dark, and she was laying on her side, looking exceptionally groggy. Her eyes were half-shut in the blinding light of her linkpad.

"What the hell?" Siuv muttered.

"That's no way to say hello to your friend and your sister," said Aeiko.

Siuv blinked a few times and opened her eyes wider, before squinting them again. "Alani?" she said.

"Hi," Alani said meekly. She waved, her hand barely making it into the frame.

"So you made it," said Siuv. Alani nodded.

Aeiko cut straight to the chase. "We need to see your tattoo," they said.

Siuv's face scrunched up. "Why?" she said. "It's late. I'm

tired. I was sleeping soundly before you so rudely woke me up."

Alani was a little disappointed that this call was going to be so short, but it was already nighttime here, and she knew Hurrathsa was several hours ahead of the Volukho Isles.

"I just learned that you never told your sweet little sister here about it."

Sweet little sister?

"Did I not?" said Siuv.

Alani shook her head, tearing her attention away from Aeiko's descriptor.

Siuv groaned dramatically, loud enough that Aeiko scrambled to lower her linkpad's volume. They had to immediately turn it back up, though, to hear Siuv speak. She was saying, "Fine. If I show you, can I hang up and go back to bed? Is that really the only reason you called?"

"I mean, we'd love to chat with you, but if you want to go to bed after, that's okay," Aeiko said.

Another groan, which was mercifully quieter than the first. Then Siuv turned her linkpad to show her torso. She pulled down her blanket then lifted her shirt up to reveal her ribcage. It was decorated with a colorful bird in regular ink and a line of text that was illegible on account of the linkpad's camera quality combined with the dim lighting.

"Happy?" said Siuv off-screen.

"What's it say again?" asked Aeiko.

"'On tired wings, we still can fly,'" Siuv recited.

Alani and Aeiko both stifled laughs.

"Thank you," said Aeiko. Siuv lowered her shirt and turned the camera back to her face.

"Goodnight," she said. Then, "It's nice seeing you, Alani."

Alani smiled. "Same," she said. "Love you."

"Love you too." Then Siuv hung up.

Aeiko put their linkpad away, and finally the two could laugh at the tattoo.

"What a dweeb!" said Aeiko. "Your tattoos are way cooler than hers."

"She's only got normal ink, too," Alani pointed out.

"Yep, good point. *Man,* that quote is funny."

They scooped up some more of the pork-filled rice dish and shoveled it into their mouth. They chewed, swallowed, and sighed contentedly. The bowl's bottom was becoming visible.

"Should we order one more of these?" they asked.

"You read my mind," Alani said.

14
THE BRACKET

FIVE DAYS LATER, ON THE FIFTY-NINTH OF SUMMER, THE sun was blazing down blisteringly hot on Makanuele City.

Sixty-four Summoners from all over the world—though a majority were from the Volukho Isles—marched across the length of the Xatetu Crater and filed into the enormous stadium where, starting tomorrow, they would commence pummeling each other.

The past five days all had roughly the same shape: wake up after Aeiko and Holly were already gone, hang out around the city with Alani and Niona all day, then spend the entire evening training with Niona before lumbering back to the apartment in a fatigued haze.

Even with hours upon hours of practice under his belt now, Balt was unbelievably nervous about the tournament. Aside from Wasaaru (if his cousin had even made it in time), he positively *had* to be the most inexperienced Summoner in this throng of people. Why had he done this to himself? As he walked across the crater's neatly cut grass, looking at the stern faces around him, he wondered which of them he'd be facing in his very first match.

Niona clapped him on the shoulder, laughing at him. "Chill!" she said. "You look like you're constipated. Relax, have a good time!"

"Easy for you to say. You're not the one who's gonna get eliminated and humiliated in the first round."

"Yeah, that's true."

Normally, her faux discouragement was amusing to him, but not in that moment. It was making his stomach flip.

Do not throw up in front of these people, he commanded himself. *You would look like a fool. Do not do it.*

The competitors were instructed to return to the stadium to see the initial bracket as well as get their memory cards scanned by tournament officials. There were guidelines about what kind of Jekuas one could use in the competition, so they had to be sure everyone was adhering to the rules. Hybrids were allowed, but a Summoner could only use up to three modified Jekuas in their team of four.

Balt didn't know where they got that number from or why, but he only had one modification anyway: the Barrier ability he'd installed on Milton. And as far as he knew, the only modded Jekua Niona was using was Glom with his extra speed. When he gave it some extra thought, he remembered that Pops was also outfitted with that Refraction mod and Garbo could use a Thermal attack. She didn't seem to use the Nuri's mod all that much, though.

He turned to Niona to ask a question. "If they're scanning our memory cards now, does that mean we can't change our team later in the tournament?"

"Why? You plannin' to run out and imprint some new dudes in between matches?"

He shook his head. "Just curious," he said. His four-man team was locked in regardless, but he wanted to know. He'd seen his grandmother compete in tournaments where she and others used a different team every match, and he'd watched plenty of competitions like that on TV, but evidently he'd missed what the Makanuele Rumble sign-in form said. He'd been reading over it carefully, line by line, but at a certain point he grew self-conscious about Niona and the other woman watching him read it so he'd just signed and turned it in.

"You shoulda read the rules, big boy."

"Come on." His stomach did another somersault. It was becoming a gold medal gymnast.

Niona quirked an eyebrow and dropped her jokey arrogance. "Yeah, we can't change teams. Once we're scanned, we're locked in to whoever we chose. That's why I was giving such thought to the team I picked last week."

"Why are they doing things that way?" he then asked. It definitely wasn't the norm.

She shrugged. "Just the way they want things done, I guess."

The Summoners at the head of the pack were beginning to enter the stadium. They all flowed through the wide open doors and spread apart in the entry halls to gaze up at the bracket.

It was on display right there in the entryway for everyone who stepped foot in the stadium to see. The bracket was on a brightly illuminated electronic screen that extended down from a slit in the ceiling. The background was a shade of purple that matched the ocean, sporting sixty-four rectangles with rounded corners that alternated between light blue and light gray as it went down the list. As the tournament wore on, the screen would update automatically with the winners and losers, so everyone who passed by would be able to see the most up-to-date information. Balt imagined this was not the only bracket screen in the stadium, and that they could be found on every floor.

He squinted, trying to read the names and find his own. It was dizzying, seeing all the Summoners' names in one long list like this.

The two names paired up at the very top of the list were Renata Tohm and Wasaaru Vana.

So he made it after all, Balt thought to himself. He was surprised his cousin hadn't made his presence known yet.

Did being the first people listed mean that Wasaaru would be part of the first match in the whole tournament? Or were these randomized? There was no indication anywhere that the order mattered one way or the other. Balt continued reading.

He spotted Niona's name before his own, too. Her first opponent was a woman named Justine Tesh. At least it wasn't his own name coupled up with hers. He nudged her and pointed at her pairing.

"Ever heard of her?" he asked.

"Nope," she said.

Balt wondered if he would be able to find footage of all these Summoners battling online. That might give him an advantage in battle, seeing what their style was. If nothing else, that was one good thing about being a newbie: there was nothing online about his fighting style. Yet.

He continued looking up and down the list, frantically searching for his name. Had there been some kind of error? Was something wrong with his application so they had to toss it? Was he literally too inexperienced to compete?

There were a few familiar players from the Tanepke Tussle several weeks back. He recognized Yakka Dho, the guy who'd foolishly pushed himself to soulsickness right off the bat. There was also Desi Taewao, the hometown hero who'd lost to Olli Berrap. He spied Olli's name further down the list, too.

He even found someone named Kallon, and he was curious as to whether that was the same Kallon who had been in their tour group in the Volukho Wildlife Center. None of the other names he saw matched anyone from the group, and he was admittedly a little let down by Valentina not being there.

Finally, just as he was losing hope that his entry form had been counted, Balt found his name just before the halfway point on the board. It was listed before Niona's name, so he didn't know how he'd missed it. But there it was, matched up with someone named Rei Yor.

"You know Rei Yor?" he asked Niona.

"Nah," she answered.

"What good are you?" he joked.

"Sorry. I might have seen some of these people fight before, but I'm not good with names. If I saw their face, I'd remember better."

That was alright. He would have to look up Rei on his linkpad later, see if he could glean anything useful.

He scanned through the list of names again, but didn't recognize anyone else aside from Toby (listed as Tobias), the Summoner he'd latched onto during the elimination round. There was somebody simply listed as "Uil," with no surname, which was odd. He balked at the sight of Mr. Dia's name on the list of competitors, and immediately pulled out his linkpad to tell Alani.

Mr. Dia might have several decades on him and most of the other competitors, but a person's mana reserves deepened at a slower rate the older they got, so older Summoners didn't necessarily have an unfair advantage there. Not all of them trained to deepen their reserves as frequently as Balt did, either. And a powerful attack was still a powerful attack—there were plenty of moves that could decimate a chunk of mana from a Summoner, no matter how many years of summoning they had under their belt.

And besides all that, Balt was familiar with Mr. Dia's summoning style and his limited retinue of Jekuas. The old man was going to get absolutely pulverized. He couldn't help but laugh as he typed a message to Alani.

"Welcome, Summoners!" came a booming voice resounding through the hall. Sixty-four heads turned to the left to examine the source. It was the same red-haired woman from the registration desk, speaking into a microphone. "I trust you have all taken a good, hard look at our bracket here. As you can see, you are all divided into different pairings. The order, from top to bottom, is the order in which you will be competing."

So Wasaaru would indeed be in the kickoff match. Balt was entertained by the notion of Wasaaru being eliminated almost immediately, but he also knew his cousin would no doubt boast about being one of the first competitors. That was going to make Balt's blood boil. It was only a matter of time.

"The first round will be spread over two days, the sixtieth and sixty-first, with sixteen battles on each day. The sixteen matches that comprise round two will be held on the sixty-second. The sixty-third will be an off day for all those who are still in the competition. Then, the following day, we will continue with the third round, followed by the fourth the day after. On the sixty-sixth, we will have both the fifth round as well as the finals."

The timeline had been described in the sign-in form, but there were probably many Summoners who had only skimmed it, like Balt had. He appreciated the refresher.

"If you'll follow me, please," the woman then said, "we'll get your memory cards scanned and logged, then you can be on your way. I know you all must be anxious to get some last-minute training in before the first matches kick off tomorrow!"

People shoved past Balt and Niona, making their way down the hall behind the stout woman. Niona grabbed him by the hand and pulled him along before he was trampled by the crowd.

On all sides were anxious, excited murmurs from his fellow Summoners. Nearby, he spotted Yakka Dho, with his signature (and ridiculous) coifed orange hair.

Balt grinned. Just a short while ago, he had been relegated to the stands, watching someone like Yakka Dho compete. Now they were side by side, duking it out for the top spot in a real tournament.

His stomach did another flip, but his heart buzzed with excitement, too. He could scarcely believe he was standing here, with so many bona fide Summoners. Counting himself amongst them.

They were instructed to wait outside a set of heavy metal doors, with only five Summoners allowed to enter at a time. Balt and Niona were near the middle of the group, so depending on how long it took to scan each person's memory cards, they might have to wait a while.

"So," Balt said, "I guess we're both up tomorrow."

"Yep," said Niona. Both their pairings were in the top half of the bracket. They would be two of tomorrow's sixteen matches.

"You nervous? Or excited?"

"A bit of both, I guess. I'm not worried or anything, but you never know what's gonna happen. Should be fun either way, though." With a grin, she said, "I'm lookin' forward to making people deal with Glom, I can tell you that much."

Balt grinned too. He hoped he would have a good vantage point tomorrow to observe Niona's match. He loved watching her battle.

Then he realized that whenever he watched Niona's fight tomorrow, at that point he would already know if he was out of the tournament or not. Weird.

The crowd inched along as more people were funneled into the room. Balt's linkpad vibrated, and he pulled it out to read a message from Alani: *You have got to be joking.*

Nope, he replied. Mr. Dia's match was another that he

could not miss for anything in the world. He would crawl on his hands and knees through a trail of acid to see that man in a bonafide tournament battle.

They shuffled up a few more feet, and then someone else from Tanepke nudged Balt from behind.

"I honestly cannot believe you're doing this," came Wasaaru's voice.

Balt turned around to glare at his cousin. "Why's that?" he said.

"I've seen you fight," Wasaaru sneered. "Enough said."

"I beat you in our last battle," Balt reminded him.

"You know that was only because of the bad massage I got."

He was still leaning on that pitiful excuse. "Right. Have you already got a spa picked out in town that you can blame your next loss on?"

Wasaaru huffed a mirthless laugh. He ignored the snide remark and said, "I take it you saw who's competing first tomorrow?"

"Yep. You ready?"

"Of course."

"Who've you got on your team?"

Wasaaru laughed again. It was a hollow sound, and it still infuriated Balt. "Like I'd tell *you*! You'll have to wait and see like everyone else. What've you got, a pack of Suelus?"

"I don't know why you keep clowning on Suelus when you have one yourself," Balt pointed out.

"And what's wrong with a Suelu?" said Niona, butting into the conversation. She had to defend Pops's honor.

She looked Wasaaru over and said, "Who's this charming gentleman with a distaste for Suelus?"

"Wasaaru Vana," Wasaaru introduced himself, holding out his hand for Niona to shake. He smiled politely at her, and Balt wanted to slap the expression off his face.

"Another Vana?" said Niona, her curiosity piqued.

"He's my cousin," Balt said flatly.

"Ahh, the infamous cousin," Niona nodded.

That amused Wasaaru. "You've been talking about me, huh?" he said to Balt.

"Only bad things, I assure you," said Niona.

"My team isn't all Suelus," Balt said.

"Not that there's anything wrong with that," Niona chimed in.

"Well, I guess we'll see what the other's working with tomorrow," Wasaaru said. Then, "Where are you staying while you're here? I've got a room at the Venmont."

Niona whistled. "That's a nice-ass place," she said. Wasaaru grinned smugly, having baited her for such a reaction.

"I'm staying with a friend of Alani's," Balt replied.

"Who?"

"You don't know them."

"Maybe I do."

"You don't."

"Just tell me. Stop being weird."

"I just know you don't know them, so why do you care!"

"Just say it then!"

"Aeiko Fentao," Niona finally said, ending the inane debate.

"I don't know them," Wasaaru said.

"I told you," Balt grumbled.

But then Wasaaru's eyes narrowed. He was processing the name. Balt knew he was about to put two and two together.

"Wait a second," his cousin said slowly. "Fentao? As in *Tin* Fentao?"

Balt sighed, then confirmed.

"You're shacking up with the *enemy*?" Wasaaru snarled.

"Aeiko is not the enemy!"

"Tin Fentao is our eternal enemy, and therefore any offspring of his is the enemy too!"

"Aeiko is fine! They are a different human being than their dad!"

"He called us Rockboys for years!" Wasaaru took a breath, then said, "Wow. I just…wow. Who would've thought that someday you would be shacking up with Tin Fentao's kid. I can't believe it."

"Stop saying 'shacking up,' it's gross."

"Am I wrong?"

"I feel like the phrase has a certain connotation that is inaccurate here," said Niona.

Wasaaru huffed again, turning his attention away from Balt's perceived betrayal and focusing on Niona. He smiled and said, "Anyway, it sounds like you're familiar with the Venmont. If you want to come by and have a few drinks at the bar sometime, just ask the reception desk to ring me."

Balt stared at his cousin with horror.

But then, without a moment's hesitation, Niona

laughed at the invitation. "Yeah, okay," she said, her tone mocking.

Her reaction obviously rubbed Wasaaru the wrong way. He grimaced and said, "I'll see you later." Then he shoved past them to get closer to the front of the crowd.

When he was out of earshot, Niona asked, "Is he even old enough to drink?"

"No, he's my age. I wouldn't be surprised if he had a fake ID, though."

Niona laughed some more. "Dumb little boy," she said.

The words were directed toward Wasaaru, but they stung Balt slightly, too.

Another half an hour passed before it was their turn to walk through the metal doors. On the other side were five technicians standing by to scan each Summoner's memory cards.

A few of them were occupied with people who had previously entered. Balt walked over to one of the free techs, a skinny man with a short black beard that had a streak of white in it. "Cards, please," the man said bluntly. There was no warmth in his expression. He had a job to do, and he wanted to get it done.

Balt held up his wrist and ejected the four memory cards from his kayet. They were small enough to all fit in his palm. He handed them over to the bearded man, and he was taken aback by how uncomfortable it felt giving his memory cards to a stranger. It didn't feel natural.

The man held a device that appeared similar to a kayet, but it wasn't strapped to his wrist. He simply held it in his hand. He glanced up at Balt and said, "Name?"

"Balt Vana."

He typed Balt's name onto the device, then held it up to his kayet. He scanned it, and a shrill tone alerted him that it was finished doing whatever it was doing. Probably marking down his KIN, Balt guessed.

Then the bearded man slid the first of Balt's memory cards into a slot on top of the device. The screen lit up with numbers and waveforms that Balt did not understand in the least, but they seemed to make sense to the man.

After examining the information for a short while he removed the memory card, which Balt knew to be the Tottaworm's, and returned it to him. The short, easy process repeated for all four of his memory cards. The waveforms and numbers all varied wildly from Jekua to Jekua, and Balt was impressed by the man's ability to discern anything of value from the information. There was probably something tucked in there with the rest of the data that indicated whether a Jekua was modified.

All in all, only three or four minutes had passed before Balt was once again in possession of all his cards and the disinterested man informed him he was set.

"That's it?" said Balt.

"That's it," the man said.

So that was it.

All his information was registered and his name was on the bracket.

And tomorrow, the tournament would finally commence.

15

CONVERSATION AT KONATARI

THE GROUP STOOD ON THE SIDEWALK OUTSIDE KONATARI, the restaurant Holly had spoken of where customers cooked their own food, waiting for a table. There were five of them: Alani, Balt, Niona, Aeiko, and Holly. The latter had invited herself along to dinner, returning home from work just as they were about to slip out. They had almost made it.

The outing had been Aeiko's idea. With the tournament kicking off the next day, they thought it would be nice for everyone to go out and enjoy a big, fancy meal together. It was their treat. When everybody involved said that such generosity was not necessary, Aeiko insisted with a cute smile.

Alani felt bad, given that she and Balt had already taken up space in their apartment for nearly a week, but Aeiko seemed to truly not mind. Maybe she was getting into her own head too much.

So, once Holly had changed out of her work clothes,

Aeiko booked a car on her linkpad and it took them across the city. It would've been a thirty- or forty-minute walk, and all of them were too hungry to spend that much time walking.

Tonight, Konatari was packed. According to Holly, it was always a popular restaurant, but she'd never waited this long for a table. Since it had been such a last-minute decision, they were unable to secure a reservation.

"Guess everyone else had the same idea as us," said Balt, leaning against the building and knocking his heel against the wall. He rubbed the bare spot on his wrist where he usually wore his kayet. Back at the apartment, he was confused when Alani told him he probably should refrain from wearing the bulky device out to a nice restaurant. It took several minutes for him to relent. It wasn't like he had any particularly fancier clothes to wear either, but at least his casual outfit wasn't punctuated by a kayet.

Alani eyed Holly suspiciously. The woman was wearing a skin-tight black and white striped long sleeved shirt that accentuated her curves. She had lightly applied blue eyeshadow with hints of pink mixed in and thin streaks of white eyeliner. She rubbed a hand over the bright blonde stubble on her scalp, laughing heartily at something Aeiko said.

She looked extremely hot, which sucked.

Alani fumed silently, standing away from the pair and half-listening to whatever it was Balt and Niona were blabbering about. She had no right to be jealous, since she and Aeiko were nothing more than childhood friends, but she was anyway. Over the past five days, she had gleaned no further clarity about the relationship between Aeiko and Holly. All she could be sure of was that Holly still wanted Aeiko. Or, at the very least, she wanted them to think she did, for whatever reason. She was still strangely flirty with Niona too, who was either oblivious or unreceptive. It wasn't clear which.

After nearly half an hour of waiting out in the chill air, the hostess called Holly's name. She had appointed herself the leader of their little group. The four of them followed behind her and the hostess to their table, past dozens of tables that were topped with sizzling meats and vegetables. The smells were beyond scintillating. Alani cursed Holly for picking a good place to eat.

The group was seated at a round table that provided all of them with ample room to reach the center, which housed a small black grill. The hostess departed, saying their waiter would arrive shortly. Balt and Niona sat near each other, naturally, as did Aeiko and Holly. Alani sat in between Balt and Aeiko.

"This is gonna be fun!" Holly beamed, tapping her fingernails on the table excitedly.

Balt reached out a hand and quickly patted the grill in the middle of the table. The rest of them stared at him as he retracted his hand.

"What are you doing?" Niona asked.

"Seeing if the grill was hot."

"And what if it was?"

He shrugged.

"They'll turn it on for us when they bring out the food," said Holly. "And that brings us to our decision: what should we get?"

The restaurant offered four types of meat. In order of price, low to high, they were: chicken, beef, pork, and Gomingo. Nobody wanted to make Aeiko pay Gomingo prices, so that was out.

"What do you recommend? You're the expert here," said Niona.

Holly batted her eyelashes and said, "Their seasoned chicken is really good. Their pork belly is the bestseller, though. That's what they're famous for."

"Sounds like we need to get at least one order of that, then," Balt said. Alani chuckled at him; he was practically drooling.

Soon the waiter came by to take their drink order. The three people over the age of twenty ordered themselves cocktails, while Alani and Balt were relegated to just water. Alani was briefly tempted to get an iced tea, but she didn't want to increase the bill. They also placed an initial order for two things of chicken and one pork belly, just to start with. Holly assured them ("them" primarily meaning "Balt") that they could always order more.

While they waited, it was of course Holly who initiated conversation. "It's been so long since we've been here, huh?" she said, flicking her eyes toward Aeiko.

Aeiko stared at her for a second, then said, "Oh, yeah. That was, uh, a long time ago."

"Not *that* long!" Holly laughed lightly. "We came here for an anniversary like two years ago," she said, placing a hand on Aeiko's shoulder. "We nearly ate ourselves sick that night."

"Yeah," said Aeiko quietly.

Holly squeezed their shoulder but did not remove her

hand. "It's a good thing they weren't as busy then as they are tonight. We nearly lost our reservation as it was! We were late because we got a little distracted back at the apartment, if you know what I mean." She gave Aeiko's shoulder yet another squeeze.

"I do know what you mean," said Niona. "You mean sex, right?"

Her bluntness made Holly giggle even more, while Aeiko looked absolutely mortified. That was confirmation enough.

Holly's frankness was making Alani's skin crawl. She knew Niona was trying to joke around and point out how absurd it was that Holly would mention that, but it didn't exactly work. It just made Alani even more uncomfortable.

After the waiter brought everyone's drinks, things only devolved from there. Holly slurped hers down with fervor, emboldening her to place every conversation's spotlight directly on her.

If Aeiko was asked about their job, inevitably Holly would jump in to answer for them and then steer the subject toward what she was doing at Lakahlo instead (which, in Alani's perfectly humble opinion, was far less interesting than Aeiko's mana absorption research). Holly was part of the team that designed the UI for linkpads.

"Admirable work," Niona said, her words laced with sarcasm. Holly took them at face value, though, and thanked her with a smile and a bite of her lower lip. That time, even Balt looked weirded out.

The waiter then brought out a collection of tiny white dishes that were filled with various side items. There were cold potatoes in a sweet, sticky glaze; pickled and fermented vegetables; tiny, triangular cuts of bread; the list went on. All told, there were maybe fifteen different little plates of food placed on a rolling circular platform in the middle of the table, surrounding the grill, that they could swivel around to grab whatever they wanted. The waiter also flicked the grill's flame on and informed them he would be back soon with their meat.

"Not many people do this, but I think grilling the bread makes it super tasty," Holly said. She began to snatch a few different sides and plopped them onto the plate in front of her.

Everyone else followed suit, and a minute later the waiter returned with three plates piled high with raw, marinated meat. He set them down gently and said, "Give the grill about...five more minutes to heat up, then enjoy!"

As they waited for the grill, Alani took a bite of some pickled cucumber. It had a hint of spicy tang to it that she found odd but enjoyable. None of the small dishes contained much food, and they were all almost depleted already. They would need to get more; she suspected she might enjoy the sides even more than the meat itself.

Again, Holly took it upon herself to take charge. Once the grill was sufficiently heated, she used some tongs to grab strips of meat one by one and placed them on the hot surface. They immediately started sizzling, and the aroma was intense. As Alani breathed it in, she briefly doubted whether she would indeed enjoy the sides more.

"After a couple minutes, we'll flip them," Holly said. All the meat was sliced thin, so it wouldn't take very long to cook through.

Balt was given flipping duties. Everyone could tell he was eager to devour the pork belly. It was a wonder he didn't grab a handful of the raw meat and gobble it down.

While the food cooked, Holly scrambled for more attention. When Aeiko asked Balt and Niona about the tournament, Holly was somehow able to turn *that* on herself too. They spoke for a minute about their first round opponents, until Holly started blathering about a friend of hers who competed in a different tournament in a different city six years prior.

To her credit, she was able to go on and on about every little detail. What the arena was like, what food they offered, which Jekuas her friend used, which ones they fought against—every question Balt or Niona had was met with a hasty reply. Alani thought the woman was probably fabricating at least half her answers, but that might've been her own biases talking. Those were talking just as much as Holly herself.

Alani shoved aside her annoyances and grabbed a few pieces of chicken and one slice of pork belly off the grill. She wasn't a huge fan of pork, but if it was the restaurant's specialty, she couldn't *not* try it. But first, she took a bite of chicken, which was amazing. It was juicy and succulent, with a bit of sweetness from the marinade combined with a mere hint of smokiness from charring on the grill. Chasing that with one of the cucumbers would be divine, and so that was what she did.

Meanwhile, Balt was losing his mind over the pork belly. He gnashed it in his teeth, moaning about how delicious it was. He then tossed a slice of bread on the grill, taking care to place it far from where they'd cooked the raw meat.

"Oh, this is good too," Holly said, sticking some of her fermented cabbage next to Balt's bread. It instantly started crackling, and she had to turn it over after less than a minute. When she took it off the grill, it left behind sizzling remnants of the red liquid that it was marinated in.

Balt shifted his bread over a few inches to soak up the errant marinade. He couldn't let it go to waste.

"So," Holly said after swallowing her grilled cabbage, "Alani! Tell me about this pilgrimage you're on. What's the deal with that?"

Alani ate another piece of chicken before detailing to Holly what "the deal" was with her pilgrimage. Aeiko appeared genuinely interested as she talked about how two Veptists, Conbreas and Duremjul, both vied for her undying devotion. Now she had to travel to the archipelago's five shrines to determine which path her life would follow.

"Hmm. That's pretty weird," said Holly.

That was one way of putting it.

She said, "I remember being your age and not knowing what it was I wanted to do with my life either."

Alani faltered, then said, "That's…not quite what the situation is here." It wasn't as if she was having trouble deciding between the Architect and the Sculptor. If anyone was being fickle, it was the Veptists.

Holly waved a hand, dismissing her words as if she were a child. In Holly's eyes, she probably was. Holly was twenty-three, a couple years older than Aeiko. Alani cast a glance at Aeiko, who looked at her briefly before returning their attention to the food on their plate. In that moment, Alani did feel like a child.

"I was interested in art, but I was also really into tech," Holly went on, bringing the conversation around to herself yet again. "I entered so many art contest things in school, and my professors always loved my work. My pieces garnered big crowds at all the end-of-semester showcases. I don't have any of them anymore, though. I gave them all away to friends and family."

"That's very generous of you," Niona said, her mouth stuffed with chicken and bread. Alani knew she was teasing again, but with her mouth full, the sarcasm was probably impossible for Holly to detect.

"Well, everyone just kept asking me if they could have one of the pieces, so how could I say no?"

"You couldn't," said Niona.

"Of course not. But anyway, when I wasn't painting, I was always on the computer. I was kind of an introvert all throughout school."

Based on how much she dominated the conversation, Alani genuinely would have never guessed that Holly could have once been considered introverted. Perhaps it was another impulsive lie.

"I was always fiddling around on there. I guess I was kind of a nerd," Holly said, chuckling.

Alani wanted to smack her gorgeous face.

She felt the impulse to smack Holly yet again when she returned her hand to Aeiko's shoulder. There was no real reason this time, she just did it to do it. Aeiko ignored it, continuing to eat their food without comment or objection.

"I realized I could combine the two, though! I got an internship at Lakahlo doing graphic design for some of their apps. That was how we met, actually," Holly said, moving her hand from Aeiko's shoulder to their back, rubbing it for merely a moment before removing it. "We were both interns at the same time. You weren't an art hoe like me, though."

"No, I wasn't," Aeiko said, grinning ever so slightly. Then they took a bite of potato, saying nothing further.

"What was it you were doing, exactly? I never understood. I'm a techie, but the stuff you were into was way beyond anything I'm capable of."

Aeiko said, "I was helping write some of the Artificial Ability code."

Niona perked up at that. "Really?" she said. "What'd you make?"

"I didn't do anything on my own," said Aeiko, "I only assisted other, much smarter people. But I had my hands in, uh…Smog, Whiplash, and just a tiny, *tiny* bit in Plasma Skewer."

"Wow…" Niona muttered. "That's so rad." Balt nodded fervently, but he was too busy chewing his grilled bread to add anything.

"The Plasma stuff was too complicated for me to ever really get a good handle on it, but it was cool," said Aeiko. "Smog was really more my speed," they said with a chuckle.

Clearly too much time had passed with focus aimed away from Holly, so she had to jump back in. "Like I said, way crazier stuff than what I was doing!" she grinned.

If Alani had to put a descriptor on it, she'd say "grinned manically."

"Our first date was in the Lakahlo break room, though," Holly continued. "We were just two little interns struggling to get through our workload. We were both working late and ate dinner together in the break room. It took us forever to get back to work 'cause we were so caught up in our conversation, ha! I don't know about you, but I ended up staying at the office way, way later than I intended to."

Alani shifted in her seat and pushed food around on her plate with her fork. She didn't understand why Holly kept bringing up her and Aeiko's history. What was the point? What did she have to gain?

"Yeah, I did," Aeiko said. "I don't really know if that would count as a date, though. We were kind of just both in the same place eating food at the same time and talking."

"Isn't that what a date is?" Holly said brightly.

Aeiko didn't have any fight in them. They let Holly have it.

Alani looked at Balt and Niona to her left. They were both preoccupied with stuffing their faces, though she and Balt exchanged a strained look. She could tell that he too had no idea how to react to anything Holly was saying. Niona probably wanted to toss out more awkward quips, so Alani was thankful for the woman presently being distracted by food.

If only we'd gotten out the door just a minute sooner, Alani thought to herself as she watched Holly gleefully pop a cucumber in her mouth, biting down with a loud crunch.

Balt and Holly placed the remaining meat onto the grill and relished the side dishes while it cooked.

"Should we order some more?" Holly asked.

Alani noticed Balt glancing at her for a split second before saying, "Probably so. I think I need some more of that pork belly." Niona nodded her assent.

Holly turned to Alani and said, "That sound good to you? Should we order more of the chicken?"

Alani wanted nothing more than for this weird, awkward conversation to be over, so she resented the fact that she was admittedly still pretty hungry. She had not filled herself up on the tiny chopped vegetables and thinly-sliced meat.

"Yeah," she replied, disheartened. She put on a smile to hide her frustration. "Let's order some more."

16
OPENING CEREMONY

It was a genuine miracle that Niona awoke the following day without a hangover. Maybe the Veptists really were pulling the strings from deep within the Vept after all. In order to get through the evening, she'd had to order (and consume) several drinks. The buzz kept her in a light mood, one that was able to tease Holly without sounding outright mean. That woman was exasperating, though.

Drowning herself in alcohol the night before the tournament had been a calculated risk, and Niona was grateful it paid off. She felt great. She pulled herself out of her bed, which had been tucked in too tight when she drunkenly climbed into it the night before. Now the sheets were astray, crumpled up in a heap from her unconscious movements.

She walked over to the window and pulled the curtains open. Morning sunlight poured in, and she gazed blearily out at the city streets. An old, hunched over man was hobbling down the sidewalk with his tiny little dog on a leash. It started yapping at a nearby Suelu digging through a pile of trash that had fallen beside a dumpster. The Suelu stopped rummaging and stood on its hind legs, staring down the dog, totally unbothered by the noise.

Niona grinned at the fearless Suelu. It made her think of Pops. She chose to believe that was a good omen.

She moved away from the window, glancing at the bedside clock. They had planned to meet at Aeiko's apartment in about ninety minutes. There was still ample time to ease into her day before she needed to get ready.

Eventually, she got herself cleaned up and dressed, after a long time spent playing some dumb games on her linkpad. She always felt that they helped her mind to focus before a match, without getting too wrapped up obsessing over small details and strategies. She needed her mind sharp, but still loose. Ready to adapt and improvise, not married to any single plan. Over-preparing could be just as deadly as under-preparing.

The last thing she did was strap her kayet to her wrist. She double-checked that the four correct memory cards were loaded, though there was no reason why they wouldn't be. Still, her brain told her she needed to be sure.

And there they were. Her intrepid team. Pops, Glom, Garbo, and Boombox.

What a crew, she thought.

They would hopefully be the four Jekuas that carried her to victory.

She left the hotel early enough to walk to Corsseo Court. Fresh air would do wonders with centering her mind as well. As she passed the crater at Makanuele's center, she noticed a huge stage had been erected in the middle of it. All the entrances to the crater were currently closed off, and stadium employees hustled all over the field like little rats, running through last-minute preparations for the opening ceremony with its mysterious special guest.

When she got to Aeiko's apartment, it was Brine who answered the door. The unexpected and sudden sight of the purple coral golem nearly made her yelp. Instead, she gathered herself and said, "Hi, Brine."

Brine waved his yellow hand, as always, then stepped aside so she could enter. He closed the door (slightly too hard) behind her.

It seemed that everybody was ready to get a move on, though the opening ceremony wasn't set to begin for another hour. They were all gathered around the kitchen table, with the exception of Holly.

"Hey," Balt greeted her, smiling. His orange kayet was resting on the table in front of him, next to a half-eaten bowl of cereal. There were bright pieces of cut-up fruit mixed in with the beige cereal squares.

Also, amazingly, he was clean-shaven. It was the first time she'd ever seen him without scraggly facial hair.

"You shaved," Niona said, joining them at the table.

Balt nodded, and Alani said with a dramatic sigh, *"Finally."*

"Hey," he said, feigning offense.

"You look much better," Niona said, flashing him a grin.

He blinked a few times, then said, "Thanks."

"Got your dudes loaded up?" she asked, nodding at Balt's kayet.

"Of course," he said. "They're the only dudes I've got."

She almost asked where Holly was, but she didn't want to stir the pot. She found Aeiko extremely difficult to read, and could not figure out what their feelings were toward the woman. Did they like her, or were they just as irritated by her antics last night as the rest of them? She didn't know, and she did not want to prod. The relationship between the two roommates seemed complicated, to put it mildly.

"I saw the stage being set up," Niona said. "Smack dab in the middle of the crater. Gonna be a real bastard to walk through there once they start lettin' people in."

But Balt didn't seem to care about the crowd logistics. "Who do you think the special guest is?" he asked eagerly.

"I dunno," Niona shrugged. "The organizers could probably afford a pretty big name, but I have no idea what they're plannin' to do. Maybe they got a juggler."

"Who's a big-name juggler that you know of?" Balt asked, scooping up a milk-laden slice of strawberry.

"Pontius Gloom," Niona replied without skipping a beat.

Balt narrowed his eyes at her, then stuck the spoon in his mouth. He chewed and swallowed the strawberry before finally saying, "I don't know enough about jugglers to know if that's a joke name or not."

"Guess you'll find out in an hour," she said.

By the time they made it down to Xatetu Field, it was already packed with people. There were guards posted at each entrance, scanning tickets to the event. Since Niona and Balt were competitors, they wore special lanyards around their necks designating them as such. Being a part of the festivities also granted each of them a guest pass to the tournament, which they had naturally handed over to Alani and Aeiko.

They carefully descended the steps into the crater, with Aeiko lamenting the large crowd gathering around the stage.

"Our view is gonna be terrible," they sighed.

"Probably won't be anything worth seeing anyway," said Balt nonchalantly.

Scanning the crowd, Niona could see a handful of the Summoners with whom they'd be competing. The audience contained all sixty-four of the competing Summoners, but also hundreds of eager Jekua fans who had bought tickets to the tournament. She saw Justine Tesh, the woman who would be her first opponent, sitting underneath a tree, uninterested in whatever was unfolding on stage. Niona only recognized her because she'd looked her up online after dinner. It seemed that this would be her first time participating in a big, televised tournament; the miniscule amount of footage Niona had unearthed was just from some local contest on Kou Tekkis that Tesh had competed in a couple years ago. Not enough there to get a good feel for the woman's style.

She even spotted Balt's fool of a cousin standing by himself on the left side of the stage, but she didn't point him out to the others. She didn't want to cloud Balt's mind before everything kicked off.

The group wandered up to the edge of the crowd that surrounded the stage, but no one could see much beyond other people's heads. Niona was the tallest of the four, and even she couldn't see much. While she wasn't super invested in the tournament's special guest, she *did* want to find out if it was a juggler or not.

Sure, there was a full drum kit on the stage now, but she didn't let that deter her dreams of a world-renowned juggler wowing the audience with their ball-tossing expertise.

"Let's move further back," she said over her shoulder, thinking of Justine Tesh sitting far away under her tree. "We'll be able to see better."

They found a decent spot somewhere halfway between the stage and the staircase they'd descended, next to a flowing water fountain. Aeiko and Alani sat on the stone ledge, with Alani running her hand through the water, while Niona and Balt remained standing. They stood side by side, intently watching the stage.

As was typical for an event of this size, it started roughly twenty minutes late. They were all grumbling to each other about the lack of organization when a short, bald man trundled out onto the stage and grasped the microphone.

"Good morning, everyone!" he said, his voice a harsh rasp. It sounded like he'd just gargled gravel backstage.

The crowd cheered wildly, frothing at the mouth with eagerness to get the pageantry started.

"Welcome to the Makanuele Rumble!" the man's voice boomed across the crater. "I'm thrilled to be kicking off yet another exciting tournament here in the lovely city of Makanuele. When I moved here fifteen years ago, I never expected how much this city would mean to me..."

The man droned on about how special Makanuele was, which Niona did not necessarily disagree with, but she wasn't here to listen to some random corporate guy opine about the beauty of the city. Neither was anyone else; they were here for Jekua battles.

After several minutes of pointless blabber, the man finally ceased and took a deep breath. He said, "We also have a special guest for you all today. I figured why not start our biggest tournament ever with a bang?"

"Here comes Pontius," Niona said, nudging Balt.

"She's come all the way from sunny Qwi Island to be with us today, and wow..." The man shielded his eyes as he looked upward. "How appropriate it is that there isn't a cloud in sight..."

"No," Balt muttered in disbelief, his eyebrows raised.

He turned to Alani so fast, Niona was scared his neck might snap.

"No!" he said again.

They both stared at each other with wide eyes.

"What?" said Niona. Apparently the clues this old man were dropping were too subtle for her.

Balt ignored her question. "It can't seriously be her," he said.

"Please welcome to the stage...*Zawé*!"

Alani shot up from the fountain, rushing to Balt's side. She gripped his arm, shaking it up and down. They were both mumbling inaudibly to each other.

On stage, a young, thin woman trotted out to the microphone, thanking the bald man as she passed him. She was wearing a purple leather crop top and matching skirt, flaunting her toned midriff. Big poofs adorned the top's shoulders, and her exceptionally long hair was pulled up in two bouncy buns. She clomped across the stage in tall, shiny boots with thick wedge heels. She looked like something out of a pulp science fiction novel.

"No way! No *way*!" Balt continued to shout.

Over by the stage, the crowd was absolutely losing their minds. The woman, Zawé, gripped the microphone stand and smiled cutely, with a dimple on only one of her cheeks. She was probably around Niona's age, but Niona had never once been that thin or petite in her life. Zawé looked over the crowd, giggling into the microphone.

Niona had heard of the popstar, of course. She was one of the biggest names on the radio right now. She'd be hard-pressed to name one of her songs, though. And she had no idea the woman was such a little sprite.

Zawé started to speak as her band filed out onto the stage. "Hi, everyone!" she said. The crowd screamed as one massive entity. "Thanks for coming out today!" Another earsplitting screech. "I think you might know this one."

The drummer started playing a beat and the bassist started plucking along, and an instrumental backing track emanated from the towering speakers on either side of the stage. An electric guitarist began playing alongside the others, grinning at his fellow musicians on the stage.

Then Zawé pulled the microphone close to her lips and began to sing.

The crowd went wild.

As did Balt and Alani. They jumped up and down excitedly next to Niona, and she couldn't help but laugh at their infectious enthusiasm. Still sitting on the fountain, Aeiko was chuckling to themselves too.

Now that she was hearing it, Niona did recognize the song. She'd heard it a couple times on the radio, and she had to admit it was pretty catchy. It was called *Cloudless Skies*, so that explained the bald man's clues that had tipped off Balt.

"She's no Pontius Gloom, but…" Niona muttered to him.

He had no time for her japes. He was too drawn in by Zawé's lilting melodies and the bopping instrumental.

But then he suddenly turned to her, and his head swiveled back and forth between her and Alani as he spoke hurriedly. "We have to get closer! What the hell are we doing back here?"

Niona turned from him to the palpitating crowd. Every person was bouncing along to the beat, screaming along to the lyrics. It did not look like something she yearned to be a part of. She was not a Zawhead, or whatever it was her fans called themselves. Surely it couldn't be "Zawheads," but that was her best guess at the moment.

"I don't know about that," she said.

Balt wasn't taking no for an answer. "Let's go," he said to Alani. She nodded enthusiastically, her expression brighter than Niona had ever seen it before. They were true Zawheads. To Niona, he said, "C'mon, it'll be fun!"

While he worked on her, Alani scurried over to Aeiko and pulled them off the fountain. They were initially as reluctant as Niona, but they quickly relented.

"Fine, fine," Niona said, pretending to put up more of a fight than she actually was.

Balt grabbed her by the hand and pulled her across the field like a tugboat. She nearly tripped over herself, but she managed to stay upright.

The four melted into the crowd, instantly jumping along to the song's rhythm alongside everybody else. As soon as they were enmeshed, Balt and Alani were screaming along to Zawé's vocals. Niona could hardly tell what anyone was singing, but she would be lying if she tried to claim the audience's zeal wasn't leaking into her.

By the end of the song, she was screaming excitedly with the crowd, pumping her fist in the air as she and everyone else all shoved against each other. They organically made their way further up toward the stage just through sheer dancing, being pushed along by others' jubilation.

The sun basked them in warmth, and sweat poured down Niona's face and arms. If she was this sweaty after only one song, the audience was going to be drenched when the set was over.

During the short interim between songs, the crowd calmed down a little. Not by much, but they at least no longer had a beat that they could pulsate to. Everyone stood swaying in the heat, catching their breath.

The smiles on Balt and Alani's faces had not faded in the slightest. Aeiko was on the other side of them, and they looked just as bewildered as Niona, but they were definitely enjoying their time.

Zawé then broke into her second song, and it all started again.

All told, Zawé performed only five songs, but each one felt like it lasted a lifetime. And not in a bad way, either, like Niona might have expected. It was a truly joyous experience, lost in the crowd with nothing but the music in her ears, time stretching on and on as the beat pounded away at them.

They were all absolutely soaking with sweat as the lithe popstar slinked off stage, waving tiny little waves to her fans. She blew a few kisses before disappearing backstage. Niona caught Balt staring at the singer with admiration, and she chuckled knowing that if one of those kisses was directed at him, he would've fainted on the spot. That, or spontaneously combusted.

While everyone in the crowd came down from their Zawé-inflicted high, the bald man tottered out onto the stage again and grabbed the microphone. He did not look nearly so stylish holding it as Zawé did. He started saying something, but Niona would have wagered a great deal of money that she wasn't the only person standing there whose ears were ringing too much to know (or care about) what he was saying.

The crowd dispersed once the man was finished speaking. Most filed through the stadium's row of glass doors, looking to purchase their snacks and merchandise before the first match commenced in little over an hour's time. The Summoners, however, had been given instructions about a side door through which they were meant to enter. It would allow them swifter passage through the stadium's winding halls to the locker rooms where they could rest and prepare for their battles. There weren't any tai dair or fry stands along that route, though, which was a hefty detractor in Niona's opinion.

"Well, I guess this is where we part ways," she said,

throwing her arm over Balt's shoulder as they stood before Alani and Aeiko.

"Good luck!" Aeiko told them.

"Go win out there," Alani smiled.

"I will," Niona said. "No worries there."

"I'll try," said Balt. "Many worries there."

They tore off from Alani and Aeiko, who followed the mass of people entering Xatetu Field. As they walked away, Niona overheard Aeiko talking about wanting to grab some tai dair before the match. Damn them. She had worked up a good appetite bouncing around to the music.

Up ahead, she saw some of the other Summoners rounding the corner of the stadium. It wouldn't be a far walk to the side door.

She looked at Balt, offering him a smile. He smiled back, but she could see his anxiousness hidden behind the expression.

"Here we go," she said.

"Here we go," he echoed.

And so they went.

17

WASAARU VS. RENATA

XATETU FIELD BOASTED TWO DIFFERENT LOCKER ROOMS TO accommodate the sixty-four Summoners. Squeezing thirty-two people into each one was still quite more than each room was accustomed to, but luckily not all the competitors were present. Most of them were, caught up in the thrill of the tournament's commencement, but a few who wouldn't be battling until the following day had opted not to come down just yet.

Balt and Niona were in what was dubbed the Diwepti Room. The other was called the Staman Room. While they chose their lockers (with Balt wondering what he would even store in it), he glanced around the room to see who else had gone with the Diwepti. Personally, he had chosen this room because of their encounter with Khonoti when the Jenu had leapt into the sea and snatched up a Diwepti. For whatever reason, that made it seem like the right choice to him. Hopefully the confluence would bring him some measure of luck, or something.

There were a few people he knew. Desi Taewao, for one. He wanted to say hello, but Desi had no idea who he was. There was also Yakka Dho, as well as Niona's upcoming opponent, Justine Tesh. Balt had been unable to find any information online about his first opponent, Rei Yor, which was both a blessing and a curse. Having nothing concrete out there meant that Rei probably wasn't a super experienced, established Summoner, but it also meant that he couldn't do any specific prep for the battle.

He *did* find a user on the Jekua forums with the username "OutOfYorRei," which he suspected might be Rei (although the username was baffling), but they didn't have any posts in their history that were illuminating in the least. If that was the correct Rei Yor, Balt was just glad they weren't the type of person who was on there concocting insane conspiracy theories.

He also spotted Kallon from their VWC tour group in the locker room, so that confirmed the Kallon he'd seen on the bracket was the same one. Balt waved to the man, who returned nothing more than a curt nod before turning away.

Fair enough, Balt thought.

They hadn't interacted much in the jungle anyway. Maybe at some point he'd be interested in hearing what happened with Reno, if there was ever an opportunity for them to sit around and chat. And if Kallon even remembered or cared who Reno was.

Balt stood in front of an open locker and stared into the metallic void. He truly had nothing to put in there. Other Summoners were stuffing items into their lockers, making him feel inadequate somehow. What did *they* own that they needed to store in a locker before a match that *he* didn't?

Niona set up shop right next to him. He leaned over and asked her, "Are you putting anything in there?"

"Just my linkpad and wallet, I guess," she said. "Keep me loose on the battlefield."

"What the hell else do people put in these things?" he asked, looking around. Someone was shoving a hoodie into their locker. Why in the world did they wear a hoodie in the height of Summer to begin with?

"Believe it or not," Niona said, "some people have normal brains and actually take their kayets off when they're not using them."

"Doesn't sound normal to me," Balt replied.

"I would never deem you the arbiter of normalcy."

Farther down the row of lockers, past Niona and three or four others, he saw Wasaaru standing in the corner of the room. He was wearing his kayet and reading something on his linkpad, with his face scrunched up in concentration.

Balt took out his own linkpad to check the time. It wouldn't be long now before Wasaaru was on the battlefield. On television, too. That was bizarre.

In a few hours, Balt would be on TV as well. Did his parents know that? Should he send them a text?

He banished the thought. The last thing he wanted right now was to get sucked into a conversation with his mother and father. That would not help with his nerves at all.

Talking to Wasaaru would probably just rile him up

too. He decided to leave his cousin alone, let him get ready for his own match. Balt needed to keep his mind clear, and speaking to his family would achieve the opposite result.

Before long, it was time for the first battle of the Makanuele Rumble.

Balt never found anything else besides his bag to put in his locker. There was no way he'd be removing his kayet in between matches, that sounded ridiculous. But when the time came, he followed along behind Niona into a dugout on the side of the arena where Summoners could sit and watch the matches.

Being the first battle of the entire tournament, it was drawing a lot of attention from their fellow competitors. Everyone wanted to see who would come out on top. Balt and Niona were quick enough to get a good seat at the front, granting them a clear view of the whole arena. Almost all the other Summoners from the Diwepti Room filed in behind them, as well as several from the Staman Room.

On the far end of the battlefield stood Wasaaru, and on the end closer to the dugout was Renata Tohm. She was possibly a year or so older than Balt and his cousin, but she looked very young. She was a solid half a head shorter than Balt, with her dirty blonde hair pulled up in pigtails.

She was also wearing a denim jacket, which led Balt to wonder what these people knew that he didn't, in regards to wearing jackets in the Summer. Did it grant some mystical summoning power that he'd never heard of before? Why else were they subjecting themselves to such extreme discomfort?

Between the two of them, Balt was getting his first good look at the environment setup for the initial round of matches.

It was nothing super fancy. Apparently the organizers wanted to keep things relatively simple for the start of the tournament. The arena was covered in rolling hills, with tufts of (fake?) grass blowing in the wind from the open-ceiling stadium. A few boulders of varying sizes were scattered about the plain, as well as a decently wide river that cut diagonally across the length of the battlefield.

Not much for a Jekua to work with. Not that Balt could see, anyway, but he was far from a terrain specialist. He was always impressed by Summoners who could make great use of their environment, but he'd yet to feel confident in his ability to do so. It would be nice if that changed over the course of the tournament.

Balt turned his attention away from the hills and scanned the stands. From this distance, it was impossible to make out anyone's distinct face, but still he tried to spot Alani and Aeiko in the vibrant sea of onlookers.

He failed spectacularly in tracking them down. What he succeeded in, however, was making himself even more anxious about his upcoming fight.

Looking out at the enormous audience, he wondered how it was even possible to fit so many people into one place. Could it be a trick of the light? Were some of them holograms? They couldn't all possibly be real, living and breathing people. There were too many of them.

Almost every single seat in the stadium was filled. Adults and children alike were packed together tight, sporting their Summoner merch and chowing down on stadium grub. He even caught one guy spilling his oversized bucket of popcorn onto the person in front of him, inciting a small conflict. Balt laughed.

Suddenly, a deep male voice boomed throughout the stadium speakers. Thankfully, it was not the same jarring rasp as the man who'd spoken before Zawé's performance.

"Welcome, one and all, to the first match of the Makanuele Rumble!"

Boisterous applause from the crowd. Even the popcorn duelists set aside their differences to cheer.

"Thank you for joining us at Xatetu Field on this absolutely beautiful Summer day," said the disembodied voice. *"In our first round, Summoners will be required to switch Jekuas when their opponent switches. Summoners in the Makanuele Rumble are allowed to use four Jekuas, only three of which can be modified."*

The voice continued laying out some of the ground rules for the audience that the Summoners already knew. Balt eyed his cousin while the announcer spoke, watching for any sign that Wasaaru was nervous about the match.

But Wasaaru stood there, steel-faced, glaring across the grassy expanse at the petite woman on the other end. If he was feeling panicked at all, he certainly wasn't showing it. Even Balt was a little worried on his cousin's behalf, and he loathed the guy.

"Our first competitor hails from a small village on Totta Island. Please give a warm welcome to Wasaaru Vana!"

The crowd cheered for Wasaaru, who did finally crack a smile. He lifted his arms in the air, inviting the attendees to scream even louder for him. They acquiesced, eliciting an even wider grin from him. Balt rolled his eyes, knowing that Wasaaru was pleased as punch about being the opening act.

"Today, he'll be going up against Na Tana's own Renata Tohm!"

There were even wilder cheers for Renata. Na Tana was the biggest island in the archipelago, and the announcer hadn't even indicated that she was from Makanuele, but still the residents felt some degree of hometown pride with her competing.

Across the way, Wasaaru's smug grin curved into a deep frown. Balt laughed at him.

He was too busy laughing at his cousin's irritation and missed what the announcer said next, but when he tuned back in the man was saying, *"Summoners, when you're ready..."*

The crowd quieted, and tension filled the arena.

Everyone watched silently, waiting for one of the Summoners to make the first move.

Balt knew it was going to be Wasaaru. His cousin wouldn't be able to resist putting on a little show.

He was right.

Dark orange soulclay burst from Wasaaru's silver kayet. It splashed onto the artificial grass and started taking shape.

Balt squinted, wishing he was closer to the other end of the battlefield so he could get a better look at his cousin's Jekua. The orange soulclay bubbled and shifted, forming a long torso and wide, flapping wings. The monochromatic color faded to show a pale gray insect's body, with light blue wings and glittery green eyes.

His first Jekua was a Nullfly, a Gravity-Type. Something he had to have imprinted in the Qwisdeep. He'd traveled through there after all.

Balt was glad they never encountered him. That would've been another unfortunate incident to add to the too-long list of terrible events in the VWC.

Renata waited to see what Wasaaru had summoned before channeling any mana into her kayet. She finally began summoning as the Nullfly flapped its wings, leisurely making its way across the field.

Her soulclay was yellow, and it took the shape of a Pairrot. Another flying Jekua with Gravity abilities. Kind of an unorthodox choice, and infinitely less interesting than Wasaaru's endangered butterfly. Everyone and their mother had seen a Pairrot before.

Balt immediately ate his words, because no one had seen a Pairrot do what Renata's did.

Both heads immediately spewed torrents of fire across the field at Wasaaru's Nullfly. There was a lot of ground to cover, so he had ample time to flutter out of the way, but it was an intimidating display nonetheless.

Nullflies weren't equipped with a ton of natural abilities. They could alter another Jekua's gravity, sending them soaring into the air, but that wouldn't be effective since the Pairrot was flying already anyway. That might have been why Renata chose the bird: it might not have any specific advantages over the Nullfly (aside from the massive streams of fire), but it at least wasn't at a *dis*advantage, like her other Jekuas might be.

He could also understand Wasaaru sending out the Nullfly first. If it truly didn't have much up its sleeve, then it was to his benefit to get it out of the way first to allow his heavy hitters to end the match.

Wasaaru sent the Nullfly careening toward the Pairrot. It dodged another flaming stream, though the tip of a wing was singed. The two flyers then collided, but the Nullfly crumpled against the Pairrot's bulkier body.

The Nullfly shot up into the air, then circled back toward the Pairrot for another tackle.

Balt knew what was happening. He knew his cousin well, but it also seemed to him like the obvious strategy. Was Renata going to maneuver correctly, though?

Evidently not. As Balt expected, the Nullfly crashed into the Pairrot with incredible force, sending both Jekuas slamming into the ground. Wasaaru had increased his own Jekua's gravity mid-flight, effectively making the bug much heavier. He might've also decreased the Pairrot's, but Balt was at least sure of the former.

Renata's Pairrot struggled to free itself of the Nullfly's increased weight. It fired a blast of flame, though, that warded off the Nullfly. The insect flew away hastily, its antennae smoking and its face charred.

The Pairrot was attempting to get back up, but Balt noticed Renata grimacing with the effort. A Pairrot's body was pretty fragile, and it was entirely possible that the magically-enhanced tackle had broken a lot of the bird's bones.

That was what Wasaaru wanted. While the Pairrot tried and failed to right itself, the Nullfly used its magic to decrease a nearby boulder's gravity, sending it flying upward.

It was still too far from the other Jekua, though. The Nullfly positioned itself behind the boulder and started frantically flapping its wings, kicking up a heavy gust of wind. The boulder shot forward, but Balt doubted the trajectory was right to land on the Pairrot.

As the boulder moved through the air, arcing downward, the Nullfly once more enacted its magic on the rock. It started to plummet faster and faster toward the earth.

While Balt didn't think it was going to hit, Renata wasn't taking any chances. Her Pairrot seemed ruined already, anyway. Not a great first outing for her. The bird lit up in yellow before returning to her kayet.

The boulder crashed into the ground, several feet away from the tiny crater the Pairrot had left behind. Some people in the audience booed at the poorly judged trajectory.

Their jeers rattled his cousin, Balt knew. He saw that frown etch deeper into his face.

As per the tournament's rules, he withdrew his Nullfly. Orange soulclay glided across the hills back to the device on his wrist. Balt was eager to see what he would summon next.

"The crowd pissed him off," Balt said to Niona. "He's definitely mad that they booed him even though he beat the Pairrot. He might go big on the next one just to shut them up."

It was unfortunate for Renata that she'd already blown one of her modified Jekuas, and one with such a powerful attack too. This time, she was the first to summon her new fighter. It was a Scrypto.

Why was Balt suddenly seeing so many Scryptos everywhere? Were they gaining newfound popularity, or was it just frequency bias?

Either way, it seemed possible that Renata had an affinity for Jekuas with Thermal abilities. Or Jekuas that could fly. Or it was just a funny coincidence that both of her creatures just so happened to fly and breathe fire.

Wasaaru's next Jekua was a Dewrat.

"What the hell?" Balt muttered. His cousin spent so much time talking shit about Suelus, and he was bringing a *Dewrat* to the table, of all things?

Honestly, he'd expected way flashier creatures from his cocky cousin. This was a surprise.

One of his four had to be that Eclipse Jackal, so there was only one more mystery on his team. Balt wondered what it was.

His cousin's Dewrat scurried across the field, running up and down low hills, dodging fireballs from Renata's Scrypto. The beast hovered high in the air, its purple scales gleaming in the sunlight bearing down on them all. It whipped its spiked tail back and forth as it surveyed the land below.

The Dewrat seemed to be a good call, for now. It was a pretty small target for the Scrypto to hit. Blackened patches of dead grass were left in the Dewrat's wake as it dashed out of the way of the Scrypto's blasts.

The tiny rodent was heading straight for the river cutting through the field. It was a Tidal-Type Jekua, but it needed a water source to pull off any of its Tidal moves. In most cases, a Dewrat wasn't an animal that could generate its own water the same way a Scrypto could generate fire. Some Tidal-Types could, like Tottras or Wortens, but not all of them were capable. If the Summoner was highly skilled, they could probably conjure water out of the air with a Dewrat, but clearly Wasaaru wasn't at that level yet. It must not have been his Dewrat that Balt saw during the elimination challenge.

Balt leaned forward in his seat, angling for a better view of the Dewrat. It was a small Jekua, and though its brown fur stood out from the lolling green grass, it was still difficult to see.

The rat dove into the water, disappearing beneath the surface. Renata's Scrypto swooped in closer, trying to spot the thing. It shot off a useless fireball, evaporating some of the water. Steam rose into the air.

"Quit hiding!" Renata yelled. "Get your rat out here and fight!" She popped off another fireball that sizzled as it struck the water. Not the smartest idea, wasting precious mana on pointless gestures.

Although, Wasaaru was so arrogant, such things could usually bait him into doing something stupid. He seemed to have a plan, though, and he wasn't letting Renata's taunts distract him.

He stood still, waiting. The Dewrat didn't surface.

The Scrypto swooped even lower. Its body erupted in flames as it divebombed at the stagnant river. If Renata could peer through her Jekua's eyes, she might be able to see where the Dewrat was exactly, but Balt still wasn't sure how common that power was in other Summoners. In all likelihood, she was diving blindly. Throwing her Jekua and praying it hit something.

It swiped at the surface of the river, its attack completely ineffective.

But then a huge wave rose up from the river and engulfed the Scrypto. It flapped its wings, trying to scramble away, but the Jekua was swiftly encased in a column of water.

Damn, he's actually kinda good with that thing, Balt thought as he observed Wasaaru's control of the water. If he'd only imprinted the Dewrat recently while he was on Qwi, he must have been spending a ton of time training with it.

What impressed Balt even more was Wasaaru's next move.

The Dewrat leapt out of the water just below the Scrypto's flailing body, and as it landed safely in the grass nearby, the column of water hardened to ice.

It was how wild Dewrats captured insects: trapping them in water and then either letting them drown or freezing them. Just on a much bigger scale, and with a flying monstrous lizard instead of an ant.

Wasaaru must have been doing a *lot* of training with that Dewrat. Maybe he wasn't that far off from conjuring his own water.

Renata had already demonstrated how rash she was when she jumped straight into the fray shooting firestreams with her Pairrot. Wasaaru had been banking on that rashness again, using it to get her to bring the Scrypto closer so he could trap it.

The Scrypto was frozen solid inside the block of ice. Renata balled her hands into fists and groaned loudly. She kept trying to break her Jekua free, but it was no use. She couldn't even wag its tail.

To add insult to injury, Wasaaru made his Dewrat scurry up the side of the ice block and plop down atop it. The Dewrat gazed out at the crowd and waved adorably to the onlookers.

That got him a cheer. People loved seeing that little rat acting all cutesy while a creature more than ten times its size struggled underneath its furry ass.

Renata did not love it.

She continued fighting against the ice, while Wasaaru did nothing. Everyone watching knew that the mana required to summon a Jekua as small as the Dewrat was far less than what was necessary for a Scrypto. It seemed that Wasaaru's strategy was to just wait out his opponent, let her mana slowly drain until she had to forfeit. After the brutal hit on her Pairrot and the wasteful use of fireballs, there was no telling how low Renata's mana already was. It might not take much to finish this.

Again, Balt was surprised by his cousin's play. This was nowhere near as extravagant or arrogant as he expected Wasaaru to act. He was valuing winning over making himself look cool. Balt knew it was always a savage fight to the death between those two impulses, but usually "looking cool" won out.

It became increasingly clear that Renata was not going to get her Scrypto out of Wasaaru's ice trap. If she wanted to continue the fight, she would have to swap Jekuas again.

She raised her kayet and begrudgingly began to withdraw the Scrypto. Fury painted her features.

Something that Renata probably wasn't expecting happened next, however.

The magical force from returning the summoned Jekua to its soulclay form was enough to burst apart the ice block. Shards of ice exploded outward, some pieces splashing into the river and others piercing the earth around it.

Wasaaru's Dewrat went sailing through the air, landing with a harsh *thud* on its back a dozen feet away.

Renata let out a pained yelp and dropped down to her knees. Her breathing was heavy and she clutched a hand to her chest while her soulclay returned to the kayet.

"What just happened?" Balt asked.

"Your soulclay can still get damaged, even if it's not technically in the form of a Jekua," said Niona. "The things we summon are just made out of soulclay anyway, it just looks like a Jekua. When a Jekua gets slapped, it's your soulclay gettin' slapped."

So the explosion of ice had still inflicted damage on Renata, most likely draining her mana by a considerable amount. Balt was curious to know if Wasaaru had been planning on that, or if it was simply a happy accident.

They all watched with bated breath, waiting to see what Renata would throw onto the field next.

But instead, she raised her hands in surrender.

"We have our first winner!" the announcer roared over the crowd's fervor. *"Congratulations to Wasaaru Vana!"*

Balt blinked. It was over, just like that. Wasaaru was moving on to the second round in a couple days.

And he hadn't gotten to see that final mystery Jekua.

"Dammit," he muttered, both for being robbed of that answer and also for his cousin's victory.

Out on the field, Wasaaru was charging into the center of the arena. Surrounded by the grassy hills, he once more raised his arms into the air, urging the cheering crowd to whoop and holler even louder for him. In the dugout, the other Summoners were clapping too.

Balt reluctantly joined in.

18
DOUBT

THE NEXT FEW MATCHES DID NOT END QUITE AS QUICKLY AS Wasaaru's had. The Summoners involved put up a bit more of a fight than Renata Tohm.

Cole Illiom beat Misty Nomomicha when they had summoned their fourth Jekuas. The final assault involved him using a Vinetail, a Growth-Type creature that was akin to a large green fox with slender, intertwining tendrils that comprised its tail. He used the Vinetail to reach roots down into the ground, with which it then grasped several boulders from below and threw them all at Misty's pitiful little Togatam. She'd been trying to use its Tidal abilities to shoot powerful streams of water at the Vinetail, but it was too fast. She never stood a chance.

Mr. Dia was absolutely flattened by a Summoner named Kentaro Kao. In fairness, Mr. Dia lasted way (way, way) longer than Balt ever would have thought he would. Being that old, he had countless years to build up deep mana reserves. But in the end, his Bombat was snuffed out by Kentaro's Urud without Kentaro breaking a sweat.

The last match Balt was able to watch was between David Woollis and Xander Roth. Xander stuck strictly to using Sonic-Type Jekuas, starting with a Bobbol. The weird cat-bug thing didn't do much damage against David's Yissoon, but things got a little spicier when Xander summoned a Sunkin. He was much more skilled with it than that guy was who Niona had battled a couple weeks earlier. With the arena directly exposed to the sky, there was plenty of sunlight for the Sunkin to absorb and turn into a Sunbeam attack. But still, David was able to take down the Jekua along with the subsequent Koutix that Xander summoned. He didn't get a chance to summon any other Sonic Jekuas after that.

There was one more match before his own (between Olli Berrap and Zende Fao), but Balt wanted to head back into the locker room to mentally prepare himself for his battle. He knew Olli was going to wipe the floor with Zende, anyway.

Niona remained in the dugout to watch the ensuing match. She offered to join him, but he declined, saying he wanted to be alone for a few minutes. He hoped that Olli would put on a good show, but give him more than a mere two or three minutes to collect himself.

He marched through the desolate stadium halls back to the Diwepti Room. He swung the door open and ducked inside, breathing heavily. It slammed against the doorstop, a loud smack reverberating through the room.

The few people who were inside turned to glare at him. One of them was Misty Nomomicha, who was still trying to cheer herself up after her devastating loss. She was actually sitting with Renata Tohm, the two of them commiserating. Balt wondered if they'd previously known each other, or if they were only bonding over their first-round eliminations.

Balt moved past the two women and came to a bench near his locker. He sat down on the cold wood, staring down at the floor. He tapped his feet softly, not wanting to disturb anyone but unable to control himself.

Tap, tap, tap, tap—

With each tap, his breathing grew more ragged and his heartrate increased.

Was this a panic attack? He'd never had a panic attack before. He wasn't someone who got panic attacks. It didn't feel severe enough to be a panic attack, but he was panicking.

He couldn't stop envisioning himself out on that battlefield, amongst the verdant artificial hills. Dipper out in the thick of things, being obliterated by some Romproar or Urud or Sleethog or some other huge, absurd thing he didn't have the slightest chance of beating.

He could perfectly picture himself out there, in front of thousands of people, foolishly pushing himself too far or getting hit just *slightly* too hard and spiraling into soul-sickness. Out there, on his hands and knees, vomiting profusely while tens of cameras broadcasted the career-ending footage from every possible angle.

Above the lockers, mounted on the wall, was another electronic screen showing the current status of the tournament's bracket. It was nowhere near the size of the one in the entryway, but it was useful. On another wall was the actual broadcast of the battle taking place, but Balt did not want to see that.

He stared at the bracket. On the left side were several green-tinted names: Wasaaru, Kentaro, Cole, David. Below each of them was an accompanying red-colored name.

In the slot with Olli and Zende's names, both were still a neutral white. The match had probably started by now.

At the end of the bench, a guy in a wheelchair had just retrieved his kayet from his locker. He then summoned a Wallago, and the muscular feline started slinking around the locker room.

A Wallago could destroy me, too, Balt thought miserably. The opponent didn't have to be some giant, hulking beast. A medium-sized Jekua could blast his crew away without trouble.

Hell, even a dumb little Juntoo could probably whoop all their asses. Why not? He had hardly any battles under his belt. He was no real Summoner. He couldn't do this.

The Wallago strode past him, its furry paws brushing against his restless feet.

"Sorry," said the Summoner. Balt didn't recognize him. "Excuse me." The Wallago continued down the length of the aisle, curving around the bench then coming back toward the man.

He was excited. Of course he was excited. This was what he wanted for the past ten years. It was finally happening, and that was exciting, but it was also terrifying.

This was going to be his debut as a Summoner. Not

just some idiot on the side of the road, having a friendly match with other random dudes traipsing around.

He was going to be on television. He was going to be the center of attention for however many minutes it took for him to either win or lose.

And he was Remisti Vana's family. Following in his world-renowned champion Summoner grandmother's footsteps. Joining the family business, as it were.

Wasaaru had already gone out there and proved he had what it took to compete in a legitimate tournament. His opponent hadn't been the brightest bulb in the drawer, sure, but that was irrelevant. What mattered was that he'd won a tournament match.

Now it was Balt's turn to try.

Balt told himself he'd done plenty of training. For the past week, he'd spent hours upon hours at the gym every night with Niona. She didn't go easy on him, either. Those were some of the toughest sparring matches they'd ever done, and he'd even won a couple of them. Not to mention the numerous attack combinations he'd tried with the dummies, or the amount of times he'd run each of his Jekuas through the obstacle course. He'd even tried getting Milton across that dangling ceiling bar thing, and while that was ultimately unsuccessful, he'd at least gotten the bear across a couple bars. They practiced and practiced, building up their teams until their mana was almost entirely depleted, then chugged Thunderjolts so they could do it all over again.

He chuckled, thinking about how he'd summoned Dipper when they rode in that car in the VWC. He reached into himself and felt his mana reserves. They were full, and they were deep. Easily four or five times deeper than when he'd first imprinted that little sleepy Puffolin in the forest surrounding Tanepke. His grandma's training tip had paid off.

He thought back to all the times he had watched his grandmother walk out onto some battlefield in the midst of a tournament. The confidence in the toothy grin on her face, the determination in the furrow of her brow.

Seeing her out there always filled his young body with excitement. He would practically vibrate in his seat, screaming enthusiastically, ready to watch his grandma knock out another effortless win.

Did she ever doubt herself like this? Or did she always know she would be a champion?

Either way, she was gone now. She wasn't out in those stands, waiting to watch him battle. Waiting to see what maneuvers he pulled, what strategies he implemented. She wasn't out there, vibrating with excitement and anticipation.

She wasn't out there.

Balt took a deep breath, failing to calm his nerves. His feet continued *tap-tap-tapping* on the floor. The Wallago slipped by again, this time avoiding his feet. The wildcat's body heat warmed him somewhat as it passed, but that warmth disappeared as quickly as it came.

He took a deep breath, then stood for a moment to open up his locker and pull out his bag. He fished around in the front pocket until he found what he was looking for: the small, thin teleporter card he carried with him.

When he sat back down, he angled himself away from the man in the wheelchair so that he couldn't see Balt was in possession of a teleporter card. But he flipped the rectangle around in his fingers, watching its surface gleam under the locker room's fluorescent lights. He stared at the date marked on the card: 04/Spring, 2897. Eight years past.

Holding the card soothed him. Made him feel closer to his grandparents, and to his grandmother in particular. He ran his thumb over the text on the front of the card. He closed his eyes and envisioned himself in Paluopa City, standing across from his grandmother, the two of them summoning their most prized Jekuas. Grinning at each other as their soulclay slithered through the air.

Then he opened his eyes and took another breath. He smiled, looking down at the card.

His linkpad vibrated in his pocket. He inhaled deeply, then checked to see what it was.

It was a message from Alani.

Good luck out there! the text read. *Make our girl Dipper show them who's boss! :)*

Balt read the message twice, smiling stupidly at his linkpad. It took him a second to realize he'd stopped tapping his feet on the floor. His breathing grew easier, and his heart no longer felt like it was about to burst out of his chest.

He was good. He was fine.

He'd done all he could to prepare for today. If he won, then that'd be spectacular. If he lost, then that would be unfortunate, but he'd be okay.

Balt read Alani's message one more time.

He really wanted to win, though.

Dipper was going to show them who was boss. She

had to, now that Alani requested it. And Alani was the leader of this whole expedition, after all; Balt had to listen to her.

He glanced up at the screen just in time to see Olli Berrap's name light up in green, while Zende Fao's faded to red. Like he'd expected.

That meant it was time to get up and go. People would be waiting on him.

Unfortunately, Olli had only given him a few minutes to gather his thoughts, but it turned out to be enough time.

The Wallago passed him by again as he was standing. The man nearby asked him, "You up?"

Balt nodded and said, "Yep."

"Good luck."

"Thanks."

As he left the locker room, he took one more deep breath.

19

BALT VS. REI

FOR THE ENTIRE DURATION OF THE THREE-MINUTE WALK from the locker room to the archway under which he would pass to enter the battlefield, over and over again Balt looked within himself to check on his mana reserves. They were full; of course they were full. He hadn't spent any mana today. That concert had tired him out, but it hadn't used up any mana. And besides, that was hours ago, and he had since recovered. There was no reason to think his mana was not in prime condition.

But he kept checking anyway.

The tournament official brought him underneath the pristine white archway that led out to the field. The man held up a hand, indicating for Balt to stop walking. Balt stood still, peering over the man's shoulder to look out at the hilly battlefield beyond.

He watched the technicians reset the battlefield. As he did so, Balt somewhat regretted missing the previous match. Olli Berrap and Zende Fao seemed to have really done a number on the place. There were shattered boulders, great big craters in the earth, and chunks of hill missing. He spied smoke drifting upward behind one of the farther hills, but he couldn't quite see what was on fire.

It took only ten or fifteen minutes for the workers to get the field set up the same way every other Summoner had experienced it. The artificial material used to create the hills could regrow quickly, with the help of some sort of fancy fertilizer that Lakahlo had developed specifically for this purpose. What took the longest amount of time was hauling out the chunks of destroyed boulder and bringing in new, similarly-sized-but-not-blown-up boulders.

The guy placed a finger to his ear, pressing against his earpiece as he listened to someone speaking to him through it. Balt wanted to know if that actually did anything, or if people just did it when they were wearing earpieces because they saw other people with earpieces doing it. He suspected it was one big conspiracy.

Regardless, the man said, "Alright, you can go." He stepped out of the way.

Balt stood for another moment, inhaling deeply.

"Go," the man said irritably.

He let out the breath and sputtered, "Okay, yes, jeez, I'm going!"

There was some light hollering from the crowd as he stepped out into the arena. Sunlight blazed down, warming his skin. Along the outer rim of the hills was dirt, with a ring of tile separating the two areas. He kicked up small clouds of dust with every footstep, which made him strangely self-conscious. Could the cameras pick up that dust? Did he look messy or something? Had everyone else kicked up dirt too, and he just hadn't noticed because it didn't matter? Or was he just very heavy-footed?

Quit freaking yourself out, he told himself.

He walked over to the spot where he'd seen all the other Summoners stand, near the dugout. He looked over, seeking out Niona's round face. She was there, pressed up against the edge of the dugout, waving exuberantly at him. He waved back.

Then he looked across the expanse of green hills and gray boulders and saw his opponent standing on the opposite end, mirroring him.

Rei Yor.

She was a few years older than him, it appeared. Her hair was long and straight, a rich black that was oddly shiny in the sunlight. She had a supremely narrow face with thick, dark eyebrows and a fierce glare that would do more damage to the battlefield than any Jekua. Her kayet was silver, one of the more expensive models, like his cousin's. Her red shirt had cutouts on the shoulders, exposing tan skin which bore a jagged scar on her left shoulder.

Rei looked ready to kill him, in a very literal sense. Balt was worried she was going to race across the battlefield and throttle his neck. Why did she look so angry? He hadn't even done anything to her yet.

"Up next we have two dewy-faced competitors! This is each Summoner's first time competing in an official tournament, so let's give them a healthy round of applause, folks!"

The crowd roared in cheers and claps, and at that

precise moment Balt was acutely aware of just how many people were in the stands surrounding him. He looked up, craning his neck in all directions to examine the mass of people, a multitude of colors in their clothing and skin tones. People from all over the world had come to watch this.

Why? he then thought to himself. *Why come see this? Why do you care? Just go home,* he begged.

"Hailing all the way from Kou Tekkis, we have Rei Yor!"

Cheers for Rei. Unlike Wasaaru, who had egged the crowd on, Rei remained as still as a statue. Balt briefly doubted whether he'd actually seen her walk out there, or if she'd been wheeled out on a dolly.

"And from Totta, we've got ourselves another Vana! Give it up for Balt Vana!"

Was the other Vana his grandmother, or Wasaaru?

Either way, Balt wished the announcer hadn't drawn extra attention to his name.

But the crowd cheered wildly, and the sound got his heart pumping. He started bouncing up and down on the balls of his feet, amping himself up.

Let's go, he thought.

As always, the announcer then said, *"Summoners, when you're ready..."*

Balt lifted his arm, preparing to channel mana into his kayet. He glanced downward to ensure the correct memory card was primed. Then he waited for Rei's cue, wanting her to dip into her mana reserves earlier than he did, even if it was only by a second or two.

Like he expected, Rei was not one to wait. Mucusy green soulclay poured out of her gleaming kayet, taking the shape of a fairly large, six-legged beast. The soulclay shifted into a darker shade of green, and Balt instantly recognized the Jekua: a Korbir.

Korbirs were great big Growth-Type wildcats with six legs and a two-pronged spiked tail. They had sleek, narrow heads much like Rei did, with four beady black eyes that were barely visible amongst their fur. A Korbir's fur (if it even was technically fur, Balt wasn't sure) looked like sharpened leaves, granting it the appearance of a living hedge sculpture.

Balt momentarily wished he had a Thermal Jekua that could set this leaf-cat on fire, but alas. He pushed mana into his kayet, directing it toward Milton's L2 card.

Soulclay shot out of the device, taking the thick-bodied shape of his Mirrorbear.

There Milton stood in all his glory. Green grass reflected dimly off his strange, reflective underbelly, while the top of his body was tinted blue from the sky overhead.

Balt had given a lot of thought about which Jekua to send out first. The Tottaworm seemed obvious, since it was his weakest fighter and also cost the least amount of mana to summon, but he decided to go with a different approach. He wanted to try battering his opponent a good deal right out the gate, then let himself reserve some mana when they sent out their second Jekuas.

Now, in the moment, he wasn't sure if that logic checked out—but at the time he'd decided it, it made sense to him. He was rolling with it.

The two Jekuas charged toward each other. Rei's Korbir was much faster, bounding across twice the distance Milton did in the same stretch of time.

Milton possessed no long-range abilities. This fight would have to be up close and personal.

Balt switched to the Mirrorbear's perspective. If they had to fight in close quarters, he needed the fastest reaction time he could get. He nearly tripped after shifting into Milton's eyes, not quite anticipating the bear's weight and momentum, but he recovered swiftly and continued running.

The Korbir veered left, and Balt followed. Milton's paws beat against the ground, tearing up tiny clumps of dirt as he raced across the grass.

For a second, the Korbir was out of sight behind a hill, but the cat quickly ascended and leapt off the peak.

Milton reared up as if to catch the Korbir. At the last second, just before they collided, Balt activated the Barrier.

The Korbir smacked against Milton's purplish shield, curved claws outstretched, but the attack didn't penetrate the magic. It did not go both ways, though—Milton was able to land some powerful blows on the cat. Bits of leaf tore off the Korbir's body, littering the ground.

One thing the Barrier couldn't guard against, unfortunately, was the Korbir's weight. The cat pinned Milton to the ground with its deceptively muscular frame. Balt felt weighed down in his own body, like some Gravity-Type Jekua was inflicting its magic on him. He tried shoving the Korbir off, but it was too heavy.

They swiped at each other with razor-like claws, but they each only had one free paw. The Korbir was using one to hold down one of Milton's arms. Balt kept the Barrier up, so every one of the Korbir's attacks bounced off Milton uselessly, though he could already sense he wouldn't be able to maintain it for much longer.

He reached Milton's head forward, as far as his thick neck would reach, and chomped down on the Korbir's cheek. Fang pierced flesh. He ripped away a chunk of meat, and the Korbir jumped off him, tumbling on its back.

Milton righted himself and barreled toward the Korbir. It got back up before he could reach it, and two ropey vines extended from its back, reaching out for him.

One slapped him in the face, while one wrapped around his front right leg. Another thing the Barrier would not have protected against, if Balt had even managed to put it up in time, which he didn't.

All it took was one rough yank, and the Mirrorbear was off his feet. Milton came crashing down, smashing his chin on the ground. Pain reverberated through Balt's head and there was a faint ringing in his ears. He blinked away dizziness.

The Korbir growled viciously, yellow blood dripping from the hole Milton had torn in its cheek.

Balt jumped back to his own perspective to look at Rei, and confirmed she was sporting a similar scowl. He returned to Milton's point of view.

A wound that severe had to drain a decent amount of Rei's mana, and the more it bled, the more her mana would deplete. If he focused on that spot and worsened the wound, it was possible he could make her gradually lose enough mana to withdraw.

The tendril around Milton's leg tightened its grip, and the Korbir tugged again. Milton barely moved. That vine was strong, but evidently not strong enough to pull the Mirrorbear's impressive weight.

Milton bit down on the tendril, his huge fangs easily severing it from the Korbir. It went limp, flopping uselessly on the ground.

He stood up again and surged at the Korbir. It whipped at him again with its remaining tendril, but Balt ignored the pain and pushed onward. Each lash clipped at his mana, but not by much, and he was able to put up his Barrier in time to absorb at least half of the attacks. Each use of the Barrier sliced away at his mana, but not nearly as much as accepting one of the blows would.

The Korbir dodged Milton's headbutt, pouncing to the right.

But that was what Balt had been betting on. The Korbir could only dodge one of two ways, and he hoped it would be the way that exposed its wounded cheek to him.

He held out Milton's right claw, reaching toward the Korbir, which was jumping right into his trajectory. The bear's long, sharp nails caught on the wildcat's cheek wound, ripping across the rest of its face.

More blood poured from the gash. It was then Balt realized that the Korbir could have jumped backward or even leapt over Milton to avoid the headbutt, but thankfully that had not been the case.

It would be stupid of Rei to keep her Korbir out for much longer, with the amount of blood it was losing. There was no way of knowing how much mana she possessed, though. Balt knew there was a possibility he had barely put a dent in her reserves, but he didn't think that was likely. She was no Mr. Dia, with decades of mana deepening under her belt.

A collection of leaves rose from the Korbir's body, and Balt immediately knew what was about to happen. He'd done it plenty of times with Dipper. The leaves shot toward Milton, traveling too fast for Balt to raise the bear's shield.

He didn't want to, anyway.

Their sharpened edges tore at his glimmering reflective skin, leaving behind thin trails of blood. Not nearly as bad as the injury he'd given Rei's Korbir, but it wasn't ideal.

As the leaves hit, he'd activated Milton's one magical ability and absorbed the Korbir's move. Doing so had also decreased the amount of damage it had done. It didn't totally nullify the mana loss, but it was lessened.

Before Rei knew what was happening, those same sharpened leaves burst from Milton's back, raising into the air.

Again, it was a move that Balt was intimately familiar with.

He spread the leaves wide and fired them at the Korbir. Spreading the leaves thinned them out, so less leaves would strike the Korbir, but they were also harder—if not impossible—to completely avoid.

Rei let out a growl of frustration as her Korbir was sliced up with its own leaves. None of them cut deep enough to make the cat bleed, but the reflection had to do a bit of damage in addition to aggravating her.

Balt readied Milton to charge again. If he could just land one more powerful blow—

But Rei wasn't giving him the chance. The Korbir suddenly melted into a puddle of green before flying across the field, back to its Summoner.

Balt withdrew Milton as well.

He couldn't stop himself from grinning. If nothing else, he had at least made his opponent withdraw her first Jekua before he did.

While he had nothing summoned, he did a quick check on his mana reserves. He was still doing pretty good, only having lost a touch more than a quarter of it. Next, he'd send out the Tottaworm; surely whatever Rei summoned would expend more mana than his Elastic Jekua. Much like Wasaaru's strategy with the ice block, he might be able to pull off a win just by running down the clock.

Both Summoners unleashed their next Jekuas simultaneously. Rei seemingly didn't want to waste any time, and Balt wasn't overly concerned about the Tottaworm's mana consumption.

Much to his chagrin, the Jekua that Rei was summoning was similar in size to his Tottaworm. It wouldn't cost her much mana to use, unless of course it came equipped with powerful attacks.

Her green soulclay was taking the shape of a human hand, which Balt found exceedingly disconcerting. When it faded into its true colors, the shape made sense.

The thing was vaguely handish, walking on five legs that looked like fingers. Its entire body was covered in glowing burgundy pustules, like every inch of skin had a bloody wart.

It was a Palmegranate.

Another Growth-Type, Balt noted. Did she only use Growth Jekuas?

The Palmegranate skittered across the grass like a spider. Given its stature, it was much harder to see from a distance. Its glowing red body helped it stand out, but it easily disappeared behind hills and boulders.

Well, Balt could hide too.

He arced the Tottaworm downward, chewing through the earth and disappearing underground. He remained in his own perspective, not particularly wanting to know what Lakahlo's weird artificial material tasted like.

Even in his own body, he could feel gentle vibrations on his skin thanks to the Tottaworm's Sonic affinity. He could lightly sense the Palmegranate scampering across the ground, despite the fact that he couldn't see it. His Jekua was getting close.

At a certain point, the Jekuas were too small and too far away for him to get a good look at anything that was going on. He could probably just walk around the edge of the battlefield, but he switched to the Tottaworm's view.

He was pleasantly surprised to find that the fake earth tasted like literally nothing. It was a little jarring, but far from the worst taste he could have experienced.

Now he had an even better sense of where the Palmegranate was above him. Balt was momentarily amused, thinking of how boring this must be for viewers.

It was time to strike.

The Tottaworm shot upward, exploding out of the ground directly beneath Rei's Palmegranate.

The bubbly red creature was flung through the air along with chunks of dirt and blades of grass, slamming into the side of a hill. It rolled down the steep incline, but halfway down, Rei was able to get a handle on things. It came to a stop on its five meaty legs and scuttled toward Balt's Jekua.

It came to a stop at the bottom of the hill. Then it extended its legs, standing as tall as possible. It arced its body, raising its back half, and some of its pustules shot off and flew toward the Tottaworm. Most of the globs landed on the ground, but a couple hit the worm's body. Each and every one of them popped upon impact, spraying bright red juice everywhere. The liquid sizzled on the ground and on the Tottaworm's flesh, sending an intense, hot itch through Balt's body.

He tried shaking off the acidic liquid, but it burned deep into his Tottaworm's skin. Maybe he would not be saving as much mana as he thought, feeling it slowly drain from his reserves.

For a few seconds, he feared that it would be like the Korbir's bleeding wound and that it would continue draining mana over time, but it soon stopped. There was still a sharp pain every time he moved the Tottaworm, but it wasn't depleting additional mana.

That was something, at least.

But even if it wasn't literally costing him mana, Balt wasn't sure how long he could keep the Tottaworm summoned if every tiny movement sent a jab of pain coursing through him. He needed to do some damage to the Palmegranate, and fast.

The thing was on the move again, growing closer to the Tottaworm. If Balt had to guess, he'd say Rei was moving it closer so that her next batch of acid bombs wouldn't contain so many misses.

Balt needed to neutralize it somehow. He thought about how the Jekua had to stand tall and curve its body a bit before it fired the globules. Was that a necessary part of the attack? Would it be unable to do it if he pinned it down?

It was worth a try. He had the perfect thing to pin the Palmegranate in place from a distance, too.

He kept an eye trained on the Palmegranate as it creepily crawled across the battlefield. The second it came to a stop, beginning to rise up on its tiptoes (or fingertips, rather), Balt acted.

Feces fired from the Tottaworm's rear, smacking into the Palmegranate's body just as it arced its own rear end. The impact sent the creature toppling backward, and Balt shot off a few more clumps of feces at it, which all landed on its legs.

The clumps were too thick and sticky for the Palmegranate to quickly free itself. While Rei struggled to get it back on its feet, Balt elasticized the Tottaworm then sprang forward.

It landed atop the Palmegranate just as the Jekua had freed two of its five legs. Balt decided to give Rei a little help and wrapped the Tottaworm around the Palmegranate's body, hoisting it to its feet. Then he coiled the worm's body around, gripping it tighter, before going fully rigid.

Rei fought against the worm's binds, but she could not get her Palmegranate out. The Tottaworm's body was rock solid thanks to its Elastic magic.

Once again, Balt planned to simply wait her out. Using the Elastic magic to make his Jekua's body go rigid had spent some mana, but now all he had to spend was the itsy bitsy trickle of mana required to keep the Tottaworm summoned. A pittance. Meanwhile, every thrash of the Palmegranate's limbs was draining Rei of more and more mana.

Balt's dreams were short-lived, however, because a mere moment later the Palmegranate essentially self-destructed. Nearly every single pustule on the creature's body burst all at once, covering the Tottaworm in its vibrant red acid.

He let out an involuntary scream, instantly jumping back into his own body. A painful shudder rippled across his skin, and his muscles suddenly ached intensely. He tried blinking away the pain and wiped away a stray tear running down his cheek.

He did a quick check on his mana reserves. While the attack had been extremely painful, he was lucky that the extra defense granted by the Tottaworm's rigidity decreased the amount of actual mana damage he had taken. Still, it was considerable, making him dip below the halfway mark. He couldn't imagine how much it would've cost him if he hadn't upped his Jekua's defenses.

It was probably time to recall the Tottaworm. He needed to lay some powerful moves on Rei and end this. He could only pray that the Palmegranate's full-body explosion had required a lot of her mana.

Light yellow soulclay drifted around the hills, back into his kayet. His breathing was still haggard from the acid bombs, but the pain was slowly fading now that he had withdrawn the Tottaworm.

If he wanted to end the match with his next Jekua, Pistachio might be the smarter play. The Mosstopus packed more of a punch than Dipper did. And if his suspicion about Rei being a Growth Summoner was correct, the Puffolin's abilities wouldn't be as effective on whatever Rei summoned.

There was some mild guilt about leaving Dipper on the sidelines during his first tournament match, but he had to do what he had to do. He summoned Pistachio.

The Mosstopus's appearance in the arena garnered some *oohs* and *ahhs*, which admittedly gave Balt a burst of pride and confidence. He started running the Mosstopus across the field on its ten spindly legs before Rei's soulclay had even shown itself.

Her next Jekua was a Vinetail. Another Growth-Type, as Balt had predicted. And not a very big one, either, compared to his Mosstopus. Hopefully he could crush it with ease.

He found her approach interesting. It seemed like she had sent out her biggest and baddest Jekua first, hoping to hit him hard and fast and end the match quickly. It was lucky that he'd torn that hole in her Korbir's cheek, ruining her whole strategy.

That would be his strategy now, though: Balt was going to hit the woman's cute little Vinetail hard and fast with his Mosstopus. He wanted to finish this as swiftly as possible.

The Vinetail was an agile little thing. It darted across the grass, dodging every slimeball Balt fired its way. He nearly tripped over it as it weaved through Pistachio's tangle of legs. It ran a bit further, then turned around and headed back. Balt spat more slimeballs, but none of them connected.

He cursed as the Vinetail was once more underfoot. He wanted to trap it in Pistachio's legs, but that would probably just cause him to fall over.

As the Vinetail ran underneath Pistachio, it twisted its head to look straight up at the Mosstopus and three sharp spikes flew out of its mouth.

By the time they all pierced Pistachio's underbelly, the green fox was already several feet away, never losing a step.

Each spike bit out a chunk of Balt's mana. They probably wouldn't have been too bad if they'd struck Pistachio's back or one of his legs, but the more sensitive underbelly being hit drained his mana a bit more.

Shit, Balt thought. He didn't know if he could say it out loud. Nothing had been explicitly stated about swearing in the tournament's rules, but couldn't you not swear on TV? Was that accurate? Would he have to pay a fine?

That wasn't important right now. He needed to focus on keeping Pistachio's more vulnerable areas safe, and he needed to decrease this fox's speed.

The Vinetail curved into a turn and was making its way back toward Pistachio. Its snake-like tail slithered in the air behind it as it ran.

Balt spewed forth the kinetic energy-draining fog from Pistachio's mouth. The Mosstopus's foul breath enveloped Rei's Vinetail as it surged through the thick fog, undeterred in its purpose. With every step, though, the Jekua was slowing down.

It was subtle at first, but became increasingly obvious. The Vinetail was running directly through the whole cloud of nasty breath with reckless abandon, leaving Balt to reap the full benefits of the move.

Rei's Vinetail was moving hardly faster than a light jog by the time it reached Pistachio again. The Mosstopus, though, had gained all of the speed that the Vinetail lost. Balt could hardly control the Jekua, it was moving so fast now. But he managed to move Pistachio out of the Vinetail's way, as well as slipping past a trio of spikes that the Vinetail decided to fire at him.

Balt stretched one of Pistachio's arms out at the fox, and with their swapped speeds, the Vinetail had no hope of getting away. The fuzzy tentacle wrapped around the fox's slim belly, raising the lightweight animal up and up and up.

And then it came down.

Pistachio's limb swung downward with immense momentum, slamming the Vinetail's backside into the earth.

A loud shattering sound cut through the air. Balt winced at the sight of the Vinetail's legs crumpling beneath its own body.

Only one more time, he thought. There was no way Rei could take much more.

He tightened Pistachio's grip on her Vinetail even more and brought it back up. The green fox writhed against the backdrop of blue sky, frantically swiping its front paws while its lower body dangled flaccidly.

It was a pitiful and deeply saddening image, and Balt genuinely had to remind himself that the Vinetail he was holding was not a real, living creature.

And so with that, he smashed it on the ground again.

There was another splintering in the air, with both Rei and the Vinetail letting out agonized shouts.

When he started to lift Pistachio's arm again, the Vinetail melted into soulclay and drifted back to Rei.

Balt eyed her for a moment before he withdrew Pistachio.

She lifted her arms in surrender.

The match was over.

He had won.

He didn't even realize he was withdrawing his Jekua. He was lost in a daze, standing there on the battlefield while the crowd erupted around him.

Across the hills, Rei was wearing that same furious scowl that she'd started the match with. That expression might set the whole arena on fire now.

But Balt didn't care. He blinked, trying to ground himself. Bring himself back to reality.

"I won," he muttered.

He looked up at the stands, wishing he could make out Alani in the sea of faces. While he looked, a cameraman pressed in on him.

Again, he said, "I won." Then, "Holy shit."

He really hoped there would not be a fine for that.

But he also didn't really care.

20
AN INTERESTING CONUNDRUM

SHE JUMPED AND YIPPED EXCITEDLY, TRYING TO MAKE OUT the expression on Balt's face while he stood on the battlefield stupidly, trying to process his win. She waited and watched until at last he stepped away and out through the exit. Then Niona's footsteps pounded through the stadium halls as she swerved around corners, winding her way through the mazelike corridors on her way from the dugout back to the locker room to meet Balt.

Surprisingly, she beat him there. It was probable that some stuffy tournament official was congratulating him and explaining to him what the next step was, when he'd be competing next and all that nonsense. Boring stuff.

The only other person in the locker room was a guy in a wheelchair, rolling around in pursuit of a Wallago that was walking ahead of him. He sputtered and looked embarrassed when he caught Niona staring. The Wallago melted away and returned to the man's kayet. "Howdy," he said with a meek wave.

"Don't mind me," she said, grinning.

The man composed himself, trying to act as if he wasn't just chasing his big wildcat Jekua around the room. "You just finish out there?" he asked after clearing his throat.

"Nah," Niona replied. "I'm goin' up after this next match. My buddy just won, though, so I'm waitin' for him to get back."

"Oh, nice. Congrats to him."

"Mhmm."

"Was he that little dude in here earlier? The one freakin' out and shit?"

"Probably. Sounds like him. Platinum blonde hair? Too shaggy, needs a haircut?"

"Yeah, that's him. He looked like he was losin' his gourd in here. Glad to hear he got through it alright."

Given the fact that there were multiple screens in the room broadcasting the matches, Niona wasn't sure how the man hadn't seen who the winner was. But then she realized he was obviously caught up in whatever game he was playing with his Jekua.

The guy rolled toward her, and Niona moved out from the doorway.

"Anyway," he continued, "I oughta get goin'. I'm not even battling today."

Niona pulled the door and held it open for him. "What's your name?" she asked him. "I'll try to catch your match tomorrow."

"That's mighty kind of you," he said. "Name's Andy Lowe."

"Niona Daneo," she said, holding out her hand.

Andy shook it and said, "Sorry I can't watch yours. I've already been here too long as it is. Procrastinatin' some stuff I don't particularly wanna do. You know how it goes."

"I do indeed," Niona chuckled. "Take it easy. And good luck tomorrow."

"Thank you." He pressed through the doorway and turned to her in the hall. "Hey, tell your buddy I said congrats on the win, eh?"

"Will do."

He nodded, smiling warmly, and started down the hall.

Niona sat herself down on the bench near the doorway so that she could scare Balt when he walked in. Hopefully no one else would come in before him. She didn't need to be humiliated in front of her fellow Summoners before she even set foot on the battlefield. There was plenty of time to make a fool of herself during a match.

For a moment, she had the impulse to start walking her Nuri around the room like Andy had been doing with his Wallago, but she knew that'd be a pointless use of mana so soon before her battle. So instead, she sat and stared at the door, thinking about nothing. She was thirsty.

Two minutes later, the door started to creak open and Niona immediately let out a bloodcurdling scream.

The person on the other side yelled *"Shit!"* and stumbled backwards into the hallway, the door slamming shut on them. It was a male voice, and it sounded like it was Balt, although she wasn't a hundred percent sure.

Niona got up and opened the door to find Balt pressed

against the opposite wall, gripping his chest and breathing raggedly. She laughed hysterically at the sight.

When he realized it was her, his eyes widened and he said, "What the hell was *that*?"

She stopped laughing, caught her breath, and shrugged. "Just wanted to scare ya. I dunno."

"What the hell? Why?"

"I dunno," she said again, then laughed some more. "Come on in, it's safe in here. I promise."

"I don't know if you can be trusted," he said shakily, then chuckled. He moved away from the wall and followed her through the doorway.

As soon as he stepped through, Niona threw her arms around him and squeezed tight. "Congratulations!" she said, shaking him back and forth. He nearly lost his footing, but he hugged her back.

"Thank you!" he said. When she pulled away, his tans cheeks were tinged with red.

"Am I the first to congratulate you?" she asked.

"No, actually. I got a text from Alani on my way here. It was written in all caps, which is extremely out of character, if you're familiar with her writing style."

"Texts don't count!"

"Yes they do. We're living in the future."

"Fine, whatever. Anyway, good job not losin' out there."

Balt said, "That Palmegranate exploding almost screwed me."

"Yeah, that was pretty wild. Piss came through clutch, though."

"Stop calling him that."

"You were savage with that thing. I was convinced Rei's legs were about to snap too!"

Balt winced at the mention of what he'd done. "Yeah, that was, uh...yeah. Brutal."

"Hey," she said, "that's far from the most intense thing I've seen in a battle. I'm sure you've seen some gnarly shit in all the tournaments you've watched, too. Your grandma would throw fools around like it was nobody's business."

He nodded. "I know," he said. "It just looks so extreme. Could Lakahlo not alter the kayets to, like, censor that stuff? Just let it magically blur out or pixelate the broken bones and gushing blood and stuff. That would be fine by me."

"Some people are payin' to see that stuff," Niona pointed out. "They like the spectacle. The *grotesquerie*."

"Is that a word?"

"Of course it is. Don't doubt your wise mentor. Anyway, congrats! Your first tournament win!" She pulled him in for another hug. After they separated, she asked him, "How's it feel?"

"It's weird," he said. "It's cool, though. It's awesome. I'm just in disbelief still, I guess."

"How's your mana?" she asked. There were a ton of vendors selling Thunderjolts in the stadium, but he wasn't going to be battling again that day, so he could just let his body reabsorb the mana naturally.

He took a second to check his reserves, then said, "Not too bad, honestly. Less than half left, but still."

"I bet that self-destruct thing took a huge bite out of you, didn't it?" she said.

"Yeah, that shit sucked. But I could've gone a little

while longer without worrying too much about running out, I think. Most of what I can do with Pistachio is physical attacks, so they don't drain a whole lot. Neither does that slimeball move."

Niona grinned. "Round two's gonna be harder. You might have multiple exploding Palmegranate type situations on your hands. We'll have to hit the gym hard to make sure you're up to snuff."

"It's gonna be embarrassing for you if I made it to round two and you don't," Balt said. "The student becomes the master..."

She flashed another cheeky smile. "Don't get ahead of yourself," she said. "Pops could still whoop any one of your Jekuas."

Then she glanced at the bracket on the wall and saw that the next match was between someone named Zu Jerat and someone named Ima Daugherty. Whoever won that match would be going up against Balt in round two.

She gestured at the screen and said, "Let's go check out the match, see who you're gonna be fighting next. That'll help us devise a good strategy."

Balt groaned. "More work? I don't get to relax even a little bit?"

"All you gotta do is sit and watch, you big baby. It's just mental work."

"That's the worst kind!"

"Get used to it, pal. Oh, also, there was some guy in here with a Wallago who said congrats on the win. Seemed like he knew who you were."

"Oh, yeah," said Balt. "He was in here before my match. He was still walking that Wallago around?"

"Chasing it, actually."

"...why?"

"Who knows. We've all got our training techniques. Anyway, let's hurry before things kick off."

They made it back to the dugout as the announcer was declaring the two competitors' names. Zu Jerat was from Na Tana, while Ima Daugherty hailed all the way from eastern Hurrathsa. That explained the name "Ima," which Niona had never once heard of in her almost twenty-four years of life.

"Just in time," Niona said as they shuffled past some of the other Summoners. A few people had left the dugout, so it wasn't hard for them to secure good seats.

Less than a minute later, the match commenced.

Zu was the first to get a Jekua onto the field. His soul-clay shot out of his kayet with the speed of a bullet. Niona couldn't recall ever seeing a person summon so fast.

His first Jekua was a Whissler, which was a relatively unassuming name for something so ghastly. It was an uncommon Hybrid between a Hiss and a Whifflit, combining their Radiant and Sonic abilities into one horrifically ugly package. The Whissler was only an upper body, humanoid with abs and muscular arms and a feline face. The Hiss's floppy ears were replaced with the Whifflit's large, pointed ones, and protruding from its back were two enormous wings. It was covered in white fur with orange streaks.

The Whissler flapped its wings and screeched shrilly. Everyone in the dugout slapped their hands to their ears to drown it out. Then the creature balled its hands into fists and flexed its muscles, its fur suddenly shining bright.

Moments later, the arena was engulfed in pitch-black darkness.

A literal dome of blackness covered the hilly area at the stadium's center. Nobody could see within. Niona hadn't even caught what Jekua the girl Ima had summoned.

"What did he just do?" Balt asked by her side. He sat up farther in his seat, as if that would allow him to see within the dark dome.

"I don't know exactly," Niona confessed. "I guess some sort of Radiant power that creates a dome around an area that's devoid of light."

Zu Jerat was grinning contentedly at the edge of the dome. On the other side of the field, Niona saw Ima Daugherty beginning to freak out. She ran around the curve of the dome, trying to find a better vantage point, but it was impossible. If she couldn't see inside, she couldn't effectively control her Jekua. It seemed Zu wasn't perturbed by the dome and could probably somehow see his Whissler just fine.

Niona said, "If she's smart, she'll—"

Before she could even finish the sentence, Ima did exactly what Niona would have done. She withdrew whatever Jekua it was she'd summoned, forcing Zu to do the same.

With the Whissler's withdrawal, the black dome disappeared as well. It was disappointing, to be sure; Niona was looking forward to watching the Whissler fight. It was a weird Hybrid that she had not seen much of. But this was probably for the best anyway, since she wouldn't have been able to penetrate the dome it created.

"Ahh, a hasty swap! Our fastest yet this year!" the announcer said over the stadium loudspeakers.

This time, Ima got her second Jekua out before Zu. It was a Romproar.

Niona let out a low whistle. Ima Daugherty was not to be trifled with if she had a Romproar in her coterie. Now more than ever Niona wished she had seen the first creature the woman sent out.

Zu's second Jekua was another Radiant-Type, so a clear pattern was emerging. It was a Conuto, an insect that was around the size of a small dog. The thing was wiry, with six spindly limbs that looked more like hairpins than legs. Long, frilly antennae extended out from its tiny round head. It had a thin, brittle exoskeleton, so it was easy to crush if it took a good hit. But it was exceedingly fast, and it could use Radiant magic to camouflage itself to sneak up on other Jekuas before latching onto them. If it got its fangs in something, it could then send a nasty shock to their nervous system with its secondary Electrical abilities.

The Conuto skittered across the grass toward Ima's Romproar. The huge cat was true to its name and roared magnificently before bounding forward.

Romproars had a ton of strength. One swat from the beast's meaty paw would possibly be enough to put a Conuto out of commission, if Ima could manage to land a hit on the speedy little bug.

Zu's Conuto suddenly leapt forward, tucking into itself. It rolled along the field for a couple seconds before propelling itself upward, unfurling its body as far as it would stretch, emitting a quick pulse of light. Then it landed on the ground and continued heading for the Romproar.

But the Romproar was no longer moving. It came to a faltering stop in the middle of the arena then stood there like a statue.

Niona looked to its Summoner and saw that Ima was waving a hand in front of her face.

She couldn't see.

The Conuto had used a Radiant ability that blinded her. When Niona pointed it out to Balt, he cursed under his breath.

"I am not liking this guy," he then said.

Niona agreed. It was not technically legal to use a Jekua's ability on a Summoner instead of their Jekua, but a Summoner seemingly as skilled as Zu would be well aware of that. More likely what had happened was the ability affected a target area, and Zu deployed it so that it affected the Romproar but Ima also *just so happened* to be within the area.

It was a scummy move, to be sure, but he hadn't explicitly broken any rule, so it wouldn't get him disqualified. And, admittedly, it was impressive that Zu's range for the ability could cover half the battlefield.

And another pattern was emerging. Zu used his Radiant Jekuas to, in various ways, blind his opponent so that they couldn't even fight back.

The Conuto finally reached the Romproar a moment later and leapt onto the cat's back. It sank its fangs into the Romproar's neck and sent a staggering jolt of electricity coursing through it.

Ima could clearly tell what was happening, feeling her

mana rapidly draining away with every passing second that electricity was poured into her Jekua. She tried to blindly shake the bug off, but it was latched on tight and refused to let go.

Balt slumped in his seat, frowning at the battling Jekuas.

He said, “How am I supposed to fight against someone if I can’t see them at all?”

It was an interesting conundrum, and one that she did not have an immediate solution for. Niona noted that he was already working off the assumption that Zu Jerat was going to win this match. She could not bring herself to disagree with his assessment.

“I guess we’re gonna have to figure something out,” she said.

They sat together and waited for poor Ima Daugherty to lose.

21

NIONA VS. JUSTINE

NIONA STOOD AT THE EDGE OF THE ARENA'S HILLS, watching Justine Tesh standing across the way while the unseen announcer informed the adoring crowd who they were.

She did not care that Justine was from Na Tana, but she intently observed the woman while waiting for the match to start. At a glance, Niona would guess that Justine was maybe in her mid-thirties. She didn't like that age gap between them, but hopefully Justine had gotten a later start as a Summoner. She had shoulder-length curly red hair, and she was wearing a yellow sundress with flat, pink shoes. She bounced lightly on her heels, her hands interlocked behind her back.

If Niona had to sum her up in a single word, it would be *bubbly*.

The whole time Niona watched her, Justine did not stop moving. *Restless* would be another good word for the woman.

"Summoners, when you're ready..." the announcer intoned.

It was only then that Niona decided on the first Jekua she would summon. Her plan was to gross out this bubbly chick with her nasty pal Glom. She clicked the button on her kayet to prime the Muggish's memory card and began funneling mana into the device.

Her bright pink soulclay took the form of the Muggish, which was essentially just an amorphous blob like the soulclay itself. It gained a little definition in the upper body, though, before the pink darkened into a murky brownish-red. Even from fifteen or twenty feet away, she could faintly feel the heat coming off the Thermal Jekua. Niona lifted Glom's arms over his short, wide head and waved them at Justine.

The woman's lips curled at the sight of Glom. Niona giggled to herself.

She pressed forward. Glom slowly slithered across the battlefield, with Niona silently thanking herself for installing a Speed mod as she watched the creature's tepid pace. He was still moving so slowly, without the mod it would be simply nightmarish. She circumnavigated the hills so that Glom wouldn't have to move on an incline.

Meanwhile, Justine was finally summoning something. Blue soulclay shot out of her kayet and took the form of a Tonnit. Niona didn't know much about Tonnits, only that they were Sonic-Types and that she'd seen some scurrying around the grounds of a hotel she and her father stayed at in eastern Na Tana a couple years prior. They were little rodents, hand-sized mice with pale blue fur and naked pink tails that looked like worms. Their ears curved and spiraled, almost like Garbo's horns, and their noses came to a sharp point as well.

Poor little mouse was going to be melted by Glom's big, dripping palms.

If she could catch it, anyway. One unfortunate advantage that Justine's Tonnit had over Glom was agility.

And it was an extreme advantage, at that. The mouse bounded over the hills, its tiny feet not even kicking up any dirt. As Glom crawled across the field, he left behind a streak of charred, smoking grass in his wake.

The two Jekuas were fast approaching each other. Niona began lobbing fireballs at the mouse, but it of course dodged all of them with ease. Then the Tonnit leapt to the left, not anywhere near Glom, and pierced the ground with the tip of its pointed nose.

Suddenly the earth beneath their feet began to shake.

Niona had to regain her footing, but she remained upright. If Justine had been attempting to knock Glom over, she had abjectly failed. The Muggish's viscous liquid body was mostly unaffected by her mini earthquake.

The earthquake ceased as quickly as it began and the Tonnit was on the move again. But it ran straight past Glom and rammed its nose into another hill, which was followed by yet another quake.

While the mouse was stationary, Niona turned Glom to face it and shot more fireballs the Tonnit's way. Two of them struck the ground around it, burning the grass, but the third connected.

The second earthquake stopped as the Tonnit screeched and fell over, its back aflame. It rolled across the ground, rubbing the molten liquid off its body. The action was not entirely successful, but evidently it had recovered enough to keep running.

Niona did not understand Justine's strategy here, but she continued trying to assail the Tonnit. While it ran around stabbing the ground and sending shudders through the arena, Glom rained down fire on the hills. A couple of them hit the Tonnit as it scampered around, but for the most part, Justine was able to weave her Jekua around the molten rainfall.

She took a moment to reassess what she was doing. Justine wasn't even trying to cause her any damage, but Niona was wasting mana trying to hit this tiny target with her fireballs.

The Tonnit wasn't letting up, though. Niona pondered what she could do for a moment, then an idea came to her.

It probably wouldn't work, but Jekua battles were all about adaptation and experimentation.

Instead of trying to hit one small area with one small fireball, she would try to cover a bigger area with a bigger piece of lava: Glom himself.

She made Glom go flat on the ground, looking more than ever like he was melting into the earth. Soon the Muggish looked like no more than a puddle of lava, bubbling and smoking, and she started to expand his body outward.

Her thinking was that if she could stretch Glom's body out far enough, the Tonnit would have to run through him at some point. The damn thing was running all over the field, and Niona figured she could cover a pretty good portion of it with her Jekua's dangerous body.

Justine's Tonnit pierced a few more pieces of earth, but then it stood still. All of a sudden its pale blue brightened, and the woman's soulclay was flying across the arena.

"Dammit," Niona muttered to herself. She didn't even get a chance to try out her new strategy. She cursed again as she withdrew Glom.

It was a weird and unsatisfying first round. Justine hadn't inflicted even a minimal amount of damage, but Niona had expended a lot of mana trying to hit her Jekua.

What the hell was she doing? Niona wondered, trying to decide who to send out next.

She waited a moment to see what Justine's next Jekua was. The answer was a Dompring, a Gravity-Type.

Domprings were huge beasts, their bodies the size of a car and covered with shaggy brown fur. They walked on four spidery legs that were similarly hairy, and long, curved tusks protruded from their ugly faces.

They were formidable foes, despite the fact that in the wild they were herbivores. Domprings lived in the mountains of Na Tana, altering their own gravity to scale terrain that other creatures could not. Their magic was powerful, as were their bulky bodies.

She needed something that could pack a powerful punch too, something that could actually do some harm to the Dompring beneath its thick layers of fur and muscle. Pops could electrify it, which might be good; or Boombox could land some mindblowing punches on the thing. Not to mention, both would bring a ton of speed to the table, which she would appreciate after controlling Glom.

A choice needed to be made fast. She was starting to

look like a fool, just like she told Balt he would if he delayed swapping Jekuas.

She went with Boombox. She wanted to punch something.

The Bruiserweight appeared before her, standing on her muscular, green-scaled legs. Boombox blinked her bulbous yellow eyes as Niona assessed the Dompring's movements, absorbing the residual heat from all the charred grass Glom left behind. A Bruiserweight's natural habitat was a desert over in Hurrathsa, so Boombox was accustomed to the heat.

Boombox darted across the field toward Justine's Dompring. Again, though, the other Summoner seemed to not even be paying a modicum of attention to what Niona was doing.

The beast was scuttling around the field, enacting its Gravity magic on the hills. Some parts were flattened completely, others reshaped, curving the earth even more.

It didn't matter what she was doing.

Boombox reached the Dompring and swung her tightened fist. As the blow landed on the Dompring's face, Niona increased the friction between the two Jekuas and a spark ignited, lighting the Dompring's face on fire.

The Dompring stumbled backward, shaking its head manically in a misguided effort to extinguish the flames. They dissipated on their own a few seconds later, leaving behind a bald patch on the Dompring's otherwise furry cheek.

In an instant, the Dompring was in the air. Its gravity was lessened to fling it upward, and Niona feared the massive beast was about to cannonball onto her Bruiserweight.

But her fears turned out to be misplaced. Justine did bring the Dompring down again, but not with any particular intensity and not on top of Boombox.

The Dompring landed several feet away and continued its task of inflicting its magic on the terrain instead of on Niona's Jekua.

It then dawned on her what had happened. Justine had used her Tonnit's Sonic magic to send several earthquakes coursing through the battlefield, loosening and weakening the soil. Then she sent out her Dompring, which could now easily reshape the arena thanks to the weakened earth.

Why, though?

Boombox ran toward the Dompring again. As she grew nearer, Boombox leapt into the air, extending her leg in a flying kick. Once more, she used Boombox's inherent Friction magic to increase the friction between them and ignited another spark.

The Dompring's ass caught on fire, but the flames sputtered out almost immediately as Justine withdrew it.

"Dammit!" Niona swore again, louder this time. She withdrew her Bruiserweight, grumbling to herself as the pink soulclay returned to her kayet. It felt like Boombox had spent even less time out there than Glom.

The woman was not giving her the opportunity to do any significant damage. She had landed several decent blows with both Boombox and Glom, at least, and all the magic that Justine was doing had to be draining her mana a good amount.

Now that her Tonnit and Dompring had gotten to it, the arena looked completely different from how the tournament officials had set it up. Resetting it for the next competitors was going to be a huge headache.

Instead of rolling hills, the arena was filled with steep ramps and deep recesses. It was more akin to a skate park now than anything else, albeit one comprised of grass and dirt. Justine had to have used up a lot of her mana just to change the way the battlefield looked.

Niona still was not totally sure what this woman was doing, but she wanted to end the match before she had to find out. Her most powerful Jekua was Pops, so she summoned the Toolu next.

Pops's disconcerting black-shelled body skittered onto the battlefield, seeking out something to electrocute. Yellow fur peeked out through the Toolu's carapace, sparking and buzzing with static.

Whatever Justine was about to summon, Pops was going to absolutely paralyze it. Niona would not let her continue on with her weird plan.

Justine's third Jekua was a Toryoth. What was she going to do now with a Wind-Type?

Thankfully, Pops was a fast little devil. He had crossed the makeshift skate park by the time Justine finished summoning her hulking bird. Pops leapt through the air, covered in electricity, and rammed his head into the Toryoth.

It flapped its wings angrily, kicking up a strong gust of wind that sent Pops tumbling backward. Then it lifted itself into the air and started toward one of the ramps that Justine's Dompring had crafted.

Niona righted Pops and began firing thunderbolts at the bird. Justine was not as agile with it as she was her Tonnit, plus it was a bigger target overall, so several of them hit. The Toryoth came crashing down on the ground close to the ramp, and it took a few seconds for it to stand again.

Just hit the sucker again, Niona told herself. That was all she could do. Pops stood and dashed in the direction of the bird.

The Toryoth was flapping its wings again, but at nothing. It was building up wind at higher and higher speeds, until a funnel of wind remained stationary in that spot, sending high-velocity gusts pointed directly at one of the ramps. When it was done, it flew upward and moved to one of the other ramps.

It was clear what was happening now. If Niona was a betting woman, she would put money on Justine's next Jekua being something that could move around fast. Probably a Friction-Type.

All of this was just setup for whatever her fourth Jekua was.

Could it really be worth it? Had she done this before to great effect, or was this her first time trying out the strategy?

Niona did not want to find out if it was going to work. She needed to ground this bird post-haste.

The Toryoth lifted off again, and Niona opened Pops's tiny mouth in a shrill screech. Soundwaves blasted through the air, but they had dissipated a great deal by the time they reached Justine's Jekua. Niona had hoped to disrupt the bird's flight by using Sonic magic to vibrate the air molecules, but it didn't work. The soundwaves could not travel that far.

There was something else she could try, though.

Pops fired another thunderbolt at the Toryoth (which hit), then ran toward the funnel of wind it had just created. Niona tried the technique again, sending a shriek of soundwaves at the funnel.

Being at a much closer range, the vibration of the air molecules produced by Pops's soundwaves was strong enough to dissipate the wind funnel. And, when checking her mana levels, Niona was pleased to discover it cost her very little mana to perform the ability. That made some amount of sense, given how weak and ineffective it was in most use cases.

Niona grinned when she saw Justine's bubbly demeanor falter momentarily.

Pops ran over to another of her funnels and wiped it out, though it took two shrieks to fully erase that one.

While the Toryoth continued flying around creating wind funnels, Pops followed behind trying to disperse as many as he could. Finally, Justine called it quits and withdrew her Jekua.

Unfortunately, Niona had to withdraw Pops too and could not run around screaming at the wind funnels until they were all gone. She'd only managed to get rid of about half of them, but it would have to do.

Hopefully focusing on that instead of on attacking the Toryoth would not prove to be a mistake. Niona felt a little stupid, having gotten caught up in wanting to thwart Justine's plan rather than quickly ending the match. But what was done was done.

Niona summoned her Nuri, Garbo, the last Jekua on her team. Whatever Justine's grand plan was, Garbo would have to be the one to bring down this last Jekua.

Admittedly, she did not know if the Nuri had what it would take. She had to try, though. It really would be embarrassing if Balt moved on to round two and she didn't.

Justine's final Jekua was, as Niona expected, a Friction-Type. It had some Sonic abilities too, but Niona suspected she would primarily be seeing it implement its Friction powers.

It was a Wheelburrow, a mole-esque creature with rough black and gray skin that could curl up on itself and roll around, looking much like a tire.

In truth, it was a Jekua that Niona had always found to be pretty stupid. Ugly, too.

Some good extra motivation for her to crush the thing.

For the moment, Garbo stayed put while Niona waited to see what the Wheelburrow was going to do exactly. No need to spend more mana making the Nuri an easier target to hit.

The Wheelburrow immediately curled into a ball and began rolling across the terrain, headed straight for one of the remaining wind funnels. They had to dissipate over time, but for now they were self-sustaining thanks to the Toryoth's powerful Wind magic.

It veered directly into the back of the funnel, and Justine must have decreased the Jekua's friction the moment it hit the wind. It shot through the funnel like a bullet and was propelled off the ramp the Dompring had shaped.

Niona bit her lip, watching the Wheelburrow shoot into the sky.

What's next? she wondered to herself. What was all this for?

At the peak of its trajectory, the Wheelburrow unfurled itself, stretching its four limbs out as wide as possible, exposing its belly to all below. Then a spear of crackling dark pink and purple energy shot out from the creature's stomach, and it headed right for Garbo.

Niona was briefly stunned by what she was seeing, but she was able to muster up the cognitive awareness to move Garbo out of the way just as the bolt of plasma impacted and exploded on the spot where the Nuri previously stood.

So Justine had modified her Wheelburrow with a Plasma ability. That was good to know.

The Wheelburrow rolled back up before landing with a loud smack and immediately taking off across the field, still juiced up by its decreased friction. It zoomed straight toward Garbo and was suddenly encased in electrical energy.

It had some kind of Electrical mod too. Great. Superb.

Her Nuri was not fast enough to dodge the Wheelburrow's tackle, even if it hadn't increased its own speed by so much. It slammed into one of Garbo's legs, sending a jolt of splitting pain through the Jekua.

Surprisingly, the electrically-charged tackle had not depleted much of her mana. Whatever mod Justine had used to give the Jekua Electrical power was not very strong. It might have been a more general "Electrical" mod rather than a concentrated Ability mod, which would have likely done more damage.

Niona was still operating at about fifty percent capacity with her mana. A lot had been spent trying and failing to hit Justine's creatures, but at least she had lost very little from being hurt herself.

The Wheelburrow rolled off, heading toward a funnel-less ramp. It gained more and more speed then shot off the top, landing with a *thunk* and using the extra momentum to curve around in Garbo's direction.

Niona started to move Garbo out of the way. Regardless of the lessened Electrical power, that Wheelburrow had gained a frankly insane amount of momentum and even a plain tackle would send her Nuri sprawling.

She wasn't fast enough. The Wheelburrow struck Garbo, and he was sent smashing into the ground on his side.

This was not going well.

As the Wheelburrow turned to start toward another ramp, from the ground Garbo extended one of his spiral horns. It reached across the gulf between them and just barely pierced the creature.

It surely could not have done much damage, she had basically just tapped the thing, but it was enough to discombobulate the Wheelburrow. It came to a skidding halt, untucking itself and tumbling stupidly for a few feet.

Justine looked annoyed again. Niona enjoyed annoying her.

The Wheelburrow stood back up and continued rolling away. Garbo rose from the ground and began galloping after it. It was heading for one of the wind funnels, trying to regain the absurd momentum it had achieved before.

It was also probably going to use that Plasma Skewer ability again. Plasma abilities were notoriously potent; one hit from that could be potentially devastating for her mana.

She stopped Garbo again, waiting for the Wheelburrow to head up the ramp. As soon as it was blasting up the grassy ramp, too late for Justine to change course, Garbo ran forward.

The Nuri stopped right beside the ramp just as the Wheelburrow took flight. It once again went spread-eagle and fired a bolt of plasma at the earth, but Niona had situated Garbo too close to the ramp. Justine could not angle the Wheelburrow properly to strike.

Plasma exploded uselessly on the ground, leaving behind yet another circle of blackened grass. Between the Wheelburrow and Glom's earlier feats, the entire place would soon be black.

The Wheelburrow landed and continued rolling around like the dumb little tire that it was. It once more veered in Garbo's direction to strike with an electrified tackle, but Garbo reached out with both of his horns to stab it.

His horns jabbed into the Wheelburrow, halting its charge. Its skin was tough, but it wasn't tough enough to stop the Nuri's sharp horns. Blood spurted from the holes Garbo created, and Niona swung the Nuri's head to fling the Wheelburrow to the side.

It flew through the air like a discarded doll and slammed into the ground with heavy force. Justine was quick to stand it back up, though, and moments later the Wheelburrow was rolling around again. She was relentless.

Continually breaking its momentum was good, but none of the hits she was landing could be doing all that much damage to the Wheelburrow and a single hit from its Plasma mod might bring Niona to her knees. She needed to do something different.

An idea came to her. It was risky, but she thought it would work.

The idea would require her to act fast and precise. Precision was going to be the key part of this. If she miscalculated, it might spell the end of her tenure in the Makanuele Rumble.

So she would just need to be fast and precise. Simple as that.

She watched Justine's Wheelburrow, saw the ramp it was headed for. Another wind-aided one. That bastard was going to be moving fast. Niona would have to move faster.

Garbo raced across the field toward that same ramp. At a certain point, she knew that she was not going to get as close as she wanted, and that if this was going to work she had to stop. Garbo came to a halt still tens of feet away, while the Wheelburrow charged into the wind funnel.

Niona eyed the scene carefully.

At the height of the Wheelburrow's jump, it was going to stretch its body out, and there would be a split second when its soft belly was exposed before it unleashed the Plasma Skewer.

All Niona had to do was calculate exactly where the Wheelburrow would be unfurling itself in the sky and make sure Garbo's two horns extended out and met it there.

Easy.

In theory.

If she missed, though, then Garbo would just be an idle target for Justine's plasma blast, which was not the best position to be in.

At the exact second the Jekua hit that wind funnel, Niona started extending Garbo's Elastic horns. The spiraling keratin stretched out, tan orange against the blue backdrop of sky.

The Wheelburrow shot forward, rolling up the ramp at a mindboggling speed.

Then the world felt like it was in slow motion.

Garbo's horns continued stretching out, and Niona tilted the Nuri's head ever so slightly to shift their position.

The Wheelburrow hit the edge of the ramp and went soaring into the air. It flew higher and higher up, reaching heretofore unseen heights.

Niona kept pushing her Jekua's horns. Again, she moved his head, pulling the horns' tips to the right.

Justine's Wheelburrow unfurled itself. Its little gray hands and feet stretched outward, spreading its fingers and toes wide.

The round, gray belly began to sparkle with plasma energy. Rich pink and purple hues shimmered around the Wheelburrow.

Then, with one more minor adjustment, Garbo's horns pierced the thing's stomach.

The world around Niona sped up again and the plasma energy emanating from Justine's Wheelburrow disappeared instantly. The mole was skewered on the goat's horns, held fifty feet off the ground. Blood drained from the wounds in the Wheelburrow's stomach, dribbling down the ridges of Garbo's horns.

I've got electricity too, Niona thought. *And mine's the real deal.*

She shortened the horns about a quarter of the way, then immediately extended them again with great speed while sending a shockwave shuddering through them.

The Wheelburrow was simultaneously electrocuted and flung off the ends of Garbo's horns, careening through the air while electricity coursed through its body. Justine cupped her hands to her mouth, watching wide-eyed as her Jekua was catapulted a hundred feet in the air.

It landed on the edge of the arena with a wet smack.

The crumpled, bloody heap that had once been Justine Tesh's Wheelburrow lit up in vivid blue before returning to the woman's waiting kayet.

She sadly had no more Jekuas left.

Niona was the victor.

22
SIUV'S YOUNGER SISTER

NEITHER ALANI NOR AEIKO WERE ESPECIALLY INVESTED IN the tournament apart from Balt and Niona's matches. When those two weren't competing, they actually spent most of the time chatting with each other rather than paying any attention to the battles happening below; it seemed like it mildly irritated a few people around them in the stands, but Alani was sure it was fine. Xatetu Field was the noisiest place she had ever been; noise was noise was noise. They could easily watch a monkey get squashed by a house-sized raccoon-beast while two people talked nearby.

When their friends were on the field, though, their gaze could not be torn away for even a mere instant. Alani literally screamed in fear when that gross hand monster exploded all over Balt's Tottaworm. She was also exceptionally confused throughout most of Niona's fight, and she did not know if that was a normal reaction or if it was only due to her general lack of experience with Jekua battles.

But now, with the two of them finished and moving on to the second round, Alani and Aeiko felt no need to stick around the stadium for the rest of the day. Alani texted Balt and they met up at the stadium entrance to say congratulations in person and head out.

What surprised Alani was that while the four of them stood there, a few passersby stopped to exchange a few words with both Balt and Niona. The first time it happened, Balt seemed taken aback too. When the stranger walked away, he looked pleased with himself. He enjoyed the tiny bit of adoration he was already receiving.

The tournament had only gotten through half of its allotted matches for the day, and Balt and Niona wanted to stick around to see how the rest played out. Not only because they simply enjoyed watching Summoners duke it out, but because they wanted to obtain any information about their potential opponents that they could. It made sense to Alani, but she was ready to split.

So they said their goodbyes, and the two pairs separated, with Alani and Aeiko departing through the stadium's wide doors and back into the sunny crater outside.

They had eaten some snacks at the stadium, and Alani was not particularly hungry—all that fried junk was really filling—but she was craving *something*. It took her a second to put her finger on it.

"I am in desperate need of something fresh," she said.

"What does that mean?" asked Aeiko.

"Food, I mean. Sorry. A nice piece of fruit would really hit the spot right now, don't you think?" They'd both pigged out on some fries and mekki during the battles. Aeiko had bought a corndog too, which Alani had taken a couple bites of. And they had also split a plate of nachos drenched in cheese sauce and pickled jalapenos. And also they each ate a single tai dair.

Aeiko nodded. "You're not wrong," they said. "I know a good place. There's a little market thing over by Fontaro Street." They checked their linkpad, then said, "It should be open for another couple hours."

The market they were thinking of was in the south central part of the city, a good thirty-minute walk from the crater. Alani had not quite expected such an arduous trek, but the weather was nice and even though there was the typical din of the city streets, it was much, much quieter than within the stadium. Even with the honking car horns and pounding footsteps on the sidewalk and building doors opening and slamming shut, it felt downright peaceful compared to the mayhem of Xatetu Field.

Plus, Aeiko was good walking company.

The two had spent a lot of time over the past few days strolling through Makanuele together, with Aeiko showing Alani some of their favorite spots around the city. Today was their first official day off of work, so presumably their time together would only increase from here.

As the days wore on, Alani was starting to feel less self-conscious around them. On occasion, she still caught herself feeling less like *Alani* and more like *Siuv's Younger Sister,* but for the most part those feelings no longer lingered.

The Fontaro Street Market was a cute setup, with fruit

and vegetable vendors lining a narrow alleyway. Handcrafted signs sat propped up against their wooden stands, while people sauntered up and down the alley examining everyone's wares. There was also one person selling pickled vegetables, and another with a rack of spray-painted and bedazzled shirts.

They spent a minute rifling through the shirt rack. The designs were all extraordinarily flamboyant, ranging from illustrations of cartoon characters to aspirational quotes to abstract colors. Alani had to stop herself from laughing as she looked at them all. Not at the designs themselves, but at the notion of wearing one of them in front of a Church Elder. Elder Poul would have an aneurism seeing an initiate wearing something like that.

"These look like the types of weird-ass things Holly would love," Aeiko said as they checked out the absurd shirts.

A question was on the tip of Alani's tongue, but she wasn't sure if it'd be weird to ask. Apprehensively, she said, "Can I ask you something?"

"Of course."

"It might be kind of awkward."

"Go for it," said Aeiko amusedly.

Alani's face scrunched up, uncomfortable with the question that was about to pour from her mouth. She screwed up her courage and asked, "What is the deal with Holly?"

Aeiko huffed, their expression light. "With the whole living situation, you mean?"

"Yes."

They said, "I know, it's weird that I live with my ex."

"...yeah, kind of," said Alani.

Aeiko looked at her, putting the ugly shirt back on the rack. "Trust me, it's weird for me too. We've been broken up for a while, but it's...I don't know, it feels wrong forcing her out of the place, and I'm too busy with work and stuff to go apartment hunting. Plus, having a roommate makes the rent so much cheaper, and I don't really know anyone else who's looking for a roommate..."

"So it's all about convenience," said Alani.

"The trade-off of convenience for awkwardness is not always the best, but yes," Aeiko said. "Convenience is the name of the game. Until I can figure out something else."

"She seems awfully clingy," Alani then said. She surprised herself by blurting it out. She almost wanted to take it back.

Aeiko chuckled. "Yeah, she is," they said. "I don't know what else to say. That's just Holly."

It was somewhat of a relief to Alani that the two were only still living together because it was easier than the alternative. If the reason had been because there were leftover feelings between the two of them...well, it wasn't like that would realistically change anything for Alani, but she knew it would have saddened her.

When they were done inspecting the clothing, they moved on to the various fruit stands. Pretty much anything Alani could dream of was at her disposal, and she waffled between buying a crisp apple and a fresh, juicy mango. Ultimately she went with the apple, since it would be a far less messy endeavor while they walked.

Aeiko bought themselves a banana, another good choice for avoiding messiness. Alani really wanted a kiwi, too, but she did not see how she could easily eat it without going back to Aeiko's apartment first.

"What next?" Aeiko asked as they peeled their banana. The peel's yellow flaps dangled over their hand.

They stepped out from the alley, not wanting to obstruct other paying customers from being able to navigate the narrow walkway. Alani chomped into her apple with a hugely satisfying crunch.

She pondered the question for a moment, relishing the tart sweetness of the fruit. Then she had it.

"There was a park we walked through when we first got here," she said, trying to remember if she had seen the name of it. "We're in the south part of town, right? I can't imagine it was terribly far from here."

"Big-ass place? Lots of different pathways and trees and stuff?"

"Most parks have trees," Alani pointed out, "but 'big' is definitely an accurate word. It was enormous."

"I think I know what you're talking about," Aeiko said. They set off down the street and Alani followed, taking another bite out of her apple.

Aeiko did know the place she was referring to. How could they not, though? It had to be the largest park in the city, perhaps aside from the area outside the stadium.

Just as before, Alani was mesmerized by the wide open space of the park. Squirrels and Dewrats scampered around, climbing up trees; butterflies fluttered amongst the shrubbery; flowers bloomed vibrantly in the sunlight. She breathed in the park's fresh air with a smile.

"There really is nowhere like this in Tanepke, huh?"

said Aeiko. They were holding their limp banana peel down by their side.

Alani's eyes lit up. "That's exactly what I thought when I first saw it," she said.

Aeiko chuckled. "We've got this, and Tanepke's just got the Undertow," they said wistfully.

"I'll take this any day."

"Same." Aeiko walked forward, toward a trash can that had attracted a curious squirrel. "I gotta get rid of this nanner suit," they said, indicating the peel they held.

As the two approached, the squirrel ran away. It stopped behind a nearby tree trunk and peered around the edge to watch them, its tiny fuzzy chest heaving wildly. Aeiko threw away their peel, and Alani tossed her apple core.

"You're lucky you have a place like this," said Alani. "Honestly, it depresses me every time I have to walk past the Undertow."

"You don't live there anymore?" asked Aeiko. They began walking through the grass, veering off the stone pathway.

Alani said, "I guess it's technically still my home? A lot of my stuff is there, but I spend most of my nights at the Church. They have bunks and stuff there."

"How's the food, though?"

She chuckled. "It's, uh…" She searched for the most diplomatic term. "It's passable."

"Passable!" Aeiko exclaimed. "That's just a longer word for *bad*."

"I think that was a loaded question," Alani said. "You knew what the answer was going to be."

"Of course I did. How could the food that some dumpy old Elders make be anything but passable?" After a beat, they said, "Sorry, I didn't mean to badmouth the Elders. My bad."

"It's okay," Alani assured them. "Elder Poul could probably be described as dumpy." The old man's ear-shattering snores still haunted her dreams.

Off in the distance, there was a lone ball sitting nestled in the grass. Its rubbery red surface stood in stark contrast to the verdant green.

Aeiko pointed at it and asked, "Wanna play some wicker?"

Alani laughed. "Seriously?" she said. "That's not our ball."

Aeiko shrugged. "Seems abandoned to me."

"What if the owner comes back for it?"

"Then we'll give it back. No big deal. C'mon." They hurried off toward the abandoned ball. Alani jogged behind them.

Aeiko leaned down to pick up the ball then held it at their waist. "You remember how to play, right?" they asked.

"Of course," said Alani. "It's just hitting a ball with your head. How could anyone forget that?"

"Fair. Alright, we'll do some solo play against each other. Balt and Niona aren't the only ones with competitive spirits." They grinned then said, "You're going down, Temel."

Alani laughed again. "Whatever you say, Fentao."

In her youth, Alani had played wicker with Siuv and her friends hundreds of times. Neither she nor Aeiko were ever the winners. They were both awful at the game.

"Anyway, back to what we were talking about," said Aeiko, lightly tossing the ball in the air. "Do you like it there?" they asked. They immediately missed the ball and it landed with a bounce on the ground.

"In Tanepke? Of course not," Alani replied, laughing at Aeiko's failure. She liked her hometown just fine, she supposed, but she did not feel any real, deep attachment to the place. "I wish I could move somewhere else, like here. You've got way better food here. Far beyond passable." She retrieved the ball and readied herself to toss it.

"Yeah, well, that's because I know all the best places to eat," said Aeiko. "But no, I meant at the Church."

Alani was startled by the question and completely missed the ball too. It didn't even come close to her head. She quickly said, "Yeah, yeah, of course I do. Yeah."

Aeiko tried to suppress a laugh, but failed. "That sounded very convincing," they said.

"I mean..." Alani trailed off, not sure what she was trying to say.

"It just doesn't seem like something I ever expected you to do," Aeiko said. "I mean, I know I was closer to your sister than to you, but I feel like I knew you pretty well, yeah? I just didn't see the Church in your future, that's all." They picked up and held the ball at their side.

"Things change, I suppose," said Alani. "It's been a few years since you moved away."

"That's true," they conceded. "It's just that you also don't...I don't know how to explain. You don't really ever talk about it. Not that you should be spending every conversation expounding on the virtues of the Church and the beauty of the Veptists or whatever, but I don't think you've talked about what you do with the Church at *all* this past week except when I've asked. I guess what I'm saying is that you don't seem passionate about it, that's all."

Once they finished speaking, they tossed the rubber ball in the air. It came down on their head and they shot it back upward. They managed to hit it again, then again. They were on a roll. After six hits, the ball tumbled to the ground. Alani moved to pick it up, her thoughts wandering.

Passionate. Was she passionate about the Church?

It wasn't something that she had ever actually sat down and asked herself. In her mind, it didn't really matter. The Church was an escape.

So she said as much. "It's a good way to get out of the house."

Aeiko shot her a dubious look. "I mean…I think dedicating your entire life to a religious practice is at least a level higher than 'getting out of the house,' it's not like going to a movie or grabbing some coffee or whatever. But I can completely understand why you wanted to do it."

That last sentence was tinged with sorrow. Alani knew they didn't intend to minimize her feelings; she assumed Siuv had talked to Aeiko about their parents at some point, but she didn't know to what extent.

And it was true that going to a movie or buying a cup of coffee would distract her for a couple hours, but then she'd always end up right back at home. The Church of Salt and Sanction provided her with a lifelong distraction.

Alani picked up the ball. She tossed it in the air and it came back down on her head, bouncing skyward again. She scrambled to position herself underneath it as it descended, but she miscalculated.

"I'm winning," said Aeiko.

"I know. I'll get it on my next go, though."

"I don't think you will."

"Just wait and see."

"Alright, Temel, you talk a big game. Don't change the subject, though."

Alani sighed. "I don't see what there is to say," she said. "It's a way to occupy my time. It's a way to get away from my parents. You know how they are."

Aeiko nodded, grabbing the ball. "There are lots of ways to get out, though," they said, holding the ball and looking Alani in the eye. They appeared concerned. "I get why you'd want to, but…is this the way you want to do it? Truly?"

Maybe it was true that she wasn't passionate about the Church. Maybe she was stressing out about how these Veptists were judging her pilgrimage even though she didn't *really* care what they thought about her. Maybe.

But what else *was* there in Tanepke?

The Church had opened its doors to her, and she had walked through. They had given her a safe space for the past three years, and for that she was eternally grateful.

Alani folded her arms across her chest and looked down at the white shineink tattoos traced along them.

The manastreams glowed dimly in the bright natural sunlight.

"I don't know," she finally said aloud.

An awkward silence hung between them for a few moments. It was one of those occasions where she once again felt like Siuv's Younger Sister. A child who didn't know what she wanted out of life, who didn't know how to act like a proper adult.

At last, Aeiko said something. "I'm just saying, there are, like…endless possibilities for you to choose from. For real, there are so many paths your life could go down."

Their choice of words struck Alani. Elder Fanareot had only presented her with two paths: that of Conbreas, or that of Duremjul.

And even then, those choices were handed down to her by someone else. Chosen by an Elder. And they weren't even really choices at all, it wasn't as if she was allowed to decide whether she wanted to follow the Architect or if she wanted to follow the Sculptor. The whole reason she embarked on this pilgrimage was so that some unseen forces would make the decision for her. It was all entirely out of her hands.

Alani had never really thought of herself as someone with choices. She had grown up in the Undertow, after all. With a lack of support from parents like hers, what could she really do with her life? And with her older sister gone, she had to look after herself. She was all on her own. Her options were more limited than ever before.

She had never thought of herself as someone deserving of anything more than a distraction from her circumstances. Someone who could make a real life for themselves doing something that they loved. Something that brought them joy.

All her life, she could only ever think about getting away, and the Church had been the first and only opportunity to do that.

"I'm sorry," Aeiko said. "I don't mean to say anything out of line or weird or anything like that. Forget I said anything."

"No, it's okay," said Alani. Her head was swimming.

"No, it wasn't my place," they said.

"Really, it's okay," Alani told them.

She really did want to change the subject now, though. This was all too much for her to process at the moment. She nodded at the ball in Aeiko's hands.

"Let's keep going," she said. "I need to beat you before someone comes looking for their ball."

Aeiko smiled, and the expression warmed Alani a bit. Even after the uncomfortable conversation, their kind eyes soothed her.

"You're not going to win," Aeiko said confidently. "You're out of your mind if you think you can beat six."

Alani smirked and said, "Well, I've gotta try."

23
SENSORY OVERLOAD

After their victories the day before, Balt and Niona were both exhausted. Balt had never engaged in such a physically taxing battle, not even when he was fighting Reno in the Qwisdeep.

When Balt opened his eyes after a night of restful sleep, he was greeted by the sight of Brine staring down at him with his featureless coral face.

"Good morning, Brine," he said to the golem.

Brine waved to him, then walked away.

Balt shifted underneath the covers, breathing in deep and savoring the warmth. He could hear Alani, Aeiko, and Holly chatting in the kitchen not too far away, but they hadn't noticed him stirring.

He looked within himself, checking on his mana level. His reserves had refilled by the time he went to bed, and this morning he could now sense that they had also deepened after his match.

It felt hugely satisfying laying there with deep, full

mana reserves and a bunch of warmth trapped underneath the blanket. His muscles ached after being pummeled by Rei Yor's band of Jekuas, and every tiny movement made him creak like an old house.

He bravely reached his arm out from underneath the covers to grab his linkpad, which was plugged into the wall beside him. He clicked the screen on and had to squint with the bright light.

An idea occurred to him. He headed over to the forums and pulled up the user profile for OutOfYorRei, wanting to see if they had posted anything incendiary about the match yesterday that could confirm for him that it was Rei's account.

Unfortunately, the owner had not posted anything in several days, so he could neither confirm nor deny that it was the woman's account. If it wasn't, though, then that username was a hell of a coincidence.

He was in the middle of trying to learn whether Zu Jerat had an account when a notification popped up on his screen and the device vibrated. It was a new message from Niona, asking if he was awake yet. Then six more texts came rolling in, all in fast succession, every single one saying *WAKE UP!* His linkpad didn't even have a break in between each text, it sounded like one long vibration as they came in.

He told her yes, and then told her to calm down. It did make him chuckle, though. She knew the ceaseless vibrating would wake him up if he wasn't already. He wouldn't be sleeping in on her watch.

Despite his and Niona's incredible fatigue, they could not spend their entire day off lounging in bed (or, in Balt's case, lounging on his pallet on the floor). They also couldn't spend the whole day simply watching the other half of the first round, although they would definitely need to watch some highlights online later.

Before he got up, he decided to do one more search on the Jekua forums. He stopped his fruitless search for Zu's profile and instead tried finding anything about fighting in darkness.

He found a couple of decent suggestions. In retrospect, they made a lot of sense, and Balt didn't know why he hadn't thought of them himself.

One user said they always used their Bingst when battling at night, since the creature was nocturnal and therefore had pretty good night vision. Puffolins were mostly nocturnal too, so maybe Dipper's vision would be good enough to combat Zu's dark dome. He also noted that users discussing using a Jekua's night vision was the first time he'd even obliquely seen someone referring to the technique he used, switching into the Jekua's perspective. They didn't outright state that was what they did, but how else would they make use of the creature's natural vision?

Another user said that they went with Sonic-Types for nighttime battles. Something like a Whifflit could use echolocation to navigate the battlefield, and Jekuas that burrowed could sense vibrations in the ground to seek out their opponent. Both required a lot of skill to use effectively, but they were good options. Balt didn't have anything with echolocation (and he did not want a Whifflit), but the Tottaworm might prove useful. He'd used its

Sonic prowess to great effect in the elimination round, after all.

Those were two good avenues for him to explore when he met up with Niona in a little while. He was most adept with Dipper, so if she could secure him the victory, that would be swell.

Balt sat up and stretched, letting out a deep yawn. The loss of his blanket's warmth was unbelievably devastating. Everyone at the table greeted him, and he waved back as his yawn concluded. Then he crawled over to his bag and retrieved his grandmother's bestiary.

He wanted to skim the pages to make sure there was nothing in there that could help, but he'd already gone through the book countless times. He knew it inside and out, especially the pages for the Jekuas he'd imprinted. While he knew there would be nothing new to actually glean, the act of reading through it still helped to put him at ease.

The pages for each Jekua in his crew were dog-eared. He scanned the page for the Puffolin, then the Tottaworm. On the Mirrorbear's page, he started to wonder if Milton's power to absorb abilities could be used to turn the tide in some way. Although Zu would also have to use a light-based Radiant ability in order for Balt to then ward off the darkness, which seemed unlikely. Absorbing the dark dome power or the flashbang wouldn't be especially useful, except to blind Zu too with the latter. He decided Milton might not be the most useful combatant in his next match.

He flipped to the page detailing the Mosstopus, and he

stared at the detailed black and white illustration on the page.

It didn't have any eyes. The creature's gigantic, round head was dominated by its vicious maw.

Balt recalled how disorienting it was shifting into Pistachio's perspective the few times he'd attempted it. He couldn't spend more than a few seconds that way without wanting to vomit. Perhaps there was a way to gain finer control of it and navigate the world using whatever senses the Mosstopus used.

That would have to be a last resort, however. He didn't want to risk nauseating himself in the middle of Xatetu Field in front of thousands of people. Using Dipper's naturally enhanced vision or the Tottaworm's delicate senses would both be far easier.

About an hour later, he met Niona at the gym between Aeiko's apartment and her hotel. She was waiting for him outside the entrance, holding two steaming plastic cups.

"I got you a coffee with all the fixin's," she said as he approached.

He grabbed the cup, which was hot to the touch in spite of the protective cardboard sleeve around it. "Thank you," he said, taking a sip and burning his tongue. He didn't know what else he had expected to happen.

"How'd you sleep?" Niona asked, slurping from her own cup. She did not wince as if it had harmed her, like Balt's had. She truly was the master and he was the student.

"Like a log," he replied. "Out cold the entire night."

She grinned. "First sleep after your first match is pure bliss, huh? It never changes. I was dead-ass asleep as soon as I got back. I barely managed to get dressed after my shower; I almost collapsed into my bed."

That image sent heat rushing to Balt's face. He took another scalding sip of coffee to distract from that fact. Then he said, "My body is sore as hell, though."

"Ahh, damn. That sucks."

"Is yours not?"

"Nope, not really."

"Any advice for me?"

"Nope, not really."

Niona proceeded to swipe him in with her guest pass and they strolled to the center of the gym. There was only one other person there, a man with a Halaua that was shocking a dummy over and over.

"I've been thinking about my Radiant magic dilemma," Balt began.

"So have I. I've got no ideas for you."

"Some mentor you are."

"Hey, I at least brought a Radiant Jekua from my stash for you to practice against. That's somethin', ain't it?"

"Alright, you're not the *worst* mentor. Anyway, I had a few ideas." He explained in detail what he wanted to do with Dipper and the Tottaworm, and she was receptive to the ideas. She did have to point out that he could not exactly burrow the Tottaworm through the gym's floors, so they might have to find a spot outside to practice that.

He refrained from bringing up the Mosstopus pitch just yet. He wanted to see if he could yield positive results with Dipper first.

"Hold on," Niona said. "How does a Puffolin havin' night vision help you?"

Balt's mouth hung open stupidly. He figured now was as good a time as any to explain his unique ability to her. When he finished, she stared at him with one eyebrow raised.

"You've been able to do this the whole time we've known each other?" she asked.

"Yeah."

She scoffed, folding her arms across her chest. "How could you keep this from me!" she demanded.

"I dunno," he said. "It just felt weird to mention. I didn't know how common it was."

"It's not the most common thing in the world, but I've heard of a few people who could do it," Niona said. "Weird thing to keep secret, Vana. Hey, that's *two* secrets! Your name and your ability! But I'm jealous, honestly. Wish I could do it. And I bet that's the only way you've ever gotten the upper hand on me, too. Usin' stuff like that that I don't even know about!"

"Anything to win, right?" he smirked.

"That's true," she nodded.

They moved over to one of the sparring rings. Balt readied Dipper's memory card, while Niona loaded up the Radiant Jekua that she had brought along. He was excited to see what she summoned.

His enthusiasm was immediately dampened when she summoned a Gujjy into the ring. She cackled at his downtrodden expression.

"You got a problem with Thompkins?" she asked him.

"You named it *Thompkins?*" Balt shuddered, incredulous.

He stared at the Gujjy. It was a slug that was roughly

the size of a cat. It had absolutely no distinctive features. Just a girthy, slimy green body and two probing antennae on the end of its head.

"It's a good name," said Niona. "Goes well with 'Milton,' I'd say. And it's way better than 'Piss.'"

"His name isn't Piss," Balt shot back. "You've got me on the Milton thing, though."

The Gujjy trundled forward, leaving a trail of viscid slime on the mat. Balt stared at the creature, still dumbfounded.

He said, "You truly have no discernible taste when it comes to imprinting Jekuas, do you?"

"What's that supposed to mean!"

"You'll imprint damn near anything, it seems like," he laughed.

"I'm sure your palate is so much more refined," she said. "Did you wanna summon your ugly little worm, or…?"

"Okay, fine, you've got me again. That was only my second Jekua, though."

"How do you know Thompkins wasn't my second?"

"Was he?"

"I'll never tell."

"I don't think he was."

On their own, Gujjies were not especially useful Jekuas. Most of the time, they were used as Hybridization fodder. They could use Radiant magic to refract light so that it seemed like there were a lot of copies of themselves, which was a neat trick, but not very helpful if the Jekua couldn't do anything after that. It was a great ability to combine with something more powerful, though.

"Don't matter," Niona said. "What matters is that I can do some Radiant shit with him. I can do that blinding light thing that Zu's Conuto did, and I *think* I can pull off somethin' similar to that dome. Not exactly the same, but in the same ballpark. You're wastin' my mana sittin' there gabbin', though."

Balt summoned Dipper, moving the Puffolin out of the way of Niona's encroaching Gujjy. Even if it was all fake and magical or whatever, for some reason Balt still did not want to get the creature's slime on Dipper.

"Ready?" Niona asked.

He nodded.

Thompkins's gelatinous body began to ripple, but then nothing happened.

Niona let out an exasperated sigh and said, "Sorry, hold on. Haven't really done this before, but I was reading up on it earlier."

She tried again. The Gujjy's skin vibrated intensely, but still nothing. On the third try, she finally got something.

A small orb of perfect blackness emerged from Thompkins's back. It floated outward, bouncing along the ground in Dipper's direction.

"Let it hit you," Niona said, her voice weak. Pulling off the new, unfamiliar technique must have taken a lot out of her.

The orb bounced a few more times before colliding with Dipper. She was enveloped in darkness, her entire body disappearing into the sphere of black. When Balt moved her, the orb moved too.

"What is this supposed to do?" he asked.

Niona cleared her throat. "Well, to be honest, it's supposed to be bigger," she said, "but I dunno. It's the best I could come up with on short notice."

The ability wouldn't deter anyone who controlled their Jekua in the typical way, but it would work for his training purposes. Balt shifted his perspective into the Puffolin's, looking out at the world through her eyes. His skin was suddenly filled with an intense chill, like slipping into an ice bath.

He couldn't see anything, though. There was the faintest outline of what lay ahead, but it was mostly indistinguishable. He blinked Dipper's eyes, hoping they would adjust to the darkness, but no luck.

"I can't see anything," he said.

He took a few cautious steps forward in Dipper's body, but nothing came into clearer view. Suddenly something wet and sticky smacked against the Puffolin's face, and he jumped back into his own perspective. He instinctively wiped at his own face, though of course nothing was there.

"What the hell was that?" he asked.

"Just wanted to check that you really couldn't see," said Niona innocently.

"Why wouldn't I be telling the truth?"

"I dunno. You love keepin' your little secrets!"

Balt didn't know what he was doing wrong. According to those forum users, the Puffolin's natural vision should have been enough to let her see in the darkness.

But then he realized all the users' word choice. Everyone who talked about this had said it was their technique when battling at night. No one ever specifically mentioned darkness that came from Radiant magic.

That had to be the key difference. A creature could use its natural night vision to see in the dark, but magic-based darkness was an entirely other matter. Something about the Radiant energy made it impenetrable.

When he said all this aloud, Niona nodded along and said, "Yeah, I guess that makes sense, now that you put it that way."

"Shit," he grumbled. So Dipper was probably not going to be particularly useful against Zu. Maybe he could send a few Petal Showers at the guy's Whissler and pray that some of the petals hit, but that was grasping at straws.

Balt withdrew Dipper, and Thompkins's orb dissipated into nothingness as the soulclay returned to his kayet.

"Wanna go outside and test the Tottaworm?" he asked.

Niona shook her head. "Let's save that for later. We're already in here. Is there anything else in particular you wanted to practice?"

He inhaled deeply then sighed. "I had one more idea for how to deal with the Radiant shit," he said. "Pistachio doesn't have eyes, right? So he wouldn't be affected by anything Zu used to screw up my sight."

Niona nodded, but said, "If he doesn't have eyes, how do you see through him?"

"That's the problem. Every time I've tried, the experience has been…bad. It's just sensory overload, an experience unlike anything else. It makes me incredibly nauseous."

"You're not gonna throw up in here, are ya? That might be a literal and figurative stain on my record."

"I hope not."

"Might as well try it out, see if you can wrangle it at all."

She was right. Balt thought back to the bestiary entry on the Mosstopus. The only illuminating piece of information written there was that the creatures navigated by scent, but he wasn't sure how to translate that into something useful for himself.

"It senses things with smell," he said.

"Alright," said Niona.

"Nothing to suggest?"

"Nope. Only that it's funny this dude sees through scent even though he doesn't have a nose either."

Balt switched memory cards and channeled mana into his kayet. Again, he stepped his Jekua away from the approaching Gujjy.

There was no need for Niona to cast any magic this time around. His sense of sight would be altered immediately upon entering Pistachio's point of view. He switched over, and the effects were immediate.

He was met with a disorienting, mottled vision of the world. Nothing he could see made any sense whatsoever to his human brain. He jumped back to himself and said, "Okay, that still sucks."

"Your mouth's hangin' open," Niona said.

He looked at her. "What?"

"Piss's mouth is hangin' open."

"So?" Balt said. He looked over at the Mosstopus's gleaming fangs and wet tongue.

Niona was looking at him like he was an idiot. "Are you serious?" she said. "You said he sees with scent. He ain't got a nose, though. I would figure that makes him kinda like a snake, don't you think?"

"Snakes have noses," Balt said. Then, "But they detect scent with their tongues."

"Now you're gettin' it. Maybe you need some more coffee, wake you up a bit. You've always got this dude's mouth hangin' open with his tongue floppin' around all over the place. Could be the reason why everything seems so insane when you switch over to him. Maybe not, but it's a theory."

It was a salient point. Worth experimenting with.

Balt closed Pistachio's mouth and shifted back into his perspective. This time, there was no immediate assault on his senses. His head still had a dull ache, and his vision was a swirl of monochromatic purples. Overall, though, it was a hundred times more tolerable than before. Almost soothing, in fact.

When he flicked the Mosstopus's tongue out, the mottled colors flashed in his vision. They remained there even after he closed his mouth again, dancing around like the streaks and spots one saw after looking directly at the sun.

A jolt of pain course through his head, but after a few seconds the dizzying colors faded and he was left with the sea of lavender. He recollected himself, then shot Pistachio's tongue out again.

He did this several times, trying only to adjust himself to the jarring sensation. He wasn't attempting to actually make sense of anything just yet. The whole thing must have looked exceedingly foolish to Niona, who could only see him standing there idly while his imposing Mosstopus flicked its tongue around every few seconds.

"You alright over there?" she finally asked him.

"Yeah, yeah," he answered distractedly. He didn't bother explaining what he was doing, instead trying to focus on Pistachio's senses. He didn't want to lose his concentration.

He switched back to his eyes and closely examined the sparring ring, taking in every detail, noting the placement of everything in relation to where Pistachio stood. Then he jumped back and flicked the Jekua's tongue, soaking up the colors.

His purple vision was filled with bands of orange, faint streaks of green, and pulsating reds. There was also an absurd amount of yellow. He had no idea what was going on in the Mosstopus's body to translate the scent particles its tongue picked up to the colors he was seeing, and he was not going to question it.

He did this a few times, making note of the different colors' positions in his range of vision. A lot of them blended together, so it was hard to know for certain what each color corresponded to, but he had a few suspicions.

Balt laughed at Niona's bewildered expression when he returned to his perspective.

"Are you actually accomplishing anything?" she asked from across the ring. Almost fifteen full minutes had passed since he'd started his experimentation. Those minutes must have been excruciatingly boring for Niona.

"I think so," he answered, still unsure himself. Then he

started moving Pistachio, sequestering him in the back corner of the ring.

He shifted perspectives again and tasted the air with Pistachio's tongue. Those same colors flashed again, this time rearranged after the Jekua's change in orientation.

Some of his theories were proving to be true. The orange streaks were Niona and Thompkins. He didn't know what that meant, exactly, especially since the smudge that designated Thompkins was also muddled with green. He figured the yellow was the rubber mat on which they stood, but he still wasn't sure what the pulsing red meant.

The orange was a good start, though.

Still in Pistachio's perspective, he said, "Could you summon something else?"

"Sure," said Niona.

Then he hastily added, "Don't summon it in the same spot. Let me try to find it."

Balt flicked his tongue out the same moment Niona withdrew Thompkins. The Gujjy smudge flashed in an extravagant white, which sliced across his vision. That had to be her soulclay. He had never detected even the faintest smell from soulclay before, but obviously a Mosstopus had a far greater sense of smell than he did.

He could hear something else being summoned, but he had no idea what. He smelled with Pistachio's tongue, and one of the orange smudges was in the same spot as before. That had to be Niona. There was another, though, on the far right edge of his vision, almost out of sight. He turned Pistachio's body, flicking the tongue out again, and he got a better look at the new orange blob.

Then he spat a slimeball at it.

He heard the wet smack of it hitting Niona's Jekua, and she laughed. "Wow," she said. "Good job."

Balt returned to his own set of eyes and looked at what he'd done. Pistachio was directly facing Garbo. The Nuri shook his head, dispelling the sludge dripping from his cheeks and horns.

"You figured it out," said Niona.

"Eh," he mumbled uncertainly. "I think I figured out the basics, but I don't know. I wouldn't really call myself a master or anything. And it's one thing doing it here with a stationary target, and another thing trying to fight a moving opponent."

Not to mention the massive crowd that the battle was going to draw. He was going to need to practice a lot more if he wanted to avoid being overwhelmed and getting sick all over himself in the arena.

A mischievous grin broke across Niona's face. "Why don't we try out a moving target, then?" she said.

Balt bit his lower lip, then said, "Okay." It was the logical next step, but it stressed him out.

"If you can hit me with another slimeball, I'll buy our first round of Thunderjolts. If you can't after three minutes, though, then you buy 'em."

Balt looked at the Nuri's broad body and said, "Sure. Deal."

Niona then suddenly withdrew Garbo and instead summoned her tall, skinny, agile Bruiserweight.

He mentally prepared himself to buy their drinks.

24
THE BLITZ TRIO

ALANI WAS THANKFUL FOR THE BREAKFAST THAT NIONA treated them to the next day. She was in no mood for yet another bowl of soggy cereal. When Niona arrived at Aeiko's apartment, she came bearing paper bags full of breakfast burritos stuffed with various delights. They all had scrambled eggs, then they came with any combination of potatoes, bacon, sausage, cheese, black beans, onions, and bell peppers. There were enough for each of them (including Holly) to eat two, which was the most ludicrous thing Alani had ever heard of. A single burrito was practically as big as her forearm.

Everyone tried to read the messy scrawl on each of the foil wrappers to determine what fillings each burrito had. While they attempted to decipher the restaurant employee's shorthand, Niona dumped a vast collection of salsas in small plastic containers onto the kitchen table.

"They swear this shit's their specialty," she said,

pointing at a thicker, lime green salsa. The other kind was red and runny.

"What's in it?" Balt asked.

"Don't know," said Niona.

"You didn't ask?"

"Of course not. It's their specialty, I had to get some and try it. Who cares what's in it?"

He then asked Aeiko if they knew what it was, being the local, but they had never been to the restaurant. "I've always heard they're good, but I haven't gotten anything from them before," they said. "Maybe Holly knows?"

Holly had yet to emerge from her bedroom, but they expected she would soon. Today was her day off, but much to Alani's relief, she would not be attending the tournament with them. The event was already sold out, and they couldn't get her a guest pass. She had no idea how Holly would occupy her time otherwise, but that was neither here nor there.

Alani was also relieved to have looked in the mirror that morning to find the bruise on her left cheek had faded. It had been a little over two weeks since she'd gotten kicked by that Facet member, and while it hadn't really hurt for over a week now, she was glad to see it was no longer visible either. No more borrowing makeup from Niona or Aeiko to cover it up.

They all once again thanked Niona profusely for the hearty breakfast, then they dug in. Balt and Niona had spent almost all of the previous day training, and it was apparent in the way they ravenously devoured their food. Niona must have been basing her purchasing decisions on her own appetite, because it was clear they'd both be reaching for a second burrito soon.

The two of them poured the mystery green sauce on top of their overstuffed burritos before taking giant bites. As they chewed, they screwed up their faces, processing the flavor of the sauce. Then they looked at each other and nodded. Evidently it passed some sort of test. Each of them grabbed their plastic container and dabbed more sauce onto their next bite.

While they ate, the topic of the tournament naturally cropped up almost instantly. Both of them would be competing in the second round later today, alongside thirty other Summoners.

Alani did not think she had it in her to watch sixteen straight matches, even after taking yesterday off. "Do you guys know the schedule yet?" she asked, praying to the Veptists that Balt and Niona's matches weren't terribly far apart.

Balt nodded, his mouth full. He wiped a small smear of sauce off his chin. He said, "Tidus Wight and David Woollis are first up, but then Niona's after that. She's facing Yakka Dho, actually."

That meant nothing to Alani, until Balt reminded her that they'd watched Yakka battle at the Tanepke Tusslers tournament before they left town. He was the guy with the goofy orange hair who'd started with his Suelu.

"A fellow Suelu lover, eh?" said Niona.

"He's good, but I think Pops has him beat easily," Balt said.

"His Suelu got beat pretty badly by a Juntoo," Alani recalled.

"Yikes," Niona muttered. She took another green-soaked bite of burrito. An errant chunk of scrambled egg tumbled down onto her plate.

"To be fair, the Juntoo had some Gravity mods," Balt said, "but yeah, it got wrecked." He ate some more burrito, then said, "Actually, the person who beat him is in the tournament, too. Desi Taewao. If you go up against her, just know she's super into Gravity stuff."

"Good note."

Balt took out his linkpad to pull up the rest of the bracket. He scrolled through for a second, then said, "I'm about halfway through the day, it looks like. Wasaaru goes right after me, against someone named Amara Y'nit."

"Oh!" Niona suddenly exclaimed. "Did Andy make it through yesterday?"

Alani had no idea who Andy was, but Balt confirmed that he had indeed moved on to round two.

"He's battling Nakira Mun today. Ever heard of her?"

Niona shook her head and took the last bite of her first burrito. She crumpled up the thin foil that had held it and tossed the aluminum ball onto her plate before grabbing her second. She needed an additional sauce container, as well.

The two Summoners continued going through the list of today's competitors. Alani and Aeiko exchanged conspiratorial glances, knowing that neither of them had anything to contribute to the conversation. They chuckled lightly to themselves as Balt and Niona droned on.

"Desi Taewao made it through. No surprise there," said Balt. "Goin' up against someone named Kia Notowe. No idea who that is, probably gonna get crushed."

"Kia came up around Makanuele," Niona said. "We trained at the same gym. She's good. Might put up a good fight, who knows? Time will tell. Did you catch anything from the battle between Anesk Pauz and Bi Kalakao?" she then asked excitedly.

Balt shook his head. So did Alani and Aeiko, but Niona probably did not register them doing so. She and Balt were always in their own world when they talked about summoning.

"Alright, you've gotta pull that up before we head down there. There's some wild shit in there with his Vintrist. Probably the best use of that river I saw in any of the matches."

"Who won?"

"No spoilers."

Balt was finished reading through the day's bracket after noting a few more match-ups (Grant Deere vs. Mair Lambt, Nock Brynn vs. Aubrey L'al, Cole Illiom vs. Cassidy Simms, a ton of others), all of which meant nothing at all to Alani. If the person was not Balt, Niona, or Wasaaru, she hadn't the faintest clue who they were.

At least it sounded like she and Aeiko only had to sit through half the matches before they could split again. She was not super compelled to sit and watch some person strangely named Uil battle against Tobias Screet, whoever that was.

"Huh," Balt said, furrowing his brow at something on his screen.

"Hmm?" Niona grumbled, her mouth full of egg and bacon.

He took another second to fully read whatever it was,

then started speaking. "Rika Yonomi was spotted in town," he said. "She was getting lunch with Bill White."

"Okay," said Niona. "By the way, how in the hell did Bill White get dropped in the first round of this thing? I was *sure* he was goin' to the finals. That dude Jin must be a force."

"That isn't weird to you?" said Balt.

"Yeah, it is. I just said I thought he was gonna make it farther."

"No, the Rika thing."

Niona shrugged.

While they bantered, Alani tried to remember where she'd heard the name Rika Yonomi. It was extremely familiar. She of course knew that Rika was one of the most popular Summoners in the Volukho Isles, but where had she read the woman's name recently?

Then she remembered. She'd read a news article about Rika several weeks ago, way back on Totta Island, when she was chilling in her hotel room in Himony. It was a big news story about Rika pulling out of the Makanuele Rumble. Much like Bill White, many spectators had anticipated her reaching the finals.

"She was originally in the tournament, but she dropped out," Alani said.

Balt nodded and pointed at her, then started to read more labels on the unclaimed burritos. He was ready for seconds. The mere thought of eating another burrito gave Alani a stomachache.

"So?" said Niona.

It was Balt's turn to shrug. He selected a burrito and unwrapped the foil. Unlike Niona, he still had some of his initial green sauce left. "I dunno, I just found it odd," he said. "She pulled out because of a scheduling conflict or something, but she's still here? Why? I would've thought she'd be stuck somewhere else, wherever the conflict was."

"Maybe the conflict's here."

"I guess so," he conceded.

Aeiko chimed in, much to Alani's surprise. "Maybe she's shooting a commercial?" they suggested. "I know Lakahlo's launching some new Artificial Ability chips soon and they're doing a big promotional push for them. They're supposed to shoot sometime this week, I believe. I don't know who they've hired for the campaign, but maybe it's her."

"Ahh. That sounds likely," Balt said. "I wanna be in a Lakahlo commercial," he then whined.

"I deserve to be in a commercial before you do," Niona said.

"Must everything be a competition with you?" Balt asked.

"Only when it comes to Jekuas."

"Can't we do a cool team-up promotion or something?"

Niona pretended to ponder his offer for a moment before saying flatly, "Nah." Then she asked Aeiko, "What's the new chips?"

"There's three of them, all with similar effects, but for different Types. They're calling it the Blitz Trio."

"Not a great name," said Niona.

Aeiko giggled. "No, I guess the marketing department was slacking. But that's what they went with. Anyway, there's a Thermal Blitz, an Electrical Blitz, and a Growth

Blitz. The Jekua shoots a powerful blast of whatever—fire, electricity, uh...what would the Growth one be?" they wondered. "Seeds? Vines? I don't know. Point is, they shoot a blast of whatever, and it damages the enemy a ton as well as inflicting a long-term ailment. Thermal has burns that'll continually hurt them over time, Electrical has the chance to paralyze them, and Growth wraps them up in thorny vines that make it harder to move as well as inflicting damage."

"Those sound insanely overpowered," Balt said.

"No doubt they're priced to match," Niona cut in.

"Oh, for sure," Aeiko said. "They're some of the most expensive mods the company's released yet. And there are downsides for the user, too. They all cause recoil damage on the Jekua using them."

"Damn," Balt muttered.

"I want all three," Niona said. "And I sound like the perfect spokeswoman for them, too. We need to get Pops on TV blastin' some idiot with an Electrical Blitz!"

Balt said, "I'm not crazy about the recoil damage, but I wouldn't mind tossing around a Growth Blitz with Dipper..."

"When are they on sale?" Niona asked.

"I'm not sure," Aeiko said. "They've been in production for a while, but I'm not really sure when they're hitting the market. That's not really my purview. They haven't even been officially announced, so keep all that hush-hush."

It was then that Holly finally stepped out of her room. "Divulging company secrets?" she said cheerfully.

"Only some," said Aeiko.

Holly greeted everyone with a smile and came over to

inspect the pile of cylindrical foiled things on the table. "Burritos?" she said.

"Help yourself," Niona said in reply.

She grabbed one of the burritos at random and stood over by the counter, since all the chairs were occupied. "So, how's everyone feeling this morning?" she asked, beginning to unwrap it.

They all mumbled that they were feeling good.

Then Alani's linkpad began buzzing in her pocket. She pulled it out and her face lit up seeing Siuv's name on the screen. Her sister was initiating a video call.

She answered and Siuv's face filled the tiny screen. "Hi!" her sister beamed.

"Hey!" said Alani. "What's up?"

"Nothing, just on my lunch break," Siuv said. "Sorry it took so long to get back to you. Life, y'know?"

It had been almost a week since Alani and Aeiko called and accidentally woke her up. The huge delay in getting back to her was not anything new to Alani, so she hadn't even noticed how long it took. The annoyingly vague "life, y'know?" excuse was a regular occurrence for Siuv, too.

But all she said was, "No worries! Here, you can say hi to everyone." She turned her linkpad around so that everyone could wave to Siuv.

When it reached Alani again, Siuv said, "Was that little Balt Vana I saw?"

"I'm not little," Balt said off-camera.

"You'll always be little to me, kid," said Siuv. Then she said, "Was that Holly, too?"

Alani knew her sister well enough to realize from her tone that Siuv had been attempting to hide how weird she found Holly's presence, but she did not entirely succeed. Niona chuckled by Alani's side, and Balt stuffed his mouth with burrito to somehow avoid the awkwardness.

"Yep!" Holly said from the counter. "How are you, Siuv?"

"I'm fine," Siuv said, her tone still wavering.

On the other side of Alani, Aeiko looked slightly embarrassed by the quick exchange. She hoped they could figure out a way to move out sooner rather than later. The situation seemed to make them fairly uncomfortable. Holly, on the other hand, did not seem to care at all, even when others were blatantly weirded out by it.

Alani did not want to dominate the morning by awkwardly just chatting with her sister, but luckily Aeiko joined in a bit and Siuv also threw out some more jabs at Balt. "She's keepin' you on your toes, gettin' your mind sharp for the fight later," Niona said. Balt's response was to roll his eyes. Holly interjected whenever she could squeeze herself in, but she was mostly preoccupied with eating her breakfast.

Soon, Siuv had to wrap up her break, and so she bade the group farewell. After she hung up, Alani realized they would need to leave for Xatetu Field soon.

"Are we sure we need to go down there?" Niona asked, standing up to throw her trash away. "Is it possible I can pull out for scheduling conflicts and Aeiko can get me into that commercial shoot?"

Aeiko laughed and said, "If I had that kind of power at the company, you can bet your ass I would be living in a bigger apartment than this. I probably also would not have a coral golem as a roommate."

Brine stood motionless near the front door and waved at the mention of him.

"Oh well," Niona said with a dramatic sigh. Then she pointed at the three remaining burritos on the table and asked, "Are any of those up for grabs?"

25

NIONA VS. YAKKA

ALL NIONA KNEW ABOUT YAKKA DHO WAS THAT HE LOOKED like a video game character. Huge, coifed orange hair with cartoonishly round blue eyes that glimmered against his tan skin. He also wore a matching blue bandana that was streaked with an intricate white pattern that looked like traditional Volukhan symbols.

She did not know how he fought, but she would be finding out momentarily. Balt gave her a rundown on his loss at the Tanepke tournament a while back, but there wasn't much information there that she could make much use of. She knew the guy had a Suelu. Great, who didn't?

The first match of the day had been between some guys named Tidus Wight and David Woollis. Woollis was a well-known Summoner, a man from Hurrathsa who competed in almost every major tournament for the past seven or eight years. He had swept the floor with Tidus, who truly floundered throughout the entire duration of the match. In round two, Summoners could switch out their Jekuas at any point and however many times they wanted, but Woollis only used a single Jekua against Tidus. Meanwhile, Tidus continually switched between his four Jekuas, scrambling to gain purchase in the battle. Nothing ever worked, though. Tidus was out.

Now Niona stood in the dim hall at the threshold of the arena, waiting for final touches on the environment reset. The tournament employee standing before her was a woman in her fifties whose shirt collar was flipped straight up, covering her neck.

While she waited, her belly churned. All those burritos she had eaten sat like bricks in her stomach. Perhaps it had not been the wisest decision to eat her body weight in eggs and starch right before a lot of strenuous activity. That green sauce had just been so *addictive,* though…

At last, she was allowed to enter the arena.

After the first round of any tournament, the audience now knew who you were, and sometimes you garnered a temporary fanbase. As she took to the battlefield, Niona was met with twice as many cheers as she had been two days earlier. Their shouts of affirmation warmed her, pumped her up.

For round two, the battlefield was a city block.

These were always Niona's least favorite environments, the super urban ones. How often did people actually battle Jekuas on city streets? What were they trying to emulate here? Distantly, she realized that maybe that was the point: to see an exciting Jekua fight in an uncommon locale. Still, she did not enjoy it. They were always full of obstacles that got in the way. That was the definition of an obstacle, she knew, but they weren't even the fun kind.

Just the annoying kind that served no other purpose but to be in the way. What was anyone going to do with a neon sign?

The Summoners were even more hidden from each other than they were with the hill setup. The street they'd be fighting on was L-shaped, with numerous narrow alleyways spiking off of the main street. From where she stood, Niona was looking at a few different alleys that would lead to the main street, which had to mean that Yakka's view was of the main thoroughfare. Neither of them would be able to see what the other summoned at first, and without Balt's cool ability to see through his Jekua's eyes, Niona would have to run through the city herself to battle proficiently.

That was the trouble with city battles, too: she couldn't just stand in place. These people were going to make her run around. And for what? The audience couldn't even see the battle as well! Most of them would have to watch the jumbotron!

The announcer announced them, and Niona readied herself.

The only thing she had to go on was that Yakka was maybe using a Suelu, so she might as well act on that intel. She'd hold back on Pops for now, and she didn't want to wait on Glom lethargically crawling to the main street.

Garbo could stomp a Suelu pretty easily, and the Nuri offered one other advantage too…

Niona channeled her mana toward Garbo's memory card, and soulclay poured out of her kayet onto the concrete in front of her. It rippled and shaped itself into

Garbo's form, with his shaggy white fur and long, glorious horns.

Then Niona hoisted herself onto the Nuri's back. It took more effort than she anticipated, which was humiliating, but she positioned herself on the Jekua and started making him trot forward.

The crowd surrounding her let out a collective gasp, followed by some excited screams. Was riding a Jekua really all that thrilling? Niona did not think so, but she kicked up Garbo's pace, hoping it would further entertain the masses. A Nuri had to be more interesting to watch than a Suelu, for sure. Spearing the little rodent would elicit quite a reaction.

Streetlights flickered above her head, the electrical buzzing filling her ears. It was a surreal feeling, being surrounded by streetlights and tall buildings and trash cans and parked cars while still being able to hear the roars of a stadium crowd. It created a strange dissonance within her. She tried to shake it off and continued trotting toward Yakka's Jekua.

When they neared the main street, Niona hopped off Garbo and walked alongside the Nuri. They stepped out onto the shorter street in the block's L-shape, approaching the corner to see what Yakka was working with. She hadn't heard any movement, so it was possible that whatever Jekua he'd summoned was small. Something like a Suelu wouldn't be heard over the crowd's din, and it could easily hide in the innumerable nooks and crannies the city block provided.

Garbo rounded the corner first, but Niona followed

right behind him. Her brick-filled stomach dropped when she saw Yakka's Jekua.

I definitely should not have eaten all those burritos, she immediately thought.

The reason she had not heard Yakka's Jekua moving wasn't because it was small. The reason was because it was standing still, and the thing was actually not small at all. In fact, it was very, very big.

The bastard had summoned a Bingst. It was a creature the size of a house, with a portly body and pointed face much like a raccoon. Bingsts were covered in pastel blue and pink fur, soft to the touch and radiating warmth. They had long, straight whiskers poking out from wet black snouts and sharp, skinny fangs. In spite of what their coloring might make a person think, they were Thermal-Types. Their tails were wide and flat and scaly, possibly to stamp out any accidental fires they set, given their limited mental capacity.

Yakka had summoned a giant, fire-breathing raccoon to terrorize this city block.

It was just standing there idly, waiting for her to show her face. It stood at the same height as the buildings on either side of it, a bakery and a comic book shop. The designers really put a lot of unnecessary detail into the environment.

The sight of the Jekua made Niona utter a swear word, and then she leapt into action.

Garbo charged forward, while Niona stayed hidden behind the convenience store on the corner. Yakka's Bingst began lobbing fireballs from its mouth, all of which Garbo nimbly dodged. As he grew closer to the Bingst,

Niona used his Elastic magic to rubberize and shorten his graceful legs, giving him the proportions of a pony, then immediately extended them again, springing him upward.

Her plan was to then extend his horns out to stab the Bingst's eyes, but the giant varmint swiped one of its enormous paws through the air to swat Garbo away.

The Nuri did somersaults as he tumbled through the air, smashing through a window. A huge chunk of her mana was instantly gone, just like that.

Shattered glass pierced Garbo's flesh, and he stood gazing out the window on wobbly legs. Niona had to duck him out of her line of sight to avoid more fireballs from the Bingst.

She could just barely make out the Nuri's outline in one of the still-intact windows. She bent his head forward and broke that unbroken window with his horns so that she could see him better, as well as grant her the opportunity to fire back at Yakka.

Garbo's horns crackled with electricity, preparing to fire a thunderbolt. That was not the Nuri's specialty—his Electrical powers were much more potent when making direct contact with the horns—but it would have to do in this case. They could manage long-range attacks, but those were not the most effective use of a Nuri.

A bolt of lightning shot out from Garbo's spiral horns, a loud *boom*! resounding through the stadium as electrical energy cut across the space between the two creatures. It connected with the Bingst's head, which was a pretty massive target and hard to miss.

Yakka, down by the Jekua's feet, looked a little rattled by the hit. A Jekua so large had to be immensely resilient, but still, a blast of electricity to the head had to cause some damage.

The man doubled down and his Jekua took a few beleaguering steps forward, the whole arena quaking with the beast's stomps. He swung another massive claw, effortlessly tearing through the building's shoddy construction. The top floor of the building was ripped off, crashing into the building next to it.

Before he could be swept up in the debris, Niona made Garbo leap out of the window. As he plummeted toward the earth, she made his body go rigid. The Nuri crashed into the street like a meteor, creating a small crater in the concrete. Using up some mana for that cost her less than it would've if the Nuri slammed into the ground and was seriously hurt.

Bits and pieces of building then rained down on Garbo. Glass, steel, iron, whatever the hell it was people constructed buildings with crashed all around the Nuri, and Niona had to make his body rigid again to increase his defense. Chunks of walls and shards of glass bounced right off his body, but each impact still siphoned a bit of mana from her reserves.

Garbo ran forward, away from the mess, charging up more electricity in his horns. She was going to ram into the Bingst's leg and send a jolt coursing through it.

But the Bingst swirled around before Garbo could reach it. She cursed herself for not increasing the length of his horns. The Bingst's flat, hard tail lifted and swiftly came down.

Niona knew that was what Yakka was planning as soon as the Bingst started to turn, though. She veered

Garbo out of the tail's trajectory, and it came down on the street with an earth-shaking shudder. There was a distinct tailprint on the ground when the Bingst lifted it back up and turned back around.

That hit would've knocked off at least a tenth of her mana, she wagered. Maybe even a quarter of it if Garbo's defense wasn't hardened at all.

Garbo had nearly reached the Bingst's leg now, but the creature's maw was opening as it turned around again. Embers flickered around its mouth, and then a stream of fire spewed forth.

She had to bail on her plan. *"Shit!"* she shouted from her position behind the convenience store. She dared not get any closer, seeing how much destruction was left in the Bingst's wake. This might not be a real city block, but she could really be hurt by a building falling on top of her.

Garbo stumbled out of the way, avoiding the stream of fire but tripping over his own legs in the last-second effort to run away. The Nuri fumbled forward, crashing into a food cart that was equipped with a fryer filled with mercifully cold oil. His white fur was drenched in the liquid, and it dripped off tangled strands as he stood.

The Nuri's lack of ranged attacks was killing her. Pops and Glom both had ranged abilities, but she doubted the Muggish's Thermal powers would do much good against the Bingst. Being a Hybrid, Pops cost her the most mana to summon, so she wanted to hold off on using him just yet if she could.

That only left Boombox. While Garbo was fairly fast, the Bruiserweight beat its speed easily. Not to mention the Bruiserweight's body required less mana to manipulate, too. Boombox possessed no ranged abilities at all, but she might be able to get close and scale the Bingst, then deliver some powerful blows.

It was worth a shot. Niona began funneling mana through her kayet to Boombox's memory card, and when it was full, she withdrew Garbo then primed the other card.

Soulclay shot out of her kayet. She summoned Boombox next to her, and together they ran around to the back of the convenience store.

In the alleyway, Niona spotted a ladder leading up to the store's roof. She and Boombox both climbed up, listening to Yakka's Bingst clambering down the street. It swiped at another building that was only a few down from the roof on which they stood.

Niona hurried to the edge of the building to watch the Bingst. Its pastel fur was illuminated by the multitude of neon signs hanging off every building lining the street. It was still a few buildings down, but that was no problem.

She remained on top of the convenience store, which was a much better vantage point than down on the ground. It would be hugely devastating if Yakka knocked the building over, though, so she stood tall, in plain view of him. He would be out of his mind to blatantly attack another Summoner.

Meanwhile, Boombox got a running start and leapt across the gap between the convenience store and the next roof. While she ran, she lessened the Bruiserweight's inherent friction, increasing her speed with every passing moment.

Niona did not have a solid plan, and that worried her.

It was not often she was worried during a Jekua battle, which made the worry turn to fear. But she had to keep fighting.

The Bingst was still slapping away at the buildings as it passed them by. Luckily it was not outright destroying them like it had that one building, but it was still causing a considerable ruckus. The ground shook with every step the Jekua took, and Niona hoped the convenience store had a relatively solid foundation.

Finally, Boombox and the Bingst came head to head, so to speak. Without missing a beat, Boombox surged forward and jumped off the roof of the building, flying toward the beast's furry face.

But again, Yakka swatted her Jekua away in mid-air.

Boombox flew all the way to the buildings at the end of the street, her thin frame as lightweight as a doll to the huge raccoon. Her back smacked into a streetlight before she quite reached the buildings, and it was enough to send a jolt of pain running down Niona's back, which was rare. Unfortunately for her, Boombox's defenses were nowhere near as robust as Garbo's.

While Boombox slid to the ground, Niona's mana plummeted in tandem, dipping below the halfway mark.

Summoning Boombox was obviously a huge mistake, and it had cost her dearly. Glom's Thermal attacks wouldn't put a dent in the Bingst, and the Muggish was far too slow even with his Speed mods to avoid any of its crushing blows. That tail would squash him in an instant.

She had to pull out Pops. She had no other choice.

Clearly, that was what she should've done from the start, but oh well. Onward and upward.

The Bingst breathed a torrent of fire up the street, but Niona withdrew Boombox just before it reached her. The oil that Garbo had spilled caught fire, sending smoke drifting up through the stadium's open ceiling to mix with the clouds above. There was also a magazine stand that burst into flame near the entryway of the convenience store.

A mighty roar loosed from the Bingst's lips and it stomped its feet a few times, sending some loose pieces of building crumbling to the ground to break apart.

Show-off, Niona thought bitterly. She couldn't let this stupid animal beat her.

She didn't know whether that was referring to the Bingst or to Yakka, but either one worked.

The city street was covered in debris and fire from the havoc that Yakka's Bingst wreaked. Even at this distance, Niona could feel the heat emanating from the Thermal Jekua's fur. It was uncomfortable, and it made her skin slick with sweat.

Then she summoned Pops, before any officials could think she was throwing in the towel. The bizarre little creature stood by her side on the convenience store roof, his fuzzy yellow fur peeking out from his hard, black carapace. He stood on his six spidery legs, waiting for her to do something.

She thought for a second about what to do. There had to be some way for her tiny little bug-rodent to bring down Yakka's towering beast.

The guy was undoubtedly draining mana at an exponential rate. Something as big as a Bingst put a huge strain on a Summoner's mana, and he'd been breathing fire and punching buildings every chance he got. The pointless displays of bravado would be chipping away at his reserves, too. Niona remembered Balt's story about how he'd even been pushed to soulsickness just using a Suelu, so no doubt he would be hitting his limits soon with this thing. She would be surprised if he wasn't running as low as she was.

She could wait him out, or she could deliver one huge push to send him over the edge.

The former was easier, but the latter was possibly less risky, in a roundabout way. She could try waiting him out, but her own mana was so low and Pops was so small, just one stray hit from the Bingst might take her out. Trying to avoid attacks rather than being on the offensive might not be the smart play.

She leaned over the edge of the building and surveyed the area again. The Bingst's body was so wide it took up the entire street, its shoulders nearly brushing against the buildings on both sides. It had caused damage to a lot of those buildings, but it had only toppled that one still, and only partially at that. The rest stood intact, albeit worse for wear.

Every storefront was designated with a neon sign. Niona did not know why, since it was fairly unrealistic; perhaps it was merely so that the audience could see those details more clearly from far away.

She couldn't help but chuckle to herself. She was about to demonstrate what someone might do with a neon sign.

First things first, she emitted a shrill shriek from Pops's mouth. The cacophony of sound reverberated throughout the arena, sounding as if there were dozens of Toolus running all over the place.

Yakka blinked wearily down on the ground, disoriented by Pops's Sonic distraction. The ability was inflicted on his Jekua, but it coursed through his soulclay and back to him, confusing him as well. He could not easily discern where exactly her Jekua was.

As soon as she could see the confusion on his face, Pops scampered along the edge of the building. He passed over the store's neon sign, and Niona charged it up with some of his Electrical energy. Not too much, but enough that the sign shone brighter and its electrical buzz grew louder.

Then Pops jumped from one roof to the next. It was a closer call than when Boombox did it, but she could latch onto the side of the building with Pops's claws and clamber up. He continued skittering along the edge, and he charged the sign hanging off the side of that building as well.

She continued this along the entire row of buildings while the symphony of Toolu screeches echoed throughout the city block. Soon they died out, and Yakka's dizziness wore off.

By that time, though, Pops was running along the buildings behind him. He looked around the street, past the flickering flames and around his massive Jekua's furry form, but he could not find Pops anywhere. Niona grinned.

Pops let out another Sonic-enhanced shriek, and Yakka pressed his hands to his ears in irritation. His Bingst did the same thing, and Niona did not know if it was intentional or simply instinctive, but either way she was glad to see him waste mana with the action.

Regardless of whether he could see Pops or not, Yakka decided he needed to strike. The Bingst's arms fell back down to its sides and the creature spewed fire at the base of the buildings, filling up each and every alleyway with walls of flame.

Meanwhile, Pops was high above the fire, sending electrical energy into every neon sign that he passed. With the extra light that his Bingst's flames were providing, Yakka seemed to not notice the signs brightening one by one. His obliviousness pleased Niona.

She stopped at the sign that was closest to the Bingst. Her plan didn't require the signs beyond it, and she was losing enough mana as it was.

This next part would be tricky, and she was down to less than a quarter of her mana, so she was worried about overexerting herself. She was self-aware enough to withdraw when she got too close to empty, though; she wouldn't let herself get soulsick.

Pops stood on the building directly across the street from her. She steeled herself, knowing that this move would drain most of her remaining mana. This was her one shot.

Please let this work, she begged.

Pops charged forward and jumped off the roof.

He soared past the Bingst's head. Yakka was still too distracted by the chorus of fake Toolus screaming, so he did not swat away at her Jekua like he did all the others.

When Pops reached the center of the street, in the middle of the two neon signs on either building, Niona sent out a powerful electrical shockwave from the Toolu's body.

She had practiced this move countless times with Pops when he was still just a Suelu, and now that he'd been Hybridized it was even stronger. Its area of effect extended outward to both signs, as well as the two signs on the next buildings over. That of course meant that it enveloped the Bingst's head, too.

Electricity surged through the Bingst's head and simultaneously overcharged the four neon signs her shockwave touched. The signs burst apart, and given the Bingst's proximity to them, it did not go unharmed.

Fire, electrical energy, and glass shards exploded onto the Bingst from either side. Its fur caught fire and the multiple shocks of electricity coursed through its body, while glass pierced its skin and its eyes and its lashing tongue.

It breathed fire as it stumbled backward, flailing about and spraying blood from its face. As it staggered backward, the extra magical electrical energy given off from the explosions as well as the Bingst's natural heat reacted with the next set of supercharged signs, which proceeded to explode just like the first ones.

A chain reaction went off, with the Bingst stumbling down the street in sync with the exploding signs, being assaulted with fire and electricity and glass over and over again.

Yakka screamed in anguish as his behemoth toppled, crashing onto its back with a resounding quake. The Bingst then lit up in rich blue soulclay and swam through the air back to the Summoner's kayet.

Niona's eyes widened, watching Yakka drop to his knees as he let out another piercing scream. He leaned over, retching, then coughed up a sticky black substance.

The combination of the mana used to summon the Bingst along with her chain reaction attack had fully depleted his mana. He was soulsick, just like he apparently was during that Tanepke tournament.

Pops stood in the middle of the decimated street, until Niona withdrew her trusty Toolu.

Medics streamed onto the street from the narrow alleyways, rushing in on Yakka's location.

Niona stood on the convenience store roof, reveling in the crowd's booming cheers.

26

FLOOR PEOPLE

THE DIWEPTI ROOM WAS EMPTY WHEN NIONA RETURNED to it after her match. All the other Summoners must have still been hanging out in the dugout, awaiting the next battle.

She was absolutely exhausted. She needed to lean on something. She yearned for it. The backless bench was not going to cut it.

A set of lockers would do. She pressed her back against her locker and slid down to the ground, which she hoped had been cleaned recently. She made a mental note to do some laundry at the hotel tonight anyway.

She checked her mana levels while she sat leaning against the locker's cold surface. Pops's shockwave gambit had brought her down to around a tenth of her mana.

That was way too close for comfort.

She had wasted too much time trying to take down that Bingst with her other Jekuas when she should have believed in her boy Pops all along.

But it was fine. In the end, she had won. That was what mattered.

To put a bow on that fact, she glanced up at the electronic bracket hanging up on the wall. She smiled, seeing her name lit up in green with Yakka Dho's name in blood red just below it. By now, he had to be tucked away in an infirmary somewhere in the labyrinthine stadium. Niona did not plan on ever finding out where it was located.

"Hello?"

Niona looked to the doorway. The voice was unfamiliar. She hadn't even heard the door open.

"Hi?" Niona called back.

A tall, black-skinned woman with a short afro came around the corner and smiled when she spotted Niona on the floor. "Hello," she said again, her voice low and calming.

"Hi," Niona repeated, unsure if this was going to be the extent of their conversation.

The woman approached her, reaching a hand out. "My name is Vanessa Ren," she said, never breaking that smile. She was wearing a blue, striped suit that looked crisper than anything any of these Summoners had ever worn.

Niona grabbed her hand and shook. Vanessa's palm was extremely cold, in stark contrast to Niona's which felt like it was dripping with sweat. She hoped that was an exaggeration in her mind and that Vanessa's hand wouldn't come away wet. She didn't know who this woman was, but from the air about her, she seemed important.

"I'll get right to the point," Vanessa said.

Something an important person would say, Niona noted.

"Ms. Daneo, I work for a talent agency called Atoll Talent. I'm not sure if you've heard of us, but we represent Summoners such as Nona Tonomos, Brian Deerheart, and Kalika Lowa. Our main office is on Kou Tekkis, but we check out tournaments all over the islands, as well as occasionally scoping out ones in Hurrathsa and Tollush. I'm a scout for the agency."

Niona nodded. "I've heard of Atoll," she said. She had only distantly heard about the agency; she didn't really know any details, but she'd heard the name before, and the three Summoners that Vanessa mentioned were all pretty famous.

Her heart suddenly beat faster. Why was a talent scout talking to her? There was only one reason for a talent scout to talk to a Summoner at a tournament, right? Surely she wasn't just asking where the bathroom was.

Vanessa smiled again. Her teeth were the whitest teeth Niona had ever laid eyes on. It was almost unnatural. She said, "I saw both your matches so far. If I'm being honest, I really thought that Bingst had you there."

"You and me both." Niona refrained from mentioning just how low her mana was at that precise moment.

That comment garnered a light chuckle. "I like your style, Ms. Daneo. I really do."

"You can call me Niona," she interrupted.

Vanessa nodded. "I think you're a great Summoner, Niona. You're clever, you're highly adaptable, and you've shown great range with your selection of Jekuas. Those are all qualities we look for in our Summoners over at Atoll."

Niona smiled. This woman was definitely not looking for the bathroom.

"I want to be completely honest with you, though. I don't have an offer for you right now. I simply wanted to introduce myself to you." That deflated Niona a bit, but she nodded, and Vanessa continued. "But that isn't to say I'm not very interested in what you have to offer. I'm going to keep an eye on the rest of your matches, and if all goes well, we might be having another conversation here in a few days." She once more offered her abnormally bright smile.

"Well, I'm certainly happy to meet you," Niona said warmly. She tried not to reveal how out of breath she was.

"The feeling is mutual," said Vanessa.

Another thing someone important would say. If it were Niona, she would've just grunted *"Same!"*

"I'll get out of your hair for now," Vanessa said. "Get yourself some rest. You deserve it after that whole ordeal."

"Thanks, Ms. Ren."

"You can call me Vanessa. First-name basis feels right, right?"

Niona nodded. "You got it, Vanessa. Thanks for stoppin' by. I hope we'll talk again soon."

"Me too."

With that, Vanessa glided out the door as quietly as she had entered, leaving Niona alone.

Her heart fluttered thinking about all the possibilities signing to an agency would present. Having an agent meant she could more easily get into better, higher-paying tournaments, which the agency would be paying for anyway (as well as any travel expenses). Agents were also key in securing endorsement deals with brands, which was how a lot of Summoners earned a great deal of their money. And the better she did in tournaments, the more those sponsorships would pay out.

This was the logical next step she needed to take in her career as a Summoner. With an agency backing her, her name would be in front of a lot more eyes, both inside and outside actual competitions. She would also finally start earning money consistently rather than only from the sporadic tournaments she was able to enter.

It wasn't that she couldn't afford to get herself to Hurrathsa for a tournament, or that she couldn't pay entry fees, but that was still all with her father's money. She didn't want him paying for every part of her life forever. She wanted to build her career off her own worth, not his wallet.

If she was picked up by Atoll Talent, that could be the first real step toward financial independence from her father. She deeply appreciated all the help he'd given her over the years, but she wanted to make it on her own. She didn't want to be indebted to him anymore. Metaphorically speaking, anyway; it was not as if he expected her to pay him back for anything.

Everything was riding on these next few matches now. She'd already wanted to win, of course, but now the stakes were much higher. If she could make it to the finals, or even somehow miraculously win the whole thing…

She sat there, imagining herself as a real, agented

Summoner. She would *kill* for a Thunderjolt endorsement deal. Her chest swelled with excitement.

Only then did it dawn on her that she'd spent that entire interaction sitting on the floor of a locker room like a freak.

"You moron…" she muttered to herself.

A minute later, she heard the door slowly creak open. Then came an apprehensive call: "…hello?"

It was Balt. Niona said back to him, "What are you doing? Come in here."

She heard the door open more, followed by slow, cautious footsteps. Finally, Balt appeared around the corner. His face was tensed, but he visibly relaxed when he saw her.

"What is wrong with you?" she asked. "Why are you being weird?"

"The last time I came to see you in here, you screamed and scared the shit out of me."

"Oh. Fair enough." She laughed.

He walked over to the bench in front of her and sat down. "You're a floor person now?" he said.

"Yes."

"Okay. Hey, that match was amazing. My view of your Jekuas wasn't really the best for most of it, but I could definitely see that Bingst walloping the city. How'd you take it down, exactly?"

The dugout did not provide a great view of the city block's main street, so it checked out that he wasn't sure how she'd won. She explained to him the maneuvers she'd pulled off with Pops, and he grinned like a little kid the whole time.

"That is awesome," he said when she finished. "Good use of the environment. Yakka clearly is not the type of person to make use of his environment with magic and stuff."

"Nah, he's more of the brute force type," she agreed.

They clowned on Yakka for a few more minutes, before their attention turned to the television screen broadcasting the matches. The stadium crew was still cleaning up the Bingst's extraordinary mess, and they probably would be for a while yet.

Niona nodded at the screen and said, "Wanna just watch from here?" It seemed like with the stadium's aerial camera crew, they'd get a much better look at the following matches there than in the dugout.

"Yeah, sure," Balt said.

She was glad he was fine with it, because she was way too tired to get up and trudge back to the dugout. The high energy of all the other Summoners around her would likely drain her completely.

"Can you do me a favor?" she asked him.

"Sure," he said.

"Could you grab me a Thunderjolt?" She was craving the energy boost as well as its sugary sweetness.

Balt nodded. "I'm gonna get you a grape one, though."

"Don't you dare."

"Can't stop me. You're a floor person now. There's nothing you can do."

She grabbed for one of his ankles, but he hopped out of the way, leaving her to snatch nothing but empty air.

"If you get me a grape one," she warned him, "I'm

gonna do to you what I did to that Bingst, whether you're a Vana or not."

"I ain't scared of you."

"Yes you are."

He laughed, then left to fetch her drink. He returned a couple minutes later with a blueberry Thunderjolt and a paper tray of mekki for them to share. The sugar rush was going to do her a lot of good. She thanked him and accepted the drink.

Balt joined her on the floor, banging his back into his locker before sliding down and landing with a hard thump on his ass. "Jeez," he muttered, placing the container of mekki between them. They were both floor people now. She bit into one of the crunchy little balls of fried dough and moaned delightedly.

The next match was starting soon. They both stared up at the screen, munching on their mekki. The tray would be empty before the match even began, at the rate they were going. Unfortunately, neither of them possessed the self-control to stop eating until then.

Niona raised her eyebrows and pointed at the screen as the first Summoner marched out into the arena. "Doug!" she said excitedly, jabbing her finger toward the screen.

"Hmm?"

"It's Doug!" she said. "The guy I battled who sucked eggs and had the Sunkin."

Balt glanced at the bracket, then burst out laughing. "His name isn't Doug," he said.

"Huh?" she mumbled, turning from the screen to check the guy's name.

According to the bracket, he was going up against Olli Berrap, who was going to obliterate him. And, according to the bracket, his name was indeed not Doug. It was Fennerick D'yel.

"Damn," she said. "I was *way* off."

"His last name's got a D in it, at least," Balt said. "None of the other letters, though, and of course he never told you his last name, but hey. You got that D right."

They watched as Olli proceeded to decimate every single one of Fennerick's Jekuas. The man tried the same trick on them that he'd failed to beat Niona with, which was using his mediocre Sunkin to blast away their team with sunbeams.

Thankfully, Olli was already represented by Black Shore Talent, Niona knew. Otherwise, she would be worried about Vanessa extending an offer to them instead of her.

"Oh," she said, "almost forgot to mention. A talent scout talked to me."

"Wait, what? How could you forget to mention that!"

"I was thirsty."

"What happened? What'd they say? Do you have an agent now?" He sprayed sugar dust out of his mouth with every syllable.

"Nah, nothin' big to report yet. Just said that she dug my style and is gonna keep an eye on me. If I do well in the rest of the tournament, Atoll Talent might sign me."

"Damn! They've got Kalika Lowa, Nona Tonomos, Zantara Wei...I think Rika Yonomi was with them too, until Bill White convinced her to move to Black Shore. It was Atoll who pushed her name hard and got her where she is now, though. They could do great things for you over there."

Niona nodded. "I'm excited about it. Tryin' not to get my hopes up too high, though. We'll see what happens."

As expected, it did not take long for Olli Berrap to send Fennerick D'yel packing. While she watched him amble off the field, head held low, Niona couldn't help but still feel that *Doug* was a much more fitting name for the guy.

Balt huffed out a laugh and pointed at the bracket with a sugar-coated fingertip. "How did I not notice that before?" he said. "There's some dude competing name Johnny Fierce."

"Oh, yeah," Niona giggled. That name had made her laugh when she'd first read it, too.

"That can't be his real name, right?" Balt said. "That has to be a pseudonym or something. Or do you think his KIN is literally registered to, like, *Jonathan Fierce*?"

That made her laugh. She nodded at the bracket and said, "Maybe you'll get a chance to ask him yourself. Looks like if he beats..." She paused, struggling to pronounce the person's name. "...Fola'h Notor'eh, and you win your match too, you'll be up against each other in round three."

"Oh, jeez," Balt groaned. "Am I really gonna have to fight someone named *John Fierce*?"

"*Johnny*," Niona corrected him. "And don't get ahead of yourself. Worry about Zu Jerat first."

They watched the rest of the battles preceding Balt's from their position on the floor.

After Olli and Doug came the guy Balt said he knew,

Kallon, up against Kentaro Kao. Kallon ended up winning and moving on to round three, but it was a close match.

Niona rooted for Andy Lowe when he came up against a woman named Nakira Mun. She'd given Fifine Marc a good pounding in the first round, but Niona believed in her buddy Andy, and he came through with a swift victory. When Niona checked the bracket after his match, she saw that it was possible his third round opponent would be Desi Taewao, which concerned her. Desi had a pretty strong reputation, if Balt was to be believed.

The battle after that was pretty spectacular. It was between Hana Minir and Ti Kiro, and they both sent out Uruds to fight each other. Ti Kiro actually appeared to possess the same ability as Balt, not needing to enter the city to observe the battle; presumably he was seeing it through his Urud's eyes. The giant beasts tore apart the city street with their powerful Gravity magic, until Hana swapped hers out with a Slopape and put an end to Ti. The guy threw an unholy fit as he was ushered off the battlefield, which made Niona and Balt cackle.

The final match before Balt's involved someone named Mair Lambt, who was going up against a man who Niona recognized. She learned from the bracket that his name was Grant Deere, and he was the old, roughhewn man she'd seen training in the gym when they first arrived in Makanuele. The guy who had been impressively swinging his Whirlcruel up on the ceiling handlebars. She wanted him to win, solely based on the fact that she had seen him before.

If she had put money down on the match, she would've hit it big. Grant's Whirlcruel (along with his Harkmare) tore apart Mair's measly flock of birds. Niona clapped giddily as he was declared the winner.

In round three, Grant would be going toe to toe against David Woollis, who was a commendable opponent. Anyone who made it to round three had to be pretty skilled, really.

And then it was time for Balt to head out to the arena while the city was reset again. He stood up off the floor, wiping the mekki's sugar off his hands with his pants. It rained down onto the locker room floor. If it was still there tomorrow, Niona would know for sure how frequently those floors got cleaned.

"You good?" she asked him, still sitting on the ground and looking up at him.

He shrugged. "I dunno," he replied honestly.

"Know what you're gonna do?"

"I know what I'm gonna *try* to do," he said.

She grinned. "That's the most any of us can do, I guess. Good luck out there. I'll be cheerin' you on from in here, if that's alright."

He thanked her, then headed out to the battlefield.

Niona's eyes were eagerly glued to the television screen.

27

BALT VS. ZU

WATCHING THE OTHER MATCHES HAD GIVEN BALT A FEW ideas about how to handle Zu Jerat. The city block environment offered plenty of places for his smaller Jekuas like Dipper or the Tottaworm to hide, thereby potentially avoiding any blinding Radiant magic from Zu.

Another advantage he had was his perspective-shifting technique. That meant he could stay far from the pageantry, away from danger, but also away from Zu's blinding spell with the Conuto. Whoever he sent in would still be vulnerable to the Whissler's weird black dome ability, but at least that was the only thing Balt would need to worry about.

Staying out of the way would be his best bet, he figured. He would send out Dipper first. His Puffolin was strong; perhaps she could whittle Zu's mana down enough to finish him off. He only wanted to use Pistachio's peculiar scent sights as a last resort. Yesterday he had gotten a decent handle on them, but he still kind of felt like a toddler learning how to walk. He might be able to make do, but he didn't fully trust himself not to screw up.

Balt stood at the edge of the fake city block, trying to build his confidence. His starting position was at the end of the main street, where Niona's opponent had stood for the duration of their fight. The crowd was partially obscured by the towering buildings, which helped. Their presence filled him with more dread than he'd been anticipating. That was still something he needed to get used to.

He took a deep breath and began channeling mana into his kayet, clicking the button for Dipper's L1 memory card while the announcer's voice rumbled in his chest. Then, finally, the droning died down and all that was left was the din of the crowd and the pounding of his heart in his ears.

The match began.

His soulclay poured from the kayet as he dashed to the right, shoving past a glass door and retreating into a comic book shop. He ducked behind a shelf filled with gay romance graphic novels. He glanced around for a second and saw that every shelf in the store was filled with books, and every glass display case was crammed with figurines. He wondered why the designers had gone through such extraordinary efforts to genuinely stock this store with products. There were even t-shirts hanging from the walls with the fake store's logo on them.

Dipper stood out on the street, standing on all fours with her pink and purple flowers blooming on her back. Balt realized he was being an idiot watching her through the window and ran to the very back of the store, as far from the street as possible. He hurried behind the cash register, and then a thought occurred to him. He popped it open, and there was indeed about thirty dollars inside. Would it be insane to take it? Was that unethical? Was it even real money or was it fake? It wasn't like the books were fake books, they were real books brought in to the set…

He pocketed the money. Just in case.

Then he crouched down below the open register and shifted his gaze into Dipper's.

Ahead of her, the city street was devoid of activity. Again, Balt felt like a fool, wasting mana having her summoned while he waited for Zu and his Jekua to show their faces.

He might as well make good use of the time. By his estimation, he had probably half a minute before they wound their way through the alleys and onto the main street. Probably less than that, in actuality, but it was enough for him to work with.

Dipper ran forward, racing toward the end of the street where there was a sharp turn. There were a number of alleyways that emptied out onto the street, and there was no way of knowing from which Zu and his creature would emerge.

Balt moved the Puffolin over to the first alley and shot off a Petal Shower in all directions. The razorblade flower petals fired at the buildings on either side of the narrow alley, shattering their windows. Dipper hopped backward, out of harm's way, as shards of broken glass littered the walkway.

He then proceeded to do the same thing on the next

three alleys before deciding that was all he had time for, pulling Dipper back down the main street. Hopefully Zu would choose one of those paths and his Jekua would be damaged running across the broken glass.

For a second, he considered doing the same thing on the main street, creating even more hazards for Zu's Jekuas. He probably would be able to avoid the glass just fine in his own Jekua's perspective, but it could easily turn disastrous if Zu blinded him. And, in all honesty, that *if* was almost certainly more of a *when*.

He heard something. A shuffling down one of the alleys. It sounded like it came from one of the ones he'd booby-trapped, too.

It was stupid to stand there out in the open, just waiting for his attacker to show up. Dipper ran to the side, hiding behind a food cart. Balt wished he could attain a higher vantage point, but Puffolins weren't exactly built for climbing.

He could still see the alleys from where Dipper hid, but even so, he almost didn't spot Zu's Jekua.

It was one he hadn't seen the guy use a couple days earlier: a Muntoo. Balt had to admit he was not expecting to see something like that here, a Jekua that was typically only found on Yuluhu.

A Muntoo was basically like a shadow Juntoo. It took the same shape as the monkey, but its body was entirely black with piercing yellow eyes and no other facial features. It didn't have fur, exactly; whatever it was made of seemed inky and unnatural. There were rumors (mostly perpetuated by edgy teenagers) that Muntoos were the spirits of dead Juntoos, ones that were corrupted and trapped on this plane of existence. The more likely explanation was that they used to be regular Juntoos that were infected by the disease that spread on the island and had evolved to be this way.

"This way" meaning incredibly unnerving to look at. Balt had never seen one in person before, nor were they detailed in his bestiary. He'd only read about them online.

The Muntoo barreled forward, scraping its knuckles and feet on the scattered glass in its path. The Jekua screeched and fell forward, while Zu stopped a few feet back, wincing in pain. He managed to get the Muntoo up again and out onto the street, while he carefully navigated around the mess.

It probably hadn't done a huge amount of damage, but some was better than none. And it probably hurt the Muntoo more than it would've the Conuto or the Whissler. A positive result, all in all.

Zu and his Muntoo both glanced around, seeking out either Balt or his Jekua. The two of them stood befuddled in the street, the Muntoo's strange black flesh forming small puddles at its feet.

From behind the food cart, Balt fired another Petal Shower at the Muntoo. Petals zoomed across the battlefield, slicing the Muntoo's face and arms. The monkey jumped up and down before running to the opposite side of the street, where it was sucked up into the shadow of a building.

It was using the same technique that Wasaaru's Eclipse Jackal had used, the move Balt had dubbed the Shudderstep. There were countless shadows all over the street, so there was no telling where it would crop up next.

Including right behind Dipper. Balt ran forward out of the cart's shadow, onto the street that was mostly illuminated by streetlights and sun. The Puffolin was somewhat more vulnerable out in the open, but at least she was away from any shadows, so theoretically he'd be able to see the Muntoo coming.

Only he saw it coming too late to dodge. When he looked up and to the left, the Muntoo was flying through the air toward Dipper. It must have jumped out of a shadow higher up on the building somewhere.

Balt curled Dipper up into a ball and hardened her petals. The Muntoo's claw swipe glanced off her back without leaving a scratch, and Balt quickly unfurled to whip the Jekua with a vine.

But the Muntoo grabbed Dipper's vine as it lashed out and yanked hard, sending Dipper tumbling forward. The world went upside down in Balt's vision as Dipper was thrown onto her back, and he started kicking her legs to right her.

The Muntoo grabbed one of her legs, and its hands were oddly warm. It leaned down and bit her on the leg, its fangs tearing her flesh, sending blood dribbling down her leg. At the same time, Balt's vision went dark.

Of course the Muntoo possessed some kind of ability to blind its opponent. All of Zu's Jekuas did.

Despite being unable to see, Balt flipped Dipper back over and shot off another Petal Shower. He didn't need to see anything to aim the attack. Flowers exploded out from Dipper's body, and although he couldn't see it happen, he knew that a fair amount of them had to hit the Muntoo given its proximity to her.

That wasn't a reliable strategy, though. While Dipper was still on the field, he started channeling mana into Milton's card.

Before he could do anything else, he felt another swipe of the creature's claws, which ripped through some of the petals on Dipper's back. Over in the comic shop, Balt's back coursed with a sharp heat. Then it happened again, and then one more time.

He did one more Petal Shower before withdrawing Dipper. His soulclay floated through the street, into the comic shop, and he quickly summoned Milton. As soon as he did, he shifted into the Jekua's perspective.

The Mirrorbear trundled through the comic store's front door. It was a tight fit, but it caused less damage than bursting through the large glass window would have. That would've been a lot cooler and more dramatic, but Balt opted to prioritize maintaining his mana in this particular instance. Hearing the crowd's reaction probably would've been fun, though.

Zu's Muntoo swiveled around to face Milton. It paradoxically let out a high-pitched screech from its mouthless face, then swung both its claws, one at a time.

A half-circle of dark, shadowy energy flew from each of the creature's arms. They were like boomerangs slicing through the air toward Milton.

One came after the other in quick succession. The first struck Milton in the left shoulder, then the second was nullified by his Barrier. Balt was glad to find that the first hit hadn't really caused much damage anyway.

The Muntoo performed the move again. This time, Balt readied the Mirrorbear's absorption ability. He was too slow to absorb the first hit, which drained another small piece of his mana, but he could feel the creature's dark Radiant magic running through Milton's body with the second one.

He didn't know what to do with it now, though. And he was also suddenly aware that Zu knew his position, having seen his soulclay return to his kayet. That left him open to a blinding from the man's Conuto.

That was a problem for later. He charged forward with Milton, but quickly veered to the left. He didn't want to risk another blinding bite from the shadow monkey.

Instead, he headbutted a car that was parked on the side of the road. It set off an incredible pounding in both his own head as well as Milton's, and it did not even have the desired effect. The Mirrorbear was strong enough for the force to send the car moving a few feet, but it was not flung wildly through the air to crash atop the Muntoo like he'd planned.

So now he had a headache, lost some mana from the impact damage, and everyone thought he was a moron. *Excellent work, dipshit,* he scolded himself.

Milton stood up on his hind legs woozily. He was about to fall over from the dizziness, and his vision was slightly blurred. When he blinked it back into focus, he didn't see the Muntoo anywhere. It must have slipped back into the shadows.

When he shot a look over at Zu, though, he spotted the remnants of his soulclay returning to his kayet.

More began to pour out onto the sidewalk a second later, conveniently taking shape underneath a massive neon sign for a boutique hotel that read RENUE.

Balt watched through Milton's eyes, waiting until the other man's soulclay started to take a recognizable form. After a moment, he could tell it was going to be the Conuto. Its six wiry legs were starting to extend out from its torso.

A few seconds before the soulclay would fade into the Jekua's natural coloring, Balt swiped Milton's claws in the direction of the hotel sign. Two curved shadows cut through the air, each one smashing into the sign with intense force.

It came undone from the side of the building, its yellow and blue lights flickering out, then it plummeted to the ground just as Zu's Conuto was fully formed.

The sign splatted the bug in an instant.

Zu let out a howl of anger at the decimation of his Jekua. Its brittle exoskeleton couldn't stand up to the sign's weight. The bug's shell cracked and split, all six of its legs snapping. Blood and guts and other viscera oozed out from breaches in the shell.

The audience completely lost their minds. Screams filled the arena, both of terror and of excitement. Balt laughed to himself, still hidden behind the cash register in the comic book shop.

Zu had no choice but to immediately withdraw the Conuto. It was as good as dead, there was no coming back from that. With the extreme amount of damage done to the Jekua, it had to have depleted an enormous amount of the guy's mana, too. A blow like that could completely wipe out a lesser Summoner. Hell, it might have even pushed Balt into soulsickness if it happened to him.

But Zu evidently had ample mana left in the tank to

continue the battle. His lip curled into a snarl as his soulclay went back into the kayet on his wrist.

Balt knew that Zu was too clever to fall for the same trap twice. Whatever he summoned next, he would make damn sure that it was not beneath a giant falling hazard.

It was also plain to see on the man's face that Zu was growing aggravated with how the battle was proceeding. Balt wasn't succumbing to his tactics as easily as Ima Daugherty had. He probably expected every round of this tournament to be relatively breezy.

If Balt was going down, it was not going to be easily.

Zu's soulclay was taking on the form of his Whissler. It was easy to tell, considering the substance was floating in mid-air but taking on a humanoid shape. Soon the big, nasty wings would sprout from its back.

Balt had seen Zu's other Jekua during his first match, and it was just a Gujjy and Coaltoad Hybrid. Not a super useful Jekua, all things considered; kind of a throwaway. A surprising pick for a tournament, honestly.

But that meant that the Whissler was his heaviest hitter, now that the Conuto was out of commission. Zu was wanting to finish him off.

Balt's mana levels were looking pretty solid, though, even after the hits Milton and Dipper had both taken. He was feeling better about his chances now than he did at the start of the battle.

A *little* better, anyway.

He was still scared of that Whissler and its intimidating black dome.

Was that something Milton could absorb, rendering it useless? Could he turn it back on Zu?

He found out very quickly that the answer was no. The Whissler roared, and he braced Milton to absorb the ability. But it didn't matter, because whether it wasn't possible or because Balt timed it wrong, Milton was enveloped in the dome's unrelenting blackness. From his position in the store, he couldn't even tell how much of an area the dome covered.

Balt blinked Milton's pearly blue eyes, but his vision was totally shot. He returned to himself back in the comic store and muttered, "Dammit." He really hated Zu's tricks.

They were undeniably effective, though. And clever. But that was precisely why he hated them.

It was time to bust out a trick of his own, assuming he could pull it off. He withdrew Milton then primed Pistachio's memory card, pushing mana into his kayet. A few seconds later, the Mosstopus was standing before him.

Looking at the size of the beast, he knew that Pistachio was not going to fit through the door. He would have to make that dramatic exit from the shop.

But Zu wasn't even going to give him the chance. The front window suddenly burst in a shower of glass, which all thankfully clattered to the floor without striking Pistachio or Balt himself. The gay romance shelf was ripped to shreds, and Balt was silently thankful he'd had the foresight to move earlier.

The Whissler flapped its thick wings right outside the broken window, its fangs bared and its muscles flexed. It unleashed another shrill shriek, its fur blazing bright.

Then all Balt knew was darkness.

It wasn't a darkness like being in a dark room at night, something that his vision could progressively adjust to.

Somehow, it was darker than that. It was as if all the world was blackness, like no light or color or anything at all existed. He was in a black void, completely and utterly helpless.

He truly loathed Zu's tricks.

"Shit, shit, shit," he mumbled, pressing his back against the counter. He pulled his knees to his chest, his breaths staccato. He'd only injure himself if he tried to blindly retreat through the destroyed comic store. His heart raced, and he could feel himself starting to panic with every beat of the Whissler's wings.

He was hoping he wouldn't have to do this so soon, but he had no choice now. Even if he withdrew Pistachio and summoned the Tottaworm, they'd still be stuck in the enormous black dome, rendered blind by the Whissler's Radiant magic.

Well, here goes nothing, he thought wearily.

Balt shifted into Pistachio's perspective, taking care to keep his giant maw closed.

Thankfully, when he flicked his tongue out, he saw all the bizarre streaks of color and stuff like he'd seen in the gym. Part of him was irrationally worried that the dark dome would somehow nullify this effect too, even though it was based on scent.

He knew from experience that he couldn't last very long in Pistachio's head. He'd grown slightly accustomed to the way the Mosstopus processed the world, but it still made him nauseous after a few minutes. He needed to bring down Zu before that happened.

Pistachio's tongue shot out of his mouth again, filling the purple void with bands of color. There was only faint red above, and in front of him he could see a floating orange mass, which he assumed to be the Whissler. The rest of his vision was mottled with yellows and greens and a hint of blue. He'd ascertained that, generally speaking, those cooler colors signified inanimate objects. The shelves, flooring, the door, and so on. He was not adept enough to tell any of them apart, necessarily, but it was enough for him to form a decent mental map of the area. Orange was usually something giving off a lot of heat and body odor, so usually it was either a human or a Jekua. Again, there were most likely a ton of subtleties that were lost on him, but he had learned enough to get by.

The Mosstopus surged forward. He moved out of the way of the big green rectangles that he assumed to be shelves, heading for the open window. He bumped into a few things along the way, and he stupidly forgot about all the glass on the floor. It tore into Pistachio's tentacles, but nothing stuck, and it didn't suck away at his mana too much. Still, he should have been smarter, so the mistake grated on him.

The orange Whissler blob floated upward out of his way as he tripped over the window's frame and out onto the street. The colors were beginning to fade, so he flicked his tongue out again and was met with a rainbow of streaks. A quick flick was sufficient to pick up on enough detail for him to navigate. There was a ton of blue and green now, along with dabs of red all in a straight line on either side of the street. Red had to indicate light, somehow, and those were the streetlights. The colors faded farther down the street, but his senses could pick up a pretty huge range.

He looked up and saw the Whissler hovering above him. Suddenly a black streak burst out from the orange. Balt had no clue what it was, but he moved Pistachio out of the way and it exploded on the ground. Whatever it was, it radiated cold.

Pistachio's mouth opened wide, and Balt could feel phlegm traveling up his own esophagus. Mottled streaks filled his vision while the Mosstopus's mouth was open, sending a jabbing pain into his head.

He fired the slimeball he'd been building up, and it splashed into the Whissler. It was knocked backward, into the building, leaving a dent and a crack in the facade.

Balt closed his mouth again, giving himself a second to acclimate. The disorienting swirl of colors quickly faded, leaving him with the monochromatic purple void of the Mosstopus's vision.

Shit, he thought. He was going to make himself sick much faster if he kept lobbing balls of mucus at the Whissler. He'd only practiced attacking a few times back at the gym, and his vision hadn't been assaulted with nearly so many colors in there.

That was basically the only attack he could do with Pistachio, though, aside from physical strikes. The Whissler was solely an airborne Jekua. How else would he hurt it without ranged attacks?

He flicked Pistachio's tongue and just barely dodged another black blast that he could suddenly see. Then he noted that the Whissler was still hovering pretty close to the comic book store.

The other thing he could do with Pistachio was alter the Mosstopus's friction. He used its magic to increase its natural friction, and he began climbing up the side of the building. It was a feat that Pistachio could have accomplished already, to a certain degree, but the increased friction made it ten times easier. There was no slippage whatsoever as Balt ascended the wall like a spider.

Then he quickly sprang off the wall, opening his mouth wide. Colors flashed in his vision, and he could see he was aiming right for the Whissler, which was still flapping its wings nearby.

Pistachio's gnarly fangs came down around the thing's right wing, and Balt shuddered at the sound of its flesh tearing. He wrapped Pistachio's limbs around the Whissler as he gnawed on its wing, sending them both crashing to the ground.

Balt's head was pounding as he chewed on the Whissler, his tongue scraping against its coarse fur. Orange and white filled his entire view, and it was enough to blind him in an entirely different way.

The Whissler shoved Pistachio off its body, just as Pistachio belched his kinetic energy-draining breath. Balt stood on shaky legs and watched the orange blob rise falteringly into the air.

Two more black streaks followed, neither of which Balt avoided. They hit Pistachio in two of his legs; it was quite a feat for it to miss the Mosstopus's huge, round body.

Balt quickly checked on his mana reserves. Those blows knocked him under the halfway mark, but that meant he still had a good amount left. If anything, the headache and nausea would knock him out of the fight before his mana did. His stomach churned now with every flick of the tongue.

But flick it he did, and he saw the Whissler haltingly flying away. Between the ravaged wing and the draining of its kinetic energy, its pace was slow.

The energy that Pistachio absorbed really only brought him back to his baseline, after the way he'd altered himself to scale the wall. Balt scurried forward a ways, until he was standing on what he believed to be the wide open street. There should be nothing there for him to trip on or hurt himself with.

Then he raced forward, his ten long legs cutting the distance between him and the Whissler in no time.

The orange blob stopped momentarily and a strange reverberating noise filled the air, then Balt—or Pistachio, rather—was knocked flat on his ass. Or what constituted as an ass for the Mosstopus, which now lay with his legs sprawled out around his spherical body like a cartoon sun.

It took Balt a second to understand what had happened. The Whissler must have used some kind of sonic blast ability, drawing on the Sonic powers it gained from the Whifflit side of it. Obviously, there had been no scent for Pistachio to pick up on, so he hadn't seen it coming.

Balt was scrambling to stand up when three more of those black streaks came flying toward him. All three cut across Pistachio's flesh, knocking his mana down several pegs in the process.

Hopefully that made Zu think that any attack was viable, and did not reveal the fact that sonic attacks would be invisible to Balt. It was possible Zu still had no idea how he was controlling his Jekua so proficiently in spite of the black dome surrounding them.

He dodged out of the way of some more black streaks as he finally got Pistachio up on his feet, then he hurried forward and shot another slimeball at the Whissler. It tried to flap out of the way, but its injured wing hindered it. The weight of Pistachio's mucus pulled the other wing down, sending the Jekua spiraling to the earth.

It was time to move.

Balt couldn't sustain too many more sonic attacks, nor could he stave off this overwhelming ache in his head for much longer.

He conjured up another slimeball, ignoring the stabbing pain in his brain, and it coursed through the air before slapping wetly against the Whissler's right arm, sticking it to the ground. Or, at least, that was what Balt thought he was doing. It was unclear in his color-vision. But either way, the orange blob wasn't getting up, so *something* was keeping the Whissler on the ground.

Pistachio was upon the blob a few seconds later. He began thrashing the thing, slamming as many tentacles as he could spare down on the thing's immobile body. Then he reached forward, opening his mouth wide, and clamped down on what he thought to be the Whissler's head.

It certainly felt like its head. Pistachio's mouth was filled with fur and sharp points that he assumed to be whiskers and teeth. He chewed, digging his many, many fangs into the Whissler's neck. They tore through skin and muscle, tapping against bone, and the metallic taste of blood gushed into Balt's mouth.

Combined with his headache, that was enough to nearly make him puke. He lurched forward in the comic shop, clutching his roiling belly in his hands.

The taste was too much. He had to stop. He pulled away from the Whissler, then flicked his blood-soaked tongue out to catch a glimpse of what the Jekua's condition was.

He saw the orange blob burst in a stunning flash of white light.

Just like Niona's Gujjy when she had withdrawn it.

The white smudge streaked across his field of purple, before disappearing into the ether.

He shifted back into his own body, and was relieved to find that he could see again. There was also an abrupt roar from the crowd outside.

Balt stood up, banging his head on the open cash register drawer. He swore, then cautiously stepped through the piles of broken glass and out the window frame, onto the street. Halfway down, he saw Pistachio standing there, completely still.

Beyond the Mosstopus, Zu was sitting on the ground, his head on his knees. He was done.

Balt had won.

And he needed to get off the damn street before he vomited all over it.

28
IN WHICH A STAGGERING REVELATION IS MADE

The floor of the gym was cold. Sitting on one of the rubber mats in a sparring ring or one of the target practice areas would've been (only slightly) more comfortable, but Balt did not want to become the latest victim of Glom's Molten Rain.

It was the day after their second-round matches, the last off-day of the tournament. After this, it would be three straight days of battles. It was hard to imagine that within the next three days, the champion would be crowned. Balt's mind raced, wondering what opportunities might arise from this. A talent scout had approached Niona; who's to say the same wouldn't happen for him?

They had both slept pretty late into the morning, after how rough the previous day had been. Balt was endlessly grateful that Alani hadn't woken him up and that Holly's big mouth hadn't disturbed his slumber. Now Niona was spending the afternoon getting a bit of training in with Glom, since she said he was the weak link in her team.

Balt had been practicing a bit with all four of his Jekuas, but now he was seated on the floor flipping through his grandmother's bestiary while he waited for his mana to refill.

Yesterday, when his match had concluded, several people thought he was suffering from soulsickness. Even he did, for a second, before double-checking his mana levels and seeing that while they were close to empty, they weren't quite there yet. And anyway, his nausea and dizziness were nowhere near as debilitating as the times he'd actually gotten soulsick.

Being in Pistachio's head was just too overwhelming for him still. He'd pushed himself to his limit fighting against Zu. He was glad he'd won, but it made him feel like complete shit. Niona had helped him get back on his feet, texting Alani continuous updates since she wasn't allowed back in the locker room, but in the process they both missed the following two battles. The first was a victory for Wasaaru, and the second was a win for the absurdly-named Johnny Fierce.

They were able to watch the rest of the day's matches, at least, once they got Balt's stomach settled and his headache dulled around the middle of the third battle. Uil—who was becoming the new favorite to win the tournament—handily beat Tobias Screet, much to Balt's disappointment. He'd wanted his Nonnim-summoning buddy to win, feeling some strange sense of comradery with him.

Plus, the ferocity in Uil's expression as he battled scared the ever-loving shit out of Balt. Unfortunately for him, if both he and Uil won their next matches, they would be facing each other in round four. That would surely spell the end for him in the Makanuele Rumble.

Desi Taewao won her second round, naturally, and would be battling Niona's pal Andy Lowe the next day. Niona's upcoming opponent was a man named Winston Knox, a huge, beefy guy who fought with huge, beefy Jekuas. Balt found Winston to be unbelievably intimidating, but Niona appeared totally unbothered.

The rest of the battles were pretty standard fare between evenly-matched Summoners. There were no huge blowouts like Uil against Toby. Cole Illiom beat Cassidy Simms and would go on to fight Kallon next. Balt hoped Kallon would win; Cole seemed like an idiot. His main Jekua was a big, white spider whose body looked like a rose. It was a Jekua from Peliq, and that country's Jekuas were the least familiar to Balt, so he wasn't sure of its name.

Between Nock Brynn and Aubrey L'al, Nock was the winner. Balt had been wanting Aubrey to win, because he thought she was very cute, and he would be sad to see her leave the tournament. Nock was pretty cute too, though, so it wasn't a total loss.

The most intense match of the afternoon had been between Anesk Pauz and Alo Darwi. The two men and their Jekuas covered every inch of that city block, rubberizing street lights and throwing cars and creating cyclones of shattered glass. It was anybody's guess as to who would come out on top, but in the end it was Anesk Pauz. He was another summoner from Peliq, with a retinue of Jekuas that were uncommon to Balt. One of them, though, was a regional variant of a Puffolin. It was still called a Puffolin, and it was still a Growth-Type, possessing almost all the same moves as Dipper. The differences were really only cosmetic, with its scales being a creamy brown and its flower petals being a different shape. Anesk and his Peliquan Jekuas would be Wasaaru's next opponent.

Balt had wanted to watch the battle between Johnny Fierce and Fola'h Notor'eh to see what Jekuas he'd be up against when he fought whoever won that match, so he was planning on pulling up some footage of Johnny's matches later tonight when he was back at Aeiko's apartment.

For now, he was trying to expand his repertoire with Dipper. After that blinding match with Zu Jerat, he wanted to gain more abilities that he could use without having to worry about precise aiming. The Puffolin's Petal Shower was good for that, but he knew there was more he could do.

His inspiration was another Growth-Type Jekua, a thing called a Mushcap that lived in the forests of Totta, Kou Tekkis, and previously Pakree. It was a walking green mushroom with little stubby arms and legs and six eyes that circled around its entire body. Balt had to assume that looking through a Mushcap's perspective would be just as disorienting as it was with his Mosstopus.

Mushcaps specialized in the *decay* aspect of their Growth energy, much like Gunkskunks. A lot of their abilities were based on poisoning their enemies or absorbing power, either from the earth or from another Jekua.

The moves Balt was most interested in were what he referred to as the Fungal Spore and the Sleep Spore. The former more so than the latter, but either one would be fine. With the Fungal Spore, the Mushcap released an airborne spore that latched onto the enemy and sprouted tiny fungi all over their body, which then leeched their health (in other words, the Summoner's mana) over time. Eventually the fungi would fall off the body and the effects would cease, but that took a while.

The Sleep Spore acted in the same way, but instead of draining mana it simply put the Jekua to sleep, rendering the Summoner unable to manipulate their soulclay to attack.

He had yet to really tap into the decay side of Dipper's magic, and he thought one of the spores would be a good place to start. Continually leeching mana from Zu would've been a good way to batter him without needing to see anything, and it was an area of effect attack. As long as the other person's Jekua was within range, it would hit. The closer they were, the more spores would latch on, but even one little fungus could turn the tide of a battle.

So he was reading through his grandmother's notes on the Mushcap. Other Growth-Type Jekuas were capable of learning the ability, but she had written her notes about it on the Mushcap's entry.

Like when he was learning the Vine Whip, what would make this extra difficult was the fact that producing spores was not something natural for a Puffolin. Dipper would be fully capable of doing it, given her Growth magic, but it would not be as easy to pull off as it would be with a Mushcap or a Bontobi.

What his late grandmother suggested was not especially useful, he was sad to see. It was all about the Mushcap's anatomy, how to maximize the amount of spores that latched on to the enemy, things of that nature. Nothing about how to actually produce the spores.

He closed the book and wracked his brain for other solutions. He'd read through this bestiary countless times; was there anything in there that he could reread to give him an extra boost?

Then he remembered a note in the entry for the Serroj, of all things. They were primarily Electrical-Types, but their secondary Type was Thermal. In the wild, those Thermal powers were pretty much only used for altering their body temperature or the temperature in a small area. But having that magic meant that, theoretically, even though their main form of attacking at long range was with lightning bolts and such, they *could* breathe fire or ice, if the Summoner wanted to put in the work to make it happen.

He checked the book's index to find the page number for the Serroj, then flipped to that page. He grinned, seeing his grandmother's messy scrawl at the bottom of the page, squeezed in with tiny, cramped text in the margin. If there had been an illustration of the Jekua, she would have not had enough space to write what she wanted to.

Can shoot icicles that shatter on impact. Hard, but worthwhile. Easiest method I found was to go through motions of conjuring bolt, then shift the focus of your soulclay from Electrical energy to Thermal energy. And make it cold, not hot. Duh.

It was not the most detailed instruction, but it was something to go off of. While it wasn't the exact same case, since he was not trying to use a different type of magic, it was probably a similar enough concept. That was his hope, anyway.

The power closest in form to what he wanted to do with the Fungal Spore was Dipper's Petal Shower. It was possible he could start to use that ability, but manipulate his soulclay in such a way that it produced those spores instead of the sharp petals.

"Whatcha readin', nerd?" Niona asked him as she left the Thermal target practice area. The rubber mat and the Juntoo-shaped dummy were covered in scorch marks. She sat down beside him, leaning over to scan the page he was open to. They were floor people yet again. "You lookin' for a Serroj?" she said.

"No," he replied. "Do you have one?"

"Nah."

"I was just reading this note from my grandma about teaching yourself new techniques." He pointed at the note, and Niona read it over.

"Weird," she said. "I guess that makes sense. Usually when I can't figure out how to do an ability, I just buy a mod chip for it."

"How do you ever enter tournaments if, like, all of your Jekuas are modded?"

"When they scan your shit, the only Artificial Abilities flagged are ones that don't match the Jekua's Types."

"What about something like that Blitz Trio they're about to launch? Moves that strong fit the Type, but I'd still think they would count as a mod, since they're so overpowered."

"Okay, yeah, that's true. I was generalizing. There are some moves, the strongest ones you can buy, that'll come up in a scan too. But, like, if you installed that petal thing you do with Dipper onto another Growth-Type, it wouldn't pop up since that's a more common move."

Balt nodded, then said, "Well, it's all irrelevant to me anyway, since I can't afford to go out and buy mods whenever I want them." He hadn't meant it as a slight, but he noticed her mouth take the slightest dip into a frown after he said it.

But she said, "It seems like your grandma left you with a bunch of good notes. I think that'll work." She tapped a finger on the note three times for emphasis. Then she asked, "How come your granny left *you* with this thing and not that cousin of yours?"

They hadn't really talked about Wasaaru since Niona had met him. Balt said, "I dunno. She just gave it to me one day when I was alone at her house. Wasaaru and his parents were on a trip, otherwise he probably would've been there that day, too." He took a breath, then continued. "She, uh...she *did* say for me and Wasaaru *both* to make good use of it. We were supposed to share it, I guess. Hand it back and forth, or something. I was a little jerk kid, though. I was only nine. I was obsessed with her Jekuas, and with this book, and so I was just stoked that she'd given it to me. I didn't wanna share it."

He didn't want to look at her. He'd never admitted that part to anyone before, not even Alani. And definitely not Wasaaru. All these years, Wasaaru had been under the impression that their grandmother had specifically gifted the bestiary to Balt and Balt alone. He felt somewhat ashamed of the fact that he'd never told Wasaaru, lying by omission.

"Is that why you two don't get along?" Niona asked. "You two seemed to snap at each other a lot for cousins. I thought cousins were always pals, while it was siblings that fought."

"Yeah, well, neither of us has any siblings, so maybe we had to turn to each other for squabbles."

"So is that why?" she asked again.

Balt shook his head. "We were friends for a few years after I got the book," he said. He was still staring at the Serroj page, not wanting to look Niona in the eye while he spoke. "We kinda just drifted apart. As time passed, it seemed more and more like he didn't want to spend time with me. There was this weird resentment between the two of us." He elaborated a little, then told her about the incident at the movie theater that proved to be the breaking point in their relationship.

Again, it was something that he hadn't even explained in detail to Alani. He didn't know why he never had. Maybe it had something to do with the fact that Alani knew Wasaaru too, so that colored his desire to spill the details to her. Or perhaps it was just that he always feared the incident was too small to justify his extreme anger toward his cousin in that moment. In the scheme of things, it wasn't a huge deal. But it was the principle of the whole thing, and that it had been building up over such a long stretch of time. If Wasaaru had just apologized for his behavior, Balt probably would have forgiven him, and they would still be friends today. Maybe still not as close as they were when they were kids, but not rivals like they were now.

"I get it," Niona said once he finished his story.

Those three little words were a great relief to him. Maybe his ill feelings toward Wasaaru were justified after all. He would certainly hope so, after holding this grudge for the past three years.

"You do?" he said, finally looking at her.

"Sure," she said. "He started actin' like he was better than you, and you got sick of it. Makes sense to me." She paused, then said, "You think it might be because he felt jealous of you?"

Balt frowned and furrowed his brow. "What do you mean? Jealous of what? He's always had anything he could possibly want. His dad's rich as hell."

"So is mine, and I ain't always had everything I want," said Niona. "Money can't get you everything." She waited again, then laughed mirthlessly and said, "Are you really that dense?" She tapped on the bestiary once more. "He was bitter about not gettin' the book, you idiot!"

He looked from Niona back down to the bestiary. His eyes wandered over his grandmother's handwriting. Wasaaru's grandmother, too.

They'd both pored over the book for years. Of course Wasaaru was mad that she'd given it to Balt instead of him, Balt had always known that. But he'd never connected the dots that perhaps that was the reason his cousin started drifting away from him.

He really was an idiot.

"I, uh..." he mumbled, not knowing what to say.

"Jeez, you're like a little baby," Niona laughed. "You gotta up that emotional intelligence, bro."

His cheeks flushed red. He felt more childish than ever. "In my defense, we literally *were* kids," he said. "And only a year later, our grandma died, so we were kind of wrapped up in, y'know, *grief*."

"All the more reason for you to share that piece of her with him."

Balt felt like he was on the verge of tears. He took a shuddering breath and composed himself before speaking. "You're probably right," he said.

"No shit I'm right. Sounds to me like he treated you shitty, for sure, but you ain't totally faultless here."

He couldn't bear to look at her again. He didn't want her to see in his face how close he was to breaking.

She was completely right, of course. He'd denied Wasaaru this memento of their grandmother, even after she passed away, making him feel less than. It only made sense that a bitter teenager would react by making Balt feel less than in return.

"I'm an idiot," he said.

"That's what I've been tellin' you for weeks."

It would've made him laugh if he didn't feel so awful.

"I do miss him," he said.

It was another entry in the seemingly endless list of things that he hadn't told Alani, but was easier to tell Niona since she was so far removed from the situation. Every time he spoke to Alani about Wasaaru, he would end up embroiled in his bitterness and rage all over again. He never felt like he was *allowed* to miss his cousin, because in his mind, he was supposed to be angry.

Probably if he had ever said any of this to Alani, the conversation would have gone very similarly. Alani was much less crude than Niona and would not have called him an idiot so many times, but the sentiment would have been the same. And really, she could be blunt when she wanted to, so maybe she would have indeed called him out for being an idiot.

"Why don't you try to mend things?" Niona asked. She said it nonchalantly, as if it was the simplest thing in the world.

"I dunno if I can."

"Of course you can. You're cousins. You were best friends, right? You've got a few shitty years between you now, but so what? You've got way more good years, I bet."

"We do," he said. Then, "I don't think I know how to talk to him anymore. We don't speak much, and when we do, you saw how generally unpleasant it is. And that was a pretty civil conversation, comparatively speaking."

Niona shrugged, her shoulder brushing against his. She said, "It doesn't have to be immediate. Honestly, it'd be weird if you went up to him and started bein' all super chummy again like nothin' ever happened. You'll both have to confront all that shit at some point, hash it all out, but you could start by just not bein' a dick to him."

"Gonna be hard to resist," he joked, chuckling lightly.

"Yeah, habits can be hard to break sometimes," she said. "Maybe you could pluck somethin' out of those good years to talk about. Break the ice, kinda."

Balt nodded. "We've got a ton of fun memories from our grandparents' house," he said.

He closed the bestiary and ran his hands over the front

cover. They sat together in silence for a minute before Balt mustered up the strength to speak.

"They died the Spring before my tenth birthday. Our grandma was always thinking ahead, though, unlike our grandpa. He forgot shit all the time. She bought him a monthly planner that they hung up in the kitchen so he would stop forgetting shit, but he always forgot to write stuff down in it, so it didn't help. Anyway, she ordered my birthday present way in advance, 'cause she was supposed to be in Tollush for a tournament and wouldn't be able to come to the party. When my mom pulled it out, gift-wrapped all nice and with 'Grandma and Grandpa' or whatever on the tag, I just lost it. Bawled my eyes out for like ten minutes straight. In front of all my friends, too. It was so embarrassing, I thought I'd never live it down, which made me cry even harder. I could tell Wasaaru wanted to cry too, but he was always better at hiding his emotions than me."

Niona chuckled. "What'd they get you?" she asked.

"A Pocket Jekua. So dumb. Did you ever have one?"

"Nah, those were after my time," said Niona.

"I could never keep mine alive," Balt sighed. Pocket Jekuas were a short-lived craze that cropped up in the Spring of 2897 and were snuffed from the public eye by Fall 2898, although they were making a resurgence as of late purely due to nostalgia. They were little round electronic devices that kids carried around, no bigger than the palm of their tiny hands. They had horribly pixelated depictions of various Jekuas, which the kid was supposed to feed and train and generally take care of. Balt always forgot to feed his and they always died within a week, no matter how many times he reset the device.

"Sounds like a nice gift anyway," Niona said, giggling at his irresponsibility.

"It was. Kind of ruined by the circumstances of it all, but yeah."

"Yeah, I gotta admit, you have me pretty beat as far as terrible birthdays go."

"What was your worst one?" he asked.

Niona inhaled deeply, then let it out with a sputter of her lips. "Alright, buckle up. I was dating this dude at the time, and I was convinced he was the love of my life. Obviously with hindsight, that was the stupidest thing I coulda thought about this dude, but whatever. Young love's a hell of a thing. So he was supposed to take me out to dinner for my birthday, right? We were meeting at this fancy place, one of Himony's nicest restaurants at the time. It's shut down now, the owner was connected to some underground drug ring, it was a whole thing. Anyway, I got there before him, told the hostess I was there and the reservation was under his last name, Wonoi. They tell me the table will be ready in a minute, all that jazz. So I sit down and wait, he texts me that he'll be there soon. Then the hostess calls out for the Wonoi party, table's ready. I stand up and go over there, but so does some other chick who's been waitin' since before I got there."

"Was she…?"

"Oh, yeah, totally. My dipshit boyfriend had made that reservation for a date with some other girl behind my back, then only realized later that it was my birthday that night."

"He could've used my grandpa's planner."

"For sure. He kept the reservation, 'cause that was easier, of course, but he didn't cancel with the other girl. Or he did, and she forgot, I dunno. Or he did and she just wanted to show up anyway to stir some shit. I have no idea."

"Man, that sucks," Balt said. "I'm sorry."

"Eh, it's fine," she said. "He was always an asshole, it just took me until then to realize it."

"How long ago was that? Which birthday are we talkin' here?"

Niona grinned. "Eight years ago to the day," she said. "My seventeenth birthday."

It took a couple seconds for her answer to compute. "Wait," Balt said. "Wait, wait. To the day? Your birthday is today?"

"Yup."

"Why didn't you say anything?"

"I dunno, who cares? I'm twenty-five. The older you get, the less of a shit you give about your birthday. It's just another day."

"Sure, I don't expect you to wanna throw a big themed party or anything, but we've gotta do *something* to celebrate! We can't just let it slip by!"

"You are oddly adamant about this."

Balt smacked the front of the bestiary, the loud clap resounding through the gym. The other Summoners were making so much noise with their Jekuas, nobody noticed. "Let's go out tonight!" he said.

"Where to?"

"I don't know," Balt said. "I can barely get past the fact that it's your damn birthday and you didn't give anyone a head's up. I don't know anywhere good here, but Aeiko must know of a place. We'll ask them. The whole gang'll go out, it'll be fun."

"Only if Holly doesn't come with," Niona said.

"Oh, of course not. She's not part of the gang."

"Good."

"I mean, she might insert herself into the proceedings, though."

"No."

"Hey, I can't control her."

"Whatever, fine. Let's do it." A grin split her face, her chubby cheeks dimpling. "You gotta practice whatever it is you were gonna practice first, though."

With all the talk of Wasaaru and his grandparents and now the staggering revelation of Niona's birthday, Balt had almost forgotten about his Fungal Spore plan.

"Okay, yes, you're right," he conceded. "I will make some fungus before we head out."

"Ew," Niona grimaced. "I don't even wanna know what you mean by that. Just do that shit now, I don't want you spoilin' my party with fungus."

Balt took a moment to check his mana, then stood and walked toward one of the sparring rings.

"Come on," he beckoned Niona, then began summoning Dipper. "Help me make fungus."

"You're nasty," she said. "You are not invited to my birthday party."

29
BARNELLO'S

No one would look at Alani Temel and think to themselves, *I bet she's a bar person. She seems like someone who would go to bars.* As soon as she started speaking, their suspicions would be confirmed.

So Alani was not especially thrilled when Balt and Niona came bounding in declaring it was Niona's twenty-fifth birthday, prompting Holly to suggest they all head down to Barnello's for a celebratory drink.

"I don't know about that," said Aeiko. "Barnello's is kind of gross."

Balt said, "I was thinking more of a, uh, a restaurant. Some place with appetizers that are priced like you should be able to share them, but the portions are too small to."

"We're only eighteen," Alani pointed out upon the woman's suggestion, gesturing between herself and Balt. Everyone else was over twenty, so they could legally get into a bar.

"Y'all don't have fake IDs?" Niona asked. They both

shook their heads. "Wow. Buncha squares, huh? I dunno what I woulda done without my fake. Had some good nights with that thing."

Holly's enthusiasm was not dampened. "Barnello's is kind of a dive," she said. "We've been there tons of times since it's only a couple blocks away, and they never check IDs at the door or inside. Well, they did once, but generally they're pretty lax."

Balt was on his linkpad, standing next to Brine in the kitchen. He said, "Hey, it looks like the place is owned by Gregory Barnello! Or it used to be, anyway. Seems like his son runs it now." He looked up and, upon seeing the confusion on everyone's faces except Niona's, he said, "Barnello was a Summoner. He wasn't the best, but he was pretty well-known. I didn't know he'd settled down here."

"Oh! Yeah, they love Summoners over there at Barnello's," said Holly brightly. "They're always playing tournaments on that dinky little TV they've got in there. Even if it's a be-sure-to-check-the-IDs night, they might let you in on sight if they've been watching the matches."

"We do need to eat some dinner, though," Aeiko said. "Well, *we* do, at least. I don't know about you two." They were referring to Balt and Niona.

"Nah, I'm starving," said Balt.

Even though Alani was positive that neither Balt nor Niona particularly wanted Holly to join, she was undeterred continuing to pitch her idea. "Barnello's has a full menu," she said. "Burgers, tacos, other greasy, filling things. You won't go hungry there."

"I still like Balt's idea," said Alani. Not just because the other idea was Holly's, but because she was still fairly dubious about their chances of getting into the bar. She was typically a person who shied away from conflict, and the idea of a figure of authority challenging her about why she was trying to get in without an ID made her skin tingle.

"Which would you rather do?" Holly asked, turning to Niona. "It's your birthday, after all."

Without hesitating, Niona said, "The bar sounds kinda fun. Seein' Balt drunk would be very funny to me. A nice little birthday treat."

Alani knew that Balt was not a drinker, but maybe he'd make an exception tonight for Niona. She wasn't pleased with the decision, but she wasn't going to be the one to break the unspoken social contract about birthdays. It was Niona's day, so they would do what she wanted to do.

A few minutes later, they were out on the street, with Holly leading the pack toward Barnello's.

While they walked, Alani asked Balt how the long day of training went. He excitedly told her about a new technique he was trying out, going into deeper than necessary detail about it. No matter how much he elaborated, she still did not totally understand the logistics of it, but that was fine. It had been a while since she'd listened to one of her friend's Jekua rants, and she found that she missed it more than she would've guessed. She was also glad to see how lively he spoke, after how fatigued that match against Zu Jerat made him. Alani wondered what exactly had happened out on that battlefield; most of it was blacked out by Zu's black dome. Afterwards, Balt had been in such rough shape, he'd barely been able to celebrate the fact that he'd made it through another round of the tournament. He had mentioned as they were going to sleep that he obviously hoped he'd make it to the end, but that he realistically never thought he'd get even this far. This night out could be a mini celebration for him, too.

Holly led them away from the street on which their apartment was located and down tight alleyways as they made their way west. They didn't see any other people once they were off the busy street, but they did stumble upon a weird Jekua rummaging through some garbage spilled beside a dumpster. It looked like a little lightbulb, with an ovular glowing yellow body and tiny red feet that looked like shoes. Its eyes were almost invisible, but they were a slightly darker shade of yellow on its face. Balt told Alani it was called a Dunceling.

"You have to be joking," she said.

"Nope."

"What a rude name."

"They're weirdly attracted to machinery and tend to hide up in car wheels. A lot of times they end up, uh... well, they're hard to spot and people don't always know they're there when they start up their cars. I'll just leave it at that."

"See? They're dunces," Niona said.

Barnello's was squashed between two empty, rundown buildings, and it wasn't looking so spiffy itself. The bar's hand-painted wooden sign hung crooked above the door, and without any nearby streetlights nor any lights of its own, it would've been nearly impossible to find without Holly's help. The name was written in thick, green, curly script, with the tail of the S underlining the whole thing.

The door was covered in scratch marks and was closed shut, completely unattended by a bouncer.

"See? No one at the door," Holly said.

That did not instill Alani with as much hope as Holly thought it would. The five of them headed inside, with Aeiko having to shoo away a Dewrat that tried to scurry in at the last second.

The indoors was at least a little nicer than the outdoors. The place was dimly lit, as Alani expected from a dive bar. There were a lot of people there, all chatting jovially and sipping from dark bottles or clear glasses. Music was playing from a jukebox over in the corner, a deep-voiced crooner over twanging guitars and pounding drums. Some people were dancing near the jukebox, but most were seated at the various tall, round tables or in secluded booths.

The bar was completely brown. Brown counters, brown tables, brown floors. The walls seemed to possibly be a pale shade of red, but with the faint lighting, they just kind of looked like another brown. It was the dreariest color scheme Alani had ever laid eyes on. If not for the lively customers propping it up, the atmosphere would have been suffocating. There were photographs hung on the walls, but from where she stood, she couldn't make out any fine details. They appeared to be of a man with some Jekuas, presumably the titular Gregory Barnello.

Two of the people at a nearby table Alani recognized from watching the tournament, a man who she thought was named Jupe and a woman named Aubrey. Come to think of it, Alani recalled that Jupe had lost to Aubrey in the first round. Were they on a date now?

A few other patrons wore kayets, though most didn't. It was amusing to her, discovering that there were in fact other Summoners as freakish as Balt, wearing their kayet no matter the occasion. Of course, he had his strapped to his wrist right at that moment. Niona had taken hers off back at the apartment.

Over at the bar, a woman around Niona's age with high blonde pigtails and a low-cut shirt was serving drinks with a huge grin plastered on her face. Behind her were rows and rows of alcohol bottles in a multitude of shapes and sizes. The mere sight of them daunted Alani. Up in the corner of the bar, shining some of its light on the bottles, was the aforementioned dinky TV. It was currently playing highlights from yesterday's matches.

Specifically, it was playing a portion of Niona's battle. Alani grinned at the sight of Pops leaping around the city, charging up those streetlights while Yakka Dho's Bingst stood around stupidly.

She nudged Niona and pointed at the screen. Niona's face lit up as the Toolu's gross little body filled the screen, zapping lights with electrical energy.

"My boy!" she beamed. "That's gotta be a sign, right? This was the right choice. Let's get us some drinks, huh?"

"I'll get the first round," Aeiko offered.

"I'll get the next," Holly said. She was probably fuming about not being the first to offer. "Birthday girl shouldn't have to pay for her own drinks tonight."

"What's everybody want?" Aeiko asked.

"They have a signature cocktail called the Tonnit's Tonic," Holly said. "It's, uh…what is it…it's gin, creme de violette, maraschino liqueur, and lemon juice."

"What the hell is creme de violette?" Balt asked. Alani had the same question.

"I dunno, but I've had stuff with it at my dad's resort bar, and it's good," said Niona.

"It's liqueur made from violets," Holly replied.

"Weird," said Alani.

"I'm not a fan," Aeiko said. "I don't like floral flavors. I'll be sticking to a ginger beer."

"Oh! They have a good cocktail with ginger beer, too. It's that, plus berry gin, raspberry syrup, and lime."

"I'll just stick with the beer."

"Why do you know the whole cocktail menu?" Niona asked. "Or at least all the gin cocktails, anyway."

"This is my go-to hangout spot with my coworkers," said Holly with a smile. She was always smiling, never perturbed by anything. It was creepy.

Niona said, "I'll try the specialty, why not. One Tonnit Tonic for me."

"Same here," said Balt.

"Me too," said Holly.

Then all eyes were on Alani. The Tonnit Tonic did not sound like the best thing to her, but it didn't sound like the worst thing in the world, either. She did like maraschino cherries with her ice cream sometimes, so that liqueur was probably good. She didn't have the first clue what gin tasted like, but she also didn't know what else was on the menu. She had never set foot in a bar before, and she was crippled with indecision.

"A round of the Tonics," she said at last, putting on a smile. She sincerely hoped she would not regret her choice.

"Got it," said Aeiko. They sauntered over to the bar, and Alani decided to follow along after them when she realized they would probably have trouble carrying five drinks.

They looked happy to see her sidle up next to them at the bar. "Fancy meeting you here," they said, waiting for the bartender to turn her attention their way.

Alani glanced up at the television screen just in time to see the giant pastel raccoon topple to the ground while Pops skittered around it. A man sitting at the bar, drinking from a frosted mug, let out a whoop and a "Hell yeah!" He cheersed to the screen then took another glug.

Before the bartender came over, Aeiko looked at Alani and said, "You sure you want that drink?"

She was surprised that Aeiko had seen right through her. "Not really," she confessed.

"Don't let Holly intimidate you," Aeiko said. "I know she's brash and it's easy to get steamrolled by her, believe me. I've been there plenty of times. Just get what you actually want, it's no big deal."

Alani smiled. "Honestly, I kind of just want a water," she said.

"A water it is, then," said Aeiko. When the bartender came over, they ordered their ginger beer, three Tonnit Tonics, and a water. The woman didn't verify their age for any of it.

"This place really doesn't care," Alani whispered while the woman got to work mixing the cocktails.

"Nope. Leave it to Holly to pick the fanciest restaurants but the grungiest bars. Pretty much encapsulates the two sides of her."

The bartender returned with the drinks. Alani's glass of water was not quite as tall as her thirst required. Aeiko's beer was in a brown bottle with a bright yellow label, so it fit right in with the rest of their surroundings. In contrast, the Tonnit Tonics were beautiful. They came in tall, thin-stemmed glasses and were a rich lavender hue. Together, they carried the drinks over to a booth where the others had set up shop. Balt and Niona were on one side, while Aeiko and Alani squeezed into the other next to Holly. Alani was pushed up against Holly, their bare skin rubbing against each other, which was not ideal. She preferred that to Holly and Aeiko sitting side by side, though.

"I only see three Tonics here!" Holly said, feigning distress.

"I was feeling more thirsty than adventurous," said Alani, taking her water. Everyone else grabbed their drinks as well.

Holly, inserting herself as their leader like always, raised her glass. "Here's to twenty-five good years!" she said.

It was not a particularly original or stirring toast, but everyone else raised their drinks because it was easier and less awkward than not doing so.

"To Niona!" said Holly.

"Niona," the rest of them echoed. They clinked their drinks together and took a sip.

Alani laughed at Balt, whose face was pinched after drinking some of his purple cocktail. "How is it?" she asked.

"Not bad, I guess," he said. "Weird."

"I like it," said Niona.

"Have you ever had gin before?" Holly asked.

"I have not," he said. "Not sure if I'm a fan."

"Well, I am," Niona said, slurping down more of hers.

Alani said, "A few weeks ago, you were convinced I was a gin and tonic girl."

"I still am," Balt said. "Now's the perfect time to find out, if you wanna." He edged his drink closer to her across the table.

"I'll pass for now," she said, taking a sip of her water.

"Fair enough." He took his drink back and took a second, more cautious sip. He licked his lips and gulped it down loudly. "*Man*, that is weird," he said again.

"Do y'all wanna play a drinking game?" Holly asked.

"Absolutely not," Niona said. "Birthday girl says hell no to drinking games."

"Fine, fine. What do you want to do, then?"

Niona huffed a laugh. "What do you mean? We're doin' it. We're here, we're drinkin', we're chattin'. What more do you want?"

"This just feels like a night out!" Holly groaned. "It's supposed to be a *celebration*!"

"I almost didn't even tell any of you my birthday was today," Niona reminded her. "This is plenty of celebration for me."

"How about Never Have I Ever?" Holly asked, ignoring her.

"No, no, no. Gross. I'm not a teenager anymore," Niona protested, shutting down that idea immediately. Alani was eternally grateful to her for that.

Holly drank more of her Tonnit Tonic while pouting about her idea being trampled by the birthday girl.

"I have never played a drinking game, either," said Balt.

"Well, that one's awful," said Niona. "Beer pong is more fun 'cause it's an actual game with at least *some* skill involved, not just a bunch of people sittin' around spillin' secrets that're better left secret. Can't play that here, though, obviously."

Aeiko said, "They've got a Block Tower set around here somewhere. Want me to go find it?"

"Why do they have Block Tower?" Balt asked. Block Tower was a children's game, where a bunch of wooden blocks were stacked on top of each other and the goal was for players to remove a block and place it on top of the tower. When the tower fell, whoever made it happen was the loser.

Niona chuckled. "You really *are* a bar virgin, aren't ya?" She was nearly finished with her first cocktail.

Alani had to imagine that comment ruffled Balt's feathers. His cheeks were tinged red as he took another sip of his drink and mumbled, "Mhmm."

"Lots of bars have Block Tower," Aeiko said. "Not the one you played as a kid, it's like a supersized version. Giant blocks. Perfect for drunk people to handle."

"That sounds exceptionally noisy," said Balt.

"It is. Should I go find it?"

"Go for it," said Niona.

"I thought you said no drinking games," Holly commented.

"No *dumb* drinking games like Never Have I Ever or

Alphabet Names or whatever. Good, skill-based ones are fine."

"I like Alphabet Names," Aeiko muttered.

"I don't think Block Tower requires much skill," Alani said.

"More skill than talkin'," said Niona.

That was true. Aeiko scooted out of the booth and set off in search of the block set.

"How do you even make Block Tower a drinking game?" Balt then asked. "When do you drink?"

"You can get some sets for playing at home that have, like, little dares or some shit written on each block, so when you take your block out you gotta do what the block says. Some of the instructions are just for people to drink, but also if you refuse to do the thing, you gotta drink instead."

"The ones at bars don't have that, though," Holly said.

"Yeah, that'd be chaos. The drinking aspect here will just be drinking whenever. The drunker you get, the harder it'll be to play. Or we can specify to take a drink before you pull, or after, or I dunno. Whatever we wanna do, who cares." She took one last swig of her Tonic, then placed the empty glass down on the table. "I'm gonna need somethin' else before we start, though."

Balt had barely gotten through any of his drink, but Holly was halfway done with hers. Aeiko was also halfway done with their ginger beer, it looked like. When had they chugged so much of it?

Holly nudged Alani, indicating she wanted to get out of the booth. Alani could foresee this being a nightmare. "I said I'd get the next one," she said. Alani got up and moved aside for Holly. "Want another?" she asked Niona.

"Nah, let's do a, uh…let's do a whiskey sour. I'm in a sour mood. This shit was good, though. I'll probably get another one later."

"Got it. How about you?" she asked Balt.

"Uh…not gin," he said. "I'll try a whiskey sour, maybe." It sounded like more of a question than a declarative statement.

Niona clapped him on the back, nearly spilling the Tonnit Tonic he held in his hand. "We'll do some experimenting tonight," she said. "We'll find you a drink you like, I'm sure of it. I will be your alcohol shepherd."

"Do you want to baa like a sheep?" Alani asked him.

"I do not," he replied.

"Baa! Baa!" Holly bleated cheerily, before cackling at herself. Then she hurried over to the bar to grab the next round of drinks.

The three of them turned to each other, dumbstruck.

"She's delightful, isn't she?" said Alani, hoping the sarcasm was apparent in her tone.

"Oh, yeah, totally," said Niona, her tone absolutely drenched in sarcasm. There was no misconstruing. "It's too bad I'm gonna drown her out with all these drinks."

"To Niona!" Balt said in an imitation of Holly's high-pitched voice, raising up his glass again.

"To Niona!" Alani and Niona both said. Balt and Alani drank.

Her plain, cold water went down smooth.

30
ACROSS THE BAR

If they had gone to a nice sit-down restaurant, something much fancier than Barnello's—nothing specific came to mind, considering Balt did not know any of the restaurants in Makanuele—he imagined they would've had utensils. Forks, knives, spoons, the classics. Maybe chopsticks, depending on the cuisine. There would have been cloth napkins, too. Ones that would catch anything falling onto their laps, ones that would really soak up whatever was thrown at them.

But they were not somewhere with cloth napkins, they were at Barnello's. Which meant that by the end of his meal, Balt's fingers and palms were drenched with grease. It seemed to make no difference whatsoever how many napkins he wiped his hands with, there was always more grease. The napkins were being dirtied, he could plainly see that, so he knew they were soaking up *some* of the grease. Yet somehow, there was always more.

He tossed his ninth crumpled napkin into his empty

food basket and stared down at his disgusting, wet hands. They looked as if he'd just taken the last bite of his burger seconds ago.

This called for more extreme measures.

Balt got up from their booth, which aside from their five empty or half-empty food baskets was littered with gigantic wooden blocks. Those were most likely covered in grease now, too. The end of one of them had even fallen into Balt's container of ketchup when it slipped from Niona's hands. It was unclear whether it escaped her due to her own greasiness or her inebriation. There was a high probability of it being a combination of the two. Balt had continued dipping fries into the ketchup anyway.

He nearly toppled over after taking only two steps away from the table. He felt extremely top-heavy. If he pitched over too far, he knew he would be unable to control himself. He'd rocket straight to the floor, forehead-first. It was a sensation he had never experienced before.

That was untrue, actually. He felt very top-heavy when he was in Pistachio's perspective, with the Mosstopus's huge, round head being held up by all those skinny legs.

He tried blinking away his heaviness. It worked for a moment, he thought. Maybe not. When he took another step, it was back. Oh well. Something new to contend with. He was a Summoner, he was accustomed to adapting to new situations.

The bathroom felt so far away from their table, but he made it there eventually. He swerved around people and tables and chairs, absolutely convinced that with every sudden jerk of his body he would be on the ground.

Ground sounds nice, he thought absently to himself, sliding out of the way of two women holding bright pink drinks. Then he thought, *Bright pink sounds nice.*

Finally, he reached the bathroom. He came to a halting stop in front of the sink, staring at himself in the mirror for a full thirty seconds before turning on the faucet. He took a deep breath, and it was quite possibly the most satisfying breath he had ever taken.

Again, he thought, *Ground sounds nice.* If he could just lay down for a minute or two…

Being drunk was weird. Never before had he felt the impulse to lay on the floor of a bathroom, but in his current state, plopping his head down on a cold, flat surface sounded like the best thing in the world.

Water rushed out of the faucet. Balt slipped his hands into the stream, shuddering at the cold.

Why does Barnello's keep its water so cold? he asked himself. *It doesn't need to be like it's cold. It doesn't need to.* If only there were some way to make the water warmer…

He wasn't exactly sure if he liked being drunk. He didn't *dis*like it, but he wasn't sure if this was something he really wanted to make a habit out of.

In truth, he had not consumed very many drinks, but compared to the few sips of beer he'd had in his youth, it felt like he'd downed a gallon of alcohol. He'd started with the Tonnit Tonic (bad), then the whiskey sour (fairly good), and then some sort of locally-brewed beer (extremely bad). Despite his rating for the latter, he still drank it all. Every last drop. This was due to him not wanting the person who bought the beverage to have wasted their money, and also because he did not want to be perceived as a baby by Niona.

That was what had sent him over the edge into full-blown drunkenness. It hadn't even tasted good, so what was the point? He deeply regretted his decision, but now he had to live with it. Now he had to stand in the bar's bathroom and resist the urge to lay down on the filthy floor.

Balt looked down at his hands and determined they were sufficiently wet. There was no soap anywhere to be seen (the plastic dispenser on the wall was broken and dangling, hanging on by a thread), so the water would have to do.

He shut off the faucet, his hands stinging with cold. He wiped them off on the thin, brown paper towels nearby, which he then tossed on top of an overflowing trash can. At last, his hands were no longer slicked with grease.

Thank you, he mentally told the bathroom.

Back outside, he tried to blink away his heaviness again as he adjusted to the dim light. For some reason, it was brighter in the bathroom than in the main room of the bar.

He took another deep, satisfying breath, and started back toward the booth. Now that they were all finished eating, they were going to play another round of Block Tower. Alani, Niona, and Balt had each lost a game so far. Aeiko and Holly were seasoned pros.

One positive thing about the alcohol was that the drunker he got, the more fun Block Tower became. And more challenging, to boot.

He was still not even halfway back to the table when

he spied a familiar face across the room. They were sitting by themselves at a freestanding table, with three empty chairs ringed around it.

It was his cousin, Wasaaru. In his hand he held a glass filled with a bubbly yellow liquid. It sloshed around as he put the glass to his lips and took a sip. Balt was not surprised to find his cousin here; even without the bar's distressing lack of security, Wasaaru Vana was absolutely the type of person to own a fake ID.

Balt's mind drifted lazily through Niona's words from that afternoon, about making amends with his cousin. She was probably right, both about how he should do it and about how it would not be easy. They had let too much animosity simmer between them. Three years was a long time for such feelings to fester.

He was tempted to make his way over there, sidle up next to Wasaaru and sit himself down in one of those empty seats.

His current state of mind would make talking to Wasaaru now either an extremely good decision or an unbelievably stupid one. There was little wiggle room there. Impossible to know which it'd be unless he went over there and just did it.

He started toward Wasaaru's table.

It was a treacherous path he walked across the bar, with many an obstacle to avoid. A chair pushed out one or two extra inches from a table was nearly his undoing. But, miraculously, he made it through the establishment unscathed.

Wasaaru's brow furrowed and his mouth hung agape when he saw Balt sit down across from him.

"Yo," Balt said.

"What are you doing here?" Wasaaru asked.

"What are *you* doin' here?" Balt shot back defensively.

"Drinking."

"Same."

"You don't have a drink."

"It's back at my table. It tastes of shit. You're drinkin' by yourself? Got no friends?" Despite his best intentions, he couldn't resist a light jab.

Wasaaru scoffed. "Better to drink with no one than with a Fentao."

"Hey, Aeiko's good people," Balt said, not totally sure whether his speech was slurring or not. "I was dubious at first, though." He took a moment to mentally congratulate himself on pulling the word *dubious* in his current state.

"I can't trust anyone related to Tin Fentao," Wasaaru grunted. "You're a traitor to the cause." His eyes flashed at Balt's kayet. "You here to battle someone?" he asked amusedly.

"No. I just came from the gym." It wasn't a *complete* lie. He just left out the part where he did indeed go back to the apartment in between.

Wasaaru laughed, taking another sip of his drink. Then he said, "I can only imagine the type of gym *you* could afford to train in."

It always came back to that. The comment riled him up, but Balt kept his cool. He was here to make peace. Or to *try* making peace, at least. He didn't want to get his hopes up.

So he ignored the remark and instead asked a question. Trying to keep things light, keep the conversation moving. "How did your match go yesterday? I had to miss it."

"I won handily," said Wasaaru. "I managed to shut my opponent down far quicker than you did with yours."

"Do you always finish that fast?"

Wasaaru smirked at the insinuation. "Do you always cry and throw up after?" he jabbed back.

"Hey, I didn't cry," Balt said. Then he chuckled. "I might have thrown up, though. But just a little bit. Only a dribble."

"Yeah, you looked like shit after your fight," Wasaaru said. "Got a little soulsick, huh? Lucky your opponent withdrew beforehand so you still got the win."

"For your information, I was *not* soulsick," said Balt. "I just made myself sick usin' Pistachio. Big diff."

"Pistachio? What kind of name is *Pistachio* for a Mosstopus?"

Dammit, Balt cursed. The drinks had made him forgot his rule about not sharing his Jekuas' names with Wasaaru. He still had "Milton" on lockdown, thankfully.

"It's a good name," he said. "He's green and round."

"You sound like a toddler."

"A toddler who won his match."

"Why did using a Mosstopus make you sick?" Wasaaru asked.

Balt narrowed his eyes. Did he want to reveal his technique to Wasaaru? How much did he want to commit to this whole "reestablish the friendship" thing? It remained to be seen whether they would end up battling in the tournament, and it might be good to have that leg up over him. On the other hand, Balt *had* been wondering if Wasaaru possessed the same skill…

He looked at his cousin's smug face as he gulped down more of his drink.

"They're just weird to use," he said, leaving it at that.

His discomfort around sharing too much with Wasaaru was still strong enough to push through the thick haze of inebriation. He wasn't quite there yet.

Balt then said, "Did you ever see one in the VWC? I saw you imprinted a Nullfly and a Dewrat in there."

Wasaaru shook his head. "I didn't," he said. "I was admittedly somewhat surprised to see you summon that thing. I don't understand how you imprinted one. You had to use some kind of bait, right?"

It was Balt's turn to shake his head. "I had to fight it, actually."

"You aren't supposed to battle the Jekuas in the VWC," said Wasaaru, acting as if he had ever been a stickler for rules.

"I know," said Balt, "but it attacked me first. I had to lay the smack down."

"Not using your Tottaworm, I wouldn't think."

"Nah, I had to bust out the Mirrorbear." He made extra sure not to say Milton's name. "That one I *did* use bait for."

Wasaaru scoffed and took another drink. "My group never saw any Mirrorbears," he said, the words laced with more bitterness than Balt's beer.

"You went with a tour group?" Balt said in disbelief. On one hand, of course Wasaaru had paid to join a tour group, because he always loved spending his father's money to be doted on by someone. But on the other, he was fiercely independent and cocksure, so Balt could have easily seen him blowing through the jungle on his own.

"No shit," said Wasaaru. "What, you think I was gonna hack my way through the jungle like some sort of jackass? No, I'd rather let someone else lead the way. That way I could focus on imprinting as many Jekuas as possible."

"How many did you imprint in there?" Balt asked, innately knowing that the number was going to be much bigger than his measly two.

His cousin never passed up the opportunity to gloat. "Eighteen," he said.

"Shit!" Balt blurted out, slapping a palm flat on the table. It was a bigger reaction than he would've liked, which he blamed on the drunkenness. He hated giving Wasaaru the satisfaction.

Eighteen was more than he'd even been expecting. Thinking about the single blank memory card he had back at the apartment, the idea of having over twenty Jekuas at this stage of his career was mindboggling to him.

Wasaaru was blatantly pleased by Balt's loud reaction. "How many did you imprint?" he asked.

There was no use lying. His cousin would see right through him, he always did. Even simply seeing him carrying around pineapple had been enough for Wasaaru to know he had been trying to imprint a Slipshark.

"Two," he said.

Wasaaru guffawed. "A pathetic showing. All those rare Jekuas in there, and all you could manage to imprint was *two*? Your bear and your Mosstopus? You couldn't even imprint a Rettelet, or something? A Rettelet was, like, first day stuff for me in there."

No way was he going to divulge his mortifying Rettelet story to Wasaaru. He said, "I bet my Mirrorbear and Mosstopus are way doper than any of the eighteen things you imprinted. You've gotta go off the beaten path to find the good stuff, y'know."

Wasaaru looked at him suspiciously. "What's that supposed to mean?"

"It means I didn't need a guide to get me through the Qwisdeep."

"Bullshit."

"Not bullshit." Balt failed to see the need to include the fact that he'd also lost a majority of their supplies and that they had to be rescued by some rangers.

Wasaaru waved away his claim with the hand holding his glass, ice clinking against the side. There was almost nothing left in it, and he swallowed the rest in one fell swoop.

"What was that?" Balt asked, nodding at the glass as Wasaaru set it down on the table.

His cousin glared at him. "Why?" he asked.

Balt rolled his eyes. "Because I was gonna be nice and buy you another one." The offer was out there before he'd given it any real thought. He was probably just as surprised as Wasaaru.

His friends would start to wonder soon where he had disappeared to. They would be sending a rescue team to the bathroom. It would be understandable for them to assume he'd decided to take a nap in there.

"...why?" asked Wasaaru.

"Who gives a shit why, you freak? Do you want one or not?"

Wasaaru still did not trust his intentions, but he said, "It was vodka and Thunderjolt."

"Quite a step up," Balt said.

Wasaaru looked confused. "What's that mean?"

Balt hesitated. He didn't know if his cousin remembered the time they'd stolen beer from their grandfather's stash. It was a fond memory for Balt, but the same might not be true for Wasaaru.

"I just mean since the last time we drank together," he said.

"You aren't drinking anything," Wasaaru pointed out.

"That's true. I've had enough tonight, I think. Your drink sounds kinda tasty, though. I might grab one too." Continuing his streak of trying what everyone else was ordering. Then he said, "I meant the time we stole beer from Grandpa. You remember that?"

Wasaaru grinned. "Yeah," he said. "You couldn't hold your booze at all."

"I don't think that's how it went," said Balt. "I just didn't like it."

"Same thing."

"It's not, though."

"You threw it up!"

"Whoa now," said Balt, raising a hand. "Let's not talk tall here. I didn't throw it up, I spit it out. Big diff." Why did he keep saying that? He went on. "It tasted *so* bad. It was worse than the shit I had here." Balt was starting to think beer was not the beverage for him.

"Of course it was," Wasaaru said. "The stuff Grandpa liked was that old, nasty, cheap shit that he grew up with. The only sort of shit that his tiny-ass hometown could get, and the only stuff he could afford, anyway. That was, like, some bottom of the barrel convenience store sort of shit."

"He could definitely afford better beer than that."

"When he was older, yeah. But that was what he grew up with. It was a nostalgia thing, I think. He had to know it tasted like shit, but he liked it anyway. It was his beer."

Thinking about his grandfather sitting in his recliner, watching a Jekua battle or a cometball game or whatever else on the television while cracking open one of those horrendous beers, made Balt smile.

"You didn't like it either," Balt said. "I don't know why you kept drinking it."

"We'd gone through all that effort to steal it, I didn't want it to go to waste. You kept spitting it out for the crabs to suck up, but I wanted to savor it."

"There was nothing to savor there."

Wasaaru shrugged. "I was trying to be sophisticated, I guess."

"There was nothing sophisticated about that beer."

"Well, it felt pretty fancy to me. Made me feel cool."

"That's because we were nine years old. Idiot children."

"That was my favorite part of that visit," Wasaaru said.

Balt smiled. "It was mine, too. Even though the drink was terrible."

"You liked that visit because it was the only time you ever beat me at wicker."

"Okay, now *that* is bullshit."

"It's not. Don't talk shit, dude. You know I've *always* beaten you at wicker."

"That's bullshit!" Balt protested again.

"It's not," said Wasaaru. "And, I have to say...you only

even won that day because I was so much drunker than you. I was actually drinking the beer, while you kept spitting it out like a baby."

"You've always got some kind of excuse when I beat you," said Balt. "First it's that you got a bad massage, now it's that you were too drunk."

"I was nine and drunk. I think it's fairly reasonable to say that my coordination was not at its best."

"Next you're gonna say the sand on the beach was too soft or something."

The memory brought something else to the forefront of Balt's mind. That trip to their grandparents' house was the last time he and Wasaaru went there together before their grandmother passed her bestiary down to Balt. Balt went back to visit again a few weeks later, but Wasaaru didn't.

Once again, he tried the blinking method, this time trying to banish that thought rather than the heaviness of his skull.

"Anyway," he said, "you want another vodka and Thunderjolt?"

Wasaaru mulled it over a moment before saying, "Sure."

Then Balt said, "There are, like, a billion different Thunderjolt flavors. Do I have to specify one, or…?"

"They just use the original flavor, you idiot," said Wasaaru.

"Alright, I'll be back in a second," Balt said, standing up. The entire bar immediately lurched sideways and he had to steady himself on the table.

"You alright?" Wasaaru asked him.

"Fine," he replied. "Just, uh…just feelin' it, I guess."

"Told you you couldn't hold your booze."

"Shut up."

"Go get our drinks."

They both laughed, and Balt walked to the bar.

31

A MAGICAL NIGHT

NIONA WAS NOT DRUNK ENOUGH TO SLUR HER SPEECH OR trip over her own feet, but she was drunk enough to admit that there was the slightest, tiniest little baby chance that she initially judged Holly too harshly.

She was not going to walk back Holly being annoying as all hell, because that was undeniably true, but the woman *was* fun to drink with. And best of all, she was a staunch believer in the idea of the birthday girl never paying for her own drinks. On her birthday, that was a stance that Niona could get behind.

The biggest surprise of the night came when Holly procured a deck of cards out of her purse.

They had just finished a game of Block Tower, minus Balt, who was nowhere to be found. Probably asleep on the bathroom floor, Niona figured. They could let him rest for a while. Not like any of them could easily enter the bathroom to search for him anyway.

Holly calmly placed the deck down, pushing aside the

pile of huge wooden blocks that Alani had just sent plummeting to the table. The blocks tumbled over each other and knocked into empty food baskets that were covered in grease and puddles of melted cheese.

Despite matching her drink for drink, Holly was holding her composure even better than Niona was, and Niona thought of herself as a pro. She glanced from Holly's hands taking out the deck up to the woman's face, and Holly grinned that wide grin of hers. "What is this?" Niona asked. "We playin' poker? 'Cause I have my doubts Alani here knows the rules."

"That is very astute," said Alani. She was still nursing her second glass of water.

"No," Holly said.

"This turnin' into a blackjack table?" Niona guessed next.

"No, no games," said Holly. Niona was mesmerized by the thin cards *thwipping* against each other as Holly shuffled them. Maybe she was just a touch drunker than she thought if such a simple action could enthrall her.

"Cards are for games," Niona said. She thought the statement was obvious, but evidently it still had to be stated.

Holly fluttered her eyes at Niona and said, "They're also for magic."

Niona slammed her hands on the table and yelled, "Wow! *Wow*! You're a magician now, too? This is real?"

"Oh, it's real, alright," said Aeiko with a hint of exasperation. This was surely not their first experience with Holly's magic, not by a long shot.

Niona guffawed. She was ready to officially revise her

judgment of Holly now. As it turned out, *somehow* she hadn't judged the woman harshly enough. How could she ever in a million years have anticipated close-up magic being thrown into the mix?

"This must be what got you two together," said Niona. Either that, or it was what split them apart. Holly chuckled, while Aeiko said nothing. Alani took another sip of water.

Holly finished shuffling and picked up the deck. "Okay," she said, spreading it across the table with every card face down. "Pick a card." Her expression was way more self-satisfied than it had any right to be.

"So many to choose from..." said Niona, anxiously tapping her fingertips on the table. She went for a card near the left end of the deck and slipped it free from the rest of the cards.

Making sure to obscure it from Holly's view, she checked the face. It was the four of diamonds. Holly's deck was Jekua-themed, with a cartoon picture of a Juntoo slinging around the diamonds. It was a child's deck.

"I take it I should show everyone?" Niona then said.

"Except for me."

"Naturally."

Holly picked up the rest of the deck and bodily turned away from them as Niona showed her card to Alani and Aeiko. They both nodded as they examined the card. Aeiko did not look amused, gulping down some of their beer.

"Got it locked in?" Holly asked.

"Yep," Niona confirmed.

Holly turned back around and extended the deck toward her. "Stick it anywhere you'd like."

Niona outstretched her card and jammed it back into the deck. It took a slight bit of effort, since Holly was clamping the other cards down tight. That had to be part of the trick, although Niona was not well-versed enough in magic to know how exactly.

"Alright," Holly said, holding the deck behind her back, "now I'm gonna find your card without even looking."

"Wow," Niona sighed. "Incredible feats of wonder, here."

Holly made a face of deep concentration for a few seconds, then shot Niona a flirty wink. She placed the deck on the table, face up, and began to slowly fan out the cards. Sure enough, she hit a single card that remained face down. She stopped, using the point of her index finger to dramatically slide the card out from the deck.

"Is this your card?" she asked, flipping it over.

It was the four of diamonds, complete with its mischievous Juntoo.

"Whoa…" muttered Alani, genuinely impressed by the trick. She leaned in closer to get a better look at the card.

Holly looked immensely proud of herself, confident that she was right.

"Nailed it," said Niona.

She returned the card to the deck and started shuffling it again. "Want to know how I did it?" she asked.

"Nope," Niona replied. She kind of did want to know how the trick was done, but not enough to listen to the woman's explanation of it.

"Well, I can't tell you anyway," said Holly. "A true magician would never let you peek behind the curtain."

"And I can tell you are a true magician," Niona said.

"Of course."

"So, is this a typical night of drinking for you? Playing Never Have I Ever and doing magic?"

"No, not always. I just thought you might enjoy it."

Niona had to reassess her behavior if something she had done or said was somehow giving off the impression that she wanted close-up magic done to her. She was obviously living her life very wrong.

"We had a neighbor who did card tricks all the time," said Alani. "Remember Mr. Pono?"

"Oh, yeah," Aeiko nodded. "He would sit on the steps outside Goi House with his deck of cards all day. He was, what? Sixty years old or something? Just some retired old man wanting to entertain himself."

"He seemed like he was a hundred, to me," Alani laughed.

"Anyone older than thirty seems ancient to a ten-year-old," Aeiko said. "Worse than just him doing magic at all—"

"Hey!" Holly objected.

"—look, the magic is lame. Sorry. Anyway, worse than just doing magic was the fact that he was set up right behind Mrs. Orlo's food cart. If you wanted any yucca fries, you were inevitably going to have to endure a trick or two from Mr. Pono."

"That sounds perfectly pleasant to me," said Holly.

"Snack and a show," said Niona. "Classic combo. Classic."

It was then that Balt finally showed his face again. He sauntered up to the table, his eyes drawn to the deck of cards that Holly was loudly shuffling. The noise was cutting through the chatter of the other patrons.

"What's this?" he said.

"Cards," Niona replied dryly.

"Where have you been?" Alani asked.

"Oh. I ran into Wasaaru," he said.

"...did a barroom brawl break out and we didn't notice?" Alani said, cocking an eyebrow.

"We were too captivated by the magic," said Niona.

"You're doing magic?" Balt asked Holly. Was that a tinge of enthusiasm Niona detected in his voice? That was no good.

"You like magic?" Niona asked.

"I don't *not* like it, I guess," he shrugged. That small movement nearly toppled him, making Niona laugh. The boy was out of his depth.

"Yes, I am," Holly said. "Want to see a trick? I just blew everyone's minds a minute ago."

"That's my brain there, on the floor," Niona said, pointing at nothing. Balt was in enough of a daze to actually look.

When he looked back up at the deck, he said, "Yeah."

"Wait, what happened with Wasaaru?" Alani asked.

"What do you mean?"

"I mean why were you gone so long?"

Another shrug. "We were just chattin'. I bought him a drink." He then turned to Niona and informed her, "I like vodka Thunderjolts."

"Me too, pal," she said.

"What do you mean you were chatting?" Alani asked.

"I dunno, we just talked a little," he said.

"Like…rudely? Being rude to each other?"

"I mean, a little, yeah. But also no?"

"Would you describe it as being 'perfectly pleasant'?" Niona asked.

Balt shook his head. "That's maybe a bit far, but it was…goodly pleasant."

"What does that mean?" said Alani.

"I don't really know."

"That's nothing," said Niona.

"Pick a card," said Holly.

Niona scooted over so Balt could sit beside her and be wowed by Holly's magic.

She was honestly proud of him for taking that first step with his cousin. The guy seemed like kind of a dickhead, but apparently they had some great times together as kids, so that was something to hold on to. She was surprised that he had acted on her advice so quickly, too. When she'd said it, she'd assumed it would be an "over the course of several weeks or a year" sort of thing rather than a "later that night" thing.

Balt was indeed wowed by Holly's magic, and that wasn't the only trick she knew how to do. She demonstrated two others, one on Alani and one on Aeiko, before finally putting the cards away and rebuilding the tower of blocks. While they played, Alani probed Balt about his conversation with Wasaaru, but he didn't have many details to offer. It was either an incredibly boring conversation, or he was too drunk to conjure up the specificities she craved.

After another two hours and a few more drinks, the group decided to call it quits. Niona and Balt had battles the next day, after all, and Balt really needed to get some sleep. He was going to feel like shit in the morning, which was highly amusing to her. According to the schedule, his match against the intrepid Johnny Fierce wasn't until later in the afternoon, so he would be fine. Her match against Winston Knox, however, was the third of the day. When Niona glanced at her linkpad, she discovered it was half past midnight, so technically their matches were today.

The group stumbled out into the darkened alleyway underneath Barnello's unlit sign. Well, in actuality, Balt and Aeiko were the only ones stumbling. Niona was definitely tipsy, but she was holding it together pretty well, as was Holly. Alani had never even gotten a third glass of water, let alone any alcohol.

"Alright," Niona said, standing apart from the others. "Guess I'll catch y'all in the morning."

Balt checked the time on his own linkpad and said, "It's pretty late. I'll walk to you to your hotel."

Niona chuckled. "How gallant," she said.

"Thank you for noticing."

"You think you can protect me like that?" she said, pointing at him. He was wobbling back and forth like seaweed in the tide.

He held up his wrist, displaying the kayet he had for some reason worn out. Dork. "Of course," he said. "I've got my four buds here."

"If you could summon Piss at all, let alone *control* him, I would be absolutely shocked," she said.

"Easy." He started to channel mana into his kayet while also blinking rapidly.

"Stop, stop," she said, stepping forward and lowering his arm. "C'mon. You can walk with me, it's fine."

"Will you make it back to the apartment alright?" Alani asked, worried.

"Yeah, it's cool," Balt assured her, taking an enormous breath and letting it out slowly before speaking again. A common sign of someone feeling good and normal. "I'll see you in a bit."

Niona and Balt started down the alley while the others went in the opposite direction, back toward Aeiko and Holly's apartment. Balt was still fairly unsteady on his feet, but the brisk night air would sober him up by the time they got to her hotel. She was sure he'd be fine for his walk to Aeiko's. If it seemed like he wouldn't be, he could crash on her floor.

The city was buzzing as they walked its streets. Loud music drifted from bars as their doors swung open; enticing aromas drifted from brick and mortar restaurants and food trucks alike; people sat on curbs smoking and laughing. It reminded her of home, of late nights walking around Himony with her friends. Getting a little too drunk when she was a little too young and having to walk around, killing time and sobering up before returning home to her father's disappointed gaze. The most common pastime between her and her friends was to go down to a joint called the Square Shack, which served little beef and chicken sliders that were shaped into square patties. She did not want to know how or why they shaped the chicken into a square, but either way, it was delicious. They were thin, dry, shitty little sliders, but with the moon above you and a belly full of beer, there was no better taste in the world. The over-salted and under-cooked fries went down a lot better when one's senses were dulled, too.

Not knowing precisely where Barnello's was located in relation to her hotel, Niona had to pull up the map on her linkpad and have it calculate a route. She and Balt followed it in silence for a minute before he finally cleared his throat and spoke up.

"So," he said meekly, "how was your birthday?"

"Not bad," she said.

"You glad you told me about it?"

"I suppose so," she grinned. "I coulda done without the magic, though."

"Aw, come on! That made it an even more magical night."

"No offense to Aeiko, I'm a fan of them, but I do not have any idea how they tolerated that girl for so long. Is Lakahlo doing secret experiments on their brain? Has Aeiko been chemically altered in some way to be able to withstand psychological torture?"

"I think 'torture' is a bit of an extreme term to throw around about card tricks."

"Is it *really*, though?"

"Fine. I'll let you have it, since it's your birthday. Although, I guess it's actually not, anymore."

"It's still my birthday night. It counts."

"Fine," Balt said again. Then, "Things went pretty okay with Wasaaru."

"Yeah?"

"Mhmm."

"I'm glad to hear it."

She wasn't going to pry, if he didn't want to talk about it. They walked down the block in silence. There was a rustling in a tree nearby, and a Suelu scampered down the trunk and off into the darkness.

"I thought my life would be different at eighteen," Balt suddenly said. "I had a whole vision for myself, which I realize is kinda weird. But I imagined me and Wasaaru training our Jekuas together all the time, havin' our grandma as a mentor."

Some of his words slurred together slightly, but she was surprised how comprehensible he was overall. "Remisti Vana woulda been a great teacher," said Niona.

"I know," he sighed. He kicked a small, broken chunk of concrete that skittered along the sidewalk, bouncing off a trash can. "I was always so excited to be spending weeks and weeks at her place on Pakree, going out each day to explore the land around Paluopa City and imprint Jekuas with Wasaaru. I figured we'd be experiencing every step of our summoning careers together."

"Well, you kinda are, aren't you? Didn't you both imprint your first Jekua around the same time?"

"Yeah."

"And you've both been traveling across the islands, and now you're both in this tournament. You've both made it to round three."

"I guess that's all true."

"You might not be strictly doin' it all together, but you *kinda* are, yeah? Just...apart."

"Those two words contradict each other, you know."

"You're *physically* apart, but *spiritually* together."

"I don't even know if that much is true."

"Eh, who knows? And who knows where you two'll be in, like, a week's time."

"Probably not much different from where we are now."

"Maybe not, but maybe you'll be one step closer together, after that first step you took tonight. It's all gotta start with those little steps, until you're together again. If that's what you even want, anyway."

"It is," he said. "I think."

"You don't sound super sure."

"No, I mean, yeah, I do want to be friends with him again. It's just hard looking past all the bullshit from the past three years."

"Yeah," she said.

They took a left turn, following the blue line on her linkpad that was leading them to the hotel. It was only six minutes away, if the app was to be believed.

"My life at twenty-five ain't exactly what I was expecting, either," she said.

Balt looked over at her. "How so?"

She smiled, wondering briefly if he was even going to remember any part of this conversation come morning. She said, "When I was younger, I thought that by now I was gonna be a manager at my dad's resort."

Balt balked. "Really?"

"Yup. Sittin' behind a desk, wearin' a nice, crisp uniform, puttin' on a big, toothy, stupid smile every time some moronic guest comes up to me with a dumb-assed issue."

"I cannot imagine you interacting with a hotel guest."

She laughed, since she had a hard time imagining it too. "My dad always talked about how he wanted the resort to be a family business, how it would all be mine someday, how we'd build a bunch of locations across the archipelago, all that shit. As a kid, I just saw that my dad was rich and he bought me whatever I wanted, so I was like hey, yeah, bein' able to buy myself anything I want seems pretty nice. Cool. I'm down."

"I definitely wouldn't turn down more money if somebody was offering. Even if it meant talking to the general public."

"It wasn't really what I wanted to do, though. It just became my dream 'cause it was my dad's dream. That's how it always goes for kids though, huh? Whatever our parents say is just automatically the truth for us. So anyway, my plan at this point was to be one of the managers at the resort, learnin' the ropes, gettin' ready to fully take over for my dad."

"But now you're a Summoner."

"Ahh, so you've picked up on that."

"I did, yeah, just yesterday," he said.

"I've always said you were a slow learner."

"Harsh. Also, I don't know if I'm just, uh…too *out of sorts* to follow your logic or if you just haven't gotten to the point yet."

"My point is two-fold. First, life might not work out the way you always pictured it, but sometimes it's even better! Like me bein' a Summoner instead of some miserable hotel manager. And a pretty decent Summoner, at that, if I can toot my own horn real quick. Second, which ties into the first, you just can't predict where your life's gonna end up. Things with you and your cousin might seem pretty hopeless at the moment, since shit got so bad and weird between y'all, but that might not be the case forever. By Winter, you might be best pals, pairin' up for team battles as you explore the wilds of Hurrathsa."

"Hurrathsa is a civilized country."

"Hey, which of us has been there?"

"Both of us."

"Oh. Well, then you should know they got plenty of wilds in between all the civilization. My point is, don't get stuck focusing on what you assume the future will be like, 'cause there's really no way to know."

"Point taken," he said.

"Is any of that helpful?" she asked. She felt like the thread had gotten away from her a little bit.

"I think so?" he said. She could definitively hear the question mark at the end of the statement, but it was better than nothing.

A couple minutes later, they came to the unmanned front door of her hotel. Niona turned to Balt, clapping her hands together, and said, "How you feelin'?"

"I'm good," he said. She noticed he could actually stand upright without tipping over now, so that was a positive sign. Then he said, "Thank you for everything today. I really appreciate it."

Niona smiled. "I gotta thank you too," she said. "This was a nice birthday. Maybe the nicest I've had in a while, honestly."

That brought a smile to his face. "I'm glad," he said. She caught his eyes flick downward, looking from her eyes to her lips then back in an instant.

Before she could fully process what was happening, Balt was leaning forward with his lips pursed and his eyes closed.

His lips brushed against hers for merely a moment before she took a step backward. He stumbled a bit but caught himself, opening his eyes wide in a look of terror.

"Oh," he said. "Sorry. Sorry. I, uh…"

"It's okay," she said. "Really, don't worry about it." What the hell was happening?

"I thought we…uh…" He was floundering.

Niona had no lifejacket to throw him. "You're great and all, but, like…I dunno." She almost outright said that she thought of him more as a younger brother, but she didn't want to kick him while he was down.

"No, I get it," he said. "Sorry, I've just had too much to drink. Just bein' dumb."

"Nah, it's okay," she told him.

"I'll see you tomorrow?"

"Are you okay to get back to the apartment?"

"Yeah, for sure," he said, nodding. Niona could only imagine how quickly this interaction had sobered him up.

"Okay," she said. "Be safe. Thanks again for tonight."

"Goodnight," he said, then started back down the street. He was practically jogging. If she could peer around the corner, she guessed she would see him breaking into a full-on sprint.

"Well," Niona sighed to herself, "that was…somethin'."

She needed to get to bed.

32

OH WELL

"YOU AWAKE?" BALT ASKED FROM THE FLOOR.

This came after the rustling of Alani's blankets as she repositioned herself. The fold-out couch bed's metal bars dug into her back, but she didn't know if the floor would be better or worse than that. She'd added an extra layer of blanket underneath her for cushioning, but it didn't accomplish much. It made her a little warmer, though, so there was that.

"Yeah," she replied, facing toward Aeiko and Holly's rooms.

There were no clocks anywhere, and her linkpad was turned off, so she had no idea what time it was. Given his usual tendencies combined with his condition the night before, she was shocked that Balt was awake before her.

"I have to tell you something," he said softly. It was almost a whisper.

Alani's heart started racing. She sat up quickly, the

motion digging her ass into one of the hard metal bars, making her wince. "What's wrong?" she asked.

Balt lay face-up, staring at the ceiling with his arms folded over his stomach. He glanced over at her, letting out a small laugh, though he remained flat on his back.

"Jeez," he said.

"What?"

"You're so serious all of a sudden."

"You're the one who said you had something to say."

"I do, but it's not any, like, bad news or anything. Well, I mean, kind of, but—"

"That's a very alarming way to wake someone up," she interrupted.

"I thought you were awake."

"Technically, yes, but I don't know if I was *getting up* yet."

"Sorry. Was it really that bad, though?"

"Who gravely says they have news for someone early in the morning when it's *not* something serious?"

"I don't know."

"If it's not serious, then what is it?"

He pondered for a moment. "Gossip, kind of?"

That piqued her interest. "What is it?" she asked. "You said it was kind of bad news."

"You can lay back down, don't worry," he said.

Alani sighed and laid back down on the uncomfortable bed. There were only two days left of the tournament after today, so presumably they would be leaving Makanuele before the week was up. Her body could sustain for that long, she thought.

She said, "I assume this has something to do with Wasaaru?"

"Why do you think that?"

She shrugged, although he couldn't see her do it. "I just didn't expect to hear about you two grabbing a drink together, that's all. Not without it coming to blows, anyway."

He laughed mirthlessly. "It wasn't totally unpleasant," he said. "I dunno. It was weird, for sure. I think that was the longest interaction we've had in three years."

"Aside from literally fighting each other, with your Jekuas."

"Right."

A beat, then, "Why did you go up to him? I would've thought you'd spot him and high-tail it back to our table. You missed out on some breathtaking magic from Holly." She said it sarcastically, but in truth Alani had been somewhat impressed by the woman's tricks.

"That's a shame, but I'll have to soldier on," Balt said. "I dunno, it was just something Niona said to me about the whole thing."

That struck her. "You two talked about it?"

"A little, yeah."

She didn't know how to absorb that. In the three years Balt had been harboring this anger toward his cousin, the two of them had scarcely spoken on the subject. She'd barely opened up about the conflicts with her parents, though, so maybe she couldn't blame him too much. If she thought about it, she would feel more comfortable talking to Aeiko about such a thing, for reasons unbeknownst even to herself. Maybe it made some kind of sense that Balt could more easily open up to Niona about it.

Still, hearing it hurt her. They were supposed to be best friends. Why were they keeping their deepest pains from each other? What was the point?

"She said you should talk to him?" said Alani.

"Yeah. She pointed out that, uh…that maybe we're both a little to blame for how shit soured between us."

Alani knew the broad strokes of their conflict, but she had never actually been told what the tipping point had been for Balt to cut himself off from Wasaaru. Had he been that specific with Niona?

"So you apologized to him?"

Balt laughed. "No, not quite."

"Did he apologize to you?"

"Hell no. You know him well enough to know he'd never do that. It'd require his ego to deflate even the teeniest, tiniest amount, which I don't think is possible."

"What did you two talk about, then?"

"Jekuas." He stifled a laugh.

She let out a giggle too. "Of course," she said. "What else would you talk about? Sure, there are millions of different things to talk about, but what's better than Jekuas?"

"See, you get it!"

"Sounds like a very illuminating conversation. At least you two have that common ground."

"We also talked about our grandparents a little."

"Oh," she said. "That's good." Alani was glad to hear that he'd been able to talk about his grandparents with Wasaaru. She hadn't really known them very well before the Pakree Island incident, so even if Balt wanted to talk to her about them, she wasn't sure what she'd say. Her grandparents had died when she was young, before she could form any memories about them, so she didn't have any stories of her own to share.

"Anyway," Balt said, "you got me off-track. I wasn't trying to talk about Wasaaru."

"Was it about how bad you feel this morning?" she asked, grinning to herself.

"No."

"How bad do you feel?"

"Pretty bad. I feel like I got punched in the head by a Bruiserweight and then stepped on by an Urud."

"Do you feel sick at all?"

"Oh, absolutely."

"I heard you getting up a lot in the night."

"Only to pee, I swear. No throwing up."

"Sure."

"Go check the rim if you don't believe me! Not a speck of puke tarnishing that ceramic."

"Ew, jeez. I believe you."

"Good. Okay, you led us astray again! Let me talk."

"Talk, then," she chuckled.

Balt took a deep breath, once more making her feel like the topic was something serious, despite his insistence that it wasn't.

Finally, he said, "I kissed Niona."

It felt like the world itself took a breath. She knew Balt was into Niona, of course, but for some reason she'd never really expected it to go anywhere. When Alani exhaled, she said, "What?"

"I mean, well—it wasn't much of a kiss," he admitted.

"That's the real reason why you wanted to walk her home?"

"No! It wasn't planned, or anything. It just sorta…felt right in the moment, I guess. We'd been having a good conversation, we were both standing there in the moonlight or whatever, she looked so pretty…" He trailed off, lost in the memory.

Alani waited a few seconds for him to go on. Then she said, "So are you two, like, a couple now?" Balt had never had a girlfriend before. He'd gone on a few dates with some people they went to school with, but nothing serious ever blossomed from those. For a moment she thought this might have even been his first kiss, until she remembered the whole Lexi Yutaro ordeal. That was a subject better left untouched.

"No, no, we're not," Balt sputtered. She could hear him rolling over, though she didn't know if he turned to face her or the wall. "It…did not go quite as well as I'd hoped."

"What do you mean?" Had this somehow gone worse than the Lexi Yutaro ordeal? Was that even possible? She didn't see how it could, but Balt had surprised her before.

He sighed deeply. "It only lasted for, like, a split second before she pulled away."

"Oh. Yikes."

"Yeah, *yikes* is an understatement."

"She wasn't into it?"

"I guess not. She pulled away super fast. I almost fell forward and busted my chin on the sidewalk, she moved away so quickly."

"Was that because she pulled away so fast, or because

you were drunk?"

"Both," he admitted.

She said, "I'm sorry."

On the ground, she could hear him rustling around again. Then he said, "It's fine, I guess." His words tapered off.

Alani sat up and offered him a frown of sympathy. He was gazing up at the ceiling again, and turned his head to look at her.

"Really, I am," she said. "I know that must've sucked."

He smiled weakly. "Yeah, it did."

"Are things…okay between you two?" Alani asked. She wasn't sure how else to phrase it.

Balt turned from her back to the ceiling. "I dunno," he answered. "She seemed kinda embarrassed after it happened, but not nearly as embarrassed as I was. I felt like such a jackass. We haven't texted each other or anything yet today, so I dunno."

"When is she supposed to come over?"

"I think ten? The tournament doesn't start until noon today."

"What time is it now?"

He grabbed his linkpad, which was sitting on the floor next to him. He never turned his off like she did. He clicked the screen on and said, "A little past eight."

"How are you awake already?"

"I don't know. My stomach hurts."

"Maybe you do need to puke."

"Probably, but I shall resist for as long as possible."

Alani said, "Are you sure you're feeling okay?"

"No, I just said my stomach hurts."

"About Niona, I mean."

He shrugged. "It is what it is," he said.

"That's true, I guess, but you can still feel upset about it."

He stared upward, not saying anything for a few moments. Then he broke into a smile. He looked over at her and said, "Wanna know the most embarrassing part?"

She couldn't help but laugh at his expression. "There's more?"

"Oh, yeah. After that whole awkward shit was over, I, like…I basically ran away."

"You *ran away*?" she said, disbelieving.

"I fled."

"That's ridiculous."

"Yeah, it was. But it felt right in the moment."

"Just like the kiss did."

"Yes. My instincts were not at their best last night."

"That might've been the alcohol."

"Oh, you think?" he laughed.

"It's possible."

"Yeah, it's possible. That's not the embarrassing part, though."

"How is that not the embarrassing part?"

Balt braced himself, then said, "The embarrassing part is that I fell."

"No you didn't."

"I did."

"Please tell me she saw you fall."

"Why do you want her to have seen that?" he said, sitting up in a flash. His mouth hung open in shock and offense.

"Because it would be funny?"

"If she'd seen, I would not have made it home last night," he said, laughing at his own misfortune. "I would've run straight outta the city and kept goin' until I hit the ocean, then kept goin' even further. Let the waves take me away."

"So she didn't see. Shoot."

"Hell no, she didn't. Well, I mean, unless she followed me, which seems unlikely. But it was after I turned the corner and was halfway down the next block. I was cutting across the street, and a Suelu zapped something on the sidewalk, and I thought the flash of light was a car. It spooked the shit out of me and I jumped mid-run and slipped."

"Was the Suelu even in the road?"

"No, it was on the sidewalk I was running toward."

"So you thought a car was on the sidewalk, barreling toward you."

"I was fairly discombobulated at that point already. I was not at my best."

"Clearly," she said, openly laughing at him.

"Shut up," he said, though he was laughing too.

"Was *anyone* around to see?" she asked.

"To see me scream at practically nothing and fall flat on my ass? Man, I really hope not."

"Wait, you screamed too?"

"Of course I did. I was scared."

"Of a little Suelu."

"It was using Electrical magic!"

"On what?"

Balt was reluctant to answer.

"On what?" Alani repeated.

He said, "A half of a half of a sandwich."

"A fourth of a sandwich."

"I guess that's the fraction, yeah."

"Why was it electrocuting a fourth of a sandwich?"

"How should I know the inner machinations of a Suelu's mind?" he asked.

"What was on the sandwich?"

"I think you're getting lost in the details here."

"I just like some good scene-setting."

"I don't need to describe every insignificant detail of every food item."

"Is your ass okay?" she then asked.

"It's just one more part of my body that hurts," he said.

"Are you going to be able to compete today?"

He nodded. "I should be fine," he said. "A little more out of it than usual, but mostly fine. Getting some food in me should help a ton, I think."

"Sorry about Niona," she said again. "Although I guess it could've been worse, if she'd seen the pratfall."

"Yeah, no doubt," he laughed.

They both took a second to laugh at the mental image of Balt falling in the middle of an empty street, barely provoked, before he continued speaking.

"I probably should've expected it," he said.

Alani blinked. "Why?" She always thought that he and Niona had good rapport, good chemistry. While she might not have anticipated Balt doing anything about his crush, part of her suspected that the crush was reciprocated. She just also kind of thought that his Jekuas would always take precedence over romance.

Balt laid back down on his pallet, twiddling his thumbs. "The age difference, I guess," he said simply. "She just turned twenty-five last night, we've got seven years between us now. That feels kinda insurmountable, don't you think?"

"Uh…I mean, I don't know," Alani said, laying back down too. "There are plenty of couples with that much of a gap between them, right? Even bigger ones, too. Aren't Wasaaru's parents six or seven years apart?"

"Something like that. I dunno, I just kinda feel like an idiot for even thinking it was a remote possibility. I should've known nothing was gonna happen between us."

Alani remained quiet. All she could think about now was the age difference between herself and Aeiko. It was only three years, not nearly as big a gap as Balt and Niona, but still. She rolled over, once again facing the closed door of their bedroom. Her heart fluttered thinking about them sleeping soundly in their bed. Then that feeling was immediately replaced with shame and embarrassment; maybe Balt was right. Maybe it was foolish to think that anything would develop between them. The feelings that had bubbled up over the past couple weeks were nothing more than a childhood crush resurfacing. A dumb kid who was bewitched by her older sister's friend.

Suddenly feeling acutely self-conscious, she rolled over to face away from Aeiko's room. Instead her eyes bored into the bathroom door, which stood slightly ajar after Balt's nighttime dalliance.

"Oh well," Balt said, then sighed loudly.

Yeah, Alani thought. *Oh well.*

33
NIONA VS. WINSTON

It had been stupid to send out Boombox first. That hadn't even been her initial plan, she'd just been rattled by Winston's intimidating frame and thought she ought to summon her fighter.

Winston Knox was an enormous man. He was the biggest man Niona had ever seen, both in height and width. Two of Alani could've fit across this guy's impressive chest, which was currently tucked within a black mesh shirt and a green jacket. He had muscles stacked upon muscles, with biceps that were practically bigger than Niona's admittedly big head. It was ridiculous how ripped he was. Almost cartoonish.

The only part of him that wasn't statuesque was his left arm, the one not sporting his kayet. It was shriveled up a bit, clear signs of repeated soulsickness. For most people, it would look like a relatively normal arm as far as girth and tone were concerned, but compared to the rest of his body it looked like a dead limb hanging limp at his side.

And that's exactly what it did; it did not appear that he had much control over that arm, and it swung at his side whenever he moved the rest of his body. It was also streaked with scars and pockmarks, more like the side of a volcano than a person's skin.

Back in the locker room, Andy Lowe had let out a whistle as he stared up at the bracket. "You're up against Winston Knox, huh?" he had said by Niona's side.

On another screen, Niona was watching Cole Illiom being pounded by Kallon. "Yup," she said absently.

"I'm scared of him," Hana Minir chimed in.

"You're going up against Uil," Andy said to the woman. "Aren't you afraid of *him*?"

"I'm scared of Uil's Jekuas, for sure. But I'm scared of Winston himself."

The exchange had not filled Niona with a huge amount of confidence.

Now she and Winston were standing at opposite ends of a typical battle arena setup. The staff did not put a whole lot of effort into the third round environment. It was simply a large, rectangular rubber mat with the Xatetu Field logo at its center and nothing else. Nothing for her to play with.

Boombox had beaten the hell out of Winston's Lemamo, a Gravity- and Friction-Type that tried to slow down her Bruiserweight, but Boombox could still pack a punch. Unfortunately, Boombox laid down such a beating on the thing that Winston withdrew it pretty quickly, and it was an odd-numbered round. That meant Niona had to withdraw Boombox too and send out her second Jekua.

So now she stood there, the tips of her shoes grazing

the blue rubber mat, struggling to land a decent hit with Glom.

Her Muggish was on the far edge of the mat, keeping his distance from Winston's second Jekua: a Bowlder. Another creature with Gravity abilities, but its primary Type was Elastic. It was humanoid, with craggy brown skin and thick, meaty limbs like its Summoner. Its ovular head sported six rounded nubs, and each of its six fingers had natural tan bands that looked like championship rings. Bowlders walked hunched over, technically on all fours, but in each of their hands they grasped huge, gray boulders that were a vital part of their fighting style.

Niona did not like this Bowlder. Glom had only managed to hit it with a couple fireballs so far, and none of them seemed to damage the thing at all. Its skin was tough to begin with, even if Winston wasn't reinforcing it with Elastic magic.

The Bowlder reared up on its hind legs, pulling its left arm back. Then it swung forward, releasing the massive rock it held. The boulder bounced unnaturally along the mat, rolling like a bowling ball straight toward Glom.

Just before it reached Glom, its rigidity increased to its natural amount and it smashed into the Muggish with immense force. Glom's malleable body burst apart and coated the boulder, with each extra roll pounding him into the ground again and again, chipping away at Niona's mana.

Then the boulder's gravity was decreased, sending both it and Glom flying forty feet into the air before increasing it again, sending them slamming into the mat with a resounding shudder.

Even Niona felt that one, deep in her chest. That drained a great deal of mana. She cursed under her breath and tried to ascertain whether there was anything useful Glom could do, or if she needed to relent and summon her third Jekua. She wanted to save Pops for last, since she was most confident with him, but she also wasn't sure what she'd do with Garbo against Winston's beefy monsters.

The Bowlder had to retrieve its rock if it wanted to use it again, it couldn't just make it magically float back. Winston started moving it across the mat toward Glom, who was still enveloping the rock.

Niona focused on increasing the thermal energy that Glom was putting out. The Muggish was essentially comprised of magma, so surely that would melt the rock, or something. If only Glom had Sonic abilities as well, she could probably use those to vibrate the particles in the rock at an even faster rate to melt it. As it stood, though, all she had was his heat, and the Bowlder was fast approaching.

With her proximity to Glom, she could feel more and more heat radiating off the Jekua as each second passed. Right now, he was no more than a puddle of bubbling red and black sludge smothering the boulder.

She glanced over at Winston's Jekua. Without its second rock to support it, it was limping across the mat. At least it was slowed down slightly.

Watching it jog haphazardly across the arena reminded her of Balt's drunken gait as he fled their deeply awkward half-kiss the night before. It was almost enough to make her laugh, but she kept a straight face as she watched the opposing Jekua.

Her eyes shot back to her own Jekua. Glom's liquid form was casting heat waves off into the air, making Winston waver in the distance. The Muggish's formless body bubbled and popped, spraying stray clumps of magma onto the mat.

The boulder shifted. It was slight, but she knew she saw it. A second later, it started sinking into the earth. Parts of it were melting.

Not fast enough, though. Winston's Bowlder was almost upon Glom.

Roughly half the rock had melted by the time Niona was forced to stop and start reshaping Glom's body. She realized then that the rock had melted down into magma as well, which she could absorb into Glom's body to bulk him up a bit. It wasn't much, but it was something. As she brought Glom's body back together, forming his upper body into the vague shape of a (tragically deformed) person, she made his lower slug-esque body crawl away from the approaching Bowlder.

Winston let out an irritable grunt at the sight of the half-melted rock. His Bowlder wouldn't be able to make much use of it as a walking implement. It would be all lopsided.

But he picked up the rock anyway and barreled toward Glom, nearly tripping over himself. Glom met the Bowlder head-on, which was actually bad news for Glom.

The Bowlder smashed its intact rock into Glom's head, splattering it all over the floor. Its arm was now covered in sizzling globs of Glom, but the Bowlder appeared mostly unaffected by this.

Glom's head reconstituted and Niona started pounding his wet fists into the Bowlder's chest. A Muggish wasn't typically used for close quarters combat, but she had to work within the unfortunate present circumstances.

Char marks were left behind after every hit, and the Bowlder reached out to choke Glom. Its fingers slipped right into Glom's viscous neck, burning the three digits as well as its palm. Regardless of the Jekua's nigh impenetrable skin, that had to be doing *some* damage to it.

Niona decided to wrap the Bowlder in a firehug. Glom leaned forward and, thanks to his extra body mass, was able to fully encase the Bowlder in himself. The Bowlder thrashed against Glom, his entire body covered in magma. Random blobs of gunk were flung across the stadium as the Bowlder flailed around.

She didn't have a plan beyond this. Why was she feeling so flustered? She didn't usually come into a Jekua battle with any sort of concrete strategy in mind, but normally she was not this confounded. Again, she berated herself for summoning Boombox too early in the match.

It wasn't because of the night before. The incident with Balt hadn't rattled her at all, it merely amused her. She felt kind of bad for him, but she tried to act as normal as possible when she saw him earlier that morning. She wanted to put him at ease, let him know that he didn't need to be uncomfortable or weird around her. It seemed to mostly work, and after a while they were back to their usual ribbing of each other. She hoped it would remain that way and he wouldn't try to bring up the kiss in conversation. As far as she was concerned, the sooner they moved past it, the better.

It wasn't because of the hangover, either. In fact, she'd barely felt it when she woke up. She must not have gotten as drunk as she thought.

So why was she performing so badly?

The Bowlder and Glom continued brawling, with more and more globs of the Muggish flying off every second. She needed to think of something to do, and fast. The pressure was building.

That was when she realized what it was: the pressure. She hadn't been explicitly thinking about it before, but now she was. Now she was aware that Vanessa Ren was watching her in the stands, judging every little move she made, making her determination on whether or not Niona should be invited to join Atoll Talent. There was suddenly more riding on this battle than there was in the previous two rounds.

She had to shake it off. She couldn't let herself be weighed down by Vanessa Ren's gaze. That was only setting herself up for failure. A recipe for disaster.

What she needed was a recipe for success, but Glom was not the best chef in her kitchen. She probably deserved some chastisement for bringing Glom into the tournament at all. There were other Thermal-Types in her arsenal that were much stronger, but she'd wanted to challenge herself. She granted herself one more mental insult before turning her attention back to the matter at hand.

The Bowlder was still covered in Glom's hot sludge.

Maybe if she turned it into not-so-hot sludge, she could turn the Bowlder into a living statue, trap it inside Glom's hardened body.

She hadn't tried using Glom's Thermal magic to decrease his body heat before, though. She wasn't sure if it would work the way she wanted it to. Nothing else was coming to mind at the moment, however, with the two Jekuas entangled in each other. His rain of fire wouldn't exactly do much here.

Degree by degree, she began lowering Glom's body temperature. It was actually much easier than she anticipated. Before, she'd never really been able to use the cooling effects of his Thermal magic, but her control over the Muggish had gotten pretty good over the past few weeks since she'd started training with him in earnest. She would kill to mod him with that Thermal Blitz Trio, if it were available already.

A few moments passed, and Glom was hardened to black rock.

Which only meant that Winston's Bowlder could now easily shatter him. The Jekua flexed and Glom's body immediately cracked, then broke apart, sending hard bits of rock tumbling to the ground. The Bowlder emerged from his rock casing like a butterfly from a cocoon.

"Shit, *shit*," Niona swore, feeling her mana drain drastically as Glom's body broke into a hundred pieces scattered across the mat.

"Ha, ha! Foolish girl!" Winston bellowed across the field. He pounded his chest with his good hand curled into a tight fist, smacking the hard metal kayet into his pecs.

His boasting gnawed at Niona, but she didn't yell anything back in retaliation. She wanted to appear professional.

Having her Muggish's body so horrifically ruined brought her down to half her reserves. That had not gone how she'd planned at all. What did Vanessa think of that dreadful display? Was the deal totally off the table already?

Stop, she told herself. Negative thinking like that wasn't going to get her anywhere. She could still win. It seemed unlikely, but it was technically possible. She had half a tank of mana left.

She withdrew Glom while starting to channel mana toward Garbo's memory card. Pops was still gonna be her last resort. She was afraid of another situation like with Boombox where she swiftly dealt with whatever Winston was about to throw out, then had to somehow finish the match with Garbo.

The broken chunks of Glom disappeared off the battlefield and were replaced with her sturdy Nuri. Garbo stood proudly, his white fur streaked with purple waving in the breeze. The Nuri's body was so muscular, Niona thought he would fit right in with the rest of Winston's coterie.

The bulky man's Bowlder disappeared and what he summoned next shook Niona to her core. How the hell was Garbo going to do anything against this shit?

What stood before her now was a Tomowori. Much like Niona's Bruiserweight, a Tomowori was a bipedal reptile, although this one was less like a lizard and more akin to a crocodile. It was covered in blue and green scales, with a long, flat snout lined with fangs. It had small, pitch-black eyes and a stout body. A long, thick tail dragged on the ground behind it.

Niona wracked her brain, trying to recall what Type a Tomowori was. She'd never fought one before, and she wasn't actually sure if she'd ever seen one in real life and not on TV. They weren't native to the Volukho Isles, but she couldn't recall if they were found in Hurrathsa or Peliq. Maybe both.

Her question was answered almost instantly. The Tomowori opened its ghastly mouth and a powerful stream of water shot out. Tidal.

Garbo's body elasticized and curved out of the way at the last second, then returned to its normal form. He dashed toward the beast, charging up an electric shock in his horns.

She fired off a lightning bolt at the Tomowori, and it hit the creature directly on its chest. The bolt crackled and fizzled into nothingness, leaving the Tomowori unperturbed.

"Dammit," Niona muttered. Another Jekua with a ton of muscles and rock-hard skin. How was she supposed to hurt this thing? Would Garbo's horns even be able to pierce its flesh?

It was worth a shot. Garbo continued charging forward, his head angled down so that his spiral horns were sticking straight out. The Tomowori's legs were too short and it was too slow to move out of the way in time. If nothing else, Garbo could easily beat the thing in raw speed.

The points of Garbo's horns glanced off the Tomowori's scales without even leaving a scratch. Niona refused to believe that was solely the Jekua's natural durability. It had to be enhanced with some sort of mod chip, surely.

While Garbo was in close range, Winston made his Jekua grab the Nuri with its long, curved claws. They latched onto Garbo, ripping into his flesh, catching him like a fish biting a hook. The Tomowori yanked him closer, opening its maw and biting down on Garbo's neck.

Niona winced, seeing blood spurt from the wound in Garbo's neck. Her mana dipped even lower, and then it drained further still as she fought against the Tomowori's grip, trying to break free. Garbo could only run away when the Tomowori let go of him, with blood dripping off its scaly chin.

As her Nuri stumbled off, Niona was dismayed to realize her mana was draining faster than it should with the simple walking movements. When she was sufficiently far away from Winston's Jekua, she stopped moving Garbo completely.

Sure enough, mana continued to drip, drip, drip from her reserves.

"Mother of hell, shit, damn," she grumbled.

Winston smiled devilishly. "We can end this now if you want, girl," he growled. Niona ignored his taunts again.

That bite had to have injected poison into Garbo's veins. It was slowly going to drain mana as time went on. It was a weak effort, though, not taking away all that much mana with each passing second. But over time, it would add up.

Between that and the Tomowori's impenetrable scales, it was probably foolish to continue fighting. She might as well withdraw Garbo and summon Pops to put an end to all this.

There was no telling what sort of beast Winston would summon last, however, and it would probably be pretty impressive to Vanessa if she could pull off a win with only her third Jekua—especially with a Nuri matched against a Tomowori.

Plus, the Tomowori was a big, powerful creature. Every movement and every ability it used probably sucked up a lot of Winston's mana. All of his Jekuas were big, nasty things, come to think of it. Just one of his Jekuas probably cost more mana to maneuver than all three of hers so far combined. It was within the realm of possibility that his mana levels were just as low as hers.

For now, Garbo would remain on the battlefield. She hoped she wouldn't regret this undeniably reckless decision. Balt's unwanted influence was rubbing off on her. Perhaps he transferred some of his stupidity with that kiss.

The Tomowori blasted another aqua jet at her, which she dodged handily. Then an array of sharpened scales lifted off its body and zoomed through the air, lacerating Garbo's flesh and cutting off strands of white and purple hair that fell in clumps to the mat.

Garbo fired another lightning bolt that fizzled pitifully on the Tomowori's skin. The move used up a fair amount of her mana, given how much energy she put into the blast, but it was all for naught. That burst had at least made the other Jekua wince, yet it still seemed mostly unharmed.

Mana continued draining away from her on account

of the Tomowori's poisonous bite. Then the creature opened its mouth wide again, exposing its fleshy pink tongue. A single bubble gurgled up from its throat, floating speedily through the air toward Garbo.

Niona ducked Garbo out of the way of the bubble and it popped uselessly in the air behind him. She had seen that move before from another Tidal Jekua; if that bubble had popped on Garbo, it would've scalded his skin.

Winston's Jekua was equipped with a ton of powerful, long-range moves. She needed to get closer, but then Garbo would be susceptible to another bite or scratch. It wasn't like his horns were making a mark on its scales, anyway.

That gave her an idea. If she couldn't hurt its exterior, then she had to go for the interior. She pictured that soft, fleshy tongue thrashing about in the Tomowori's nasty mouth.

She had a strategy now. It would require her to bait Winston, make him go in for another bite. That shouldn't be particularly difficult. The man was a highly aggressive fighter.

Garbo raced across the field, back toward the Tomowori. He left behind a trail of blood that cascaded down the gash in his neck. That open wound was contributing to her continually-draining mana, too.

While the Nuri ran, she started charging up another hefty electrical blast, one even bigger than what she'd fired at the Tomowori before. It was gonna require a lot of mana to pull off, and she prayed it'd be worthwhile.

She angled Garbo as if he was going to charge the

Tomowori's side again, and Winston opened the creature's mouth hungrily.

Perfect.

She pulled away at the last second, the Tomowori's claws grasping at nothing but air.

Garbo's body elasticized, allowing his head to rotate a full hundred and eighty degrees to face his opponent. His neck extended outward from his body, slithering through the air like a snake.

His horns jutted out and slid neatly into the Tomowori's open mouth. Niona carefully used her Jekua's finely-tuned elasticity to curve the horns downward, reaching deeper into the Tomowori's throat. They crackled with barely-contained electricity, and it was at that moment that Niona let it go.

Electrical energy exploded from Garbo's horns, obliterating the Tomowori's insides.

Its throat burst apart on both sides in a smattering of blood and sinew. Flesh tore from flesh, leaving its monstrous head dangling over its shoulder by a feeble patch of skin that ripped only a few seconds later, sending the head falling to the mat with a wet *splat*!

The Tomowori's headless body stumbled backward a couple feet before it too fell over in a crumpled heap. Garbo took a couple steps away, his face covered in gore.

Niona grinned and cupped a hand to her mouth. She yelled over to Winston, "We can end this now if you want, boy."

It would suck if he called her bluff. She was down to less than a quarter of her mana now, and she would not be able to do much with Pops if the fight had to continue.

The bulky man growled again and withdrew his mangled Jekua. Then he raised a hand in surrender.

Niona's chest swelled.

The audience roared all around her, and Niona hoped that Vanessa Ren's voice was among them.

34
GRAVITY FIELDS

The locker rooms were thinning out by the day as Summoners were eliminated from the tournament. Where before roughly thirty-two people were crammed into the Diwepti Room, there were now only ten making use of its facilities. Well, eight now, after Cole Illiom and Winston Knox were eliminated. The other six Summoners were still using the Staman Room. Niona thought briefly to herself that she was proud of her fellow Diweptians for making it through more of the competition.

What she was not proud of, however, was her performance against Winston. Her mind had been too clouded. She had secured the win, which was what mattered most, but she found her own performance to be lame. Whoever she battled next, she needed to prepare more. A spot on Atoll Talent's roster was on the line.

When she got back to the locker room, she was disappointed to not find Andy there. She barely knew the guy, but he had a good vibe. She enjoyed chatting with him in between matches. After checking the bracket, she realized that he was up next, fighting Desi Taewao.

The winner would be Niona's next opponent. That was a match she should pay attention to.

After them was Grant Deere versus David Woollis, both of whom were sitting around in the locker room. David seemed to be doing breathing exercises, while Grant was chugging a thick, brown drink from a plastic bottle. Had to amp himself up to summon that Whirlcruel, apparently.

Then it would be Balt against Johnny Fierce. Niona wondered if he was ready for that match, or if he was too caught up in what had transpired the previous night. She hoped her rejection wasn't weighing too much on him, and that he could focus on the battle. Hopefully his hangover had receded by now, too.

She didn't have long to think about it before a hand clapped her shoulder. She swung around to find herself face to face with Balt, who sported an awkward smile.

"Yo," she greeted him.

"Hey," he said. "I was just in the dugout. That was a great win, congrats." At least now he was averting his gaze less frequently than he was this morning.

She shrugged and said, "Ehh. I dunno about all that. A win's a win, though."

"I mean, I've never seen someone blow a Tomowori's head clean off."

"There ain't nothin' clean about how that went down," she grinned.

That got a chuckle out of him. "True," he said.

Niona walked over to her locker and input the code, then pulled it open. She unstrapped the kayet from her wrist, relieved at the loss of its weight. She needed a nap. Part of her wanted a Thunderjolt purely for the taste and the energy, not for its mana-related benefits. There was something mildly satisfying, though, about feeling mana trickle back into her system slowly but surely. She resisted the urge for now so she could let her reserves refill naturally. For some reason, the feeling soothed her soul after that uninspired battle.

She sat down on a bench. On the other end of it was David Woollis, doing his breathing techniques. She turned to Balt and said, "Can I ask you somethin'?"

That question alone struck terror in his eyes. "Uhh, sure," he mumbled, approaching with caution.

His reaction was amusing, and she almost told him that she wasn't about to bite his head off or anything, but she decided it would be better not to lampshade his discomfort. He sat next to her, staring down at the floor.

"How would you have done that differently?" she asked.

He looked confused for a second, then said, "Your match?" She nodded. He took a few moments to mull it over before responding. "Well, you were smart to stop focusing on the scales," he began. "Tomoworis have notoriously strong scales. Their defense is off the charts."

"That shit wasn't modded?"

Balt shook his head. "Maybe a tiny bit, but nah, that was probably mostly natural. They don't have a ton of vulnerable spots. You do the most damage by attacking the eyes, the underbelly, or the tail."

"The tail?" she said. "Is that not covered in hard-ass scales too?"

"It is," he confirmed. "The tail is what helps keep the thing balanced, though. All that extra weight helps it stand upright, and if it lost that, it'd be stuck on all fours. If you thought it was slow before, double that when it's knocked down. It's no Halaua or anything, but a Jekua like Garbo could run circles around it. It'd never land another Jetstream attack on you. Then it's easy to maneuver around it, avoiding that big mouth. After that, it's a matter of just flippin' the thing over and messin' up that belly with those horns. Not to mention the damage that's done by cutting off the tail."

Niona nodded. "That's all good and well, but how do you propose Garbo detach that tail in the first place, if it's covered in those scales?"

"Yeah, that's the tricky part," Balt conceded. "I think with an Elastic-Type, the move is to focus your magic on just the tail. Assuming you've got that much control over Garbo's Elastic magic, that is. Make it super rigid so that it snaps off easily, like breaking a twig. Either on account of the Tomowori's own movements or from Garbo stompin' on the tail, or something."

"You really think that'd work?"

"I'm not totally sure, but that's what I'd try. It's a pretty meaty appendage, so it would require funneling a *lot* of Elastic magic into it while you're also trying not to get bitten or blasted by water, but in theory I think it'd work."

She thought about it for a moment, trying to picture herself executing the strategy he'd laid out. "My way mighta been flashier," she said.

That garnered another chuckle. "Yeah. Like I said, blowing a Tomowori's head off wasn't anything I've ever seen before. I don't think I ever would've tried going *inside* the damn thing."

"At least both methods cut a piece off of the ugly sucker. How do you know removin' the tail knocks 'em over? That ain't in your book, I know they don't come from the Isles. That is so stupid, by the way. What a design flaw."

"I...do not know how I know that," Balt said, grinning. "I guess I just picked up that factoid at some point in my many hours of research."

"Nerd."

One advantage of the barebones environment setup for round three was that resetting the field in between matches took almost no time at all. Things were progressing at a great clip, and before they knew it, it was time for Andy's battle against Desi. They wandered back to the dugout to get a better look at the proceedings, since there were no skyscrapers or massive boulders or anything else to obscure their view.

Andy rolled his wheelchair up to the edge of the rubber mat and waved amiably to Desi on the other side. She responded by furrowing her brow and sternly crossing her arms across her chest.

"She's not the warmest of competitors," Balt said.

"I noticed."

The announcer announced them, and then they were off. Andy's first Jekua was his Wallago that he often strutted around the locker room. The wildcat burst onto the field, its long, wiry whiskers poking straight out from its snout.

Across from him, Desi looked unimpressed. She channeled mana into her kayet and summoned what looked like a large porcupine, although with twice as many silver quills jutting out from all over its body. Its head was small and its face was flat, almost receding completely into itself, with quills extending out over the head to protect it. The little amount of rough fur that could be seen in between the quills was an angry shade of red.

Niona didn't recognize the Jekua. She would've scanned it with her Jektionary, but that was attached to the kayet she'd left back in her locker. "What is that?" she asked Balt, knowing that he'd be able to answer immediately, especially if it was native to the archipelago.

"A Pokibuvv," he said. "Gravity-Type, like the rest of her team."

"Naturally."

The battle kicked off a couple seconds later. Andy's Wallago surged toward the Pokibuvv, leaping out of the way of projectile quills flying through the air. The Wallago reached it with haste, slashing at the smaller creature with its claws. Andy only managed to land a couple hits before his Wallago was suddenly propelled backward by the Pokibuvv's Gravity magic.

The Wallago tumbled ass over head several feet away, but quickly got back on its feet and charged at the Pokibuvv.

"Look," said Balt, pointing.

It took Niona a second to see it, but she huffed amusedly when she did. The Wallago was facing the slightest bit of resistance now as it ran toward its opponent.

"Is that some sorta gravity repulsion field?" she asked.

"I think it might be," he said.

The Wallago reached the Pokibuvv again and tackled it, with its body engulfed in flame. Wallagos were speedy creatures, and most of their attacks were done at close range. For most Jekuas, a Wallago's speed would be a death sentence, but apparently not so for a Pokibuvv. The moment the Wallago collided with it, it was once again thrown backward by the porcupine's magic.

When the Wallago shook itself off and tried to attack again, the repulsion field was even more obvious than before. The Jekua looked like it was trudging through powerful waters, fighting against the current. It spat out a fireball, which the Pokibuvv dodged, but then a second one connected. After it did, the Wallago seemed to have even more trouble moving forward.

"Seems like the repulsion field gets stronger with every hit the Pokibuvv takes," said Niona.

"I think you're right."

Andy looked frustrated. His expression grew even grimmer as the Pokibuvv suddenly rained quills on his wildcat. It was a wide-ranging assault, one that the Wallago could not easily avoid, especially given the Gravity magic being enacted on it. The quills pierced the Wallago like arrows, sticking into its shoulders and head, adding a dozen more whiskers to its face.

The Wallago collapsed to the ground, but Andy stood it up again a moment later. He tried shaking the cat's body to dislodge some of the quills, but no dice. They were in there good.

Flames ignited all over the Wallago's sleek body, replacing its fur with sputtering embers. It strode forward in a blaze of oranges and reds and yellows. The Jekua got a running start, then leapt forward, curling into a ball and rolling along the mat at high speed.

Until it hit the Pokibuvv's gravity field, anyway. The curled-up cat struck the invisible force and bounced backward, not even managing to break through it this time. The Wallago was flung back toward Andy, who had to roll out of the way to avoid his own Jekua's flaming form.

As the Wallago's flames flickered out and it stood back up on its four feet, another shower of quills rained down on it. Again, Andy had to roll out of the way to avoid the assault himself. Silver and black-streaked quills covered the Wallago's left side, almost making it look like a giant porcupine itself.

Niona did not like the look of this at all.

"I don't see how he can hit it again," she said. "He doesn't really have any long-range attacks, and even if he used the few he had and hit the thing, all he's doing is pushing himself farther and farther away. Eventually he'll be out of range and the Pokibuvv can just rain quills down on him over and over."

"Yep," Balt agreed.

Apparently Andy was in concurrence. The quill-covered Wallago lit up in the color of the man's soulclay and returned to his kayet. While Desi withdrew her Pokibuvv, he summoned his second Jekua, which was a

Toryoth. The great, ugly bird flapped its wings and rose high into the sky.

Niona and Balt both audibly groaned when Desi revealed her next Jekua. It was another Pokibuvv.

The dumb red and silver little creature waddled out onto the mat, its quills bristling.

"She's only got four Jekuas to work with, and she went with two of the same?" said Niona. "Where's the sense in that?"

Balt quirked an eyebrow. "Don't underestimate her," he said. "I've seen her fight several times, and she's always won. If she brought two Pokibuvvs with her, there's gotta be a reason."

"At least a Toryoth's got better abilities against it than a Wallago."

The Toryoth started by raining down sharpened feathers on the Pokibuvv. It seemed like most of them bounced off its durable quills, but several connected with the fur beneath. The Pokibuvv remained still underneath the Toryoth hovering above it.

Suddenly, the Toryoth began to lower. It was still flapping its wings, so Niona would've thought it'd remain stationary or continue rising, but with every flap it moved closer to the ground.

She looked to Andy, who appeared just as puzzled as she was.

The Toryoth flapped its wings harder, creating a gust of wind that shot through the air and struck the Pokibuvv. This time, its defensive quills didn't make a difference. The creature was picked up and tossed around onto its back, but Desi hastily flipped it back over, its quills gleaming in the sunlight.

A moment later, the Toryoth was being pulled down faster than before. It fired off another flurry of razor-like feathers, but the attack only resulted in the Toryoth being pulled more forcefully.

Andy's Toryoth was yanked back down toward the mat and impaled on the Pokibuvv's quills. The bird screeched and tried tugging itself away from the other Jekua, but it took several attempts, and when it finally managed to get off, it was stuck through with a ton of quills.

"Why is this one reacting differently?" Niona asked. "Every hit it takes makes it attract shit more and more, but the other one was the opposite."

"See, that's why she brought both," Balt said.

"So there *is* something innately different about 'em? She's not just usin' their Gravity magic in different ways?"

"No," said Balt. "Pokibuvvs are unique in that way. When they take damage, they either build up gravity attraction or repulsion. Then, as we've seen, they either impale their enemy or fire quills at them from afar."

Niona turned away from him and back to the battlefield, where the Toryoth was desperately fighting against the Pokibuvv's gravity field pulling it back in. After a few seconds, Andy seemed to give up and his Toryoth tumbled through the air before slamming its back into the Pokibuvv's spikes.

She said, "So obviously certain Jekuas work better against each type. How the hell are you supposed to know which type of Pokibuvv it is, though?" Both of Desi's

Jekuas had red fur and silver quills with black markings. They were identical.

Balt sighed and said, "I, uh…I don't know."

For the rest of the match, while Niona watched Andy being decimated by Desi Taewao, she tried to formulate a strategy to use against the woman. Some way to tell the two Pokibuvvs apart so that she could summon the proper Jekua to combat it.

She couldn't think of anything.

35

BALT VS. JOHNNY

EVEN THOUGH IT HAD ENDED DISASTROUSLY, BALT STILL had a lot of fun the night before. One thing he regretted about going out to Barnello's, however (well, the second thing), was that in all his excitement he'd forgotten to pull up footage of Johnny Fierce's previous tournament battles. He hadn't remembered to do it when he'd woken up either, too stunned by his failure with Niona. By the time he realized his error, it was too late to do anything about it. He had no clue what he was going up against.

He strolled out of the Diwepti Room, heading to the field. In his head, he was trying to decide which of his Jekuas to send out first. Maybe it would be best to wait and see what Johnny summoned.

And speaking of Johnny, he was currently standing outside the Staman Room, leaning his back against the cold wall. He was cheerily eating the second half of a sandwich, munching away with a wide grin on his face.

Balt approached him, waving a hand. "Hey," he said. "Guess we're about to fight."

"Oh, hi," said Johnny before swallowing his bite of sandwich. "Cool to meet you. Good luck out there."

"You too." Then Balt pointed at the sandwich and said, "What ya got there?"

"Oh, it's great," Johnny said, his eyes lighting up. They were big and blue, tucked away behind round, thick-rimmed black glasses. "Cream cheese, cornichons, some fermented cabbage, and a chocolate-hazelnut spread. It's my own creation."

Balt tried his hardest not to be visibly repulsed by what the man had just recited. That last sentence had been redundant, since there was no way he would have ever assumed the man had bought such a sandwich from any real establishment.

"That, uh..." He struggled to find something complimentary to say. Or anything at all to say, really. Any words would suffice, but nothing bubbled up. "...sounds interesting," he said at last.

Johnny nodded fervently, then took another crunchy bite of the sandwich. Balt nearly gagged.

"Well, see you out there," he said.

"See ya!" said Johnny, with a dab of cream cheese on his lower lip.

Balt continued down the hall, where he met up with the tournament official who then led him the rest of the way to the arena.

What the hell was that? he wondered. Was that some sort of bizarre tactic on Johnny's part? Some sort of mind game to psyche him out? That had to be it. There was no other explanation. Why else would a normal person concoct and subsequently consume such a vile aberration if not to freak out someone else?

The worst part was that it was actually working.

Dammit, he thought. Johnny was good.

Ten minutes later, he was walking out into the arena, greeted by the cheers and jeers of the crowd. Alani and Aeiko had told him roughly where their seats were, so he tried to seek them out, but it was fruitless. He didn't know why he thought he'd ever be able to scope out a specific section.

Balt stood at the edge of the rubber mat, with Xatetu Field's logo proudly displayed at its center. Hundreds of feet away, hopping from foot to foot on the other end, was Johnny Fierce. He noticed Balt watching him and waved exaggeratedly. Balt waved back, shuddering again at the thought of that sandwich.

"Welcome back, folks!" the announcer boomed over the stadium speakers. *"We've got an exciting match-up for you this time. Back in the arena is Johnny Fierce, hailing from sunny Kou Tekkis Island!"*

The crowd lost their shit at the mention of Johnny's full name. Their reaction almost made Balt jump. He also huffed with amusement at the announcer's statement; what island in the Volukho Isles *wasn't* sunny?

He didn't pay attention to his own introduction, instead keeping a close eye on Johnny bouncing around. Before he knew it, the man was summoning something.

Balt immediately forgot about his plan to wait and see

what Johnny was summoning and began to summon his own Jekua. He primed the memory card for Pistachio and channeled mana into his kayet.

The Mosstopus stood proud before him, raising up tall on its spindly legs. Luckily, with this wide open space, he would probably not need to jump into Pistachio's perspective.

Soulclay poured out in front of Johnny, but it wasn't shaping into anything distinct. When it faded to the Jekua's true colors, Balt understood why.

The guy's first Jekua was a Gunkskunk. A gloppy mass of dark gunk that was only the shape of a skunk if you squinted. It skittered forward on its six dripping legs, raising its green-striped tail.

What an appropriate Jekua for the sort of person who would eat a sandwich like that.

A Gunkskunk wasn't too terrible, though. He'd handled a Gunkskunk before, and with a Jekua much less powerful than his Mosstopus. Maybe he'd been worrying over nothing.

Pistachio rushed forward to meet Johnny's Gunkskunk head-on. Balt swung one of his tentacles just before reaching the creature, which connected with its viscous flesh.

Dark, wet slop covered Pistachio's tentacle as the Gunkskunk went careening across the mat. It rolled over once, twice, three times, then stood up and shook its whole body, spraying nastiness everywhere. The thing was gripped by a hacking cough, which resulted in a slimeball flying toward Pistachio.

It landed a few feet in front of the Mosstopus, splattering uselessly on the rubber. Pistachio stepped carefully around it, in case there was some sort of poison in it, and fired his own slimeball at the Gunkskunk.

The mucus-y mass smashed into Johnny's Jekua, but the Gunkskunk seemed unfazed. Instead of hitting it hard, or sticking it to the ground, the slime mixed with the Gunkskunk's naturally slimy body. If the attack had damaged it at all, it showed no sign.

Pistachio was still barreling toward the Gunkskunk, whose skin (if it could be called that) began to simmer. Balt opened the Mosstopus's mouth, readying himself to bite down on the little beast.

But an intense blast of light burst forth from the Gunkskunk's mouth, aimed directly into Pistachio's own maw. It was a pretty big target, to be fair, so it would've been hard to miss.

A dizzying pain exploded in Balt's face like he'd been punched in the jaw. Pistachio was stopped in his tracks and sent sprawling to the ground.

He should've been expecting that. Gunkskunks were partially Radiant-Types, and he shouldn't have expected a Summoner to bring one into a tournament without a few strong Radiant moves under his belt.

Balt stood Pistachio up, but the Mosstopus's muscles were spasming underneath his skin. It was hard to steady himself on the creature's many feet. He started moving forward again, intending to drain some kinetic energy from the other Jekua and then bite down hard on it.

The Gunkskunk was priming itself for another Sunbeam. Its dark skin bubbled and popped like soup on a stovetop. What sort of nasty shit would Johnny put in a soup?

Balt shook his head, casting away such distracting thoughts. He needed to focus on the battle, not on Johnny Fierce's disgusting eating habits.

As soon as the fiery yellow blast shot out from the Gunkskunk's mouth, Balt dropped Pistachio to the ground, curling him up into a ball and using his forward momentum to roll along the mat toward the Gunkskunk. Unfortunately, the edge of the Sunbeam still grazed the top of Pistachio, draining more of Balt's mana.

But once the beam dissipated, he extended Pistachio's legs and sprang forward, landing atop the other Jekua. His tentacles pinned the Gunkskunk to the ground, but only for a second. The slippery creature was able to free itself with ease, its flesh separating and pulling away from Pistachio. Balt leaned his Jekua forward to bite down on it, but his fangs tore through the Gunkskunk too easily. There was no give, no ripping of flesh, no blood. The teeth slid through the Gunkskunk's skin like moving a finger through water.

As the Gunkskunk crawled away, a light purple mist emanated from its rear end. Balt was thankful that he was too far away to smell the assuredly awful aroma. His reaction time with Pistachio was not quick enough to avoid the mist, and he swore at himself as he felt his mana start to chip away.

Poison Gas, one of the Gunkskunk's most common moves.

He'd also forgotten to use his energy-draining power on the thing, so it was scurrying away on its six short legs, leaving a trail of slime in its wake as the mist floated into the air, dissolving in the wind.

None of Pistachio's physical attacks were doing much to the Gunkskunk, and his Slimeball had no effect either. Now, to top it all off, his mana was slowly draining from the poison.

It was time to switch things up. He wanted to see what other sort of gross Jekuas Johnny Fierce was working with.

Balt withdrew Pistachio, which seemed to disappoint Johnny at the other end of the mat. But he too withdrew his Jekua, and then he was quickly pouring new soulclay out onto the mat.

As for himself, he was sending Dipper out next. He felt he'd barely put a dent in Johnny's mana, and he needed a heavy hitter on the field. Surely she could do some damage. His Puffolin strutted onto the mat, filling him with some newfound confidence.

But then he let out an audible groan upon seeing Johnny's second Jekua.

At first, he couldn't even tell what it was. It was just a tiny ball of snot sitting placidly on the rubber. It was the same hue and consistency as the Gunkskunk, but with black swirls mixed in. When it took a hop forward, Balt knew what he was dealing with.

Johnny had made a Hybrid of a Gunkskunk and a Coaltoad.

Why does this dude love Gunkskunks? Balt asked himself.

Whatever. Dipper could deal with a Gunkskunk frog thing. What was this Hybrid even called? Balt couldn't think of a time he'd ever read about such a combination. He wasn't sure if there was an official name for it.

He would refer to it as a Snotfrog. Simple and to the point.

As soon as he named the Snotfrog, it hopped up then zipped through the air on a blast of gas that propelled it toward Dipper. While in the air, its body lit up in flames thanks to the Coaltoad side's Thermal magic.

Balt hardened Dipper's Petal Shield, and the Snotfrog dinged right off her tough exterior. He uncurled her and used the Vine Whip to lash at the Snotfrog, which loosed a loud *crack!* as it connected with the creature. Droplets of dark glop sprayed everywhere, and the Snotfrog hopped then blasted away on its stream of gas once more.

This time, Balt was close enough to smell the gas. It was revolting. He gagged, then switched to Dipper's perspective to get away from it. It did not help at all.

In Dipper's body, he chased after the Snotfrog. He was surprised that the Vine Whip had worked even a little bit. Johnny still looked unbothered, however, with a goofy grin plastered on his face.

Balt reached out with two vines this time to attempt grabbing the Snotfrog so that he could slam it on the ground. But, like when he'd tried with Pistachio, the creature slipped right through, its ass sputtering out more noxious gas as it zoomed away.

The Snotfrog curved upward, igniting into flame again as it circled around and dove toward Dipper. Before Balt could get his defenses up, the Snotfrog was firing tiny blasts of flame at him.

He winced as the Snotfrog's fireballs hit Dipper,

burning the pink and purple flowers on her back. The flames spread a little, blackening the flower patch, and he had to roll her around on the ground to put out the fire. He shifted back to his own perspective while he did it, so that he wouldn't dizzy himself.

The Thermal attack had inflicted a great deal of damage to Dipper, being a Growth-Type. Pitting his Puffolin against something with Thermal abilities hadn't been the best move.

He jumped back into Dipper's eyes as she stood back up. Black ash drifted down from her back where several flowers had completely burned away, leaving behind bald patches. It was a depressing sight.

Balt's mana wasn't doing so hot. He'd hardly done anything to Johnny's Jekuas, while the combination of damage done to his plus the extra effort it took to control Pistachio had depleted him almost to the halfway mark already.

The Snotfrog finally landed several feet from Dipper, and the flames engulfing its tiny round body sputtered out. Flower petals rose from the Puffolin's back and shot toward the Snotfrog.

Sharp petals tore into the Snotfrog's liquid skin, slicing through the creature and piercing the rubber mat behind it. The Snotfrog belched a small flame, then hopped up and flew toward Dipper yet again.

Balt's defense was two-pronged. He extended Dipper's roots into the ground to steady her, then also hardened her Petal Shield. The Snotfrog wasn't encasing itself in fire this time, though. It landed softly on Dipper's back, easily sticking to her with its mucky skin. Balt tried to shake it off, but couldn't.

The Jekua croaked once, then hopped off Dipper, leaving behind a large ball of slime that was roughly the same size as the Snotfrog itself.

"Surely that's not feces," Balt said aloud as he switched back to his own perspective, seeing what the Snotfrog had done.

It didn't matter what it was. A moment later, the ball of grime faded from black to red to orange, then it exploded on the Puffolin's backside.

Pain stabbed through Balt's back, causing him to stumble forward out of sheer surprise. Dipper was thrown to the ground by the explosion, her entire patch of flowers now looking like nothing more than scorched earth.

The attack was a devastating blow to his mana. And worst of all, he still couldn't hit Johnny's Gunkskunks for any considerable amount of damage. Maybe if he had something with Tidal powers, he could wash the damn things away, but he didn't. If he had a Gravity Jekua, he could also use that magic to lift them into the air and slam them back down, not worrying at all about physically touching them.

He let Dipper lay on the ground motionless for a moment while he tried thinking through a plan of action. He'd move her if the Snotfrog came closer or shot off more fireballs.

It seemed easy to assume at this point that Johnny was working with four Gunkskunks, Hybridized or not. That was his signature: gross sandwiches and gross Jekuas.

All Balt had left to use after he withdrew Dipper—who was on her last legs, really—were Milton and the Tottaworm. Milton relied solely on physical attacks, except for when he absorbed powers from the other Jekua. There was maybe something there, using the Gunkskunk's power against it, but Balt wasn't sure that'd be too reliable.

The Tottaworm was what he'd used to beat the first Gunkskunk he encountered, after they had exited the Palowa Caves on Totta. For whatever reason, the Gunkskunk had been trapped by the Tottaworm's magically rigid body. If it had slipped through a bit, it wasn't enough to stop him from flinging it deep into the forest.

His train of thought was interrupted by the Snotfrog rearing up on Dipper again. He stood her up and dodged the blasts of fire, but he could feel how weak her body was. Her back was completely ruined; he'd still be able to use her Petal Shower attack, since it was based on magic and not the literal flowers on her back, but the Snotfrog's attacks had weakened her considerably.

Balt then thought about what he'd told Niona earlier, about dealing with the Tomowori. Using Elastic magic to make the tail rigid and then breaking it off.

The same principle could be applied to a Gunkskunk. That could be how he got around the bastard's viscosity. Make the Gunkskunk's body super rigid, then either hit it hard with a physical blow or use the Tottaworm's Sonic powers to shatter the body completely.

He pondered the idea for a few more seconds while he continued avoiding the Snotfrog's blasts. It wasn't the worst idea in the world. It might be hard to pull off, but he was pretty experienced with the Tottaworm at this point.

He thought it might be possible.

Johnny had two more Jekuas left as well, though. He shouldn't summon the Tottaworm next. He needed to save it for the final bout, so that Johnny had nothing left to conjure once Balt destroyed his fourth Gunkskunk.

It was a solid plan.

And even if it wasn't all that solid, it was the only plan he had.

Balt withdrew Dipper, not wanting his mana to suffer anymore Thermal-on-Growth assaults. He'd already been battered enough by this stupid little creature. Again, he had to ask who in their right mind would create a Gunkskunk and Coaltoad Hybrid.

Someone who'd eat a sandwich with pickles and chocolate and all that shit on it, he answered himself. He almost gagged again.

Johnny withdrew the Snotfrog, looking less displeased than he did the first time. Apparently he'd done enough damage with the little rascal to satisfy himself.

Balt realized he might be acting too hasty with his strategy. It was entirely possible Johnny wasn't using four different Gunkskunks. He urged himself to be patient, to wait and see what it was Johnny was summoning next. That would help him conserve some extra mana, too.

But sure enough, Johnny's third Jekua was yet another Gunkskunk Hybrid. Somehow, the man kept topping himself in disgusting creatures.

This one was tall and wide, like a bodybuilder, but dripping with that same gray wetness of a Gunkskunk. There was still a certain amount of shapelessness to the thing, but Balt could detect a hint of a melting head near the top of its humanoid body. It still walked on six legs, but these were huge and spider-like, almost like the Mosstopus's. And now, sticks and rocks and other debris protruded from various spots on its body. It was like a Bogbane, but worse.

Johnny had Hybridized a Gunkskunk with a Vossi. A Gunki, Balt decided to call it.

The important thing was that his assumption was correct: Johnny was evidently trying to become some sort of Gunkskunk Master, it seemed. A truly strange and awful life pursuit, but at least Balt knew what he was up against now.

He summoned Milton and immediately jumped into the Mirrorbear's perspective. He hoped he could inflict a bit of damage on the Gunki before the two of them summoned their final Jekuas, but he wasn't totally sure how he'd accomplish that.

Milton charged forward, and the Gunki scrambled away from him. Milton was fairly fast, though, and he caught up with the Gunki at the edge of the mat. Balt reared up, swiping his mighty claws through the Gunki's flesh, batting a few rocks and sticks out of its body and onto the ground.

He swiped again, but his hand got stuck in the Gunki's muck. Balt tugged and tugged, but he couldn't free Milton's beefy paw. It was trapped in the middle of the Gunki's chest, with more globs of wetness dripping from its face onto Milton's thick arm. Then the Gunki's hands started brightening, filling up with Radiant energy.

"Shit," Balt muttered, jumping back into his own body. He did not want to feel the full impact of whatever was about to happen. He yanked even harder on Milton's arm, but to no avail.

The Gunki savagely pummeled Milton, its fists alight with balls of Radiant energy. Each hit bloomed on Milton's reflective skin, burning his flesh. Balt put up the Barrier in time to soften the last five or six hits, but the first ten or so had landed in a blur.

Milton's Barrier dropped, and the Gunki released him from its chest. Milton staggered backward, but the Gunki was charging up its sun-powered fists again.

As it dealt another flurry of blows, Balt tried to time it right so that he could absorb the move and use it himself. He finally succeeded on the eighth hit, just before the ninth connected with Milton's jaw and sent the Mirror-bear collapsing to the ground. Balt cursed once more.

He shifted to Milton's perspective and stood on all fours. Then he rose onto his hind legs, inviting the Gunki to take another shot at him.

Johnny did indeed move his Jekua forward, but its fists were not lighting up now. Instead, they were growing massive spikes from where its knuckles should have been. Part of the Vossi's Growth powers.

As it grew closer, Balt started absorbing sunlight to power Milton's fists. Balls of light began forming around the bear's claws, and he took an unsteady step forward to meet the Gunki.

Both Jekuas laid into each other at the same time. The Gunki's spikes slashed Milton's cheek and his neck, while the bear's Radiant-charged claws ripped across the Gunki's chest, leaving behind glowing claw marks.

Johnny's Gunki leapt backward, hissing from an

unseen mouth, and some sort of purple liquid gushed from the open wound on its chest.

"Hell yes," Balt whispered to himself. Finally he had done some actual damage to one of these things. It was bleeding, too, so that would make Johnny's mana drain over time.

But Milton was bleeding as well, so it was kind of a wash. Blood dribbled from his neck and cheek. Luckily, the gash on his neck didn't seem to be too deep. It wasn't spurting blood or anything.

Balt checked his mana levels. They had dipped below the halfway mark at some point, and he could sense that they were draining from Milton's bleeding, but not a lot. He was in a decent position to try getting a few more good hits on the Gunki before he withdrew Milton. Hell, maybe he'd harm the creature enough for Johnny to be the one to withdraw.

Well, he could dream.

He shifted back into Milton and charged forward, head down. Just before he reached the Gunki, he powered on Milton's Barrier, then he headbutted the big, nasty monster.

It was a gamble, and it paid off. He wasn't sure it'd work, but he suspected that switching on the Barrier would create a magical sort of—for lack of a better word—barrier between the two Jekuas, preventing Milton's head from being sucked into the Gunki's body, but also stopping the Gunki from sliding around the Mirrorbear's form.

The Gunki charged its fists again and started pummeling Milton, but Balt was able to absorb one of the attacks for Milton to use. The Mirrorbear's head then smashed into the Gunki's stomach, sending it reeling backward. It tripped over its own tangled legs and fell over, slamming the back of its head on the rubber mat. Balt wished it had been concrete, but hopefully the fall still hurt.

Then he rose on Milton's hind legs, charging up the Sunclaws again. While the Gunki lay vulnerable on its back, he came down hard. Milton's bright claws shredded four of the creature's six legs, leaving them in tatters.

He stepped away from the thrashing Gunki before it could land another hit on him. More blood spilled from the fresh wounds, yet Johnny's inane smile had still not been wiped from his face.

Balt feared how much mana the other Summoner might have left. His own was getting dangerously low, especially after those potent Radiant moves.

But if his plan worked, it should be enough to take out an enormous chunk of Johnny's mana, and his Jekua would be left too ruined to fight with. He'd have no choice but to withdraw.

It was time to execute the plan, as Johnny's Gunki lit up in the color of his soulclay and returned to his kayet. A small victory for Balt before the big one. He grinned to himself.

He withdrew Milton, pleased with the Mirrorbear's performance. He had done more damage with Milton than both of his other Jekuas combined, he wagered. Then he switched over to the Tottaworm's memory card and began channeling mana into it.

Pale yellow soulclay streamed out from his kayet,

splashing onto the blue mat and forming the thick, cylindrical shape of the Tottaworm. The yellow soon faded into the worm's fleshy pink, and Balt started writhing toward the other end of the mat. The sooner he got to Johnny's final Gunkskunk and rendered it statuesque, the better.

Johnny's soulclay poured onto the mat as the Tottaworm slithered forward. More and more soulclay came out as the seconds ticked by. Balt's brow furrowed as he watched, confused as to why so much soulclay was coming out.

Frankly, it was an absurdly huge amount of soulclay. It just kept coming and coming, gushing forth from Johnny's kayet. It piled on top of itself, building higher and higher, looming over Balt's measly worm.

Then it finally stopped, and the color faded away.

Balt said a string of obscenities loud enough that the television cameras surely picked them up.

Johnny's fourth Jekua was not a Gunkskunk Hybrid.

It was a Tyrian Snail.

Tyrian Snails were megafauna that lived in the depths of the ocean. The pigment they released as they crawled around was what gave the water its lavender hue. They were gigantic creatures, even bigger than the Bingst that Niona had fought.

The snail's shell alone was the size of a house, bone white with lines of yellow and brown criss-crossing all over it. Long, thin spikes protruded from the shell, some of which dug into the rubber on which it sat while others lanced the sky. The Tyrian Snail's body was long and slimy, like a Gunkskunk's, but resolutely more solid. Its flesh was white like its shell, but with spots of extremely pale blue. Two long, probing antennae stuck out of its head, slithering through the air.

Balt stopped his Tottaworm in its tracks.

This was bad. The whole plan was out the window. A Tyrian Snail was way too big for Balt's Tottaworm to make its entire body rigid, and his Sonic magic wasn't strong enough to shatter it even if he was able to somehow pull off the feat.

"Shit, shit, shit on me," he swore. He looked like such a massive idiot, summoning his dumb little worm to battle this towering snail. What the hell was he going to do?

A whirlpool of magically conjured water began swirling around the Tyrian Snail's body. It whooshed around, picking up speed, faster and faster as it rose into the sky like a watery cyclone. After a few seconds, the snail wasn't even visible behind the tower of water.

Then it all came crashing down like a tidal wave. Water covered the entire mat in an instant, crushing the Tottaworm with its immense weight. Most of Balt's remaining mana disappeared in a flash as water swept him off his feet, sending him tumbling along the waves.

The water evaporated as quickly as it had appeared, gone just like Balt's mana.

He wasn't soulsick, but when he checked his reserves, he knew it was all over. One more hit from the Tyrian Snail would annihilate him. He couldn't let that happen. Not for himself, not for Alani, and especially not on television.

There was no other choice.

He withdrew his Tottaworm.

He lay there on the ground, his clothes soaked through and clinging to his chest despite the water disappearing. He stared up at the Tyrian Snail looming over him, caught in its shadow.

That was the end of the road.

He was out of the tournament.

36

BALT'S NEVERENDING PARADE

WALKING THE HALLS BY HIMSELF AFTER LOSING FELT JUST AS surreal as it had when he was walking them on his way to his first match. It was like he was floating just outside his body, watching himself stroll through the empty hallway like an idiot. First because he was marching toward something he had absolutely no experience with, and now because he'd so massively screwed up in front of thousands of people.

Possibly the worst part of it all was that he'd been knocked out of the tournament by a guy named *Johnny Fierce.*

It was hard to believe it was real. But, sure enough, the announcer had declared Johnny the winner and offered cheery condolences to Balt as he walked out of the arena with the crowd at his back. He kept reminding himself that he never in a million years truly believed he would make it to the finals, let alone win the whole thing, but the loss stung nonetheless.

On the bright side, he'd been given a consolation prize for making it to the third round, which he hadn't expected. When he walked off the field, someone from the tournament handed him a collection of memory cards: five L1s, three L2s, and a single L3. So that was something. There was also a gift card to a spa in the city, which he was unsure he'd get a chance to actually use.

As he rounded a corner and came into view of the locker rooms, he saw his cousin standing outside the Staman Room. Wasaaru was watching the corner, hands deep in his pockets, and he smiled when he spotted Balt.

Balt groaned as he neared Wasaaru. The last thing he needed now was his cousin's verbal jabs, his gloating and mocking. Balt already knew he was a loser; he didn't need Wasaaru to remind him of that fact.

He decided to cut Wasaaru off before he even got started. "I don't need you to tell me I'm an idiot," he said, his voice echoing down the otherwise barren hallway. "You think you could hold off for, like, a day before you start with the mockery? Would it kill you?"

"What?" said Wasaaru, looking genuinely confused.

"Just resist your base instincts, for once," said Balt.

Wasaaru frowned. The expression was halfway between sadness and irritation. "I'm not here to make fun of you," he said.

Balt stopped a few feet away. "But I just lost. Were you not watching?"

"Yeah, I was watching," Wasaaru said.

"Well, then this is the moment where you give me a mouthful about getting my ass beat by a sloppy mess and a big snail or whatever. Y'know what? I take it back. Go on, lay into me. I deserve it. I'm an idiot, I suck at being a Summoner, you're a golden god, yeah, yeah. Go ahead."

Wasaaru stared at him for a moment, casting a pitying expression on him, like he was gazing at a man who was sinking into the depths of depravity. "I'm not here to make fun of you," he said again. He smirked, then said, "Seems like you're doing it enough yourself, already."

"Alright, what do you want, then?" asked Balt, losing his patience. All he wanted to do was go grab the thickest tai dair money could buy and sit down in some grass while he ate it. If he followed that up with a bucket of shaved ice, then all the better.

"Do you mean it?" Wasaaru asked. "You think I'm a golden god?"

"Shut up."

"That's very nice of you."

"I'm seriously about to lose it."

Wasaaru laughed and said, "Alright, sorry. I wanted to catch you before you left to tell you that you did good out there."

There was a pause as Balt surveyed his cousin's expression, seeking out any sign of trickery or mischief. Cautiously, he said, "Really?"

"Really," Wasaaru said, rolling his eyes. "This isn't some sort of trap."

Usually, conversations with Wasaaru were traps. Their chat at Barnello's had been the exception to the rule. Balt wanted to get on the road to mending their relationship, but he did not yet fully trust his cousin.

"Well...thanks," Balt said faintly.

Wasaaru's frown shifted back into a smile. He said,

"Honestly, I was shocked when he brought that Tyrian Snail out."

"Had he not used it before?" Balt asked.

"I don't know. I hadn't seen any of his battles until this one. Aside from your fights, I've been keeping myself busy studying the people I'm going up against."

Balt blinked. "You've watched all my battles?"

"Yeah," Wasaaru nodded. He grinned and said, "I had to load my arsenal of insults, but you kept pulling out wins. Bastard."

Balt chuckled. "And now that I finally lost, you won't even toss *one* insult my way?"

"I'm resisting my base instincts."

"You're getting soft, I think."

"Fine, here's one. It's related to Gunkskunks. *Even janitors can wipe up a mess like that.* How was that?"

"Ehh, it was okay. It was almost clever. I think the wording needs some fine-tuning. Also, low blow on the janitors of the world. They do good work."

"My apologies to janitors."

"I was kind of a janitor, if you'll recall. Back at the movie theater."

"That's right," said Wasaaru.

Balt waited a second, thinking that his mention of the theater might trigger the memory of Wasaaru mocking him with his friends, finally eliciting the apology he'd been waiting three years for.

But it didn't come. Not today.

Instead, Wasaaru said, "I can't say I know what I would've done in your shoes. Tyrian Snails aren't quite as strong as Jenus, but they're as big as a lot of them...it's tricky trying to figure out how to topple one. I would've been stumped too. It's unfortunate all you had left was that Tottaworm."

"I intentionally saved that for last," Balt confessed.

"...why?" Wasaaru asked, incredulous.

"I thought he was gonna summon another Gunkskunk Hybrid. I was gonna use Elastic magic to basically make it into a statue, since it's so gloppy and impossible to hit for any real damage. Then I'd use a Sonic power or something to shatter it."

Wasaaru nodded. "I guess that would've worked," he said.

"Yeah. I wasn't exactly counting on him summoning a Tyrian Snail, of all things."

"They're so huge, though, I guess you could've tried waiting him out. His mana had to be draining like crazy every second he had that beast on the field. Way less than what it cost to keep your Tottaworm summoned. You could've just slithered around, avoiding attacks until he ran out of juice."

Balt nodded. "I guess that's true," he said. "I hadn't really thought of that. I was too rattled seeing that gigantic snail in front of me."

"Understandable."

"Also, kinda hard to avoid an attack when it consists of sending a tidal wave crashing through the entire damn arena," Balt pointed out.

"Yeah, fair."

Balt shifted on his feet, then asked, "Who're you up against next?"

"Anesk Pauz."

"I haven't seen any of his battles, I don't think," said Balt.

"He wiped the floor with Bi Kalakao in round one, it wasn't even worth watching. He did some cool stuff against Alo Darwi, though. That one was pretty close. You should check it out."

"I guess I will." A part of him now wanted to stay and watch Wasaaru's match against Anesk, but he also really wanted to get out of the stadium. The arena's energy was weighing him down, and he wanted nothing more than to be outside in the fresh air and sunshine.

Behind Wasaaru, Niona appeared at the other end of the hall and she jogged toward them. "Yo," she said, "I'm so sorry, dude."

"It's alright," said Balt, not meaning it in the least.

"I don't think anyone saw that comin'. Who the hell's imprinted a *Tyrian Snail*?"

"They're actually quite docile," said Wasaaru.

"But how did he even find one? They live at the bottom of the ocean."

"Our grandmother says they come closer to shore sometimes, usually during big storms."

Niona huffed, impressed by his knowledge. "Well, okay then," she said.

Balt looked to Wasaaru and said, "I guess we'll get out of your hair and let you get ready for your match."

"Okay. Sorry again about yours. I thought you did a great job."

"Thanks," Balt said. His cousin's words lightened his mood somewhat. It had been years since Wasaaru had given him anything remotely resembling a compliment. "Good luck with Anesk."

With that, he and Niona started back down the hall to wind their way to the exit while Wasaaru slipped back into the Staman Room.

"Was your cousin just nice to you?" Niona asked him.

"I believe so," he said.

"Wow."

"I know."

"Progress is being made, and it's all thanks to me."

"Baby steps."

Seeing Niona drove home the fact that Balt had suffered two major losses in the span of twenty-four hours. All of a sudden his mood was dampened further, even in spite of Wasaaru's unexpected kindness.

He glanced over at Niona. He appreciated how normal she was acting, ignoring all the tension between them. Although, maybe for her there was no tension. Maybe she was truly unbothered. Either way, her attitude toward the whole incident helped to put him more at ease. He couldn't help but feel kind of foolish in her presence, though. He hoped the feeling would alleviate as the days wore on.

She asked him if he wanted to stay and watch the rest of the day's matches, but he told her no. He was ready to stuff his face with junk food.

They were outside, basking in the sunlight blaring down on the crater, when he pulled out his linkpad to text Alani and tell her they were planning to head out. He knew that she and Aeiko probably had little interest in sticking around; they might even already be gone, for all he knew.

As it turned out, he already had a message from Alani: a heart symbol. He smiled and began to compose his text.

He was interrupted by a call from his mother. He answered and placed the linkpad to his ear. “Hi,” he said dourly. She always knew how to perfectly time her calls, to get him when he least wanted to speak.

“Oh, sweetie, I’m sorry,” she said in lieu of a proper greeting.

“Hey, bud,” came his father’s voice. “We saw your match on TV. Sorry ’bout that.”

Of course that was why they were calling. How could he not have assumed that? They’d texted after every one of his other matches.

“Yeah,” he said. That was all.

His mother said, “We’re very proud of you, you know. You did great out there.”

Balt was growing a little tired of everyone telling him that he did a great job of losing.

“When you get home, I gotta know how you won that second battle,” his father said eagerly. “We couldn’t really see anything with all that black shit the other guy was puttin’ up.”

“Okay.”

“Linda has been watching too, you know,” his mother told him. Linda was her closest friend, who also happened to live on Na Tana, albeit in a different city. They talked almost every day. “You really should visit her while you’re on the island.”

“I really don’t have time for that,” Balt said.

"Oh, come on, Balt. You're already over there. You know she would really appreciate it. She loves seeing you."

"I *really* don't have time to go all the way over there," he said. "You do know I'm in Makanuele, right?"

"It's not that far."

"It's, like, three hours away by bus."

"That's not very far."

"I cannot go there."

"Linda will be so disappointed."

"That's a shame."

"Mrs. Calantro has been watching, too," his father said.

"Great." The more people who saw him lose, the merrier.

"She was rootin' for Mr. Dia. I can't believe he got eliminated in the first round."

"Can you really not believe that?" Balt asked.

"He was a great Summoner, back in his day!" said his father.

"That was thirty years ago," his mother said.

"Whatever. What was that big thing at the end of your match, anyway?" his father then asked.

"We couldn't see it very well," said his mother. "The cameras couldn't get it all in one shot."

"A Tyrian Snail," Balt answered.

"Oh. Yuck," his father said.

"Sorry, sweetie," his mother said again. "Are you coming back home now?"

"What? No," Balt sputtered. "We still have two more shrines for Alani to visit."

"Oh, right," she said.

"You're still doin' that?" his father asked.

"What are you talking about? Of course we are."

"Ahh. Okay."

"Well, we're glad the trip is going well so far," his mother said. Then she asked, "Have you talked to your cousin lately?"

Balt stopped himself from groaning in his mother's ear. When was this conversation going to end? "Yes," he replied. "Just a few minutes ago, actually."

"Oh, wonderful!" There was nothing in the world his mother loved more than family getting along.

"I guess we're gonna be Wasaaru fans now," said his father. "We gotta have a Vana in the winner's circle."

"We wish it was you, though," his mother added.

"Oh, yeah, of course we do. But if not you, then him."

"Right," said Balt flatly.

"He's gonna have a tough time against that Anesk Pauz," his father said, clucking his tongue.

"I'm sure he'll be fine," his mother said. "He's a good Summoner."

"Yeah, but you never know."

His parents went back and forth for a few more moments before Balt interrupted by saying, "Hey, I gotta run. I'm meeting up with friends here and we're gonna go grab some lunch."

"Lunch? It's so late to be eating lunch," his mother said, concerned.

Balt inhaled a deep, calming breath that did not do much to calm him. He'd chosen that excuse since he thought it'd be the simplest one, but naturally his mother had to expound on it.

"We're just grabbing something small. Anyway, I have to go," he said.

"Alright. Well, be good, sweetie."

"I will."

"Love you."

"Love y'all too."

"Take it easy, bud," said his father.

"Bye."

He hung up, then finished typing his message to Alani and sent it.

Niona asked him, "Have you ever listened to yourself talk to your parents?"

"What do you mean?"

"Your tone with them is very...what's the word? It's very flat. Annoyed. Impatient."

"That's three words."

"Take your pick."

Alani quickly replied saying that they were on their way out of the stadium and would meet them outside. When they finally arrived, Alani and Aeiko both offered the same praise and condolences as everybody else. Balt was at the head of the pity parade and he was ready for it to come to a conclusion.

"To be perfectly honest with all of you, I feel like shit and I want to eat my feelings," he said.

"We can mourn your loss and celebrate my win," said Niona with a grin. She was already back to teasing him.

"Great," he said. "I am in the mood for some tai dair and shaved ice. Any good places nearby?" he asked Aeiko.

They nodded without a second thought. "Which do you want first?"

"Gotta go warm then cold, right?" said Niona.

"Yeah, tai dair first," he said.

"The place I'm thinking of is just on the edge of the crater, back behind the stadium," they said. "Then we can bring it back down here, and get some shaved ice at that stand." They pointed, and everyone's eyes followed to find a very obvious shaved ice stand set up nearby.

Balt had actually seen that one when he and Niona came outside. He said, "Is there another one somewhere else? I kinda…don't wanna be here right now."

"Oh, yeah, of course," said Aeiko. "We're in Makanuele. There are plenty of shaved ice joints."

"Awesome. Lead the way," he said.

Aeiko started toward one of the staircases leading out of the crater, with Niona trailing shortly behind them. Balt and Alani brought up the rear.

"I'm sorry," Alani said again.

"It's fine," said Balt. "Really. It sucks now, but I'll be alright. Especially after all this food."

"I know you will be, but I know this was important to you."

He nodded. "There'll be more tournaments," he said.

"Yeah," she said, smiling. "Maybe you can compete in next year's Tanepke Tussle."

Balt laughed. "I dunno if I can risk that," he said.

"Why not?"

"What if I lost? It'd be even more humiliating losing in my own hometown."

"But if you won, you'd be a hometown hero."

"I don't think that's how it works. I think you have to

accomplish something grand *outside* your hometown to become a hometown hero."

"Well, fine. Either way, there will be more tournaments."

"Yeah," Balt said. "I'm just gettin' started."

37
DEVASTATINGLY HUGE PROBLEMS

By the evening, their mana had fully recovered, so Balt joined Niona at the gym while she got some training in before round four the following day. They hadn't been back to Aeiko's apartment all day, and Balt wasn't eager to interact with Holly after his big loss. He wasn't keen on answering her endless questions about the event.

He also wasn't keen on doing any training, though. Instead, he was trying to convince himself that he'd put up a good effort in the tournament, and that he'd done the best he could. That he deserved a short break now. Just because he lost didn't mean he had to push himself even harder as soon as possible. He was not a failure in his grandmother's eyes.

It was challenging, but for now he was choosing to believe all that.

For now.

"You're takin' this better than I thought you would,

honestly," said Niona, standing a few feet away from where he sat on the cold floor.

Currently, she was stretching out Garbo's Elastic horns to use them as arms, swinging across bars hanging from the ceiling. The sight of a Nuri flinging itself literally head-first across the ceiling was ridiculous. She said it was helping her to gain better control of both the elasticity and the horns themselves, which had secured her the win against Winston Knox earlier.

Balt didn't know what to say to that, so he just mumbled, "Mhmm." His mood ebbed and flowed throughout the day.

He was scrolling through tournament results, seeing how everyone else had fared after they left Xatetu Field. Wasaaru won his battle against Anesk Pauz and would be moving forward, which Balt was torn on. Sure, he was kind of happy for his cousin, but at the same time it felt like another slap in the face. Wasaaru was the Vana with the talent, not him.

Wasaaru's next opponent was David Woollis, who Balt hadn't seen much of this past week. There was only so much time in the day to battle, eat, train, and watch the matches he missed. At this point, some of the matches were beginning to blend together anyway. If he had indeed watched one of Woollis's battles, he could not recall a single one of the man's Jekuas.

Surprising no one, Olli Berrap had beaten Nock Brynn. They would now be going up against Kallon in the fourth round. From what Balt had seen of Kallon's team, he knew the man was a formidable Summoner, but Olli was no pushover. He truly didn't know which way that match was going to go.

Johnny Fierce was up against Uil in the next round. Balt smirked. While it was true that Johnny had gotten the best of him, Uil was on a whole other level. The guy was an absolute juggernaut. Johnny's Gunkskunks were going down the drain.

Assuming Uil won, the person going against him in round five would be whoever won between Niona and Desi. Balt hadn't realized that until now, never really looking ahead on the bracket. That was disconcerting. He glanced up at his friend, who was still swinging her Nuri to and fro, cackling to herself with amusement.

He said, "You know you might be goin' up against Uil soon?"

Niona cast a gaze at him over her shoulder. "Hmm?"

"If you win your next match and Uil wins his, in round five you're battling each other."

She withdrew Garbo, the pink soulclay dripping down from the ceiling like a water leak back into her kayet. She walked over to where he sat and planted herself next to him.

"That sucks," she said simply.

"Got any idea how you'll handle him?"

Niona shrugged and said, "One devastatingly huge problem at a time, man. I gotta figure out how to handle what's-her-face first. Gravity Girl."

"Desi."

"Right, her."

"You'd classify her as a 'devastatingly huge' problem?"

"Nevermind, forget it." Niona pulled her linkpad from

her pocket and started searching for footage of Desi's tournament battles. The woman's match against Andy Lowe from that afternoon was already online, along with her previous two matches.

Balt peered over at Niona's screen as she hit the play button on the battle with Andy, but he couldn't make out much from where he sat. He leaned over apprehensively, trying to get a better view.

Niona's eyes flicked away from her screen, looking him over, and said, "Don't be weird, just come over here."

He opened his mouth in rebuttal but quickly snapped it shut. He scooted closer to her, their legs brushing up against each other. His heartrate quickened, and he mentally urged himself to get a grip.

The linkpad screen was now in clear view, and together they watched Andy Lowe's Jekuas get demolished by Desi's pair of Pokibuvvs.

While he watched, Balt tried looking for any sign, no matter how minor, to tell the difference between the two Pokibuvvs. The erratic camera work was not helpful in that regard, constantly cutting between different angles, but even so he came up short.

When they determined there was nothing useful to glean from the fight with Andy, Niona played the one against Kia Notowe from round two. In the footage from that match, everything was shot on drones from above, so they had even less clear images of the Jekuas. It seemed that Desi didn't especially rely on the gravity field moves in that battle anyway, instead opting to alter the Jekuas' gravity to scuttle along the buildings while planting quills. Then, when Kia's Jekuas hit certain marks, the quills would fire off the buildings like homing missiles.

So that footage was useless too. All that was left was her battle in the first round against Yunasca Imola, a veteran Summoner from Qwi Island. She was someone Balt had heard of before, an ex-Church initiate who only fought with Jekuas imprinted in the Volukho Wildlife Center. Balt knew that Desi was skilled, but still he was surprised that she managed to take out Yunasca right off the bat. That had been an upset, for sure.

In that battle, the cameramen had at least given them clearer, closer shots of each Pokibuvv skittering around the rolling hills. Desi did employ the same strategy that she used against Andy in this round, repelling and attracting her opponents' Jekuas.

But there was still no indication as to which type of field the Pokibuvv was going to use. Niona rewound and replayed the footage over and over, but there were no obvious tells.

One advantage Niona would have over both Yunasca and Andy was that in round four, she'd be able to swap her Jekuas at will, but that would drain her mana more. Plus, if she had the wrong Jekua out to begin with, she might take too much damage before she got a chance to switch up her strategy. She was in an undeniably better position, but if they could crack this puzzle, she might just be able to take Desi down.

While Niona played through Andy's fight again, Balt reached into his bag to retrieve his grandmother's bestiary. He opened it up to the index at the back, scanning through the P section until he landed on *Pokibuvv*.

He turned to the appropriate page and began to read the entry underneath the illustration:

Large, intelligent rodent with a coat of sharp quills that protect it from predators. They are typically found in forests, but on rare occasions have been found living in nearby mountains, using their Gravity magic to construct shelter out of rocks. When attacked, their bodies instinctively produce gravity fields that either repel or attract their attacker, at which point they use their quills to either fire upon or impale them, respectively. It has been found that males create attraction fields, while females create repulsion fields. Males are unable to fire their quills at predators, but it is a common technique amongst females.

So that was the difference. One of Desi's Pokibuvvs was a male, and the other was a female. Maybe she'd stumbled across them mating in the wild and had used that time while they were distracted to imprint them.

Balt blinked, wondering why in the world his mind had leapt to that scenario.

He said to Niona, "It looks like males of the species attract attackers, while females repel them."

"Well, that's dandy, but how am I supposed to tell 'em apart? They look identical. Should I run up to 'em after Desi summons one and take a peek under the hood, see what equipment they're workin' with?"

Balt chuckled and continued reading the bestiary entry. There was no other information there that said anything about how to tell the two sexes apart.

Then he noticed a small note scribbled at the top of the

page, just above the illustration. He'd almost missed it. A two-line note from his grandmother.

One line said "V = female" and just below that was "X = male." That was all.

What did that mean?

He pondered the clue for a moment, then said aloud, "My grandmother says that V stands for female. Whatever that means."

"Jeez, you're hopeless, huh?" said Niona. "V is for vagina, pal."

"Wanna explain X for the males, then?"

"You'll understand when you're older."

Balt ignored her stupid joke and continued scanning the page. There had to be something else there besides his grandmother's somewhat helpful yet still too vague note.

Nothing in the text revealed itself to him. He took a deep breath and let it out, drumming his fingers on the page. Smacking his fingertips against the black and white Pokibuvv's smushed face.

He stared at the illustration for a few seconds, then it hit him.

"The quills," he said.

Niona looked over at him. Her attention had returned to her linkpad. "What?"

Balt moved his finger over a few centimeters, pointing at the quills on the Pokibuvv illustration. Each little quill had black marks on them. He'd noticed them when he'd seen Desi summon the creatures, but thought nothing of it. Plenty of Jekuas had random colored streaks on their bodies.

But in the illustration, if one looked closely, those black lines looked like they formed little Vs.

Niona squinted, leaning against him as she examined the page. "Really?" she said. "You think that's it?"

"Pull up the Yunasca fight again," he told her. There were several close-ups of both Pokibuvvs in that footage.

She did so, fast-forwarding to a moment where Yunasca's Jekua was being drawn in toward Desi's Pokibuvv. Seconds later, the thing was skewered on its quills, and the camera cut from a wide shot to a close-up at the exact moment of impact.

"Look," said Balt.

It was hard to see on the tiny screen, but he could distinctly make out Xs all along the Jekua's quills. From where they had been sitting in the dugout, they just looked like random black lines, but with the closer view it was obvious.

"Shit," said Niona. She scrubbed through the footage until she saw Desi summoning the other Pokibuvv. This one was struck a few times by its opponent, and then the other Jekua couldn't get another hit in, being knocked back by the Pokibuvv's repulsion field over and over.

Balt feared there wasn't going to be a close-up of this one, but finally the camera cut to an angle where they could get a better look at the quills. Sure enough, the black marks formed Vs.

Niona saw it at the same time he did. "Shit," she said again. "Thanks, Grandma." Then, "How am I supposed to tell them apart in the heat of battle, though? A V and an X look too much alike, from a distance."

"I dunno," said Balt. "You may have to get up close and

personal yourself. It'll depend on the environment they set up, too."

"Yeah."

Balt looked from her back down to the linkpad, then said, "Actually, you might not need to get close at all." He pointed at the device's screen. "Depending on what the cameramen are doing, anyway. This is the same footage that plays on the big screens during the fights. If you wait a second to summon your Jekua after she's summoned hers, they might cut to a close-up of hers waiting. You can check the screen, see which marking it has, and summon whoever you need to." He grinned, then said, "You might look like an idiot waiting so long to summon something—your words—but I think it might work."

Niona nodded along as he spoke. She seemed to be on board with the plan. "Against the male, I need something that can both attack from long distance and also really ground itself, so that it's not pulled in."

"Glom seems perfect for that," Balt said.

"You're right, and I actually got some practice doin' that when I used him for the wind tunnel challenge in the elimination round. Thanks, y'all. I can definitely stick him to the ground, but I also might be able to freeze his lower half to keep him there with some extra training. Then, of course, he has tons of ranged moves."

"And then for the female—"

"Boombox," said Niona. "I was thinkin' about it already. She's a close quarters fighter, but I can use Friction magic to reduce her own friction with the air, increasin' her speed, and hopefully slip right through that repulsion field. Then I can lay into the thing with a bevy of fast, strong hits before it knocks her back again."

Balt thought about it, and it sounded like a solid plan.

"I think you've got something here," he said.

"I do too. Oh," she said, her eyebrows shooting up. "Speakin' of havin' something, I guess I can say this now that you're out of the tournament. I think you might be ready to make a Hybrid. If you want to, of course."

Balt stared at her in disbelief. "You think so?" he said.

She nodded. "Haven't you felt kinda...*different* when you summon Dipper and the Tottaworm?"

He tried to think back to the last time he'd summoned them. Maybe there was a slight difference in the feeling, but not anything that had struck him as out of the ordinary.

"It's subtle," she said, noticing how deep in thought he was. "Try summoning them, and try to notice something different."

He was unconvinced, but he stood and strode over to a sparring ring, just so he was out of the way of the other Summoners. He primed Dipper's memory card and started channeling mana into it.

When his soulclay poured out into the ring, shaping itself into the Puffolin's form, he realized there *was* something distinctly different about it. Like Niona said, it was subtle—and subtle was maybe even too strong a word for it. It was hard to describe, but he could sense it when he looked for it. Or, rather, it was like a *lack* of something that was there before. Summoning Dipper felt more natural than it ever had before. There was no barrier between himself and the Puffolin.

"I feel it," he said. "I think."

"Told ya. That sensation is only there once you've attained a certain mastery of the Jekua. And I don't mean that makes you a Master with a capital M, so don't get yourself all worked up, but yeah. Means you've gotten fairly good with 'em. Which ain't too much of a surprise, given how often you summon the damn things, even when we're just sittin' on the sofa." She laughed at him, then said, "Try the worm."

He withdrew Dipper and swapped her out for the Tottaworm. As it appeared in the sparring ring, again Balt could feel that finer sense of control that wasn't quite there before. More than ever, the Jekua was truly an extension of him.

Niona grinned, seeing the excited expression on his face. She said, "I didn't wanna say nothin' before, since it didn't really matter. You couldn't Hybridize anything anyway, on account of the tournament's rules about your team. You'd have screwed yourself."

That made sense. He wanted to test out Milton and Pistachio, too, see if he could feel it with either of them. When he summoned Pistachio, that feeling wasn't there. That was to be expected, he supposed, since Pistachio was the most recent Jekua he'd imprinted and also the most difficult to master. He withdrew the Mosstopus and summoned his Mirror-bear, and was shocked to discover that feeling was present with Milton.

"I feel it again," he told her.

"Whoa, nice!" she said, sounding genuinely surprised. Then, "So, yeah, once you hit that point with your Jekua, you're able to Hybridize it. So it seems like you could do that with any of those three, if you're interested."

He was definitely interested. He'd been thinking about making a Hybrid for weeks. Who to combine, though?

When it came down to it, part of him felt weird about combining Dipper with something else. She was his very first Jekua, and that was special to him. Maybe it was foolish, or childish, or some other –ish, but he wanted Dipper to remain resolutely Dipper.

Plus, if he kept training with her, maybe someday she'd be the most badass Puffolin anyone had ever laid eyes on.

Did he really want to make a Hybrid between Milton and the Tottaworm, though? It would mean that he'd no longer have the clout that came with summoning something as uncommon as a Mirrorbear. Although, summoning a Mirrorbear-Tottaworm Hybrid was probably even rarer. Still, he wanted to be sure he wasn't making a Hybrid just for the sake of doing so, and that it was something he'd genuinely be excited about.

It did not take long for him to decide that yes, he wanted a nasty worm-bear creature. Creating a Hybrid would also free up the memory card that currently stored his Tottaworm's data, which he could add to the stack that he'd just won from the tournament. He was already itching to fill them all up with new Jekuas.

"What do I do?" he asked. Hybridizing was a process he was vaguely familiar with, but in practice, he wasn't sure how to do it.

Niona grinned excitedly. "Okay, so, you know that trick I taught you about sending mana into two different memory cards?" Balt nodded. "You're gonna have to do that. Alright, well, I'm gettin' ahead of myself. First, summon one of the things you wanna use, then start to channel mana toward the other one."

"Easy enough."

"Sure, but we ain't at the weird part yet. Once you do that, you're gonna start to cast the imprinting spell."

Balt knew about that part, but he didn't fully understand what it entailed. He voiced this concern to Niona.

She said, "Yeah, like I said, it's weird. So, in essence, what you're doin' is, like...okay, so it's not *literally* this, but the idea is kinda like you're imprinting that second Jekua's soulclay onto the first. Y'know?"

"I mean, no, but I guess so," he said.

"I think it'll make more sense to you in the moment. It sounds kinda counterintuitive, but it feels sorta natural when you're doin' it."

"Okay," he said. "What happens after that?"

"Once you've successfully 'imprinted' one onto the other, the magic'll take it from there. You won't need to do any specific sort of crafting or anything, just keep channelin' mana and it'll do the rest."

"What if I run out of mana before it's done?"

Niona stared at him. "Hmm," she mumbled. "I hadn't thought of that. Never happened to me before."

"Oh. Wonderful."

"Don't worry your dumb little head, you'll be fine. Just relax."

That was easier said than done, but Balt started channeling his mana into the kayet to summon Milton. In reality, he had no idea how this spell worked, but in his mind the logic tracked that the simple little Tottaworm would be easier to imprint onto the Mirrorbear rather than the other way around.

When Milton stood before him with his icy blue gaze, Balt diverted some mana toward the Tottaworm's memory card. Once it was full, he began casting the imprinting spell.

He almost barked out a yelp of surprise when more yellow soulclay drifted out of his kayet, something he'd never produced before while another Jekua was already summoned. But he directed the gloppy substance toward Milton, and it started to encase the Mirrorbear's body, just like it did when imprinting a natural Jekua.

While the soulclay covered Milton, Balt's own body began warming. It was as if someone had draped a fuzzy blanket around him.

Soon the substance coated Milton's body, and as the seconds ticked by, his soulclay began shining brighter and brighter. He cast a quick glance over at Niona, as if to say *please tell me this is normal,* to which she silently nodded.

His mana was draining faster than he'd ever felt it do so before, which made sense given he was technically summoning two creatures at once. His reserves were fairly large, though, thanks to how often he built them up with random summons (as Niona had mentioned mockingly).

At first the glowing soulclay remained the same shape as Milton, but now it was starting to bubble and throb as it melted and shifted form. The warmth in Balt's body was heating up, and soon it would reach uncomfortable levels.

It was a full two minutes before his soulclay ceased

moving, and both the glow and the warmth within him began to dim.

"Here we go," said Niona.

That's it? he thought. The process was a lot faster and a lot smoother than he'd been anticipating. He still had over half his mana, too. There really was nothing to worry about.

The light continued to fade until the soulclay was its regular light yellow hue, and then that too began to fade into the colors of the Jekua beneath.

"Oh, no," Balt muttered.

Obviously he had some idea of the Jekua's shape, watching his soulclay forming it, but seeing the creature in all its glory was something else.

The thing was revolting.

Like the original Mirrorbear, it was a quadruped. But this thing's legs were long and wriggly, like it was standing on four worms, with big flat feet that ended in curved claws. Its chest was broad like a bear's but the torso tapered as it went on, ending in a long tail that swished in the air. The skin retained the bizarre reflective properties of the Mirrorbear, but the middle of its body looked segmented, like the Tottaworm. Its head was long, and it had lost its cute, round ears, but the icy blue eyes remained. Thankfully, it also kept its big mouth brimming with vicious fangs. The adorable wet snout was gone, though.

The Jekua was standing completely still, and it took a second for Balt to remember that he was in control of it. He took a couple steps forward on its tall, wavering legs, and immediately stumbled. His mana was dinged as the thing whacked its chin on the floor.

Niona laughed at him. "You'll have to get used to walkin' it, I guess."

Balt nodded. "It's pretty unsteady," he said. He stood it back up and turned it to face her. "Say hi."

"Hi," said Niona.

He laughed. "Alani is gonna hate this," he said.

She laughed too. "Yeah, that bastard's ugly."

"I know. Maybe this was a terrible idea."

"You've created an abomination."

He nodded at her kayet, with its Jektionary attachment, and asked, "Does it have a name?"

Niona raised her wrist and scanned his new Hybrid with the Jektionary. After a couple seconds, it let out a pleasant ringing sound, and Niona read the result.

She guffawed and said, "It thinks that's a Harkmare."

"How in the hell?" Balt muttered.

"Hey, they're two majestic beasts."

"Yeah, majestic." He looked over the Hybrid, turning it away from Niona to look at him. It was a few feet taller than the original Milton, with these new legs. "Should I still call him Milton?" he asked.

"If you wanna. Pops is still Pops to me."

He would keep Milton. Maybe that continuity would ease Alani's mind once she saw this thing.

"I guess we can refer to it as, uh…I dunno, a Mirrorworm?"

"It's not super worm-y, though. How about a Bugbear?"

Balt shook his head. "That doesn't feel right either." Then he suggested, "Echobear?"

Niona thought about it for a second, testing it out in her mind. "Where'd you get that from?" she asked.

"Well, it's still mostly bearish, and 'echo' works as both like a reflection of something, kinda, as well as tying into the Tottaworm's Sonic magic."

Niona nodded and said, "I'm sold. Wanna see what he's capable of?"

He really did, more than anything. But he said, "One devastatingly huge problem at a time. I gotta figure out how to walk first."

38

SIXTH FLOOR, SECTION T

UNFORTUNATELY BALT HAD NO GRAVITY JEKUAS, SO HE wasn't much use in getting Niona ready for her upcoming battle.

While Niona searched for a Summoner with a Gravity-Type, Balt experimented with his new Echobear, testing out the moves it had carried over from each of its predecessors. He was thankful to discover that it retained the Mirrorbear's Reflect power, which would have been a massive loss. The Echobear could also easily elasticize and stiffen its limbs, but Balt's testing of the Spearshot ability didn't go very well. He would have to rework how to achieve the same result but in a different way. He also chose not to try out the Tottaworm's whole "firing feces like a bullet" thing in a public gym. The size of the Echobear's would be nothing to sneeze at in a battle, though.

Niona managed to track down a Summoner in the gym who had a Jolligon that she was able to spar with, which didn't possess precisely the same abilities as Desi's Pokibuvvs, but it got the job done.

Balt's linkpad vibrated a minute after he withdrew Milton. He was planning on watching Niona train for about ten or fifteen more minutes before heading back to the apartment. When he checked his linkpad, he was not expecting to find a text from Wasaaru, but there it was on his notification screen.

Can we meet? the message asked.

He warily replied, *What's up?* Not committing, but not denying, either.

It took less than a minute for Wasaaru to respond. Balt looked away from Boombox fire-punching the woman's Jolligon to read: *I want to show you something. Also need your help with something else. If you're free, could you meet at Xatetu Field? Sixth floor, near the entrance to section T?*

Balt couldn't fathom what his cousin would want to show him at the stadium, but this was the politest Wasaaru had been in years, so he didn't want to jinx things. He wrote, *Sure. I'll head over now.*

He grabbed Niona's attention and told her he was leaving. She thanked him for his help in solving the Pokibuvv mystery, then returned to pounding the Jolligon, which kept trying and failing to slide out of the trajectory of Boombox's fists.

It was nearing ten o'clock, so Balt wasn't sure that the stadium would even be open to the public still. Wasaaru seemed confident, though, so for the moment he trusted him.

The walk through Makanuele's streets was pleasant. By this point, he still did not know any street names or anything, but he could navigate himself to a few major landmarks. The crater at the center of the city was pretty hard to miss, in any case. As he made his way there, he encountered a small flock of Barnatoos alighting on a crooked tree near a bus station. Barnatoos were nocturnal Thermal birds with extremely round heads and bodies. They looked like two tennis balls stacked on top of each other, and their bodies lit up in the dark.

There were more Barnatoos flying around the crater as he descended the steps into it, as well as a lone Yissoon that was curling up near the base of a tree to sleep. It stretched its body out so that it curved around the entire trunk of the tree, at which point it then solidified its body. With its brown fur, it blended in with the tree bark fairly seamlessly. Enough to trick another animal, at least.

Xatetu Field was lit up, even this late at night. Balt could spy some activity through the windows, which made him wonder if some sort of special event was taking place. When he stepped inside, it appeared to just be the typical guests buying food and merchandise at the vendors. The stadium was simply open later than he would've guessed, it seemed.

He strode past a few Summoner murals on the walls and found the nearest elevator. He rode it to the sixth floor, where it dinged at his destination and let him off into a silent, desolate hallway. All the vendor booths on the sixth floor were unmanned, with their security shutters pulled closed and locked tight. The scent of hot oil lingered in the air from the food stalls.

Balt walked along the curving hallway, gazing out the floor-to-ceiling windows at the crater below. He could see the pleasant glow of Barnatoos as well as a violinist who was setting up near the entrance of the stadium to play music.

When he looked back down the hall, he saw Wasaaru a short distance away, with a bag slung over his shoulder. He was staring at the wall. "Hey," Balt called to him.

"Hey," Wasaaru said back, though he didn't turn away from whatever he was gazing at on the wall.

Balt approached and stood next to Wasaaru. "What'd you wanna show me?" he asked, but as soon as he looked at the wall, he understood.

It was a painting of their grandmother. There on the sixth floor was Remisti Vana in all her glory. With her long, flowing silver hair and her steeply curved nose. Rich brown eyes, tan skin marked with a scar just slightly off-center on her chin. Balt couldn't believe a detail so small had been replicated. In the painting she wore a self-satisfied smirk, a determined look on her face as if she was in the midst of battle—and a battle she was winning, at that.

Balt didn't know the last time he'd actually *seen* his grandmother. There were framed photos back at home, arranged on the walls or on random tables, but eventually those always faded into the background of a house. Just one more decoration that your eyes saw but no longer processed.

The mural was taller than him, taking up the entire wall with its thick, vibrant brushstrokes. It could not be ignored. It would not fade into the background. It would always be seen.

The sight nearly made him choke up. He stood there, trying to find something to say, but he was lost. For a moment, he and Wasaaru merely stood there in silence, admiring the beautiful dedication to their grandmother's legacy.

Finally, he managed to speak. "I didn't know this was here."

"Mhmm. I found it two days ago," said Wasaaru. "I wanted to get a better view of the city block environment, since I knew Yakka Dho was gonna be summoning a Bingst. Dude wouldn't shut up about it in the locker room. So I came up here, and I just so happened to see it."

As they stared at the painting, words edged to the tip of Balt's tongue. He wanted to apologize for keeping the bestiary from Wasaaru, for keeping that part of their grandmother to himself. But no matter how he phrased it in his head, it sounded wrong. It sounded stupid.

Before he could find the right words, Wasaaru started speaking. "Anyway, this isn't really the main reason I wanted to see you. I just thought you'd wanna know it was here."

"Thanks," said Balt, hardly louder than a whisper. Then, "You needed something from me?"

Wasaaru nodded. Still, neither of them would look away from the painting. He said, "I don't know if you saw, but I'm moving on to round four tomorrow."

"I missed it, sorry. But congrats."

"Mhmm. I'm going up against David Woollis. Have you seen any of his battles?"

"Nah."

"Well, one of his best Jekuas is actually something that you have: the Puffolin."

"Really?"

Another nod. "I know you and I each have a win against each other, but—"

Balt interrupted him and finally turned from the mural. "Wait, are you admitting that I won fair and square and that it wasn't a bad massage that made you lose?"

Wasaaru looked at him and said, "Absolutely not. Don't get too full of yourself over there."

"Whatever you say."

"Regardless of the reason, legitimate or not, your Puffolin beat me. So I was wondering if you wouldn't mind sparring a bit tonight so that I could try out some techniques I had in mind to use against Woollis's."

Balt's mana was about halfway full, but it was replenishing by the second. It had been a long while since he'd stomped his cousin, too. There was a part of him that rustled at the idea of helping Wasaaru improve at summoning in any way, shape, or form, but he actively tried to fight that instinct. He shrugged and said, "Sure." His mildly comfortable pallet on Aeiko's floor could wait.

They both returned to looking at the painting of their grandmother for a minute more. They stood in shared silence, the lack of noise in the empty hall soothing Balt as he contemplated his grandmother's face. She looked so powerful, yet so playful. Like she knew she was the strongest Summoner there was, yet it was all a fun game to her. He still wished to be like her someday, and he wondered if there had been any trace of Remisti Vana in him out on that battlefield over the past few days.

"Ready to roll?" Wasaaru asked, breaking the silence. The sudden sound almost made Balt jump.

"Yeah," he said. He would assuredly be returning to this spot a few more times before he left Makanuele.

He followed Wasaaru downstairs and back outside. They circled around the edge of the stadium, still within the crater but out of sight of others. There was a single light illuminating the spot in which they stood.

"Alright," Wasaaru started, "the thing Woollis has been doing with his Puffolin is that move where it shoots out a seed and it explodes on impact. You know it?"

It sounded like an improved version of Dipper's Seed Shot attack. Balt was familiar with the advanced technique, but it wasn't something he was capable of performing. He'd never even tried it before; he was still struggling to learn the Fungal Spore attack.

"I know it," Balt said sheepishly, "but I don't *know* it." He was turning out to be a useless training partner for both Niona and Wasaaru.

"I figured that might be the case," said Wasaaru smugly.

He rummaged through his bag and tossed a plastic container over to Balt. It was a mod chip, for AA-037: Seed Missile.

"You bought me a mod chip?"

"Think of it as a late birthday present. And I only picked it up because I assumed you didn't know the move on your own."

"No confidence in me whatsoever."

"You did lose today, after all."

"Too soon."

"I also didn't see you ever use the move in your three matches, so I figured you didn't know it. It would've been handy, I bet."

Probably so. It was a way stronger move than the regular Seed Shot. "You're sure I can have this?" Balt said. Mod chips weren't cheap.

Wasaaru nodded. "Happy birthday."

Balt tore open the packaging (with strenuous effort) and inserted the tiny mod chip into his kayet. He loaded Dipper's memory card and began the installation process.

While they waited for the mod to do its thing, Balt asked, "What's this plan you've got in mind? I assume it has something to do with your Eclipse Jackal."

"Well, you'd be wrong."

"Oh."

He said, "I want to use my Koutix against it."

"A Sonic-Type?" said Balt. "How do you plan to use that against a Seed Missile? And where'd you even imprint a Koutix?" The mystery of his cousin's fourth Jekua was solved, and it was not a conclusion he would have ever come to on his own.

"The answer to your second question is irrelevant. The answer to your first is this: a Koutix can shoot a sticky web of varying size, which it can then use its Sonic magic on to create intense vibrations from the webbing. I don't know if this'll work, but I was thinking I could apply that webbing to the Puffolin's throat, then set off the vibrations as it's readying the seed. If my assumption's correct, the vibrations *could* set off the explosion before the seed leaves the Puffolin's mouth."

"You wanna blow the Puffolin up with its own seed."

"Correct."

If it worked, that could do some serious damage to David Woollis's mana. Balt was impressed with his cousin's ingenuity. He asked, "What makes you think the vibrations will set the seed's explosion off early?"

"I don't know for sure, but landmines work based on vibrations, don't they?"

"I guess so," Balt shrugged. He was not a landmine expert. He would be hard-pressed to consider himself an expert on *anything*. "This isn't a landmine, though. It's a magical seed."

"Thank you for informing me. I guess we'll just have to wait and see if the same principles apply."

Balt nodded, then said, "Hey, wait! This is gonna hurt the shit outta me!"

"Yeah, probably," said Wasaaru. "That's a risk I'm willing to take."

On cue, his kayet informed him that the Seed Missile chip had successfully installed. Between acquiring a new move for Dipper and creating his first Hybrid, today was turning out to not be a *total* loss. Balt wasn't sure if he would trade all that to still be in the tournament, but at least they were good consolation prizes.

"Ready to try it out?" Wasaaru asked.

"I mean, no," Balt muttered, rubbing his throat, "but let's do it."

"I expect it'll be a challenge landing the web in the right spot with Woollis, so don't make easy it for me," Wasaaru said.

"Wasn't plannin' on it."

They stepped a little further apart, then began summoning their Jekuas. Wasaaru's Koutix was as tall as he was, a bipedal orange beetle with huge pincers and a curved horn protruding from its forehead. The orange carapace was speckled with red and black, while its arms and legs were fully black. It had clawed hands that curled into fists as Wasaaru eyed Dipper.

This is gonna be very painful, Balt thought.

Right off the bat, Wasaaru's Koutix began spitting sonic webbing at Dipper. Balt dodged out of the way, curling the Puffolin into a ball and rolling her along the grass.

She sprang into the air, uncurling herself, and fired a Petal Shower at the Koutix. Her sharpened petals bounced uselessly off the Koutix's shell, which made Wasaaru laugh.

That irritating laugh again. Balt decided to give his cousin a taste of that scrumptious new mod chip he'd so kindly gifted him.

Much like with Dipper's Seed Shot, Balt could feel the seed traveling up his own esophagus just before he shifted into Dipper's perspective. Within her body, he could feel the hard seed tapping her teeth. It was roughly five times bigger than the one used for a Seed Shot, filling up her entire mouth.

He opened Dipper's mouth wide and shot the seed at his cousin's Koutix. The black seed zoomed through the air and struck the beetle on its shoulder, exploding in an array of shrapnel and sizzling sap.

The Koutix was knocked off its feet and onto its back, which Balt saw as the perfect opportunity to lay into it with some Vine Whips. He lashed at the Koutix while Wasaaru stood it back up, trying to swat away at Dipper's assault as he did so.

Then the Koutix grabbed one of her vines and

slammed its head down, slicing through the vine with its horn. It tossed the limp green rope onto the ground, where it immediately shriveled up.

The beetle swung its head, sending out a beam of Sonic energy from its horn that whirred through the air directly toward Dipper. She dodged sideways to avoid the Sonic Slash, then fired a Seed Shot at the Koutix. Then Balt had to tuck and roll forward, just barely avoiding a second Sonic Slash as it flew over his Puffolin.

They continued trading blows for a minute, and Balt was surprised to find himself grinning, despite how fast his heart was racing.

Am I actually having fun with Wasaaru? he suddenly thought to himself.

Wasaaru charged his Koutix forward, emitting pulses of soundwaves as it ran. The noise was debilitating, causing Balt's vision to go blurry. He lost control of Dipper for a few seconds, but it was enough time for the Koutix to scoop its horn underneath her and fling her into the air.

She landed with a heavy *thunk* on her back, and Balt flailed around like a turtle for a moment before the Koutix drilled its horn into Dipper's stomach. Blood gushed out and it effectively stopped any further movements.

Then the Koutix fired another web while she was on her back, and it landed perfectly on her throat. *Dammit,* Balt cursed internally.

He produced more vines to swipe at the Koutix, ushering it away while Dipper stood back up.

It would take exact timing on his cousin's part to set off the Seed Missile before Balt was able to spit it out.

Surely he wouldn't be lucky enough to succeed on his very first attempt, assuming the gambit even worked in the first place.

He was hesitant to lodge the seed in his throat again. In Dipper's throat, rather. The two still got muddled in his mind when he was in his Jekua's perspective. But he did not want a seed to explode in either of their throats, and if it did, would it be enough to fully deplete his mana?

This was what he was there for, though. He'd agreed to it.

He sighed.

The seed started traveling up Dipper's throat, and once again he felt its tough exterior knock against the back of her teeth. It was unsettling.

At that instant, Balt could feel vibrations on his throat—subtle at first, but swiftly intensifying. He leapt out of Dipper's perspective while trying to fire the missile as quickly as possible.

But the Koutix's magic was too fast. The vibrations grew more powerful, and suddenly the Seed Missile burst in Dipper's head.

The explosion was not as violent as Balt feared, but it packed one hell of a wallop. It flung her head backward, sending a painful *crack* rippling through her neck. Some of her teeth shattered, and her tongue and mouth burned with fiery sap.

The combination sent a shockwave through Balt's mana supply. He let out a gasping breath and withdrew his Jekua, leaning over to prop himself up on his knees.

"Man," he wheezed. "That was…no good..."

Wasaaru laughed at Balt's dismay. "Looked pretty good to me," he said cockily.

"You're not the one who had to feel it in your throat," said Balt. His throat burned like he'd just puked his guts out.

"That was too easy," Wasaaru said. "Next time, make it harder for me to flip you. Make me work to get that webbing under there."

"Next time?" Balt sputtered. His pool of mana was more like a puddle now. "I've barely got any mana left after that. I was training at the gym when you texted me."

Balt was still grasping his knees, breathing heavily and staring down at the ground. A couple seconds later, a can of peach-flavored Thunderjolt rolled into view, flattening the tufts of grass.

He craned his neck to look at his cousin, who then cracked a can of his own.

Wasaaru took a sip, wiped his lips, and said, "Drink up."

39
NIONA VS. DESI

ENERGY WAS HIGH GOING INTO THE FOURTH ROUND OF THE tournament. Niona could feel it in the air, a low-grade hum, a sort of invisible momentum that propelled her through Xatetu Field's halls and into the Diwepti Room.

Yesterday, things had gone exceptionally poorly for the Summoners of the Diwepti Room. Now, out of the eight competitors left, only three were Diweptians, herself included. She sat trying to calm her nerves while David Woollis did his typical breathing exercises nearby. The third member of their party, Kallon, was currently out battling Olli Berrap.

She told herself she couldn't have a repeat of yesterday's match. She needed to stay focused, stay on top of her game. Desi Taewao wasn't going down without a fight. But Desi also didn't know that Niona had figured out her trick, so she had a leg up there. That is, if she could make out those maddeningly small markings on the quills.

The locker room felt lonelier without Balt there.

Now that he was kicked off the bracket, he'd lost access to this area of the stadium. He'd texted her wishing her luck from where he sat in the stands with Alani and Aeiko.

Up on the screen, Niona watched Olli beating Kallon's ass. They were a hell of a Summoner. Niona was honestly afraid of going up against them, and she was never afraid of battling *anyone*. If she was being truthful, the notion of battling Uil was mildly intimidating as well. She hoped that Johnny Fierce would win against him today so she could battle Johnny next instead of Uil, but she did not think that was likely.

Not long after, she was out on the battlefield.

Second damn battle of the day, she thought to herself bitterly.

Why couldn't she go last? Give herself time to prep a little more and regain her mana. Her muscles felt tight, and she couldn't stop bouncing on the balls of her feet. Her body needed to move, move, move.

Don't work yourself up, she thought, which only got her even more worked up.

She felt foolish for being so nervous, especially since she knew it was solely due to Vanessa Ren's presence in the audience. If not for that woman, Niona would be feeling light and breezy. Desi Taewao? No big deal.

But alas.

The arena was set up like a patch of forest. There was thick grass, brown underbrush, and a copse of trees standing between Niona and Desi. Not ideal for sneaking a peek at those Pokibuvvs' quills. Cameramen were stationed throughout the woods, though, to capture footage for the televised fight. There were a handful of drones buzzing around, too.

Niona glanced upward, and from where she stood, she had a fantastic view of one of the stadium's mega screens. As long as a cameraperson got a decent shot of a Pokibuvv, she'd be able to see it.

She didn't hear the announcer's words this time around. She was glued to that screen, imagining Vanessa Ren's smiling face filling it up. Her perfect straight, white teeth. Her thick, rounded hair. Those gleaming, vibrant eyes. Staring down and judging her every move with that smile plastered on her face.

Suddenly, Desi was summoning something. The battle must have commenced.

As Balt had said, it would be smarter to wait and see what Desi summoned before Niona did anything. She usually liked to be on the offensive, but she knew that could get her eliminated here.

Desi's first Jekua was an Urud. They were massive Gravity-Type Jekuas; not quite as large as a Bingst, but they packed on some pretty considerable mass. It was all fat, though, no muscle. They were barely mobile creatures, spending a majority of their day (or rather a majority of their lives) sleeping. They were a rich maroon color, with patchy fur showing pink skin underneath. Their head was like a cow's, but fatter, and all their limbs were thick and stubby.

Watching the Urud actually walk would have made Niona laugh if she didn't know Desi was behind the wheel. Niona hadn't seen many Uruds fight, so she wasn't totally sure what they were capable of, nor did she know whether it was one of Desi's modded Jekuas.

Niona took a deep breath, then whispered to herself, "Okay. Here we go."

She clicked a button on her kayet and began channeling mana toward Garbo's memory card. In round four, she could swap out her Jekuas whenever she wanted, but she was going to preserve Glom and Boombox for now. Plus, forests always presented interesting opportunities for Elastic-Types.

The Nuri sprinted out into the forest, kicking up dirt with his clomping hooves. The ground shook with every staggering step Desi's Urud took.

Just to get things started, Niona shot a half dozen lightning bolts out of Garbo's horns at the Urud. The ones that hit its enormous, fleshy belly bounced off without inflicting much damage, but one hit its hand and another hit its face. Both caused the Urud to halt its forward march, stumbling backward a couple steps. Its bald, pink hand was burned by the blast, and a chunk of its floppy left ear had been blasted off.

The Urud remained still and opened its mouth wide. It started sucking inward, a great gust of wind flapping Niona's hair as the creature sucked and sucked.

Garbo stopped running, and Niona elasticized his horns immediately. She wrapped them around the trunk of a tree, praying that it would hold.

Leaves, twigs, rocks, and even a couple entire bushes were uprooted and flew into the beast's mouth. Its cheeks puffed as it sucked in more and more, until finally it had its fill and clamped its mouth shut.

The Urud looked like it was going to vomit, which was not something Niona was thrilled to endure, but at least she could let go of the tree Garbo was grasping onto for dear life. She unfurled his horns from the trunk, returning them to their natural size and rigidity.

She glared at the Urud, wishing she had Balt's annoying encyclopedic knowledge of Jekuas and their abilities. She didn't even have a guess as to what it was doing.

There was no sense wasting time, though. She trotted Garbo along, weaving in between trees, charging up another electric blast.

Then the Urud opened its mouth and spat out a gigantic ball of debris. All the rocks, branches, leaves, everything had combined into one hulking, wet ball that was now sailing through the air toward her Nuri.

It smashed through the trees' sturdy branches, sending chunks of wood and sharp splinters spraying toward Garbo. He was struck by those just before the ball of gnashed-up detritus hit him. The one-two punch knocked him off his feet, leaving a few pieces of wood stuck in his flesh in addition to several other lacerations of varying sizes.

Niona stood him back up, but it took more effort than she anticipated. The Nuri's legs were weak, but eventually he was back on his feet. She'd lost the electrical charge she'd been building up, wasting all the mana she'd imbued the move with, so she started over.

Meanwhile, the Urud was sinking its claws into a tree and tearing it from the earth. It might have reduced the tree's gravity to make it easier to rip up, but the Urud might have also just been that strong. Niona didn't know.

Regardless, she built up Garbo's lightning blast for a few more seconds then fired it at the Urud. The yellow beam of lightning hit the center of the Urud's stomach as if it were a bullseye, but the creature seemed unaffected. It simply continued its beleaguered steps forward and began swinging the tree it held like a baseball bat.

She did not want Garbo to be the baseball.

The Urud kept swinging the tree, destroying every other tree in its way as it neared Garbo. Soon there would be nowhere left to hide. That would admittedly help her in seeing the Pokibuvvs later, but right now it was not ideal.

She dodged another shattered tree and surged forward, using magic to harden Garbo's horns even more. They both pierced the bottom of the Urud's low-hanging belly, but they glanced off and left hardly more than a scratch. It wasn't even deep enough to make it bleed.

The Urud's natural defenses were too high. She needed to hit it harder.

If lightning wasn't doing much against the beast, then Pops wouldn't bring much to the table. She doubted Boombox's punches or kicks would do anything, either. Maybe Glom could melt the thing's face, but she wasn't sure.

For now, she kept Garbo summoned. A new idea was coming to her.

She circled around, running away from the Urud. While Garbo dashed through the forest, Niona surveyed the trees that remained upright, trying to find the perfect one.

Her plan would require her to accurately calculate the tree's length as well as the Urud's walking pace. She thought she found one that would work, and positioned Garbo behind it.

But as soon as she got there, the Urud began sucking things up again. She anchored Garbo to the tree, but she didn't have enough time to execute her plan before the Urud fired off its garbage ball.

The ball tore through the tree she'd planned on using, smashing it to bits and raining down more debris on top of Garbo. He sustained a few scratches, but overall it was a much less painful experience than the first time around.

Niona checked on her mana real quick, and was pleased to find she was doing well. That first major attack had drained quite a bit, but relatively speaking the Nuri did not require much mana to use, so she was still in good shape.

Unfortunately, she needed to find another tree. Her eyes flickered back and forth across the battlefield while Garbo dodged stray rocks that the Urud was tossing his way.

The Urud resumed its march the same moment Niona decided on a tree she thought would work. Once more, she positioned Garbo behind it. Then she stretched out his horns, longer and longer, higher and higher, until they wrapped around the trunk near its top.

She then pulsed Elastic magic through the horns and into the tree, elasticizing it. The process was going to take several seconds, given how tall and wide the tree was. She cast a glance at the Urud, which was still slowly approaching. That was good. As long as it didn't get too close, and as long as it didn't start sucking shit up again.

The tree was ready. She could sense it through Garbo's horns.

She hardened the Nuri's horns and began walking him backward, pulling the tree down with him. The huge brown trunk curved unnaturally, and once Desi realized what was happening, she stopped moving her Urud.

That'll have to do, Niona thought.

In an instant she unlatched Garbo's horns and the rubbery tree flung forward.

She eyed the tree's trajectory. It bent forward, propelled toward the Urud. It was going to hit.

The top of it struck the Urud's face, and the force of it sent the creature falling backward onto its frankly enormous ass. A quake rippled through the battlefield when it landed, creating a small crater in the artificial forest. It let go of its tree-bat, which rolled five or away.

That one had to impress Vanessa, right?

Wanting to grasp the opportunity, Niona raced Garbo through the trees toward Desi's downed Urud. The Nuri leapt forward, bounding across the beast's heaving stomach, until he came to a halt on its chest.

Then she charged up another lightning bolt and shot it point-blank at the Urud's face.

It thrashed underneath Garbo, sending the Nuri sprawling to the ground. Niona quickly stood him up and ducked out of the way of the Urud's flailing limbs.

The next moment, the Urud lit up in the color of Desi's soulclay and returned to her kayet.

Pokibuvv time? Niona wondered.

She withdrew Garbo as well, though it wasn't a requirement. She just didn't want to waste any mana having a Jekua out there while Desi didn't.

It was indeed Pokibuvv time. Niona grimaced as the red-furred little squashed-face idiot showed itself on the battlefield. Its silver quills pointed straight out from its piggish body.

From this distance, Niona could not discern which of the marks its quills bore, V or X. She glanced at the screen, and currently it showcased a wide drone shot of the entire arena. Not super helpful.

She couldn't dally too long, though, or it would be considered a surrender. She allowed herself a couple more seconds to see if the screen changed to a close-up, but it didn't. "Shit," she grumbled. She had to send something out there.

It was a coin toss, and it mentally landed on Glom.

Pink soulclay poured out of her kayet and took on the amorphous shape of her Muggish. He crawled along the forest floor, burning up grass in his wake, turning his featureless head from side to side.

Right now, Desi was keeping her Jekua completely still, seemingly relying on its gravity field ability to throw Niona off her game. Desi was going to let the fight come to her.

Without a close-up shot of the Pokibuvv, Niona wouldn't know if it was the male or the female until she hit it. She would have to play into Desi's hand.

She was gearing up Glom to lob a lavaball at the Pokibuvv when out of the corner of her eye she saw the big screen switch. She looked up, and it was a shot of the Muggish readying his attack.

C'mon, change, Niona urged the cameras.

Then they did.

An image of Desi's Pokibuvv filled the screen, like the people manning the cameras were waiting to capture a shot of it being hit by Glom's attack.

Niona squinted. Even on the huge stadium screen, it was hard to see the finer details of the Pokibuvv. Once again, she cursed Xs and Vs for being so similar from a distance.

She thought what she was seeing were Vs. If that were true, then that meant this Pokibuvv was the one with the repulsion field, which meant that Glom was the wrong Jekua.

"Shit," she murmured. She was going to look like an absolute idiot, but she had to do what she had to do.

At the last second, she decided not to withdraw Glom without launching at least *one* attack. She followed through with throwing that lavaball, which came up short, plopping on the ground a few feet from the Pokibuvv. The Jekua took some splash damage, though, as globs of molten lava sprayed from the impact spot onto Desi's Pokibuvv.

It caused enough damage to set off the Pokibuvv's gravity field, which was what Niona had intended. She immediately withdrew Glom, which seemed to puzzle her opponent.

While the lavaball was gliding through the air, she had begun channeling mana into Boombox's memory card.

Once her Muggish had returned to her kayet, she switched over and summoned the Bruiserweight.

Her scaly green lizard got a running start as soon as the soulclay faded away. Boombox launched herself across the arena, snaking in between trees—the ones that were left standing after the Urud's destruction, anyway—and heading straight for the Pokibuvv.

She had spotted the marks correctly. An invisible pulse reverberated through the forest, knocking Boombox back a couple feet.

At the moment, the extra resistance was not enough to warrant using any of Boombox's Friction magic just yet. She could still get through the gravity field without expending the extra mana, and she cut the distance between the Jekuas in a matter of seconds.

Boombox laid into the Pokibuvv with a flurry of blows, taking care to avoid the quills and only going for the face. The Pokibuvv's teeth shattered and its left cheek caved in slightly before its gravity field kicked in even stronger, sending Boombox hurtling backward, slamming into a felled tree.

The impact took a chunk off Niona's mana, but she was still over half full. Nothing to worry about just yet.

She stood Boombox up, brushing herself off. The Bruiserweight sprinted forward again, but met heavy resistance from the Pokibuvv's enhanced repulsion field.

Across the way, she spied Desi's look of smug satisfaction. It was about to be wiped away.

She used Boombox's magic to reduce her own friction with the air, and a couple seconds later the Bruiserweight was sliding effortlessly through the gravity field. She tried to increase Boombox's friction against the ground, which would have been the best of both worlds, but she couldn't focus enough to pull off both alterations.

Several feet from the Pokibuvv, Boombox jumped forward and extended her leg outward in a flying kick. She then increased the friction on just her foot, and when it collided with the Pokibuvv's face, it ignited in flame.

The Pokibuvv was sent sprawling onto its back, its quills digging into the soft earth below. It kicked its stubby legs uselessly in the air, and a moment later Boombox was upon it.

Again, she pounded the Pokibuvv relentlessly. The Bruiserweight's fists were a blur as they decimated the creature's delicate underbelly.

Then the Pokibuvv curled into a ball, rolling itself backward so that it was back on its feet yet still curled in on itself, and an explosion of quills shot forth from it.

Boombox was pierced with two dozen razor sharp quills at the same time she was thrown backward by the reinforced gravity field. She tumbled ass over head across the forest floor, with each bounce digging the quills deeper into her body.

Niona stood her Jekua up shakily, but there was no way to dislodge those quills without grabbing them and yanking them out one by one. She pulled out two of them, but blood spurted from the holes left behind, which she knew would continually drain her mana. They might make mobility tougher, but she decided the best thing for now would be to keep the rest of the quills in.

Her Bruiserweight looked like she had just come from

an acupuncture session. Niona winced imagining what it must feel like to have so many needles stuck in her flesh.

After her last devastating attacks on the Pokibuvv, its natural gravity field was literally impossible to walk through. With Boombox so far away, the Pokibuvv began firing quills across the forest at her. Niona dodged three of them, but one hit Boombox in the chest. A jab of pain pierced Niona's own body, and when she checked her mana levels again, she saw she had dipped below the halfway mark. And every second that ticked by, more mana dripped away, thanks to those open wounds.

Desi rained more quills down on her, all of which she dodged this time. Surely the woman did not expect her to be able to fight through a gravity field this strong, but Niona was going to prove her wrong.

She reduced Boombox's friction against the air even more, as much as she was capable, and still she was met with some resistance when the Bruiserweight ran forward. It was working well enough, though, despite feeling like she was wading through mud. This time, she was able to also increase the Jekua's friction against the ground, which helped to stabilize her.

Another quill stabbed Boombox in the arm before she reached the Pokibuvv, but it was worth it to see the horrified look on Desi's face when Niona assaulted the little beastie again.

Every one of Boombox's punches sparked a flame when it struck the Pokibuvv's face, which was now even more scrunched up than it was naturally, and blood gushed from its nose, mouth, and even its beady eyes. The thing was beyond messed up.

And Desi knew it. Her Jekua's gravity field pushed Boombox back, sending her careening through the air. Even so, she withdrew her Jekua, probably on account of the considerable blood loss.

Before Boombox could crash into the earth and lose more of Niona's mana, she withdrew her too.

The plan was going well so far. Mostly, anyway. She'd lost more mana than she would've liked, but at least she had knocked Desi down a peg or two in the process.

What would she send out next? Her male Pokibuvv, or whatever other Gravity-Type she had waiting in the wings?

The question was answered a moment later when Desi's soulclay shaped into the form of another Pokibuvv. Thankfully, Niona did not need to rely on the jumbotron to see which markings its quills sported. It had to be the male.

X marks the spot, she thought.

She channeled mana into Glom's memory card again. It was lucky that they could re-use Jekuas if they so chose. A lot of Summoners tended not to, since it was easy to assume that if your Jekua got trounced by your opponent already then it likely would again.

It felt good no longer being on the defensive. Without wasting a single moment, she had Glom bubbling up and sending a downpour of molten rain over the new Pokibuvv. Lava splashed onto the creature, melting some of its quills and burning the fiery red fur underneath.

Desi didn't look worried though, not yet. The porcupine's gravity attraction field kicked in a moment later, and Niona could distinctly feel the invisible tug on her Muggish.

Glom was yanked forward a couple feet, and she was having trouble grounding him. She'd thought his gloppiness would stick him to the ground more, help resist the pull of the Pokibuvv's gravity, but that seemed to not be the case.

Plan B it was, then.

She started to extend Glom's body outward, stretching his lower body across the forest. His torso lowered to the ground as his sludge thinned out beneath him, until finally his simmering, viscous form touched a tree on either side.

His flesh immediately started burning the tree, so Niona didn't have long to act. She hastily covered more of each tree with Glom's body, then instantly used Thermal magic to cool down his lower half. It took heavy concentration on her part, since she was inexperienced with using this side of the Muggish's Thermal powers. She much preferred burning shit.

But the trees stopped burning, and Glom's lower body fully cooled and hardened into black rock. He was successfully anchored to the two trees, no longer pulled along by the gravity field.

So he lobbed more lava at the Pokibuvv.

A lot of it missed the mark, but some of the lava splashed onto the Pokibuvv. The sizzling sound that emanated from the impact brought a satisfied grin to Niona's face.

Niona threw more and more lava at the other Jekua, feeling her mana drain with each assault. There were more abilities in Glom's arsenal, but she figured if it ain't broke, don't fix it.

With each hit, the creature's attraction field grew stronger and stronger. By now, even Niona herself was being pulled into it, and she had to step onto the battlefield and hold onto a tree to stop from being sucked in.

All the while, Glom remained stationary, attached to his two trees. Desi was growing visibly frustrated, considering that the male Pokibuvv possessed no long-range attacks. She'd wholly expected to be impaling whatever Jekua Niona threw at her.

She tossed more lava at the Pokibuvv, which was now half-melted and looked like absolute shit. Its gravity field was attracting all of Glom's lava directly to its body.

Finally, Desi decided she'd had enough and that her strategy wasn't going to work on Niona.

The gravity field evaporated and her Pokibuvv trundled forward with fury in its eyes but only half of its quills remaining. The others were now no more than black-and-silver sludge dribbling down its round body.

Admittedly, the Jekua could run faster than Niona would've bet. In seconds it was almost to Glom, and she had no time to soften his lower body again to avoid whatever attack was incoming. And even if she did, the Muggish was too slow to escape.

Once it reached Glom, the Pokibuvv jumped into the air and stabbed the quills on its back into his chest. It depleted some of Niona's mana, but the liquid nature of the Muggish's body muted some of the damage.

But it did not mute the next thing, which was the Pokibuvv self-destructing in an explosion of quills.

Glom's upper body burst apart, sending globs of lava spraying all over the forest while his hardened lower half remained attached to the trees. Bits and pieces of the Muggish lay scattered across the grass, and Niona had no choice but to withdraw him.

For what it was worth, that final attack forced Desi to withdraw her Pokibuvv, too. Niona imagined the self-destruct move had to drain a substantial amount of the woman's own mana.

When she checked her own, she saw it had dropped hers down to about a quarter left. *Please be done,* she mentally willed Desi.

But Desi wasn't done. More soulclay slithered out of her kayet and onto the field.

"Dammit," Niona sighed. She began summoning Pops and anxiously waited to see what Desi conjured next.

She summoned the Urud again.

"Well, shit," Niona muttered, not having expected that. Now that it was re-summoned, all previous signs of damage had disappeared. The looming beast was good as new.

Pops looked like an insect compared to the Urud's massive form. Technically he *was* half-insect, but still.

She knew electric shocks to the Urud wouldn't accomplish much, and if she brought out Garbo again, Desi would be on high alert for a repeat of that tree trick.

One advantage Pops had over Garbo was agility. Being much smaller, he could also go more places.

Like onto the Urud's head, for instance.

It was as good a plan as any. Her mana was low as hell,

but she suspected that Desi's was too. One of them had to fall first.

Pops scurried through the grass, scampering up trees and leaping from branch to branch, avoiding everything the Urud threw at him.

When he was close to the other Jekua, Pops jumped into the air and immediately crashed to the ground, abruptly weighed down by the Urud's damnable magic.

Niona stood him up, but the extra gravity was nearly crushing the poor Toolu's bones. She could sense her mana ticking away as she fought against the magical gravity.

Vanessa's watching, she reminded herself. Those two words filled her with both anxiety and determination.

Step by step, she moved Pops forward on his six spindly legs. He reached the Urud and pierced the thing's flesh with one of his claws, then another, and started to ascend the side of the large Jekua.

The Urud began swatting at Pops, but he batted away its paws with his tendril-covered tail, which crackled with electricity. Pops's extra weight had to be a burden on the Urud, but if it was, it showed no signs of distress. It continued slapping at the Toolu as he climbed, sometimes connecting but other times smacking itself with its claws, leaving behind scratch marks.

Soon, she would reach the limits of her mana. This gravity was not doing her any favors, and neither was having to swat away the Urud with an electrified tail.

Pops clambered onto the Urud's shoulder, then hoisted himself up onto its bovine head. The Urud swung its head around manically, attempting to throw Pops off, but with his added weight he was able to latch on tightly.

Niona wanted an even firmer grip, though.

She stabbed two of Pops's legs into each of the Urud's eyes, then another into an ear. The Urud screamed and flailed about even more wildly, and Niona could feel the extra gravity lifting from Pops's shoulders. If he hadn't dug into the Urud, he would've floated into the air like a balloon.

Blood rushed past Pops's legs, staining his black carapace. Niona started to charge up electricity in the Toolu's tiny body, the entirety of which was roughly the same size as the Urud's head.

"This has to do it," Niona said out loud to herself. If she said it aloud, then that had to make it true.

A shockwave emitted from Pops's body, electrocuting the Urud's head. Its eyeballs burst like jelly candies and its patchy red fur sizzled and burned.

As the Urud toppled over, Pops jumped off it and landed safely on the ground, skittering out of the way. Niona was pleased to find that Pops had regained his normal gravity and wasn't drifting into the blue sky.

Unsurprisingly, Desi withdrew her Urud once more.

Niona checked her mana levels again and saw that shockwave attack had knocked her dangerously low. If Desi had anything else up her sleeve, Niona wasn't sure she would make it.

On the other side of the forest, Desi looked royally pissed off. Her face reddened, and if they were in a cartoon, steam would've been billowing out of her ears.

She held up her hands in surrender.

Niona withdrew Pops and collapsed against the tree. She hadn't realized she was still clinging to it, even though the Pokibuvv's gravity attraction field had long since dissipated.

She closed her eyes and could have fallen asleep right there.

40
WASAARU VS. DAVID

BALT'S HEART WAS IN HIS THROAT FOR THE DURATION OF Niona's battle, and he only settled down near the conclusion of Johnny and Uil's match. It did not come as much of a shock, but Balt was pleased as punch to see his old nemesis Johnny Fierce be obliterated by Uil. Balt would've preferred if it were *him* on that field being obliterated by Uil, but this was the next best scenario.

The result of that match meant that in round five, Niona would be up against Uil. If the battle against Desi Taewao had been that much of a nail-biter, then facing Uil was going to be tough, to put it mildly.

That was three of the day's four battles finished, with Niona, Uil, and Olli Berrap moving on to the next round. All that was left was Wasaaru versus David Woollis.

Last night, Balt had been continually battered and bruised by his cousin's Koutix. He'd gotten plenty of good hits in himself, but Wasaaru was proving to be a pretty skilled Summoner. More often than not, he was able to pull off the early detonation move he'd been planning. Balt could still scarcely believe it worked at all.

It was time to see if he could use it to beat David.

At that moment, Balt recalled that the one match of David's he'd seen—in round one—David had easily squashed a Koutix that his opponent was using.

Hmm, he thought. Probably information that would've been useful several hours ago. Maybe things would go better for Wasaaru.

Alani sat in the middle between Balt and Aeiko. While he was no longer granted access to the backstage areas of the stadium, his pass was good to get him a seat to watch the rest of the matches. He leaned over to tell Aeiko over the crowd noise, "This next dude's my cousin."

"Oh, okay," they said.

He leaned back over and shoved a cheese-laden fry into his mouth. This was his second batch of smothered fries that he was nervous-eating.

"Your favorite Totta Island Summoner is back, ladies and gentlemen! Welcome back to the arena Wasaaru Vana!"

The crowd cheered for Wasaaru, Balt included. While he clapped his hands together, though, he couldn't help but doubt that his cousin was anybody's favorite Summoner from Totta. That was a load of shit, right? Balt wished he could catch a glimpse of that announcer.

Next, the announcer reintroduced David Woollis, who was a tall, gangly man with a long and scraggly beard. The hair on top of his head was thinning, and the clothes he wore hung loose on his thin frame.

"Summoners, when you're ready..."

Wasaaru didn't wait, immediately summoning his Eclipse Jackal. Starting off with a bang. Not a bad idea, either, since the forest environment offered a multitude of shadows for the Radiant-Type Jekua to slip into.

David's first summon was a Yissoon. It was a huge rodent, about the same height as a car, with a long, slender body. Yissoons were covered in short, golden fur and had cute, pointed faces with round ears. They walked on four legs with small, clawed paws. Their tails were long and skinny, ending in a set of keratin segments that rattled when they vibrated against each other.

"What is that?" Alani asked Balt. She had recognized a few Jekuas as the day wore on, but the ones she didn't she always asked him about.

"A Yissoon," he said. "Elastic- and Growth-Type. Primarily the *decay* side of Growth, though. Lots of poison-based moves. You gotta watch out for 'em around the hiking trails on Kou Tekkis. Their tail rattles when you get too close, so they're fairly easy to avoid if you listen."

The Eclipse Jackal instantly disappeared into the shade of a tree. David inched his Yissoon forward, rattling its tail. The display made Balt chuckle, knowing that it would not have the intimidating effect on his cousin that David was aiming for.

A second later, the Jackal shot out from the copse to the Yissoon's right, its body drenched in flame. It rammed its head into the Yissoon's side, sending it tumbling onto the ground.

Then the Eclipse Jackal opened its mouth and unleashed a Firebark, scorching the Yissoon's neck. It whipped its head toward the Jackal and hissed, sending a red liquid spraying from its eyes.

The stream of liquid hit the Jackal's face, staining its black fur red. The Jackal stumbled backward, tangled in its own legs, and fell over. Wasaaru tried standing it up and running away, but it seemed he'd lost some control of his Jekua.

"What was that?" asked Alani.

Balt explained, "Yissoons can, like, increase the blood pressure in their head and burst their blood vessels or something."

"...so that was blood it just shot from its eyes?"

"Yes." He knew that was something the Jekuas did in the wild to ward off predators (although anything preying on them would have to be pretty enormous, which he supposed was common for the Kou Tekkis mountains), but he didn't realize it had any use in a Jekua battle. From the looks of it, it seemed like it had inflicted a sort of confusion effect on Wasaaru's Eclipse Jackal, making it temporarily harder for him to control his soulclay.

He watched Wasaaru try to leap into another shadow, but the Eclipse Jackal pathetically flopped onto the grass, failing to slip into the dark. It lay there, flat on its stomach with limbs splayed, while the Yissoon approached.

The Yissoon's tail raised up behind it, and the rattle at its tip glowed yellow. Then the tail came slamming down into the earth, the rattle disappearing beneath the surface. A wave of yellow electrical energy surged outward from the point of impact, covering roughly half of the battlefield.

Unfortunately for Wasaaru, his Jekua was currently scrambling on the ground within that half, and it subsequently suffered a nasty shock. When Balt looked over at Wasaaru, he was sporting a deep scowl.

Initially, Balt had thought David modified his Yissoon with a Shockwave ability, but this was something different. The field remained electrified even after a few seconds had passed and the Jekua's tail was yanked out of the ground.

Wasaaru finally got his Jekua to its feet, but the electrified terrain continued zapping it as it staggered away. The Jackal's gait was wobbly and it zigzagged through the shimmering electrical energy, occasionally wincing from another shock. He still had yet to regain full control over it, but it was steadily improving.

The Yissoon, unaffected by its own magic, scampered through the grass and began extending its body as it moved.

Wasaaru clearly saw it coming, but between the confusion and the electricity both hampering him, he couldn't move his Eclipse Jackal fast enough to evade the oncoming Yissoon.

Its front half stretched out, cutting off Wasaaru's Jackal, curving around and wrapping the Jackal in its furry golden body. Then it undid its Elastic magic, retracting itself and squeezing the Eclipse Jackal in a tight embrace while they sat there on the electric field.

The Eclipse Jackal struggled and fought against the Yissoon, but it couldn't free itself. There was suddenly a switch in Wasaaru's expression, and Balt guessed that he now had full control of his Jekua again.

That had to be the case, because the Eclipse Jackal suddenly lit up in flames, burning away some of the Yissoon's gorgeous fur. The Yissoon let go and jumped off the Jackal, who proceeded to dash across the remainder of the electrical field, only enduring one more jolt of electricity before it was clear. Then it slipped into a shadow, leaving David's Yissoon on high alert.

Fifteen seconds passed with nothing happening. Everyone watched the battlefield with bated breath, awaiting Wasaaru's next move.

"I think he's waiting him out," Balt said to Alani and Aeiko. The latter could barely hear him, but they leaned over to listen. He said, "There's nothing the Jackal can do to counter that terrain shit the Yissoon did, so I think he's waiting for the effect to wear off."

Out on the field, David shouted, "You scared, little boy? Quit hiding! Come out and play!"

Of course, Wasaaru's pride and temper got the best of him. Before the electricity fully faded, the Eclipse Jackal jumped out of a shadow, landing directly on top of David's Yissoon.

The Jackal was small enough compared to the Yissoon to stand on its back, avoiding the ground. It reached forward and clamped its fangs down on the Yissoon's neck, the creature's eyes widening crazily.

A burst of fire exploded from the Jackal's mouth, searing the Yissoon's neck. All of its fur burned away and the pink skin beneath was charred and scarred.

David shook his Yissoon's body wildly, sending the

Eclipse Jackal flying off. Moments before it hit the ground, the electrical energy disappeared, leaving no trace of it ever being there.

Still, Wasaaru's Jackal landed on its head, smacking its skull on the hard ground. Even without a spark of electricity, that had to do some damage to his mana.

Wasaaru looked pissed off. Clearly things were not going as well as he'd hoped by summoning his strongest Jekua first. He withdrew the Eclipse Jackal and quickly started summoning something else, his dark orange soul-clay pouring onto the green grass. Balt was somewhat disappointed, wanting to see what other new moves Wasaaru had taught his Eclipse Jackal since they battled back in Himony.

What he brought out next was his Nullfly. There wasn't a ton he could accomplish with a Nullfly, so Balt was interested to see what his plan was.

The oversized bug immediately altered its gravity and torpedoed toward the Yissoon. It elasticized and curved its body out of the way, sending the Nullfly crashing into the earth, creating a miniature crater. Normally the tournament technicians would have to refill that, so they were probably glad this was the last match of the day.

While the Nullfly was momentarily incapacitated, David swerved the Yissoon around and bit down on it.

"Had to be a poison bite," said Balt.

A burst of invisible energy sent the Yissoon flying backward, smashing into a tree. The Nullfly flapped its wings and rose into the air, but it was haphazard.

"Ah, shit," Balt muttered. Probably not a poison-riddled bite after all, but rather it had ripped through one of the Nullfly's wings. It flapped once, twice more, then dropped pitiably to the ground. If Wasaaru could make it fly at all, it would take more effort, and by extension more mana.

David grinned to himself as he withdrew his Yissoon. It was never a great sign when one's opponent looked pleased.

The next Jekua he sent out was one that Balt had read more about when they first came to Na Tana, since it was commonly found around the island's shores. It was like their equivalent of Totta's Slipsharks.

It was called a Mitsip, a Tidal-Type crustacean the size of a person's forearm, with a long body and a vibrant blue carapace. It skittered around on tens of skinny legs, and at the forefront it bore two meaty claws. Frilly antennae jutted from its head just above four white, ovular eyes. It had some Sonic abilities too, but it mainly used Tidal-based attacks. Balt only really knew of one Sonic power that it had.

The Mitsip scurried toward Wasaaru's ravaged Nullfly, shooting an array of bubbles at it. They burst when they hit the insect, but did not appear to do a whole lot of damage.

Wasaaru was still trying to move his Jekua when the Mitsip reached it. Without its flight, the Nullfly was stuck, since it did not have very strong legs. It could use Gravity magic to raise and lower the gravity enacted on it, moving itself that way, but that would cost mana.

You gotta do something, *though, dude,* Balt mentally urged him.

The Mitsip reached the Nullfly and a stream of water

poured out from its mouth. Wasaaru flapped his Jekua's wings, but they were rendered even more useless as they were engulfed in water. It only took a couple of seconds before both creatures were encased in a ball of magical water that shimmered in the sunlight.

Then the Mitsip opened its claws and instantly snapped them shut. It happened so fast, Balt didn't even see them closing. One second they were open, the next they were shut.

Balt wasn't even sure what happened.

All he saw was the claws close, and suddenly the Nullfly was knocked backward, tumbling through the ball of water. It broke the surface of the bubble and splashed onto the ground, laying motionless on the ground.

That was its one Sonic move.

They couldn't hear it outside the water ball, but the lightning-fast closing of the Mitsip's claw created an invisible jet of water with a pressure bubble that, when it popped, created a sound louder than a gunshot, knocking Wasaaru's Jekua into unconsciousness.

His cousin was trying to get the Nullfly back up, but it lay limp on the forest floor. When a Jekua was knocked unconscious in battle, essentially it was like the Summoner's soulclay went numb. They couldn't manipulate it at all anymore.

He would have to withdraw the Nullfly, having accomplished literally nothing with it except losing himself some mana. That had to make him angry.

"Well, that was short-lived," said Alani.

"Yeah," Balt nodded. Things weren't looking great for Wasaaru.

What was he doling out next? The Dewrat or the Koutix?

Surprisingly, David withdrew his Mitsip as well. Balt would have expected him to deal a few more blows with the thing before switching out.

Balt caught Wasaaru eyeing David, hesitating to see what the man summoned next before choosing his own Jekua.

Soulclay spilled onto the battlefield, and Balt was intimately familiar with the shape it started forming. This was the Puffolin.

Wasaaru recognized it too. Before David's soulclay faded, he was already summoning his Koutix. In a few moments, they would learn if all that training had paid off.

His cousin wasted no time laying into the Puffolin. The Koutix swung its head three times, emitting a Sonic Slash from its curved horn with each fluid motion.

The rippling blades of energy cut through the air at immense speed, but David's Puffolin rooted itself in place before the first one hit. All three connected, but the damage was reduced by its hardened defenses.

Then petals rose from the Puffolin's back and rained down on the Koutix, though its tough exterior dulled most of the pain. The beetle started marching toward the Puffolin, swinging its head again to send one more Sonic Slash its way.

But the Puffolin jumped out of the way of the energy beam and opened up its mouth, firing a massive seed. It rocketed through the air, and Wasaaru just barely dodged it. The seed struck a tree behind the Koutix, exploding in a spray of splinters and leaves.

Wasaaru needed to get the Puffolin on its back, but it curled into a ball and rolled toward his Koutix. It slammed into the beetle's lower body, sending it falling face forward into the ground, its pincers stabbing into the earth. Wasaaru had to tug and tug to free it from the ground.

Meanwhile, behind it, the Puffolin was preparing another Seed Missile. This time, the Koutix was too busy trying to dislodge itself to turn around, let alone dodge. The missile hit the Koutix's back and burst apart, covering its orange shell in burning sap.

"Dammit!" Wasaaru swore, loud enough for a microphone to pick it up.

His Koutix's back sizzled from the acidic sap. It turned around, and Balt assumed the creature would be glaring if it had more distinctive facial features rather than tiny eyes and gigantic pincers.

The bipedal bug charged forward, head tilted down. The Puffolin moved out of its trajectory, but Wasaaru course-corrected, and the Koutix's long legs helped it move faster than the Puffolin could scurry away with its stoutness.

Wasaaru deftly maneuvered the beetle's horn underneath the Puffolin and tossed its head back, flipping the Puffolin over. David's fists tightened as his Jekua was flung into the air, landing on its back with a reverberating *thud*!

Sticky white webs shot out from between the Koutix's

imposing pincers. The first two landed on one of the Puffolin's feet and then its tail, which told Balt that his cousin's nerves were getting to him. Last night, when the pressure was off, he hadn't missed a single shot.

He fired three more webs, and one of them stuck just below the Puffolin's neck. It might be good enough, but Balt wasn't totally sure. Between the other two webs, one hit another of the Jekua's feet while the other stuck to the ground next to it.

Having done what he planned to, Wasaaru moved his Koutix away from the Puffolin. Assuming his scheme worked, he did not want to suffer any splash damage.

The Puffolin rolled back onto its feet, but two were immediately stuck to the ground and when it tried taking a step backward, it landed in that other web. Three of its feet were now stuck to the ground.

That didn't matter much, however, as far as David was concerned. The Puffolin's body emitted a warm glow, which Balt knew meant that it was absorbing nutrients from the ground it was stuck to, which would increase its attack power. Then David readied another Seed Missile.

Balt was quite literally on the edge of his seat.

He could clearly see the Jekua's mouth fill up with that hefty seed. Wasaaru saw it too. He only had a second or two.

The vibrations of all the webbings went off, the ones on the Puffolin's feet sending tremors through its body and the one near its neck detonating the missile.

Sap and seed shards exploded in the Puffolin's mouth. A chunk of black seed jabbed upward through the creature's snout, which was a gruesome sight. Balt didn't even know that was possible, and he was glad it hadn't happened to Dipper.

The Puffolin's mouth burned with acid and pieces of broken teeth dropped from its mouth onto the ground as it stumbled around, disoriented.

Wasaaru grinned toothily. He swung another Sonic Slash from the Koutix's horn, which struck the dazed Puffolin and sent it sprawling.

This was it. The end was in sight, Balt could feel it.

The Koutix lumbered over to the Puffolin. Its patch of yellow flowers was pointed skyward, and blood seeped from its mangled mouth.

The horn on the beetle's head began vibrating madly. Wasaaru was going to drill down into the Puffolin, but it remained to be seen whether he'd do so into its back or its head. Either way, it was not going to be pretty.

But as it reached the Puffolin, a massive needle burst from the patch of flowers and embedded itself deep in the Koutix's neck.

The effects were immediate.

Its horn stopped buzzing with Sonic energy, and the Koutix took two halting steps backward. The needle dripped with purple ooze, and the Koutix's orange shell started cracking.

Pus and some other viscous fluid began spilling forth from the cracks in the shell, and as the Koutix staggered then fell to the ground, Balt realized what that fluid was.

It was the Koutix's flesh. The meat of it below the shell was bubbling and popping with venom, causing it to seep through the cracks in its carapace.

Before the act could reach its grisly conclusion, Wasaaru withdrew his Koutix. For that, Balt was thankful. It would have been an unbearably disgusting sight, but one that he could not have turned away from.

Wasaaru still had the Dewrat in his arsenal, or he could send out the Eclipse Jackal again. Summoning the Nullfly a second time was probably not advisable.

But he didn't send out the Dewrat, nor the Eclipse Jackal.

He waved his arms in surrender.

"Oh, man," Alani grumbled beside Balt. "That sucks. What even happened there?"

"That was a really high-level Growth move," he answered. "The Puffolin's poison was liquefying the Koutix's body."

Next to him, Alani gagged. He almost couldn't believe what had happened. He thought for sure Wasaaru was going to take down David Woollis.

Evidently not, though. David withdrew his Puffolin and pumped a fist in the air, sending his baggy shirt billowing in the wind. The audience cheered him on, and the announcer hopped on the speakers to congratulate the final victor of the day.

"Folks, be sure to join us tomorrow for the last two thrilling rounds of the Makanuele Rumble! First up, we'll see our winner here David Woollis go up against the fire-cracker Olli Berrap. After that, we'll see who comes out on top when Niona Daneo battles the mononymous Uil. Once the fifth round concludes, there will be a short intermission, and then we'll all reconvene for the final battle! So rest up tonight and get ready for a day full of excitement

here at Xatetu Field, where you never know what'll happen next!"

As Wasaaru ambled out of the arena back into the depths of the stadium's halls, Balt was hit with an idea. He leaned over to ask Aeiko if they would do him a favor. They perked up and said, "Sure."

The three of them stood up, and he texted Wasaaru while they slowly ascended the steps behind a ton of other people, all heading to either the vendor area or the exit. He told him to meet at the mural of their grandmother.

When Wasaaru finally showed up on the sixth floor twenty minutes later, pushing past throngs of people who were leaving the stadium, Balt grinned and handed him a lukewarm bottle of beer.

"A Sand Dollar," Wasaaru said, chuckling. It was the brand their grandfather always drank. Balt couldn't believe that he'd elicited a laugh from him at all, after such a big loss. "Where did you get this?"

"An of-age friend bought 'em for me," said Balt.

"Of course they sell this swill here."

Balt said, "Sorry it's not a celebratory drink."

"Commiserations are appreciated too." Wasaaru twisted the cap off the bottle and stuffed it in his pocket, then took a swig of beer.

"Sorry," Balt said again.

Wasaaru moved the bottle away and wiped moisture off his lips. "Thanks," he said with a sigh.

"Guess we're both out now. Round three and round four. Not *too* bad for our first ever tournament, huh?" He gestured toward the painting and said, "Think Grandma would be proud?"

Wasaaru looked at the portrait, pondering the question. Then he said, "She would be proud of *me*, for sure. But you..."

He trailed off, and it was hard to tell whether he was being serious or if he was kidding around. This was still uncharted territory for the two of them. But a smirk danced across his face, and Balt chuckled before telling him to shove it.

Then Wasaaru nodded at Balt's bottle and said, "You gonna drink that?"

"Ehh," Balt said, scrunching his face up. "I kinda bought it as more of a, uh, symbolic gesture."

"Nah, c'mon. You have to drink it with me."

"Fine," he said, uncapping the beverage. He gulped down some of it and nearly spit it out like one of the Koutix's webs. His feelings on the drink were apparent from his expression.

Wasaaru laughed at him. "No good?" He took another sip.

"It is truly beyond me how you can stand there and drink that shit with a straight face."

"I mean, it's not good," said Wasaaru.

"So stop drinking it!"

Wasaaru continued drinking the beer. Balt walked over to a nearby trash can and tossed the mostly-full bottle inside.

"Wow," said Wasaaru. "So much for a symbolic gesture."

"The symbolism was over with, we'd moved past it. It was absorbed and appreciated."

"You can recycle glass, you know. But you just threw it

straight into the garbage."

"Alright, now," Balt said. "Now I *want* you to drink that shit. Go on. It'll shut you up."

Wasaaru grinned and downed a large swig of beer as they both turned to look at the mural on the wall.

41
XAMANEKI GARDEN

"I want to show you someplace."

Six words that made Alani's heart do backflips in her chest.

If someone like Balt said them to her, she would assume that "someplace" was a big state of the art gym, or a den of deformed rabbit monsters or something. Her heart would beat its usual rhythm, unbothered.

But it was Aeiko who said it, and so her heart was backflipping.

She was still preoccupied with Balt's story from yesterday morning, about Niona rejecting him. Every time she looked at Aeiko, she thought about the same thing happening between them. Her leaning in for a kiss, and Aeiko pulling back, dismayed and disgusted. Saying—either out loud or with her facial expression—*No, you're Siuv's younger sister.*

So it was annoying that she couldn't stop herself from being so excited about those six words.

There was something that Aeiko specifically wanted to share with her.

She allowed herself to get a *little* giddy.

Despite the speedbump in their relationship, it seemed like Balt and Niona were getting along fine still. Alani knew that if she were in Balt's position, she would be filled with embarrassment and self-loathing in the other person's presence. She would melt into a puddle, unable to form a single coherent thought, praying to all three Veptists that she would evaporate and float up and away from this planet.

Balt had tougher mettle than her, she supposed.

After the four of them grabbed something to eat, those two retired to the gym, as always, to get Niona ready for tomorrow's match. Match*es*, plural, if she made it past Uil and reached the finals. Tomorrow was going to be a big day.

Now it was just her and Aeiko, and Aeiko had said, "I want to show you someplace."

They led her around the curved railing of the crater, heading toward the northeastern corner of the city. An area that Alani had not explored at all in her time there.

She walked side by side with Aeiko down the street. "Where are we going?" she asked, her face turned away, briefly wondering if Aeiko could hear her smile in her tone.

"It's a surprise."

Three more words to excite her.

A light drizzle started coming down. Aeiko paused to look up at the sky, as if it would tell her something. Like, *Don't worry, I'll stop soon.* Or, *Does this work with your plans?*

They looked back down and turned to Alani, grinning.

"I guess I maybe should have warned you about the forecast first, huh?" they said.

"Yeah, maybe," Alani giggled.

"This a problem?" they asked. Raindrops dampened their hair, hanging down to their shoulders. Some slid like teardrops down their face, making their tan skin glisten in the encroaching pale light as the moon reached into the gray sky, replacing the sun. They blinked their big, brown eyes, their curled lashes fluttering.

Alani shook her head.

Aeiko's pace quickened, and Alani mirrored them.

Rain pelted down on them, splashing on the city streets. Cars whizzed by on the road to their right, windshield wipers swiping back and forth, spraying more water their direction. Headlights flicked on, rain cutting through the white beams of light.

Aeiko stopped short, checking both directions for oncoming traffic, then raced across the street. Alani hurried after them, her hair growing heavier as it became wetter. Strands stuck to the back of her neck, and up ahead, Aeiko looked as if they had just emerged from the shower. That thought made Alani's cheeks flush.

Her mental map of the city was spotty at best, so her confusion as to their location was compounded by the darkening sky and the rain. She continued following Aeiko as the rainfall increased.

Hopefully it would let up soon, but even so, she didn't mind much. The rain was oddly and pleasantly warm. As clouds moved in, obscuring the moonlight, the white manastreams criss-crossing all over her skin shone brighter.

The two slipped through alleyways between huge darkened skyscrapers, their employees having long since gone home for the day. Although, there were a few scant offices lit up, which depressed Alani. They cut across a gas station parking lot, where a Dunceling and a Suelu were getting into a tiff near a dumpster. The little yellow mongoose and the walking lightbulb both kept lighting up and crackling with electricity to intimidate the other, which did not work on either of them. The farther north Alani and Aeiko traveled, away from Xatetu Crater, the more the cityscape thinned out. Skyscrapers were giving way to one-story buildings, and eventually even those grew less cramped together. Before long, they would be at the edge of the city. It was possible that Aeiko was leading her outside of Makanuele entirely.

"We're almost there," Aeiko told her after a couple minutes more of walking. They had to shout to be heard over the rain at this point. Both of them were completely drenched, their clothes clinging tight to their skin.

Up ahead, at the end of the street they turned onto, there stood a tall stone wall from behind which came a faint glow. It was mostly blue, but with hints of green and pink. Alani couldn't see what was behind the wall casting the light.

Aeiko finally slowed down, walking leisurely across the empty street. Wherever they were, it was much less busy than the central downtown area of the city. A few shops were illuminated, namely a noodle place and a dive bar that from outward appearances made Barnello's look like a five-star restaurant. Alani skipped ahead to catch up with Aeiko and walk next to them.

"That's it," they said, pointing at the mysterious glowing enclosure.

There was a metal sign mounted just beside a gap in the wall where they could enter, but Alani couldn't read it. It was too dark, and there was too much rain.

As they grew closer, a hum filled the air. From a distance she couldn't hear it over the pitter-patter of rain, but now it was obvious that something within was making noise.

She could finally read the sign on the wall, and it read XAMANEKI GARDEN. It wasn't a word that Alani recognized; it might be ancient Volukhan, or possibly somebody's name.

"What is 'Xamaneki'?" she asked.

"You'll see," said Aeiko eagerly.

They stepped through the gap in the wall, which looked worn down by the years. At some point it probably looked constructed and intentional, but after years of weathering, it almost seemed like an accidental hole in the stone wall that had crumbled and never been fixed.

Then Alani saw what was creating the glow.

The garden was filled with gray stone sculptures. Some were very obviously Jekuas, while others were humans, and some were more abstract, such as a person whose torso ended in a wide egg shape. Flowers covered the ground, and errant vines wrapped around some stone archways that curved over paths.

And all over the garden, scrambling through the grass

and scaling the sides of the statues, were little glowing Jekuas.

Each one looked distinctly different from the next, but they were all the size of a book, no more than a foot tall. Some walked on two legs, while others walked on four. Their bodies were lumpy and misshapen, with big heads propped up by skinny necks and rounded pig snouts that took up half their face. Their eyes—if they *were* eyes, anyway—were merely huge, hollow sockets, like holes in a tree. Some had horns, while others had tusks, but all had stubby tails. And from all of them grew glowing mushrooms. Some sprouted from ears, while others had an eye replaced with a mushroom, and others walked on mushrooms instead of legs. There were a few who sprouted fungi from their backs, and others who were having trouble walking with a belly-shroom dragging its cap along the ground. Most of the mushrooms were blue, particularly on the quadruped ones, while the others had pink and green. But all shone brightly, casting a calming glow that illuminated the garden and the Jekuas' coarse purple fur.

"Those are Xamanekis," Aeiko said.

The little creatures seemed to want to get as close to the sky as possible. They were all trying to climb higher and higher on the statues, despite the lack of purchase offered by the rain. Some were climbing over others, pushing them down to reach the top first. Those who had already reached their destination simply stared upward, letting the rain beat at their faces. Water filled up the holes in their heads that Alani initially thought were eyes, but now she was even less sure.

That humming she'd heard as they approached the garden was coming from the Xamanekis. It was a strange, atonal sound, and in here it overpowered the pattering of the rain.

"Here, this way," said Aeiko.

They scurried through the garden, sidestepping the Xamanekis who were still on the ground seeking out a sculpture to climb. As Alani followed behind, she noticed the creatures crawling out of holes dug in the ground.

There was a pergola set up over in the corner of the garden with a cover overhanging to block the rain. The two of them ducked underneath, with Aeiko taking a moment to prop their foot up on a bench to tie their shoe.

They said, "Pretty cool, huh?"

Alani said nothing, but nodded. She only realized a moment later that she was watching Aeiko instead of the Xamanekis. She hastily turned her head away to look at the glowing Jekuas.

"What are they doing?" she asked.

"I don't really know," Aeiko replied, bringing their foot down and walking over to Alani. "Filling themselves up with water, I guess? Performing some weird little Jekua ritual? I have no idea." Then they said, "They only come out when it rains, which doesn't happen super often here."

They stood watching and listening to the Xamanekis. Eventually, the ones at the top of the sculptures would start to overflow with water. When they did, they would start their descent, opening up space for those who hadn't yet gotten their fill. The Xamanekis who were sloshing with water reached the ground and laid down, glowing brighter and humming louder than ever.

She'd never seen anything like this before. If it happened again while they were here, she would need to bring Balt out. Maybe he would want to imprint one of these things while it was singing and gazing at the rain.

"How long does it last?" Alani asked, wiping at her nose which was dripping with water.

"Oh, we don't need to stay the entire time," said Aeiko. "It depends on how many come out, but it can last hours."

"Have you ever watched the whole thing?"

"I've lasted, like, ninety minutes before I headed home. I used to live in a shitty little apartment down the street from here, when I first moved to the city."

"Oh, really?" said Alani. She hadn't seen any buildings that looked noticeably like an apartment, so it must have been a pretty small place.

"Yeah, it was a dump. Bugs everywhere, appliances always breaking, stuff like that. But it was what I could afford at the time on my own. I found this sculpture garden pretty soon after moving in, though, and it was where I always came to unwind. I was sitting here one night, reading a book, when it started raining. I didn't want to get myself wet or ruin my book, so I just waited under here, and the Xamanekis started coming out. I had no idea it would happen, I'd never heard of them before."

"Wow," said Alani.

"Yeah. After that, I would check to see when it was supposed to rain and come down here to watch them do their thing. Even now, living on the other side of town, I come over here a lot. My living situation's way better, but...well, you know what it can be like."

Alani did. They didn't need to elaborate. It also made

her heart swell, knowing now that this was something they hadn't even shared with Holly.

"Anyway, our conversation earlier this week made me think of it, when you were talking about wanting an escape from the Undertow. This place has always been my escape, I guess."

The sound of rain had always soothed her, and now mixed with the song of the Xamanekis, it had even more of a calming effect. The glow emitted by their mushrooms was pleasant, too, making up for the loss of the moon's light behind dark clouds.

"This is nice," Alani said. "I like it."

"I thought you would," Aeiko smiled.

They stood so close to Alani, their knuckles were nearly brushing up against each other's. All it would take was a twitch and their fingers could become entangled.

She swayed ever so slightly, letting her skin graze Aeiko's. Enough for them to feel it, but also subtle enough for plausible deniability. If necessary, she could claim that it was nothing.

I should've known nothing was gonna happen between us, Balt's voice rang through her head.

Suddenly she felt obscenely childish, standing next to her crush.

She stopped swaying and pulled her hand away from Aeiko's, grasping it in her other hand in front of her. Then she rocked forwards and back on the heels of her feet, watching the Xamanekis in silence.

"Thanks for bringing me here," she said.

"You're welcome," said Aeiko, their voice low and husky underneath the rain.

They stood there, bodies slick and sheening with rain, illuminated by the vivid glow of the mushroom caps.

For a while, nothing else existed outside the stone walls of the garden. All they could see was intermingled blue and green and pink light, and all they could hear was rainfall and the creatures' humming. There were no car horns, no neon signs, no screaming audiences, no uncomfortable plastic seats, no droning prayers, no crystal shrines. It was just them and that garden. Together, they escaped.

42

NIONA VS. UIL

NIONA SAT ALONE IN THE DIWEPTI ROOM. DAVID WOOLLIS was gone, having already lost his battle to Olli Berrap, who was now a finalist.

She was the only Diweptian left. Now Olli and Uil were probably in the Staman Room, plotting Niona's downfall.

A distinct clinking sound was coming from somewhere in the empty locker room. It had the rhythm and frequency of a leaky faucet, but it sounded metallic. Something in the walls? A pipe about to burst, exploding the entire locker room around her, engulfing her in a furious flame?

Anything to get out of this next match.

Never had she been so nervous before a Jekua battle. Usually she was smooth, cocky even, either uncaring about the outcome or instead confident that she would win. Against Uil, though, that confidence was out the door. He was the only thing standing between her and the finals, and with Vanessa Ren watching, her future was on the line here; it wasn't solely the outcome of the tournament she was worried about. If she just made it to the finals, even if she didn't win the whole thing (although that'd be ideal), that would be a victory in her book.

Her father had texted her before she'd woken up, always a pretty early riser himself. He wished her luck with the battle and said that he was going to tune all the televisions at the resort in to the tournament. That made her laugh. It was something he always did whenever his favorite Summoners were battling.

At Aeiko's place, she'd eaten a light breakfast, not wanting to weigh herself down with too much food like she had with the burritos. Everyone else sat around the table chattering excitedly, but she remained quiet. She was too wrapped up in her own head to talk much. When they arrived at Xatetu Field and had to go their separate ways, Balt pulled her into an embrace.

"Good luck," he said, gripping her tight.

"Thanks," she muttered. "I'll need it."

He pulled away, his cheeks red. The sight almost made her giggle, but she was glad to see he was able to power through his own embarrassment to do something as simple as give her a hug.

"Nah," he said, shaking his head. "You've got this. I know it. You're the best Summoner I know."

"The only other Summoner you know is your cousin, and he's a doofus."

"Hey, I know plenty of Summoners, and you're the best of 'em. For real. You're gonna crush it out there."

"How could I not, with someone as magnificent as Glom in my roster?"

"Exactly."

She smiled. Despite the self-effacement, she did appreciate his words of encouragement. If she couldn't prop herself up, at least Balt was there to give her a little boost.

Alani hugged her too and said, "Good luck! We're rooting for you."

"Kill 'em," said Aeiko. Niona liked their simplicity.

With that, the trio had wandered off to find their seats in the stands, and Niona had sequestered herself in the Diwepti Room. She hadn't even gone to the dugout to watch the fight between Olli and David, instead opting to watch it on the screen in the locker room. Her legs were jelly, she couldn't make it all the way out there.

Now she sat on a bench, gazing up at the electronic bracket while she waited for the stadium crew to reset the arena. David's name was lit up in red, while Olli's was green. Their name also now filled the final bracket, along with an ambiguous "???" that awaited either her own name or Uil's.

She sighed, then tried doing those calming exercises she'd seen David doing a few times. If those even were calming exercises, anyway. Not much good that they did him, whatever they were.

There came a knock at the door, then a man's voice on the other side asking, "Are you decent, Ms. Daneo?"

"Uh...yes," she called back. Only now that she was the last Summoner in here was anybody being polite, rather than barging in.

The door swung open and a man in a Xatetu Field

uniform poked his head inside. "Are you ready to go, ma'am?"

No one here had called her "ma'am" before either. She preferred it when the room was filled with other Summoners so she could deflect some of the attention. Regardless, she nodded and stood to join the man.

Somehow, walking those halls released her of her nervous energy. Moving her body, letting her mind empty and focus just on the simple act of *movement* helped her to stop obsessing over whether or not Vanessa Ren was going to extend her an offer.

As soon as they reached the threshold of the arena and stopped walking, the anxiety came flooding back into her. She started shifting from one foot to the other in a meager attempt to distract herself. If she just got out there and started summoning, she could lose herself in that. What was the hold-up?

A tinny crackle came from the man's earpiece, and then he said, "Alright. You're good to go. Good luck out there, Ms. Daneo."

"Thank you," she said flatly. Somehow it meant less coming from him than from her actual friends. She moved past him and strode out onto the battlefield.

For the fifth round, the arena's environment was sand dunes.

It was a mystery as to why it had taken the crew so long to reset what was essentially just piles of sand, but alas. Niona walked to the edge of the dunes, and across the sandy expanse she saw Uil doing the same.

She took a deep breath.

"Ladies and gentlemen, are you ready for the last match deciding who our finalists will be?"

The crowd roared in anticipation. They were ready.

"I won't waste your time then, folks! You already know our first competitor, coming all the way from beautiful Totta Island, Niona Daneo!"

A ton of people cheered at the mention of her name. Normally that would give her a bit of a confidence boost, but she was busy glaring at Uil. She couldn't take her eyes off him. She needed to get moving again. When she reached inside, she could feel her mana—it felt like it was practically simmering, bubbling and popping, ready to overflow. She yearned to unleash it.

Her hearing dulled as the announcer introduced Uil, who garnered even more applause, which unfortunately cut through her distracted senses.

The announcer's obnoxious voice trailed off, and finally she could move again.

Mana streamed into her kayet and soulclay burst forth. Across from her, she saw Uil was wasting no time either.

She knew what he was gonna do, since he'd done it in all four previous matches. He always came out swinging with his Shimmertusk. Something huge and intimidating, but also brimming with powerful magic. A worthy adversary.

Loads of soulclay poured out of Uil's kayet, piling onto itself more and more until it created the towering visage of the Radiant-Type elephant. The Shimmertusk had leathery yellow skin cracked with wrinkles and scabs. It stood somewhere between ten or fifteen feet tall, one of the biggest Shimmertusks Niona had personally seen.

One of its four tusks was broken, but the others curved outward from its mouth and glistened in the sunlight.

A Jekua like that expended a lot of mana, though. So if she could get him to move it around a lot and also cause some damage to it, she could hopefully take out a good portion of his mana right off the bat. Luckily, she had gone to see the Shimmertusk migration with her father in Hurrathsa, so she was somewhat familiar with the creatures' abilities.

Her first Jekua was Boombox, who was way smaller and faster than the Shimmertusk. Pops had that advantage too, but if she slipped up and the elephant got a good hit on her miniscule Toolu, that would be devastating for her mana.

The elephant marched forward, its massive feet shifting in the sands. It didn't need to walk far, though, to lay down an attack on Boombox, considering how much space it took up on the battlefield.

It lifted its impressive trunk and swung in a diagonal motion, releasing a slash of solar energy that flew across the battlefield toward Boombox. Niona altered the Bruiserweight's friction and slid through the air faster than was natural, easily dodging the massive beam of light, which barreled past Niona and dissipated just before it reached the stadium stands.

Boombox then slipped in the sand and fell flat on her face. She was having more trouble with the sand than the Shimmertusk was, which surprised Niona.

She stood her Jekua up and thought for a second. Then Boombox started running.

With each pounding footstep, she altered the sand's

friction beneath Boombox's feet. It would require far too much Friction magic to alter the entire terrain, but if she focused on just the area where her Jekua was running, she could reduce the sand's friction to create more stable ground for her to run on. The magic could fade away behind her as Boombox surged ahead.

The Shimmertusk swung another solar-powered slash, which Boombox evaded once more. Then it dug its trunk into the dunes for a few moments before pointing it straight at Boombox and spraying sand at an absurdly high velocity.

Uil was smart enough to aim the blast slightly ahead of where Boombox was, so Niona ran her Jekua straight into it. Boombox went flying backward, tumbling down a dune. Grains of sand dug into her skin, cut into her eyes, filled her throat.

When the sandy cyclone cleared away, Niona saw a few lacerations on Boombox's scaly skin. She also felt an uncomfortable sensation in her own throat. It was distant, but it was there, a mild scratchiness. She made Boombox cough up the sand that was still lodged in her throat, and the sensation ceased. She could sense that the Bruiserweight was blinded, and while she herself was not literally blinded by it, what it meant was that some of the control she had over her soulclay was reduced. Not ideal.

Boombox then continued her race toward the Shimmertusk. It was harder to enact her magic on the sand beneath her feet now, and she missed every other step, but she managed to reach the other Jekua without sending Boombox sprawling.

She sprang forward, grasping the elephant's tusks to

aid her ascent. Boombox clambered onto the thing's back, creating the bizarre image of a lizard riding an elephant.

Boombox could have altered the Shimmertusk's inherent friction from afar, but it cost her much less mana to do it while touching the beast. So now that she was on its back, she used her magic to heavily decrease its friction.

Niona could already see it starting to slide in the sand more, but that was only the first part of her plan. Next, she reached down with Boombox's arms and yanked on the creature's huge, floppy ears.

The action jerked its head back, and with more speed than Uil was anticipating. It sent the Shimmertusk stumbling to the side, unable to catch itself.

Boombox stood on its back, balancing steadily, then Niona made her leap off with an intense, fiery kick.

It charred the elephant's yellowy skin and the force of it sent the creature flying with its reduced friction. It fell over immediately, smashing into the sand and rolling over and over across the dunes until it finally came to a halt outside the sand's perimeter.

She had inflicted some damage with that kick, but her real goal had been to get that Shimmertusk's body moving. With every unexpected movement, with every tumble across the dunes, the huge Jekua was draining more mana from Uil's reserves. With its friction reduced, every simple movement ended up going past what the Summoner intended, sapping up more and more mana from him.

Uil had to return his Jekua to the battlefield within a certain amount of time, or he'd be forced to withdraw it.

It'd offer an unfair advantage if the Shimmertusk remained on solid ground while Boombox was stuck in the sands.

He wasn't interested in withdrawing yet, though, and the Shimmertusk stomped its way back into the dunes. It nearly tripped forward over its own wide feet, but Uil was seemingly getting the hang of its newfound friction. The effect would wear off soon, anyway.

The Shimmertusk seemed to brace itself, then it flinched forward. A mass of blackness shot out from its body, in the same shape as the Jekua. The huge shadow-Shimmertusk surged across the dunes and slammed into Boombox. It was her turn to roll out of the battlefield.

Niona made her Bruiserweight rise and hurry back onto the battlefield. She still didn't have as much control over Boombox as usual. If the blindness had been inflicted by an actual Radiant move, it would've probably worn off by now or would have soon. But since it was from sand, something in the physical world, she suspected it was going to last as long as she kept Boombox summoned.

It was then that Uil dug the Shimmertusk's trunk into the sand again. He was getting ready to spray her once more.

This time, Niona was ready. Trying to dodge probably wouldn't go well, with her lessened control over her soul-clay. So instead, she kept her Jekua perfectly still, awaiting the attack.

The stream of sand spouted from the elephant's trunk and shot across the battlefield, but Niona reduced the friction of Boombox's entire body. Rather than slicing up

Boombox's skin like it had last time, the particles of sand slid right over her and fell back to the ground behind her.

It looked like the Shimmertusk could move properly again. It started toward Boombox, who glided gracefully across the sands to meet it.

The Bruiserweight slipped a few times, but Niona was always able to catch her before she fell, blindness be damned.

What she couldn't manage to dodge was the Shimmertusk's trunk reaching out to grab Boombox. It happened with such speed, Niona had to assume her magic hadn't entirely faded yet. But Boombox's friction was still reduced too, so she slipped right out of the Jekua's grasp before it could do whatever Uil was planning.

Boombox slid out from the trunk and propelled herself off the broken tusk, latching onto the thing's giant, floppy left ear.

She held the elephant's thick, leathery lobe in her hand and climbed up, anchoring her foot in the crags of its inner ear. Then she reared Boombox's hand back and increased its friction just as it connected with the Shimmertusk, sending a spark of flame into the elephant's ear canal.

Uil was visibly shaken by the act, clasping a hand to his own left ear as his Shimmertusk staggered. Boombox clambered upward onto its head again, reduced the Shimmertusk's friction, and jumped forward. While in mid-air, Niona grabbed the beast's opposite ear and pulled it down with her Bruiserweight.

The Shimmertusk came crashing down to the ground,

surely emptying Uil's mana reserves by a great deal. Niona grinned to herself, pleased with her own tactics.

As a result of the act, Boombox had fallen into the sand and sunk waist-deep into it beside the Shimmertusk.

For some reason, no matter how hard she tried, Niona could not free Boombox from the sand. It didn't make any sense. Even when she spent more and more mana reducing her friction, it did nothing.

She had to peer closely at the scene to realize what was happening. Every time Boombox moved to pull herself out of the sand, her shadow pulled her right back down.

The Bruiserweight's shadow was touching the Shimmertusk's, merging to create one big black shadow on the sand. Somehow, with the Jekua's Radiant magic, it had gained control over Boombox's shadow and wasn't letting her move.

Niona was shuffling through the annals of her mind for any sort of strategy that would help her here.

While she did so, Uil stood his Shimmertusk up, being careful not to let the two Jekuas' shadows stop touching. Then he lifted its leg and brought its enormous foot down on Boombox's head.

Niona could hear the Bruiserweight's bones crunching, and even if she didn't, she would've known how awful the impact was by how much her mana suddenly decreased.

Shit, she thought. It was time to switch out.

She withdrew Boombox, which meant that Uil had to withdraw his Shimmertusk and swap out Jekuas as well. She only hoped that she'd lowered his mana more than he'd lowered hers, in spite of that last terrible blow.

Mana channeled into her kayet and filled Pops's memory card. She clicked over and began summoning the Toolu, anxious to see what Uil was conjuring next.

His second Jekua was a Noxbill. It was a Wind- and Growth-Type, a great big ugly bird with an absurdly huge head and bill that looked almost fake, somehow. The Noxbill had a large, curved, green bill and glaring yellow eyes with ink-black pupils. It stood five feet tall, with black feathers that dripped with green slime. The feathers themselves looked like sludge. With every flap of its wings, it sent noxious ooze spraying everywhere.

Immediately the Noxbill took to the skies, hurling vomit-y slimeballs at Pops.

The Toolu could easily scamper out of the way, sending blasts of lightning at the disgusting dripping bird. Uil flew the Noxbill out of the way of Pops's bolts, then the bird belched loudly.

Niona winced, scrunching up her face in revulsion. She had never seen a bird *burp* before. Could birds even naturally do that? Or did Uil modify his bird so that it could burp?

Either way, this one had burped, and in doing so it emitted a poisonous gas that she knew would steadily drain her mana if she let it touch Pops. It was starting to fill up the arena, though, and even Pops wasn't fast enough to escape it.

Thinking quickly, she started burrowing into the dunes. Sand slid down to cover up Pops as he dug deeper, until he was completely covered.

The poisonous fog settled on the surface of the sand.

Niona checked on her mana, and she could feel that it wasn't draining. The poison hadn't infected Pops.

Moments later, the fog disappeared, and Pops could reemerge. The Toolu burst out from the sand and started firing more bolts of lightning at the Noxbill.

All of them were easily avoided, however. Annoying.

Pops then screeched, creating a symphony of noise throughout the arena that sounded like dozens of Toolus. Niona caught the Noxbill falter for a moment, and knew that the disorientation caused Uil to lose his grip on his soulclay.

She blasted another bolt at the Noxbill, and this time Uil wasn't fast enough to avoid it. Black and green sludge blew off the bird's chest as the crackling yellow bolt struck it.

Uil flew the Noxbill higher, putting more distance in between it and Pops, giving it even more time to move out of the way of her attacks.

All she could do was attack at long range if the Noxbill stayed in the air. An electrified tackle would do a lot of damage, but so would a bigger thunderbolt, if she could manage to land one.

Pops started to charge up electricity, then fired off an enormous burst of lightning at the hovering mucky bird. Uil was able to move out of the way of that one though, wasting a ton of Niona's mana in the process. She swore.

The Noxbill remained high in the air, flapping its wings and expelling more of its slime. Niona knew what Uil was doing. He was waiting out the effects of her earlier Sonic move, waiting until he regained finer control of his Jekua before swooping in again.

It was a decent tactic. Aggravating, but sensible. It gave her time to keep her own Jekua still, conserving mana, while she tried to think of a plan.

Nothing definitive came to mind before the Noxbill dove downward. Balls of slime rained down on the battlefield like bombs, exploding on impact. Out of the six or seven it unleashed, only one directly hit Pops, while he suffered some splash damage from another.

Niona took a second to check in on her mana reserves. What she felt made her swear again. Already past the halfway mark, and with only her second Jekua summoned. That crushing stomp from the Shimmertusk had been rough, as had the slimebomb that just struck Pops.

Once the Noxbill finished its sweep across the battlefield, it returned to the skies, circling overhead. Niona bitterly wished that she had a rifle.

A few more lightning bolts were wasted on the thing, then it dipped lower toward the ground. It stopped, still in the air, and began flapping its wings wildly, kicking up sand and starting to create a huge gust of wind.

It was forming a cyclone that it'd send barreling toward Pops in a moment. Niona's eyes widened as the cyclone grew bigger and bigger, both in height and width.

The Noxbill hovered in the center of the cyclone, building the wind up around it. Sand was sucked up into the whirlwind, tan grains swirling around the bird.

The force of the wind plus cuts from the sand were going to hurt, even with Pops's carapace offering better defense than Boombox's scales did. There had to be a way to counterattack.

Suddenly an idea came to her. Something she thought she learned in school at one point, a decade earlier. She hoped she wasn't misremembering, which was entirely possible.

She started charging up electricity within Pops, then shot off six blasts of lightning straight at the sandy cyclone. The bolts struck the cyclone, and an instant later, the spire of wind collapsed to expose the Noxbill within.

Uil's bird was impaled on three spears of silica glass, created by Pops's lightning striking the blanket of sand sucked up in its cyclone. The Noxbill plummeted downward, smashing into the earth below.

This was her chance.

Niona raced Pops forward, his body crackling with electricity as he darted across the dunes. The Noxbill was still lying motionless on the ground when Pops reached it, and the Toolu tackled it with ferocity.

The bird's body shuddered and tremored as it tumbled away, and Pops began charging up another lightning bolt. He fired it seconds later, blasting the bird square in the beak.

Apparently that beak was made of iron, though, because the bolt left a tiny scorch mark but did not quite cause the level of damage Niona had anticipated. The Noxbill then rose, shaking itself off, sending ooze splattering onto the sand. It turned and glared viciously at her Toolu.

Glass spears were still embedded in its body, but Uil seemed uncaring. Black sludge dripped around the edges of the wounds, staining the glass. Then he started kicking up another gust of wind, this one rising behind Pops. The

Noxbill didn't build it up too much before sending it careening forward, capturing Pops in it.

The Toolu somersaulted forward, propelled by the wind, and crashed into the Noxbill's body. The impact had to have dinged Uil's mana, but evidently it was worth taking the hit.

Now both Jekuas were impaled on either end of the three glass spears. A jolt of dull pain coursed through Niona's body, and she struggled to dislodge Pops from the Noxbill, but she couldn't gain any purchase, even with six legs to work with.

Blood spewed from Pops's fresh wounds, and every painful jostle ripped another chunk of mana out of her.

Pops and the Noxbill were face to face, with the bird's big ugly beak a mere inch from the concave inverted triangle that took the place of Pops's nose. The bird's bill opened wide, wide enough almost to swallow Pops whole. Niona was glad she could not smell whatever putrid aroma was certainly wafting out of it.

Then green slime poured out of the Noxbill's mouth, drenching Pops. It melted through the Toolu's shell, burning off the yellow fur then scalding the skin beneath.

The more the acid burned Pops, the more Niona's mana drained away. She could feel her body losing more and more as the seconds ticked by.

No, no, no, she mentally pleaded.

But it was no use. Uil's Jekuas were too powerful. Their moves were too advanced. She had some clever tricks up her sleeve, but sometimes that wasn't enough to overcome raw strength.

She checked her mana one last time. She had around

ten percent left. Maybe fifteen, if she was being generous. Even if she summoned Garbo or Glom, one or two good hits from Uil's next Jekua would be enough to bring her to her knees.

Pops lit up in the color of her pink soulclay, finally sliding off the silica glass with ease. The magical substance returned to her kayet, stored safely on her memory card.

Then Niona raised her hands to signal defeat.

The match was Uil's.

Uil raised a fist triumphantly in the air, eliciting a massive response from the crowd. They now had their other finalist. His Noxbill melted back down into soulclay and flew back to his kayet as he continued to pump his fist while the audience chanted his name.

Niona's body felt as if it had turned to stone. She could hardly crane her neck to look out at the stands, imagining the disappointment on her friends' faces. She could perfectly picture Vanessa Ren sitting up there, arms crossed, clucking her tongue as she shook her head at the pitiful display.

So that was it. No chance of Atoll Talent picking her up now.

Why would they? She had lost. She was a loser.

No talent agency, no sponsorships, no independence.

All she had wanted to do was make a name for herself.

She walked off the battlefield, head hanging low, and all she could hear was hundreds of people repeating, *"Uil! Uil! Uil!"*

43
DISTRACTIONS

For the entire morning, Alani had been riding the high of the previous night with Aeiko. They had sat together underneath the pergola, listening to the rain and watching the Xamanekis, for almost a full hour while they chatted. After that, the skies started to clear, and they returned to Aeiko's home.

That infectious energy had carried her through the morning and up to the end of Niona's battle. The loss effectively dampened her spirits, and anyway, she did not want to rub her happiness in Niona's face when they met up with her afterwards.

There was a three-hour break in between the fifth round matches and the finals, to allow the crew time to set up the new battlefield and also for the competitors to replenish their mana. In that time, the stadium was emptying itself out, with spectators filling the city streets, eager to give Makanuele's economy a boost.

"You think she's gonna be alright?" Aeiko asked her and Balt as they waited near the exit for Niona to appear.

Balt said, "I dunno."

"She's usually pretty good at taking things in stride," said Alani. Based on her limited interactions with the woman, anyway.

"Yeah," Balt said, "but I dunno. It still stings."

"Let's go somewhere nice," said Aeiko. "Even if she's out now, making it to the semi-finals is pretty great. We can celebrate your accomplishment too," they added, nodding at Balt.

"I don't know if getting knocked out by a snail halfway through the tournament is anything to be proud of," Balt said.

"Oh, hush," Alani told him.

The stream of people had slowed to a trickle by the time Niona finally showed up. She stepped through the glass doors and waved meekly at the trio, approaching with a muted expression.

"Hey, y'all," she greeted them, her voice flat.

"Yo. Great job out there," Balt said.

"Man, I don't need pity or anything."

"It's not pity, it's the truth. I was super impressed. You did some shit out there that I wouldn't have dreamed of. Using the Shimmertusk's momentum against it was smart, and that move turning the sand into glass was wild."

"Well, the first didn't end up doin' much, and the second ended up gettin' me killed."

"Who cares? It was still clever battling. Way cleverer than anything I could come up with. I'm an idiot, you know that. Never in a million years would I have done the glass thing."

"That's, like, first grade science."

"I don't think *that's* true, but..."

"Hey," Aeiko interrupted the pity party, "let's go grab some celebratory food. I'm of the opinion that every accomplishment, big or small—or not even really an accomplishment at all—is deserving of a treat. What are you in the mood for?"

"There's nothing to celebrate," Niona said sourly. "Really, y'all don't have to do this."

Alani had never seen Niona act upset. Typically, even when she lost a battle, she was all smiles and jokes. She was well aware that the stakes were higher here, but regardless of that fact, Alani was surprised to see how hard the loss was hitting her.

"We're not doing anything," Aeiko said. "We're just getting a treat. A nice, everyday treat. So, what are you in the mood for?"

Niona glared at Aeiko for a moment, but her expression slowly softened. Then she said, "I could go for some nelo."

Alani said, "I've never actually had nelo." She wasn't even certain she knew what it was. She'd heard the name, and could picture...*something* in her head, but she didn't know what exactly comprised the dessert.

"You wouldn't like it," said Balt.

"What?" said Niona, gobsmacked. "How have you never had it? And why the hell wouldn't she like it?"

"She's not a sweets person!"

"I'm not, sadly," Alani confirmed.

"But it's *so good,*" said Niona, temporarily distracted from the fact that she was supposed to be depressed. "You've gotta try one. I can't believe you haven't had one."

"Tanepke's not exactly a nelo town," Aeiko chimed in. "I feel like that's more of a big city item."

"Well, let's go get some," said Alani. "I'm excited to try it."

"You're not gonna like it," Balt said again.

Aeiko led them out of the crater, then headed southwest. Makanuele's streets were bustling today. They always were, but for some reason, they seemed busier than usual to Alani. Perhaps it was because she'd just witnessed hundreds of people filing out onto the streets, but whatever the reason, the city felt crowded.

Niona nearly walked into multiple people as the group made their way down city blocks. She kept looking down at her linkpad, frantically checking her messages. From what Alani could see, there were never any new ones, but she kept checking anyway.

It would probably help if they could keep Niona's mind off the tournament and whatever she was checking her linkpad for. The stunning revelation that Alani had never eaten nelo before had done wonders, so she searched for another topic for them to ramble on about.

Once she landed on one, she said, "Hey, Niona? Do you think you'll be joining us on Yuluhu?"

Niona turned her linkpad screen off and said, "I forgot that's where y'all are goin' next. Uh…hmm. I dunno. Yuluhu kinda sucks shit."

"No kidding," said Balt.

"Well, to be fair, its people suffered a tragedy of epic proportions…" said Aeiko at the front of the group.

"I mean, I'm not blamin' 'em for their island sucking shit," Niona said. "That doesn't mean I wanna visit either, though. They've really got a shrine there?"

"All the islands do," Alani said.

"Sure. I just figured they would've closed that one off or told you that you didn't have to go there. Seems like a big hassle. Ain't there some sort of quarantine involved or somethin'?"

"Not when you go there," Aeiko said, "but when you leave, yes. There's a mandatory one-week quarantine to make sure you aren't infected."

"A whole-ass week? Jeez."

"That's how long it takes to be detectable in your system. Each gondola station connected to Yuluhu has a quarantine hotel attached. You have to stay locked up in your room, and the staff brings meals to your door."

"Room service, nice," said Balt. "You gotta pay for it?"

"The food? Yes. And I hear it's not very good."

"Wow. Bullshit."

Niona said, "I thought there was a waiting period or something before you go there, too. In my head, it's always been like you gotta factor in an extra month to your trip over there because of all the quarantining."

"It's not a quarantine, but yeah, I guess there's a waiting period of sorts," said Aeiko. "You have to submit an application to visit, and it can take around two to four weeks for that to go through the system and get approved."

Alani did not know that. "What is there to approve?" she asked.

Aeiko shrugged. "I don't really know," they said. "I just know you have to wait a while."

That didn't sound promising. Alani had to assume that her documentation from the Church would be sufficient to get their applications approved by the powers that be. If they denied her, she wouldn't be able to fully complete her pilgrimage. What would Elder Poul and Elder Fanareot say?

"Well, that sounds like shit too," said Niona. "Think I'm gonna have to pass on that."

Balt seemed taken aback. "Really?" he said softly.

Niona nodded. "Mhmm. Think I'll just head back to Himony. Help out around the resort a little, maybe take a quick jaunt into the mountains to imprint some stuff and train more. I think there's supposed to be a tournament in Bana Reyo over on Kou Tekkis in mid-Fall or something like that."

Alani had succeeded in distracting Niona from her sadness, but now Balt was sinking into a depression at the notion of Niona breaking away from their group. That wasn't part of the plan. He stuffed his hands in his pockets and stared at the ground as they continued walking.

Good going, Alani, she chided herself.

They turned onto another street and Aeiko let out a deep sigh. "Uh...that's the spot," they said, pointing at a line trailing down the sidewalk, almost reaching where they currently stood.

"We really don't have to do this," said Niona.

"No, let's get some," said Alani with a bright smile. She

wanted to cheer Niona up. She said, "When else will I have the chance to try it?"

"That's true," Niona said. "I doubt they've got nelo shops on Yuluhu."

"We've got several hours to kill anyway," Balt added.

The group walked about ten feet forward to join the ludicrously long line waiting to enter the nelo shop. Up ahead, Alani could see the shop's sign, spelling out REDONIA CAFÉ in blocky neon purple letters.

Since they clearly had a long wait ahead of them, Alani decided to try distracting both Niona and Balt once more now that Niona had resumed obsessively checking her linkpad.

The subject of nelo had worked before, and it seemed safe enough. So she asked, "What is nelo, exactly?"

Niona's mouth hung open for several seconds before she answered. "You don't even know what's *in* it?"

"You really don't understand Tanepke," Aeiko said, amused.

"I thought it was part of modern civilization!"

"Well, sometimes the Undertow doesn't feel like it is," Aeiko muttered.

Alani couldn't disagree with them, but she didn't say anything. Her thoughts drifted to those of her parents, squirreled away in Apartment 309 of Ti House. Against all odds, the topic of nelo had resulted in *her* getting depressed now. What could she bring up next to ruin Aeiko's day, so that all four of them could wallow in misery?

Niona went on to describe the contents of a typical nelo. "It's a bunch of shit in a cup that you mix up and eat," was how she started. "There are lots of different kinds, but the original is best. It's the classic for a reason. It's got ube ice cream, crispy rice, banana, coconut strings, coconut gel, jackfruit, mung beans of the regular and red variety, and date palm jelly. Oh, and some shaved ice, for good measure."

"That's a lot of stuff," said Alani, dizzied by the list. She had already forgotten half the ingredients.

"Yeah, but when you get 'em all in one bite...*man,* it's so good."

"It's pretty, too, seeing all the different colored layers," said Aeiko.

"What other kinds are there?" Alani then asked.

Niona shrugged while checking her linkpad yet again. "There's tons. Depends on the shop. I've had one that was full of lychee stuff, a matcha-based one, one with strawberry and chocolate stuff...the list goes on. Everyone's got their spin on nelo, but I'm tellin' ya, the classic is the best."

Aeiko nodded. "I have to agree," they said, smiling at Alani.

"I prefer the sweet corn one, actually," Balt said.

"That's because you're a self-proclaimed idiot," Niona told him.

"Sweet corn ice cream?" said Alani, perplexed. She had no idea people were turning corn into ice cream nowadays.

Balt nodded.

"It sucks," Niona said.

"I kind of like it," said Aeiko.

"It's delicious," Balt said.

"I regret ever giving you summoning tips," said Niona.

"Whatever, too late. Can't take 'em back. And I'm gonna get the corn one if they've got it, just to spite you."

Niona put her linkpad away and asked Aeiko gravely, "Do they have a sweet corn nelo here?"

Aeiko only nodded, thin-lipped.

"Shit."

"Beautiful," said Balt with a contented sigh.

The line inched along slowly. It seemed as if every person at Xatetu Field had come here to grab a tasty, cold dessert on this hot Summer's day while they waited to see who would be crowned the victor of the Makanuele Rumble. Maybe the line was full of saddened, defeated Summoners and their friends who were trying to make them feel better.

When they finally neared the door, there was a huge sign hung up in the window advertising the sweet corn nelo, which vindicated Balt. Niona was still telling him to shut up when it was their turn to enter the Redonia Café.

At the counter, Aeiko offered to pay for everyone. Alani thanked them profusely for their generosity, but they waved it off. "It's no problem," they said. "It was my idea, anyway."

Being so young, and never having had a true job before, Alani found it impossible to imagine having enough money to treat her friends to anything. Not that she even had that many friends to treat in the first place; besides the people she was with right now, the only other person she could think of was Laowa back at the Church. Most of the time, though, Laowa felt more like a groupie than a friend.

She admired Aeiko for pulling themselves up out of

the Undertow and making a life for themselves here in Makanuele. They may have started out in a less-than-stellar part of the city, but even there they had found beauty and happiness in it, and now they were successfully working at Lakahlo and buying their friends nelo. That was all Alani wanted too, at the end of the day.

"Hello?"

Alani blinked out of her daze. "Hmm?" she mumbled.

"Which one do you want?" Aeiko asked, presumably for the second time.

"Oh. I guess I have to go with the classic. It only feels right for my first taste."

"Good choice," Niona said behind her.

The three of them ordered a classic nelo, while Balt committed to his spite-order of a sweet corn one.

When they got their cups, Alani was mesmerized by the dessert. The colors were stunning, just as Aeiko had promised.

Her plastic cup was filled with each of the ingredients Niona previously described, each one layered carefully atop one another. There were the different shades of yellow for the banana and jackfruit, the green and red mung beans, cubed jelly that had been dyed red and blue, the white shaved ice and coconut. All of it was topped with vibrant purple ice cream that crested over the rim of the cup, with tan crispy rice sprinkled on top.

Regardless of how it tasted, on a visual level, Balt's nelo was decidedly less impressive. Aside from the white shaved ice, his layers were all just shades of yellow. Yellow ice cream, yellow corn kernels, yellow corn flakes.

Looking at it, Alani could understand Niona's disdain. Who wanted corn with their ice cream?

She turned her attention back to her own dessert. "I'm supposed to mix this all up now?" she said, taking the cup from Aeiko.

"Yeah, that's the idea," said Niona.

They all left the shop and found a curb outside an office building nearby to sit on while they ate. Alani spied a curious Dewrat amongst the branches of a tree a few feet away, eyeing their desserts hungrily.

"I really don't see how I'm supposed to mix these things together without making an unholy mess," Alani said, gripping her plastic spoon tight.

"I think that's the idea too," Niona said.

Alani set to mixing up her nelo and, as expected, melted ice cream and other drippy parts of the concoction swiftly ran down the side of her cup, making her hand sticky. The various colors swirling together with the purple looked pretty neat, though.

Niona spooned a heaping mound of purple into her mouth and moaned delightedly, rolling her eyes back in her head. "Man," she said after she finally swallowed. "I needed this, for real. Thanks."

"You're welcome," said Aeiko. They took a bite of their nelo too, although their reaction was not quite so theatrical.

Everyone had dug in already except for Alani, who was still trying to attain the perfect mix. Niona was watching her swirl everything together with her spoon and said, "Just eat some already! I'm dyin' to know what you think."

"Okay," Alani said. It was the moment of truth. She scooped up some of her mixture, doing her best to get most of the different ingredients onto her spoon. She stuffed it into her mouth before any could drip onto her shirt. It sloshed around in there for a moment, then she chewed through the jellies and fruit. She swallowed, suddenly realizing all three people were staring at her intently.

"What's the verdict?" asked Aeiko with a smirk.

Alani looked from Aeiko to Niona, then to Balt, then back to Niona.

"I'm not really a fan," she said guiltily.

"What?!" Niona screamed.

Balt guffawed. "Told you!"

"This is insane," said Niona. "Absolutely insane. Now I'm extra glad I'm not goin' to Yuluhu with you mental cases. One loves corn nelo, and the other doesn't like nelo at all."

"If you aren't gonna eat it, can I have yours?" Balt said, his mouth full of corn ice cream. The corn flakes crunched with every syllable.

"Wow. Wow. Can't believe what I'm hearing," Niona sputtered. "You absolute fool. You're admitting the classic nelo is better, huh?"

"No," Balt denied. "I just want both. I'm comin' out on top here."

"I can't believe this," Niona said once more as Alani transferred her dribbling cup to Balt.

"You better start believin'," Balt said, taking a bite of the purple nelo.

Alani saw another opportunity to spark a debate

amongst them, and she grasped it. "What flavor of shaved ice do you like best?" she asked Niona.

"Oh, easy. Orange-vanilla."

Balt nearly spat out his nelo. "No way," he said.

Niona glared daggers at him. "I am gonna kill you," she said.

The two of them dove into an argument about the best shaved ice flavors while they ate their nelo, with Aeiko ducking in every so often to offer their input. Alani smiled, pleased with her work.

She still kind of wanted a treat, though. She checked her linkpad and saw there was still a lot of time before the finals match. Surely she could find something good before then.

For now, she sat and listened to her friends argue about desserts.

44

CLOSING CEREMONY

THE FINALS MATCH BETWEEN OLLI BERRAP AND UIL WAS such a whirlwind, Alani hardly knew what was happening. She had never seen Jekuas move so speedily or cast so much magic. The two Summoners were at the top of their game, in spite of the fact that they'd battled hard mere hours beforehand.

Balt sat next to her and gave her his commentary while the battle ensued, as he always did. He favored Olli Berrap to win, mostly because they were not the one who'd kicked Niona out of the tournament. From what Alani had heard over the past week, however, Uil was who most believed would be crowned champion.

Personally, Alani did not care much which of them won. She would be happy to be done with this tournament, no longer having to push through crowds to find an uncomfortable plastic seat every day. If not for her friends participating, she would have much preferred spending her days with Aeiko. Although, if they were not in the tournament, the group would not have had a reason to stay in Makanuele so long. It was a double-edged sword.

In between his comments on the match, Balt loosed complaints about his stomach aching after devouring two full cups of nelo. Niona insisted it was solely due to the sweet corn ice cream, a claim which he resolutely rejected.

The environment for the final battle was preposterous. Alani genuinely didn't know how the stadium's crew had gotten it set up in the few hours between matches. It was also baffling to think that they had been storing it somewhere nearby, presumably somewhere in the depths of Xatetu Field.

Set up in the middle of the arena was a gigantic glass cube brimming with water, and anchored inside was a wooden pirate ship. It looked straight out of a storybook, complete with a skull and crossbones painted on black sails.

Alani thought the boat was absurd, and Niona thought it was gauche. Balt said it was the coolest thing he'd ever seen in his life. Aeiko did not have a strong opinion about it one way or the other.

Uil started the match by summoning his Noxbill, which caused Niona to cross her arms and sink lower into her seat, scowling. Alani was surprised she'd wanted to watch the match at all, but she supposed Niona was invested in the outcome at this point. Meanwhile, Olli had summoned their Dompring, the big buffalo-spider Gravity creature that they'd been using to great effect throughout every battle of theirs that Alani had watched.

The tussle involved Uil hovering his Noxbill in the air, like he had against Niona. As Balt explained to Alani, it then started casting Growth magic on areas of the boat to rapidly decay the wood, making it unstable for the heavy Dompring to walk on. The beast went crashing through random rotted parts of the deck, being stabbed by broken planks of wood.

Olli resorted to reducing their Dompring's gravity to send it flying into the air, where it could meet Uil's Noxbill face to face and deal some damage. The Noxbill still had the advantage, being a natural Wind-Type, and it didn't take long for Olli's Dompring to be swept away in a tornado of poisonous gas.

"That Noxbill's a real bitch," Niona said from two seats over. Alani and Balt both laughed at the jab.

Next, Olli put their Daritine up against the Noxbill. The Daritine was a snake-like creature with wings that slithered through the air and possessed Thermal abilities. It made quick work of the Noxbill, igniting the gases that the bird belched up and engulfing it in flames.

Uil was able to beat down the Daritine with an ugly thing Balt actually did not know the name of, but Niona said it was a Hybrid of a Diwepti and a Mitsip. It was reminiscent of a giant lobster, but with an eel-like body from its Diwepti side hidden within a spiky shell. The Tidal-Type made great use of all the water on the battlefield, creating whirlpools and giant exploding bubbles and powerful jetstreams. Olli's Daritine didn't stand a chance.

When they summoned their next Jekua, something ridiculously named a Yonnitu, Uil set his creature out to sink the boat on which the Yonnitu stood. The Yonnitu was a Sonic-Type found on the western coasts of Totta (as Balt explained), and it used those powers to create unnatural waves in the tank that crushed Uil's Hybrid. Its shell cracked and splintered, skewering its own flesh, reddening the water with its blood. It was a grisly sight, and thankfully the red in the water disappeared when Uil withdrew the smashed Jekua.

The pirate ship was half-sunk, its lower half now touching the bottom of the tank. The tank was not super deep, though, so the top half still jutted out from the surface, presenting its carved mermaid figurehead to the sky.

"I don't know how he's gonna use an elephant on that messed up boat," Aeiko muttered.

Balt heard them and said, "It's a Radiant-Type, and based on the previous match, it seems he's pretty highly skilled with it. He did some shadow manipulation against Niona that I've only seen high-level Summoners do before."

"I'm right here, y'know," Niona grumbled.

"Sorry. But I wouldn't be surprised if he could extend the Shimmertusk's own shadow out and solidify it to use it as a platform instead of trying to walk on the tilted boat or whatever."

"That's actually possible?" Alani asked.

Balt nodded. "It's difficult, but yeah, I've seen it before. I think Uil could probably do something like that."

His theory was not going to be tested yet, as the next Jekua Uil summoned was his Noxbill again. The bird and the Yonnitu sparred for several minutes, and it was then that Alani realized this was the longest Jekua battle she'd ever watched. Their mana reserves had to be extremely large to last this long. She wondered if maybe that was the reason Niona ended up losing, rather than spotty tactics and weak moves.

After the Yonnitu, Olli summoned Alani's least favorite Jekua of theirs. It was a huge, nasty primate made up of mud and sticks that didn't have any legs and instead bounced around on a springy tail. When she asked Balt what it was, he said it was a Slopape, a Hybrid of a Juntoo and a Vossi. She'd seen Olli use it in earlier matches, and the sight of the thing made Alani's stomach churn. Why would a person want to have a creature like that, when there were so many cuter Jekuas out there? Why use a Slopape when there were Puffolins, Suelus, Bombats... even the Crawllusks in the VWC were cuter than that thing.

The Slopape and the Noxbill slapped around for a bit, sending various Growth-Type attacks at each other. Then Uil switched back to his Diwepti-Mitsip Hybrid, trying to further sink the boat so that Olli's Jekuas had no choice but to swim in the water. Olli wasn't having it, though, using their Jekua to immediately poison the water, making it uninhabitable for Uil's without his mana draining away constantly.

At last, Uil summoned his Shimmertusk. Like Balt had predicted, he created platforms with the creature's own shadows for it to walk on. It moved far away from the boat, sending lightbeam slashes hurling toward the muddy monkey.

With the Slopape, Olli was able to use the ship's wood

to their advantage, altering its shape to create platforms of its own, much like how the Trunkeys in the Qwisdeep could reshape trees. It also attached planks of wood to itself that molded to its form and hardened, creating surprisingly durable armor that resisted a majority of the Shimmertusk's blasts.

The Slopape also hoisted what appeared to be slimeballs into the air, which then hung suspended all around the arena. Alani didn't know how that was possible.

Balt wasn't totally sure either. "A Gravity mod, maybe?" he suggested. "I haven't noticed any obvious mods on any of their other Jekuas, so maybe this one's modded to have a Gravity ability. I don't think a Slopape would be naturally able to do that, right?" he said, turning to Niona.

She shrugged. "It could also be a Synaptic mod, hangin' 'em up there with Telekinesis, maybe," she suggested.

However it worked, it was effective. As the Shimmertusk moved around the battlefield on its shadow platforms, whenever it came in close proximity to one of the hanging slimeballs, the ball went off like a bomb, spraying the elephant with acid that ate away at its leathery skin.

The length of the battle drew on and on, causing both Alani and Aeiko to lose interest. Alani sat with her head in her hands, gazing down at the battlefield, but her senses dulled as she watched and she processed very little of what was going on. Beside her, she could distantly hear Balt explaining the moves each Jekua was using. He was still heavily invested in the battle, while Niona's expression clearly stated she was ready for it to be over too.

The biggest disappointment for Alani turned out to be

the fact that neither of the Summoners ever sent out a Jenu. She didn't actually know how rare it was for a Summoner to imprint a Jenu, but she felt like two legendary monsters duking it out atop a sinking pirate ship would have made for a dramatic and thrilling conclusion to the tournament.

As it stood, the final blows came down to Uil's Scytherunner and Olli's Daritine. Apparently Olli never saw the need to summon the fourth Jekua in their arsenal. The two creatures were tangled up in each other in midair when the Daritine shot its long, thin tongue down the Scytherunner's throat. The huge insect thrashed against the Daritine, slicing up its back, but then the thing's carapace started steaming and its whole body went limp. It plummeted downward, smacking its skull against the mermaid figurehead before splashing into the water and sinking to the bottom of the tank.

"What happened?" Alani asked, suddenly intrigued.

"I think it boiled the Scytherunner's insides," Balt replied.

Alani shivered.

That effectively ended the match. Uil withdrew his Scytherunner that lay indisposed at the bottom of the massive tank, then signaled his surrender.

Everyone around them went wild over Olli's victory, with some people cheering on their favorite while others were booing and frothing at the mouth, wanting Uil to win. With the chaos erupting around them, their group of four remained unenthused. The most excited out of them all was Balt, but even his reaction was mitigated.

"That was exhausting," Alani sighed.

"Agreed," said Aeiko.

"I should've put some money down on that match," said Balt, his confidence in Olli never wavering.

"You ain't got no money to bet," Niona pointed out.

With the winner determined, all that was left was the closing ceremony, where the winner and the three runners-up were to be honored. That included Niona, so she had to excuse herself back to the locker rooms. Everyone else, meanwhile, had to once more occupy their time while the crew dragged the water tank out of the stadium and replaced it with a stage.

The whole ordeal took around ninety minutes, which was excruciating, but honestly far faster than Alani would have guessed. While they waited, she and the others milled around the stadium's halls, perusing the merchandise for sale. Olli Berrap had a booth set up, manned by a plump man wearing a loose-fitting cometball jersey. He was swarmed with fans, new and old, wanting to buy shirts and stickers and water bottles and countless other items depicting Olli Berrap and their merry band of Jekuas. They had to get in on the ground floor of the fandom before Olli exploded in popularity after their big win.

"Are you going to buy an Olli shirt?" Alani asked Balt.

"No way," he said. "I'm no shill."

"Are you not?" she teased.

One thing was for sure, and that was that Alani was getting tired of shuffling back and forth from their seats. Thankfully, this would be the last time. Now that the tournament was over, though, she and Balt would soon be on their way to Yuluhu Island. If what Aeiko said about having to wait several weeks for an application to get approved was true, then they probably still had some time to spend in Makanuele. Still, she would be sad to leave Aeiko behind, and Makanuele was in central Na Tana—they would need to travel to a coastal city first to ride a gondola to the other island.

As they wandered the crowded halls of the stadium, a deep resonance started ringing in Alani's chest. It was subtle at first, but it swiftly grew in intensity.

She tapped Balt on the shoulder, turning his attention away from a table full of plush Jekuas. He grasped a stuffed Juntoo in his hands.

"Do you feel that?" she asked him.

He pulled on the Juntoo's arms, which stretched just like the real thing. "Yeah," he said. "Not sure what it is, but yeah."

By the time they returned to their seats, a sparsely decorated stage was set up in the middle of the arena atop the same blue rubber mat on which round three had taken place. The tournament officials must have blown the majority of their budget on the giant ship and water tank, as well as Zawé's performance fee, leaving nothing left for the closing ceremony.

Behind the stage, suspended high on its dirt-covered platform, was the Veptilo. The tall, skinny pink crystal reached into the sky, bent at awkward angles with its jagged edges. That explained the resonance they were feeling. It was a relief seeing it there; Alani worried that something odd was happening to her. She was glad to see there was a simple explanation. Seeing the Veptilo here also explained why it had rested on such a strange platform underground. Evidently they raised it up above ground for important ceremonies such as this. Alani looked around, but did not see the stadium's head of security, Chief Guapora, anywhere near the shrine.

Standing on stage before the Veptilo were Olli Berrap, Uil, David Woollis, and Niona. The latter two looked somewhat miffed, standing next to the Summoners who had defeated them. Even Uil seemed bitter, with Olli right beside him. As more people took their seats, however, they all adorned fake smiles of varying believability.

"Folks, we here at Xatetu Field would just like to thank you once again for joining us for 2905's Makanuele Rumble! It's been a blast being your host and watching these heartstopping matches right alongside you. I don't know about you, but I was on the edge of my seat for that entire battle!"

The crowd clapped and cheered in concurrence.

"Give it up for this year's champion, Olli Berrap!"

Even more wild applause. Down on the stage, Niona was clapping politely as well. David and Uil stood stonefaced.

Something moved in the corner of Alani's eye. It was up above, though, which was strange. She glanced skyward at the huge opening in the stadium's ceiling and, far in the distance, she saw what appeared to be the silhouette of a person standing up there.

She quirked an eyebrow, trying to get a closer look. Why would somebody be up there? Was it someone who was part of the Xatetu Field crew? Maybe there had been some damage to the ceiling in one of the battles that she hadn't noticed. The Noxbill and Dompring had been flinging themselves all over the place, after all. It was curious that they wouldn't wait until after the closing ceremony to repair it, though.

The announcer was saying something about David Woollis when Alani nudged Aeiko and pointed at the figure, their features backlit by the sun. "What do you think that is?" she asked.

Aeiko looked, shielding their eyes, and said, "I dunno."

Just then another figured appeared beside the first, and then another, and another. After a few moments, there were easily four dozen silhouettes all standing side by side up on the roof, peering down through the enormous opening, seemingly unnoticed by most in the stadium.

Then the figures' heads all started glowing.

It dawned on Alani what she was looking at, and for a moment she couldn't breathe.

"We need to go," she said at last, though she couldn't bring herself to stand. Her legs were frozen stiff. Her whole body suddenly felt ice cold.

Balt turned to her, and she realized the announcer was now saying something about Niona. "What's the matter?" Balt asked, still clearly half-listening to the booming words detailing Niona's accomplishments.

"It's the Facet," she said. She was staring straight at the figures on the ceiling, but could not move her arm to point at them. Balt followed her line of sight upward and spotted what she was looking at.

"What do you—"

His words trailed off as beams of yellow light exploded out from the figures' shimmering faces. It was that same thin, almost translucent soulclay-esque substance that was so familiar to Alani after the encounter at Qwi's Veptilo. The beams of light shone down on the arena floor and flashed brightly, momentarily blinding Alani. Random people all around their group shouted out in irritation, some complaining that they'd spilled their popcorn.

When her vision cleared again, the stadium was being overrun by the Facet's unnatural crystal monsters.

There were a few smaller ones, like what she had been attacked by, but there were also a few that stood as tall as an Urud or even a Tyrian Snail. Every crystal creature looked different from the last, although all had the same smooth crystalline bodies comprised of sharp angles and shiny surfaces.

"We need to go," Alani said again, finally mustering up the strength to rise from her seat. Up above, the members of the Facet were now rappelling down into the arena.

A few people near them were whispering to each other, some following suit and making their way to the exits. Others clapped at the sight of the weird creatures, thinking it was a part of some performance the stadium was putting on for the closing ceremony. They quickly realized it was *not* part of any choreographed performance when the monsters started blasting fiery magical beams at the stage and at the stands, sending explosions rattling through the stadium.

The two largest monsters trundled toward the Veptilo. It would be easy pickings for them, already uprooted from the ground so many years ago. All they had to do was pick it up and carry it away.

Being so distracted watching as the crystal creatures

neared the Veptilo, Alani didn't even see the blast of energy hurtling toward their location. She merely felt its impact as it exploded in the stands, the force of it sending her flying down several rows of seats, smacking her head on the back of a chair.

Her vision wavered, then went dark.

45
IN THE ARENA

THE SHIT NIONA WAS LOOKING AT DIDN'T MAKE ANY SENSE. She was still trying to parse it when she was flung off the dingy little stage the stadium had rolled out, its cheap and flimsy wood exploding in a shower of splinters and ribbon.

Everything was moving so fast, she didn't have time to react and simply slammed her head on the rubber mat before rolling a few more feet, coming to a stop laying flat on her back. Her eyelids fluttered open, leaving her gawking up at the blue, cloudy sky.

She took a breath in and let it out, wincing at the newfound ache in her chest. She hoped she hadn't broken a rib or punctured a lung or something. It didn't feel that serious, but who knew. That was a problem for later. There were other things to address right now.

All around her was a cacophony of screams and booms. When she could make out distinct words, there were some people shouting out the names of others, trying desperately to reach loved ones. Others were yelling orders, attempting to contain the situation.

A situation that Niona still failed to understand. She tried sitting up, her back protesting against the motion. When she finally succeeded, she saw another of the unnatural crystal creatures she'd seen suddenly flash to life half a minute earlier.

It was unlike any Jekua she'd ever encountered before. That made her think this wasn't a Jekua at all, but she didn't know what else to call it. It was a magical monster that someone had summoned—typically, people referred to such a thing as a Jekua.

This one's body was made entirely of translucent blue crystal. It stood on two tall legs, with spiky shoulders that stretched up even past its blocky, featureless head. It looked much like a coral golem, albeit far more menacing.

And speaking of coral golems, where the hell were they? When they'd visited that stupid shrine a couple weeks ago, there had been dozens upon dozens of the damn things standing guard underground. Where were they, now that something was actually happening? Were they still just standing around dopily in that hallway, gathering dust?

Whatever. It didn't matter where the golems were. She needed to stop thinking and start acting.

She quickly checked on her mana levels. Thankfully, her reserves had almost fully replenished in the hours since her battle with Uil. A Thunderjolt helped speed her along, of course.

Another blessing was that the tournament officials had instructed her and the other three up on stage to wear their kayets. Not that they'd been expecting to actually summon anything, but the device would complete the picture of four elite Summoners.

Niona glanced around to see where the other three were, but in the chaos she did not immediately spot them. Oh well, that didn't matter either. The crystal golem was approaching her, and it needed to be dealt with.

She began channeling mana into her kayet. She didn't even remember which of her memory cards was currently primed, and she didn't care. She just needed to summon *something* before this creature reached her.

Pink soulclay spurted from the device on her wrist and shaped itself into the form of Pops. He'd been the last Jekua she'd summoned against Uil, so that checked out.

She didn't hesitate for another second. The Toolu skittered forward on his six spidery legs, thumping against the rubber mat. Static flickered all over his body and he charged forward, leaping and smashing into the crystal golem's chest.

The golem staggered, but was not knocked down. Pops kicked off its chest, flipping backwards and shooting a bolt of lightning at its head. The blast struck its blue head and that sent it stumbling backward, crashing onto its back.

Niona pressed forward. Pops jumped onto the golem, securing himself on the thing's body with his six legs. She then started charging up heavy sonic vibrations, intending to shatter the golem's crystal body.

But before Pops's attack could finish charging, the golem grabbed him with one of its huge hands, which was twice the size of poor little Pops. It threw him away.

Pops went skipping across the mat like a stone across a pond.

Niona was trying to stand him back up when she glanced over at the golem and saw that it had already risen and was marching toward her. "Shit," she muttered, fleeing from her position, heading toward Pops. The golem altered its trajectory to follow her.

Whoever these people were, they were not following the protocol of real Summoners. A true Summoner wouldn't sic their Jekua on a fellow Summoner, or any person at all. Never mind that these things could not actually be Jekuas—the point still stood.

That made her think that perhaps she should focus on the golem's Summoner. It was clear the thing could take a hit and dish them out, too. Its tight grip alone had squeezed a fair amount of mana from her.

Niona looked around the battlefield as she ran, trying to figure out who nearby might be controlling the crystal golem. There were too many people running around crazed to make sense of anything. A ton of bystanders had been displaced by the crystal creatures' energy blasts and fallen down into the arena, and they were now trying to find any means of escape. In addition to them, there were several figures clad in all white skin-tight outfits, with streaks of inky black slithering through the material like snakes. Their faces were obscured by glittery jeweled masks. Obviously they were her targets, but she had no idea which of them was actively trying to kill her.

She shot a look over her shoulder to find the golem had turned its attention elsewhere, but that was when she also noticed that two giant crystal monsters were making their way toward the big-ass pink crystal that had been hoisted behind them. What had Alani and those Church people called it? The Veptilo?

The golem was heading over to assist its fellow monsters in doing something to the Veptilo. Niona didn't know what their goal was, but she could assume that it was nothing good.

She skidded to a stop and sent Pops scurrying back the direction from which she'd come, veering him toward the Veptilo.

While she focused on getting Pops over there, she took another moment to seek out her fellow Summoners. Standing nearby was David Woollis, who was using his Yissoon to fend off what looked like a massive crystal spider that walked on human hands and had a gnashing wolf's head hanging underneath its abdomen. After a few more seconds of searching, she could not see Uil or Olli Berrap anywhere. Their match had been pretty recent, though, and incredibly intense, at that. She doubted that either one of them had regained much mana in the short amount of time since then. They could maybe summon one Jekua, but not for very long, and it would have to avoid any and all attacks.

That was probably why whoever these people were attacked now, she figured. If they were going after the Veptilo for some reason, this was probably the best opportunity they had. It was aboveground, and far from its coral golem line of defense. Sure, it was surrounded by Summoners now, but the two strongest ones of the bunch had depleted their mana and most of the others would not have their kayets with them. Balt was a rare breed of freak who constantly wore his.

Pops reached the three creatures that were attacking the Veptilo. The non-golem ones were easily two or three times the size of the golem, which gave Niona pretty bad odds. One of the beasts was as wide around as an Urud, but with more shark-like features and long, angular limbs that seemed to impossibly support its weight. The other was immensely tall and skinny, reminding Niona of a construction crane, but with a snake's head and crystal wings that she very much wanted to shatter.

Their immense size meant that Pops could easily slip underneath them and position himself at the epicenter of all three Jekuas. They had not yet reached the Veptilo, but they weren't far off.

The Toolu slid into position, and Niona instantly unleashed a shockwave attack. Electricity burst from Pops's body, crackling through the air and across the floor. Multiple bolts of lightning struck each of the three monsters, but only the golem was deterred. It stopped in its tracks, temporarily paralyzed, but the other two continued on as if nothing had happened.

"Shit," she cursed again. Then she fired a few more blasts at each of the creatures, to no avail. Pops's magic was not getting through them.

Suddenly a Zennekest came lumbering onto the scene, sending blobs of poisonous glop firing from its stinger tail that was raised above its head. The bipedal black scorpion then raced forward to meet the crystal snake crane. It snapped its meaty claws around the thing's tall, thin legs. Niona guessed that it was also sending out sonic vibrations as it clamped down, weakening the crystal legs before trying to break them.

Amazingly, the claws cut through, sending the crane creature toppling forward. Pops had to jump out of the way to avoid being crushed.

The shark-beast was still trundling forward, unbothered by its comrade's misfortune. The golem was no longer paralyzed, and it too recommenced its approach.

The Zennekest continued doling out sonic snaps, cutting the crane apart piece by piece. The thing kept trying to crawl forward in spite of its injuries, until the Zennekest separated its head from its thin neck.

At that, the thing lit up in a flash of light and disappeared from the battlefield. Niona followed the trail of light across the carnage and saw it returning to the shimmering mask of a nearby white figure.

Her instincts told her to run after that person and pummel them with her fists, try to extract answers about what the hell was going on, but that wouldn't help anything right now. The Veptilo was more important.

"David!" she yelled, turning to the man.

It took a few more attempts to get his attention. While she screamed his name, she used Pops to paralyze the golem again, but the shark-beast was still a big problem. It was now standing beside the platform holding the Veptilo.

"What?!" David finally replied, turning with a feral look in his eyes. His Yissoon had finally dispatched the bizarre spider-wolf-hand thing, which was stumbling away on half as many legs as it started with.

Visuals were better than words right now, so she simply pointed ahead at the creature that was starting to reach out for the Veptilo. David's wild eyes followed her finger, then nodded.

He withdrew his Yissoon and quickly summoned his Puffolin instead. Almost as soon as the Jekua was on the field, it was lobbing seed bombs in the direction of the shark-beast. Two exploded on the ground around it, unsteadying it, then the third struck its back and sent its face smashing into the platform.

But the force of the impact caused some of the dirt mound holding the Veptilo to shift, with clods of dirt falling off the platform and onto the rubber mat. Niona noticed the Veptilo tilt ever so slightly.

She did not know what would happen if the crystal fell and shattered into a million pieces, but she suspected it would not be good. Whether it released an enormous magical explosion or simply incited the wrath of the Church of Salt and Sanction, either one would be a catastrophe.

Pops was not cutting it out there. His attacks simply weren't strong enough to cut through the crystal creatures' tough exteriors. She wished she had some Plasma mods.

Niona withdrew him and began channeling mana toward Boombox's memory card. The Bruiserweight appeared before her and surged forward, but suddenly Niona was in the air, the entire world rolling in her vision.

She smashed into a pile of rubble, planks of wood from the stage and pieces of whatever the stadium was built out of. That was not going to help the already existing deep, deep ache in her body. Her eyes fluttered open just in time to see her soulclay returning to her kayet, having understandably lost her concentration after being catapulted forty feet.

In the spot where she'd previously stood was a quadrupedal crystal creature with a huge head that extended outward in a long snout, but also upward in a ridged flat arc that seemed to shield its neck. Three long horns jutted from its forehead, and its mouth seemed similar to a hawk's beak, albeit much, much larger and scarier. If all that wasn't enough, it also had a thick, lashing tail that ended in a spiked ball.

That don't look good, she thought.

And then the thing started charging toward her, which solidified her stance.

She hurriedly tried to rise, but lost her footing on the pile of loose wood and fell over again, cutting her palm on a particularly sharp edge. She swore as blood dripped red onto the debris, then suddenly she was rocketing forward, smashing her head on more wood and stone and rolling across the mat.

Blood trickled down her forehead and into her left eye. She wiped it away with a groan, urging herself to get up. The thing was going to come again, she knew it, and she needed to *hurry and get up.*

In what sounded like it was too close for comfort, she could hear wood and stone crunching underneath the beast's heavy feet. Niona finally willed herself to move, though her entire body thought it'd be a better idea to just lay down and die, maybe. Somehow, it seemed like that would hurt less.

She cast a quick look at the approaching beast and saw it start to speed up.

Then, in the distance, she saw a Wallago sprinting toward it.

Andy? she thought. She didn't see the man anywhere, but if he was here and that was his Wallago, she hoped he was hidden somewhere safe.

Even without the extra speed offered by reducing its own friction, the Wallago was fast. It caught up to the crystal beast in no time and leapt onto its back, sending the thing collapsing onto its stomach, its stubby legs splayed out. Then a powerful gust of wind generated by the wildcat sent both of them sailing upward, only for the Wallago to push itself off the other creature's back.

The Wallago caught itself on the wind and bounced lightly back to the ground, while the crystal monster plunged downward, aided by its incredible girth.

When it landed, its crystal body cracked in the center, but did not break. One of the legs cracked as well, but it was disappointing that it hadn't exploded in an array of shards.

Elsewhere on the battlefield, Niona could see more Jekuas had entered the fray. There were disappointingly few, but again, most people did not walk around wearing their kayets on a day-to-day basis. Although she *did* spot Uil's Noxbill flying around, as well as a Bowlder that was wrestling with a crystalline crustacean. David's Puffolin was still blasting away at the shark-beast, which had turned its attention away from the Veptilo to deal with the flower-covered pest, so that was good.

Up in the stands, most of the crowd had funneled out into the halls and presumably out of the stadium altogether. Some still remained, though, pushing past others and trampling over those who had fallen on the stairs. There were some crystal creatures in the stands, swiping at people and shooting energy blasts from their mouths, not aiding in the quest for the Veptilo but adding to the overall mayhem. They were being combatted by a smattering of Jekuas, but the crystal monsters far outnumbered the regular Jekuas.

By now, Chief Guapora and his security guards had also begun filling the arena, shooting at every crystal beast in sight. Introducing guns into the equation surely wouldn't be a problem. From this distance, Niona couldn't tell if their bullets were pinging uselessly off the crystal flesh or burrowing into it.

She started pushing mana back into her kayet and summoned Boombox again. Her Wallago friend was swiping at the downed crystal beast, but its claws were glancing off the purple and blue exterior without leaving the barest scratch.

It then sent the beast swirling upward in another cyclone, which blasted the monster far off into the distance. Niona followed it and was pleased to see its torso crack in half when it smashed against the wall.

A crystal wolf with a pink body, orange legs, and purple head abruptly darted into her vision, snapping its jaws around Boombox's right arm.

Niona shook the thing off her Jekua, then sent a fist flying into its snout. With such power behind the punch, the crystal wolf's nose crunched and shattered, dropping like pieces of glass onto the ground. The thing whimpered and stepped backward before pouncing forward, pinning Boombox to the ground.

The lizard kicked and bucked the wolf off, and the Wallago darted past, tackling the wolf. The two beasts were tangled up in each other as they rolled like a living tire across the field.

There was still no telling who or where the Wallago's Summoner was, but Niona was glad to have them on her side.

Then the wolf opened its mouth and shot a blast of energy straight into the Wallago's face, sending the wildcat flailing backward. Its fur was singed, and it looked as if one of its eyes was melted.

Boombox ran toward the wolf, which shot another blast of energy, this time directed at the Bruiserweight. Niona dodged out of the way, then ducked another blast, and then she was pummeling the wolf with her Jekua's fists.

Before it could pop off another shot, she punched the wolf one more time then moved Boombox away. The Wallago was standing nearby, still trying to recover from the damage done to its face. It looked toward the crystal wolf and let out a mighty roar, which sent the wolf tumbling backward in a strong gust of wind.

Suddenly Niona had an idea. *"Hey!"* she shouted. *"Wallago person! I dunno if you can hear me, but make another cyclone!"*

Hoping her command was heard, she withdrew Boombox and switched over to Glom. While doing so, she checked on her mana, which was nearing its halfway point. That was better than she'd been expecting, truthfully. But when she thought about it, she had probably taken more damage herself than any of her Jekuas.

Her Muggish splashed onto the battlefield and began his slow crawl toward the crystal wolf. A few moments later, wind started picking up around the wolf's feet, and then it was lifted into the air. The thing tumbled around in the sky, caught up in the funnel of wind and unable to escape.

Niona used Glom to hurl fireballs into the cyclone, letting the wind catch them and igniting the whole thing, creating a massive fiery tower that the crystal wolf was trapped within.

Flames obscured her view of the wolf, but she could hear it yowling as it was tossed about and seared by unbelievable heat. When the wind died down and the flames sputtered out, the wolf was no more than a puddle of colorful melted crystal that splashed onto the ground.

Its Summoner then withdrew it, the beam of light flying through the air back into a white figure's jeweled mask. Niona briefly wondered how they were summoning anything through those masks, rather than through a kayet, but there were still plenty of crystal beings to kill, so she didn't linger on the question.

At that same moment, the Wallago morphed back into soulclay and drifted across the battlefield, up into the stands. It disappeared behind a pile of rubble, so whoever summoned it had tucked themselves away where they couldn't easily be spotted or attacked.

"Thanks, Wallago person!" Niona called out to them, hoping they heard her.

Over by the Veptilo, David's Puffolin was nowhere to

be seen and the shark-beast was making another move toward the shrine.

She needed to get over there, and fast. Glom wasn't going to cut it.

The Muggish shifted from a red blob to a pink blob and returned to her kayet, then she primed Garbo's memory card. The Nuri appeared next to her, standing tall and proud with his shaggy white fur blowing in the breeze.

She climbed up onto the Jekua's back, gripping her legs tight on either side of Garbo's torso. Then she grabbed on to some strands of hair like they were reins and mentally prepared herself.

The Nuri started at a trot, then steadily increased in speed until he was galloping across the arena.

Niona bounced up and down on the Nuri, slamming her crotch repeatedly into his bony back, letting out rhythmic grunts of pain.

That pain was not doing her concentration any favors. It was difficult keeping herself positioned on the Nuri's back while also controlling its movements. It didn't feel natural, moving her own Jekua while she was on top of it. But it was getting her across the field with haste, and in less than thirty seconds she was at the base of the Veptilo.

She tried to dismount gracefully, but nothing Niona ever did could be described as graceful, and this was no different. She slid off Garbo's side, landing at a bad angle on her leg and crumpling to a heap on the ground. Really, any angle would have been bad, given how sore her entire body was at that moment.

Niona remained on the ground, shifting into a crouch, and rammed Garbo's horns into the shark-beast's side.

The crystal monster roared in anger and confusion, and Niona was pleased to discover the Nuri's horns were strong enough to penetrate the crystal flesh. The spiral horns pierced deeper and deeper until half their length was lodged in the monster's side.

Just then, a Palmegranate hopped down from the Veptilo's platform and wrapped its pustule-covered body around the shark-beast's giant head. An instant later, every bubble on the thing burst at once, covering the shark-beast's head in bright red acid.

Some of it sprayed down onto Garbo as well, sizzling on his neck and draining a bit of Niona's mana. Some unfortunate collateral damage.

The Palmegranate collapsed to the ground, its body expended, as the shark-beast clutched at its ruined face. While the crystal that comprised its head melted away, its Summoner continued manipulating its body to start clambering up the side of the platform.

Niona had to admire their determination. The Palmegranate's self-destruct move must have done massive damage to the person's mana, not to mention now suffering from a continual drain due to the acid burning away at it. Their reserves must run deep.

If they're even using mana to summon these things, she then thought. There was so much she didn't know about these crystal monsters and the people who were controlling them.

She looked up in horror as the shark-beast hoisted itself up the platform, with her Nuri still stuck in its side and dangling in the air. She started sending blasts of electricity through Garbo's horns, and this time, they actually caused some damage.

The shark-beast shuddered and let go of the platform, crashing down onto its back. Niona guessed that the horns being embedded within the creature's body made the assault more effective than Pops's attacks.

Unfortunately, the fall had also hurt Garbo and Niona's mana by extension. The shark-beast's arm had also smashed down onto Garbo, tearing away another chunk of her mana. Niona sensed that she would have trouble dislodging Garbo's horns, plus his body was pretty injured by the crystal beast's arm, so instead she withdrew him.

Then Uil's Noxbill was flung past her line of sight, smashing into the wall behind the Veptilo's platform and sending massive cracks rippling through the stadium wall. The sight did not inspire much confidence in her. That confidence plummeted even further when the Noxbill then turned into amorphous soulclay and drifted away.

There came a noise from above, and Niona looked up to see a smaller crystal creature atop the platform holding the Veptilo.

It was about the same size as a typical human, but very thick-bodied, with every piece of it a different pastel color of crystal. Horns sprouted from all around the head like a natural crown, and it walked on two clawed feet. Its wide arms reached out toward the Veptilo, with additional arms stretching forward out of the primary arms.

The thing was gross, and Niona wanted to kill it.

Given its smaller stature, she thought Pops might be

able to inflict some damage on it. She summoned her Toolu and sent him scurrying up the side of the platform.

The crowned beast grasped the Veptilo in its four hands and began tugging on it, trying to pull it out from the pile of loose earth at its base.

Bullets bounced off the creature's crystal flesh, and Niona heard Chief Guapora's voice yell out, *"Don't hit the Veptilo! I repeat, do not hit the Veptilo, you fools!"*

The gunfire ceased after that, with nobody willing to risk missing and shooting the Church's shrine.

Pops reached the pile of dirt and started blasting the crowned beast with electricity. It was paralyzed for a moment, with the Veptilo in its grasp. Niona wasn't sure she could do much else to the thing without potentially harming the Veptilo in the process.

She moved Pops forward and jumped up to wrap his body around one of the thing's arms. Pops bit down on its crystal flesh and sent a sharp sonic resonance ringing through the arm.

Her goal was to send enough intense vibrations shuddering through the arm to shatter it, but before she managed that, she herself was punted to the ground again.

She was able to keep Pops summoned despite that, but not after the next hit. The next hit sent her flying into the platform, where she smacked the back of her head and slumped over on herself.

The monster that had attacked her this time was that first crystal golem she'd faced. Security guards were firing away at it, but their bullets were accomplishing nothing.

Shoot the damn Summoners, Niona mentally urged them,

unable to bring herself to speak aloud. All she could do was cough raggedly.

The golem's high-tipped shoulderblades began glowing intensely, probably charging up one of those deadly energy beams. If it had melted a Wallago's face, she didn't want to see what it'd do to her.

She scrambled to summon something, anything, to block the blast. Even if it dipped her into soulsickness, that'd be better than taking the brunt of the damage herself.

Nothing was happening, though.

She was channeling her mana into the kayet, but the device wasn't absorbing it. Her mana dissipated into the ether, not being transformed into soulclay yet also leaving her body, depleting her reserves.

Niona looked at the kayet on her wrist and saw a massive crack cutting it in half lengthwise.

Shit, she thought. Her arm must have hit the platform too. That would explain the agonizing pain coursing through it.

Two thin beams of energy then burst forth from the golem's shoulderblades, converging into one bigger beam. Niona winced as it careened toward her, but the golem had aimed just above her head, at the platform.

The platform exploded, sending her forward to slam her face on the ground, her skin dragging against the rubber for several feet until she came to a stop. Debris fell like heavy rain all around her, mostly crashing into the floor, but some of it hitting her arms and legs and back. It all mercifully missed her head.

Niona rolled over, her face covered in blood and her

whole body shuddering in pain. She could barely move. She definitely couldn't fully sit up. But she craned her neck enough to see that the crystal golem was now in the midst of fighting a Mitsip.

David? she wondered as the crustacean enveloped the golem in a gleaming bubble.

Just beyond them, though, the towering pink Veptilo was on the ground amongst a pile of stone and dirt.

And more crystal creatures were racing toward it.

46
IN THE STANDS

BALT HAD A SINGULAR GOAL IN MIND: TO NOT LET WHAT happened to Alani at the Qwi Island shrine happen again. She was currently knocked unconscious, laying flat on her back on the floor in between two aisles, so that was not the most auspicious start.

After trying and failing to wake her up, his first instinct was to move her into one of the chairs, but then he figured she was safer on the ground, out of view. So he had gently pushed her further to the side, hiding her underneath the row of plastic chairs, getting her even more out of the way. The ground was disgusting, to be sure, littered with food crumbs and sticky with spilled beverages, but there were no better options right now.

Much to his dismay, he had no idea where Aeiko was. He'd lost sight of them after the initial explosions and the madness of everybody fleeing. None of the nearby bodies were theirs, so he could only hope that they had made it safely out of the stadium. That would be for the best; it wasn't like there was much they could do against this assault.

With Alani tucked away, he had built defenses around them to wait out the battle. Sure, he wanted to jump into the fray and fight back against these bastards attacking so many innocent people, but he needed to keep his friend safe. That was his top priority.

He'd summoned Dipper and conjured her Petal Shield, creating a huge dome of swirling, hardened petals around himself and Alani. Over the past several weeks he'd only gotten stronger with the Puffolin, and if her shield was able to deflect thrashes from Wortens before, he assumed it could withstand whatever these crystal Jekuas threw at him.

It worked. For a while.

Ten or fifteen minutes passed with little fanfare. For them, at least. Balt listened to the shouts and screams and blasts outside their protective dome, wishing he could do more, but not wanting to abandon Alani. At one point, he even felt his linkpad vibrating, and he saw that it was his mother calling him.

"You gotta be kidding," he muttered, reading the notification. He was sure his parents had been watching the closing ceremony on television and saw the beginning of the attack. Of course they would decide to call him in the middle of such a crisis.

The flowery dome surrounding them shuddered repeatedly as something on the outside pounded against it. Balt kept Dipper perfectly still, not spending any mana on moving her, and kept an eye on his levels as the dome was assaulted. Each hit only knocked a little bit of mana away.

But then came the energy blast.

It tore straight through the Petal Shield like it was nothing. Balt yelped and ducked down, covering Alani's body with his own. Dipper's petals blew away in the wind, revealing one of the crystal beasts a mere twenty feet away. It was grabbing onto one of the stadium seats, trying to wrench it free.

The creature was like no Jekua Balt had ever heard of, and not just because of its crystalline body. It looked much like a hermit crab—shell, thick little antennae eyes poking out, a full set of legs and claws—sitting on top of a stout lower body that was vaguely amphibian. Its belly was rounded and perfectly smooth, with sharply bent legs and webbed feet. The hermit crab half was two colors: purple for the shell, red for the face and limbs. Then the frog half was orange on the torso and pink on the legs.

Balt watched as it tugged at the seat with its two claws, emitting high-pitched chirps with every movement.

For a second, Balt thought the creature looked strangely familiar, which was absurd. But then he realized it wasn't because he'd seen a Jekua like this before; it was because the thing's body reminded him of the crystals sprouting out from Pakree Island.

There wasn't time to dwell on that now, though. He stood back up and turned Dipper to face the crab-frog. Flower petals rose from her back and shot forward at the thing, but they bounced off its exterior and it continued trying to pull up the chair. It utterly refused to be defeated by the inanimate object.

A huge seed traveled up Dipper's throat, and then she spat it out at the crab-frog. The seed whistled through the air and burst upon impact with the purple shell, covering the crystal creature in sticky, acidic sap. Errant globules splashed onto the nearby seats, melting some of the plastic down.

The acid was strong enough to melt through a portion of the crab-frog's exterior, and the thing hissed irritably at him and Dipper. But it was finally able to yank the seat out from the floor, which it hoisted over its head. The seat thunked against its shell as it was raised up, then the crab-frog threw it at them.

Balt was already acting, though. Vines shot forth from Dipper's back, stretching out to catch the seat. They grabbed the seat in mid-air, then Balt reared the vines back and sent the chair hurtling toward the crystal crab-frog.

It smacked the thing's face and, being so top-heavy, sent it falling backwards with ease. The crab-frog careened over the lower row of seats, hitting the ground and proceeding to then flip over the next row as well. In all, it tumbled down four or five rows until finally going over the edge of the stands and into the arena proper.

Balt had no idea where the crab-frog's Summoner was located, but that was irrelevant. He turned back around and crouched beside Alani to check on her. No change, for better or worse.

Niona, David, Uil, and Olli were all down in the arena fighting against various crystal monsters, while Balt was mostly alone up in the stands. A few more Summoners had appeared, sending their Jekuas out into battle, but they quickly hopped over the edge to land down in the arena where the bulk of the conflict was taking place.

It was then he noticed that the platform holding the Veptilo had been destroyed and the pink crystal now lay amongst a pile of dirt and rubble. There were some of the bizarre creatures striding toward it, while the white-clad figures controlling them stood idly nearby.

Of course this was the Facet, and of course they were here for the Veptilo. In the back of his mind, Balt had understood that, but it made his chest tight and filled him with dread seeing them approach the overturned shrine. The Summoners were fending them off, but there was no telling how long they could last.

By now, almost all of the tournament's spectators had fled the scene. There were a few who, like Alani, had been knocked unconscious and lay sprawled out on the floor or draped over chairs. Some were bleeding, and a few had body parts that were outright crushed by fallen debris. Balt prayed that no one was dead, but he couldn't be sure. In all honesty, he didn't want to know.

He looked around, forcing himself to tear his gaze away from the limp bodies nearby. Up near the exit, he spotted a woman rushing down the steps, eyes focused on her kayet.

It was Aubrey L'al, one of the early Makanuele Rumble competitors. She'd been beaten in round two by Nock Brynn, but she was truly a sight for sore eyes.

Seeing her made Balt smile with relief. Hopefully, she would be the first of many to return to the stadium with their kayets. If most of the other Summoners had booked hotel rooms near the stadium, then it might not be too long before they reappeared, offering aid. Probably not all of them would return, but hopefully enough to turn the tide.

Soulclay erupted from Aubrey's kayet, drifting down onto the steps in front of her and taking the shape of a Sorvana. It was a Tidal-Type, a huge red manta ray with a trio of yellow frills that could rise or flatten on its head. Or what approximated for a head, anyway.

Beyond Aubrey's Sorvana, trouble was coming. Headed their way was a rampaging crystal creature that ran on all fours, dragging its knuckles on the ground like a gorilla. Great curved wings sprouted from its back, and its head was long and pointed, reminding Balt of the Jolloms with their shovel-esque beaks. Its limbs were a yellow crystal while the rest of it was a deep, rich blue. The thing was smashing apart chairs as it barreled toward them.

Aubrey halted her descent, sending her Sorvana ahead to meet the monster. Her Sorvana swam through the air, with bubbles appearing all around its body as it neared the beaked ape. The bubbles then came together in an intense beam that fired straight at the creature, blasting it with a stream of bubbles that exploded in boiling water on impact.

The ape was unbothered by the bubbles. They were child's play, evidently.

It continued forward, reaching out as the Sorvana soared overhead. It tried to grab the Sorvana's flowing tail, but Aubrey pulled it away in the nick of time.

The Sorvana flew high into the air, curving around to head toward the creature again. This time, its long, hooked tail curled up underneath its body and fired a jetstream at the beaked ape.

Again, the attack didn't do much. Hopefully it chipped away at the mystery Summoner's mana, but the monster made no outward indication of being affected.

There was still a good amount of distance between Dipper and the crystal beast, so Balt started firing sharpened petals at it. Like the crab-frog before, they bounced off uselessly. How were they supposed to hurt these things?

Aubrey yelled something to him, but he couldn't hear what it was. *"What?"* he shouted back, but it seemed she didn't hear him either. Gunfire from the stadium's security team rang through the air, piercing his eardrums, adding an unwelcome note to the symphony of chaos.

Then her Sorvana was riding a magically-conjured wave, which quickly separated from the Jekua and swept up the approaching ape. The wave rose, lifting the crystal ape high into the air, at which point the water started to evaporate. But the Sorvana surged forward, tackling the other creature, sending it flying even higher up.

Balt jumped into Dipper's perspective so he could more accurately aim her Seed Missile. He tracked the beaked ape's trajectory for a few seconds, then felt the disconcerting sensation of the seed moving up his esophagus and clicking the back of his teeth.

He fired the seed, watching intently as it traveled through the air. It struck the crystal ape, exploding in fiery sap, and the monster came crashing back down to the ground.

Its left elbow was chipped and there was a crack in one

of its shoulders, but it stood up and shook off the damage. Then it opened its mouth and fired two bolts of energy in Balt's direction. A seat to his left exploded as it was hit, and he had to duck down to narrowly avoid being struck by the second one.

Based on what he'd seen thus far, it seemed that these crystal Jekuas did not possess many different abilities. What they had made them formidable opponents, for sure —nigh impenetrable exteriors, brute strength, and that energy blast—but at least they were predictable. He hadn't seen one pull off any other moves yet.

That meant they could plan around the limited move set, although Balt admittedly did not have any such plan in mind at the moment. Right now, he just wanted to survive.

He didn't really have a plan for that either, unfortunately. He peeked up over the seat shielding him and saw Aubrey's Sorvana repeatedly divebombing the crystal ape. If nothing else, she was effectively distracting it.

To his left, he saw a Scrypto fly past, with a flamethrower gushing from its mouth as it soared toward a crystalline boar.

"—down!" he suddenly heard Aubrey screaming.

"What?" he called again, feeling like a moron.

"Hold it down!" All the while, her Sorvana continued assailing the ape.

He nodded, but she had already stopped paying attention to him. He switched to Dipper's perspective again and leapt over row after row of seats, heading upward toward the crystal ape.

When he reached the beast, its thick yellow arms were

flailing around as it tried to swat the Sorvana like a fly. Whoever was controlling it really had a one-track mind.

Three vines sprouted from Dipper's back, sending a tingling sensation coursing through Balt. He reached toward the ape with the vines, each one aiming for a different limb. He'd love to have four, but three was all he could muster.

Two of them wrapped around the ape's wrists, while the third grabbed an ankle. Then he yanked down, sending the beaked ape to its back, pinning it onto the messy floor. It fought hard against its bonds, and Balt nearly let it slip a few times before he really got ahold of the thing.

The ape shot beams of light into the sky, which Aubrey easily dodged. One of them hit the balcony above, sending an enormous spiderweb of cracks rippling along the surface. If that collapsed, it would be bad news for all of them. He didn't even know if there were still people up there who might get hurt as well.

Balt could feel the ape starting to lose some of its fight as its body relaxed. He didn't know if the Facet member controlling it was growing bored, or if they were running low on mana; either way, it was easier to hold down.

But when the Sorvana swooped toward it, the beaked ape redoubled its efforts to escape. Balt nearly lost his grip on its right wrist, but he managed to slam the arm back down onto the floor with a reverberating *crack*!

The Sorvana avoided one more blast of energy that dissolved into the blue sky, then Aubrey brought her Jekua down half a foot above the ape's head. It was screeching at her Sorvana, its mouth wide open, and she quickly sent a stream of scalding bubbles down its throat.

That made the ape thrash even wilder as it choked on the exploding, burning bubbles. After a few seconds, it came to a jittery halt, then its body flashed into bright light. The Sorvana swam away as the light shifted into a smaller ball and drifted away.

Balt switched back into his own perspective and took a second to check his immediate surroundings, seeing that there weren't any other crystal creatures nearby. He crouched down and jostled Alani.

"C'mon, c'mon, wake up," he urged her. Nearby, Dipper shifted back into amorphous soulclay and returned to her memory card.

He lightly slapped Alani's cheeks, and breathed a huge sigh of relief as her eyelids began to flutter. Alani opened her eyes, dazedly looking around. She sat up, but immediately bumped her head on the bottom of a seat.

"Shit," she muttered, rubbing her forehead. Fried batter crumbs were stuck in her hair.

Balt chuckled. "Go slow," he told her. "You've been out for a good fifteen minutes."

"What's going on?" she asked, still clearly confused as to where exactly in the stadium she was.

"The Facet's attacking," he said simply.

Her eyes widened and her mouth dipped into a frown. "We've got to—"

"We've got to get the hell out of here," he said, interrupting whatever it was she thought was her duty to the Church and the Veptilo. He was already kicking himself enough over her getting hurt, quite possibly concussed.

There was no reason for them to stick around and invite further injury.

"But the Veptilo—"

"The Veptilo's gonna be fine," he said, not fully believing his own words. "Lots of Summoners are down there defending it. So's the security team. Let them handle the situation. What're you gonna do, anyway? Hoist it on your back and drag it outta here?" He grinned.

She did not see the humor in it. "I have to do *something*," she said.

"No, you don't," he insisted.

He was about to say they didn't have time to argue when a blast of energy exploded about ten feet away. They could feel the heat of it on their skin, but luckily they weren't even grazed.

Whatever had attacked them had its attention turned elsewhere by the time Balt tracked it down. Anesk Pauz was now on the scene, tangling with a crystalline beast nearby.

Balt took another look around and smiled at what he saw.

More Summoners had filed back into the stadium, all of them either having already summoned a Jekua or currently in the process of doing so. There were several competitors whose faces he recognized but whose names he'd forgotten; among those he did remember, though, were Bill White, Winston Knox, Mia Long, Cole Illiom, and Cassidy Simms.

"Eat shit!" screamed a man who raced out into the stands, nearly tripping and falling down the stairs before

he could even summon a Jekua. He was Brock Sesseo, a guy who'd been eliminated in round one.

Balt swelled with hope for the first time since the battle had begun. As more bloodthirsty Summoners returned to the stadium with their kayets, he couldn't help but feel like the Facet had vastly underestimated them. He imagined they'd chosen now to attack because the Veptilo was out in the open, away from the coral golems, and also because presumably there would be very few Summoners actually equipped with their kayets to fight back.

He was so, so glad that they were wrong.

Another crystal monster was flying toward his position now, though. "Stay down," he instructed Alani, who had crawled out from under the dirty seats but was crouching low to the ground. He wasn't aware of where Aubrey L'al was or what she and her Sorvana were doing.

He clicked a button on his kayet to prime Pistachio's memory card, then channeled mana into the device. While doing so, he checked on his reserves and noted that he had spent about a fourth of his mana so far. Not bad at all. He was getting more efficient.

The Mosstopus burst forth, his ten limbs holding his round, furry green body up with pride. Just for show, Balt opened the Jekua's mouth in a vicious roar, showing off the countless rows of fangs in an effort to ding the Facet member's confidence.

"Hey," came a voice behind him, "need a hand?"

He turned and saw Wasaaru standing there, soulclay already pouring out of his kayet. He sported a smug grin.

"I certainly wouldn't turn it down," said Balt.

His cousin's soulclay morphed into the Koutix, which

stood with its orange carapace gleaming in the light of the sun. Wasaaru clicked its pincers together, then the beetle started jogging down the steps.

"Can you ground that thing?" Wasaaru asked, gesturing at the creature flying toward them.

"I think so," Balt said.

"Do it."

Balt wasn't going to switch into Pistachio's perceptive, no matter how much better he'd gotten at using the Mosstopus's scent-based sight. There was simply too much going on around them for him to feel good about effectively deciphering the colorful information.

The Mosstopus crouched down and Balt reduced his friction, then sprang into the air, propelled by his ten limbs. He soared through the air with little to no resistance with his mouth wide open.

Naturally, the bird fired an energy blast from its tiny beak. The beam of light pierced the top of Pistachio's head, sending a jolt rippling through Balt's left cheek and part of his neck.

When he checked on his mana, he saw the blast hadn't depleted it too much. This bird was definitely on the weaker side of the crystal creatures. Before the two monsters met, however, the bird shot off another blast, draining away more of Balt's mana.

Pistachio continued sailing forward, and the crystal bird's head went right into his gaping maw. Balt bit down hard on the creature while wrapping all ten limbs around it.

Amazingly, the bird was powerful enough to stay in the air even with Pistachio's immense added weight. It soared higher, trying to shake him off, but Pistachio's fangs were digging into its neck and wouldn't let go.

"Ground it, you idiot," Wasaaru snapped at him.

"I'm trying!"

He reached with two of Pisatchio's tentacles and wrapped them around the bird's wings, imbuing them with the Jekua's Friction magic. He increased the friction on the wings more and more until they could barely flap, almost completely stiff like a statue.

The bird went spiraling downward, and Balt pushed Pistachio off of it before it came crashing into the stands, creating a small crater in the middle of a staircase.

Wasaaru's Koutix darted after the bird, which was already trying to stand and hop away, unable to move its wings at all. They awkwardly stuck straight out from its body in a V-shape.

The Koutix's horn began intensely vibrating with Sonic energy as it neared the bird. It couldn't fly away, but it still had two legs, so for good measure Pistachio spat slimeballs to stick its feet to the floor.

When it reached the bird, the Koutix bent over and drilled its horn straight into the back of its neck, where there were already some scratches left behind by Pistachio's teeth. The magically-enhanced sonic vibrations helped the horn drill deep into the bird's neck, sending cracks splintering outward from the point of impact.

Then Wasaaru removed the horn and placed the Koutix's pincers around the bird's weakened neck. The pincers clamped shut, meeting a bit of resistance from the durable crystal, but after only a handful of moments it shattered. They watched as the crystal bird's head rolled pitiably down the stadium steps, eventually bouncing down into the arena.

Balt glanced over his shoulder to check on Alani. Still crouching down, her knees pulled up to her chest, she gave him a thumbs up. He reciprocated.

He then gazed down into the arena, seeking out Niona amongst the confusion. He couldn't see her anywhere, but there was only a Yissoon and a Sleethog defending the Veptilo from the Facet. They were both powerful Jekuas, the Sleethog especially, but there were too many crystal monsters surrounding them.

From out of nowhere, a wave of soulclay flooded the arena and slowly took on the massive shape of a Tyrian Snail. Johnny Fierce must have arrived.

Balt hadn't thought he would ever be happy to see that damn Tyrian Snail again, but that thing would definitely cause a ruckus.

The Tyrian Snail lurched forward, sending a tidal wave splashing across the battlefield. The wave swept up Jekuas, Summoners, crystal creatures, and members of the Facet alike.

Wasaaru's Koutix returned to his side, while Balt withdrew Pistachio. The two cousins looked each other in the eye.

"I gotta get Alani out of here," Balt started.

But Wasaaru shook his head resolutely. "Are you stupid? You need to stay here and fight!"

Then it was Balt's turn to shake his head. "I can't. I need to make sure she's safe."

"She can get out of the stadium just fine on her own," said Wasaaru.

"Well…once I get her outside, maybe I can come back." It was a reasonable compromise. Once Alani was clear of Xatetu Field, there was no reason why she couldn't make own her way back to Aeiko's apartment, far from this gargantuan mess.

Wasaaru looked displeased, but he conceded. "Fine," he said.

Balt pointed at the overturned Veptilo and said, "That's what they're after. I don't know why, but they've been trying to collect the Veptilos from every island."

"The what?"

"The big pink crystal thing," Balt said exasperatedly.

"Okay."

"Go protect it. Obviously these are shady people, and whatever they're planning to do with the Veptilos can't be good."

Wasaaru nodded, then he and his Koutix started down the steps, leaping gracefully over the side of the wall and landing down in the arena.

Farther along the curve of the stadium stands, Balt spied Hana Minir and Justine Tesh teaming up to take down a staggering crystal beast that looked like nothing more than a walking rectangle.

Up above, another crystal bird circled overhead—possibly the same one he and his cousin had just dispatched, but re-summoned—and a Conuto suddenly appeared out of its camouflage on the bird's back, biting down on a wing.

There were plenty of Summoners present to distract the Facet now. It was time to move.

Balt turned around and shouted to Alani, “Alright, let’s get—”

But he cut himself off when he saw a crystal creature leap down from the balcony above. It had the pink crystal body of a large reptile, but with the long, wiry legs of an arachnid.

And it landed right next to Alani, with its jaws open wide.

47
ROWS AND ROWS

ALANI ACTED ON INSTINCT RATHER THAN WITH ANY forethought. It probably saved her life, but it also earned her an aching, bloody head.

When the crystal crocodile-spider fell into view, ferociously snapping its angular maw at her, she hopped backward out of its way. Her shins hit the top of the plastic chair in the row below where she stood, sending her tumbling over. She spun in the air, screaming, her arms outstretched and her fingers splayed wide. There was hardly any time to react, things were moving too quickly. But she possessed enough cognizance to reach out for the *next* row of seats, grabbing the back of one of those. It helped to delay her fall somewhat, but with all her momentum dragging her downward she quickly let go, dragging her fingertips across the smooth plastic and then smashing her chin on the ground, with her ass propped up in the air, draped over the seat behind her.

Blood filled her mouth, and she hastily ran her tongue

over her teeth, prodding them, checking to see if any were loose or had fallen out. They seemed to be fine, but a sharp pain was ringing throughout her whole head.

She was still trying to piece together what was even going on. She could scarcely believe that the Facet was being so bold as to attack in the middle of this ceremony, with thousands of people watching both in person and on television. It seemed that before, their movements had been in the shadows, with only the Church being fully aware of their presence. But now the whole world would know—or, at the very least, the whole archipelago. They must have truly had no other choice, with the Veptilo stored deep underground and surrounded by a coterie of coral golems. Somehow, this became their best option.

Alani scrambled her lower half off the stadium seat just as the reptilian arachnid chomped down on it, gnashing the thick chunks of plastic in its crystal fangs. It ripped through the material easily, like tearing off a hunk of bread. She screamed again at the sight and proximity of the monster.

She pushed herself to her feet, blood rushing from her chin and her mouth. Then she rushed down the length of the aisle, back toward the staircase where Balt currently stood summoning something. Yellow soulclay was pouring out of his kayet, taking the shape of a large creature that she did not recognize. The monotone shape started to run even before he was fully finished summoning it.

When the yellow faded away to reveal the Jekua underneath, Alani let out another scream as it surged forward.

The beast ran on four wobbly legs, and its broad body was gross and segmented. The head was long and rounded like a worm's, but with piercing blue eyes and sharp fangs. Its flesh had that same reflective quality as Balt's Mirrorbear; she could see the stadium seats flashing along its torso as it charged.

Is that Milton? Alani wondered as they passed each other, the Jekua bounding across the row just above her. Balt had told her he'd Hybridized Milton and the worm and that she would not like the look of it, but this was her first time seeing the thing.

She had to admit, Balt knew her well.

Alani reached the steps and came to a halt, turning to watch the ensuing fight. She ascended a couple steps to stand next to Balt as he engaged with the crocodile-spider.

It snapped at Milton, whose body continually elasticized to swerve out of the way of the thing's wide mouth. Milton swiped at its face with his long, curved claws, leaving behind dull marks on the crocodile's flat snout.

Milton stood on his hind legs, then his front legs stretched out unnaturally, coiling around two of the crystal creature's eight legs before yanking them out from underneath it.

The creature lost its balance, stumbling forward with Milton's tug. But that only brought its mouth closer to the bear, who then had to stretch and curve his neck out of the way of another bite.

A beam of light erupted from the crystal monster's mouth, which Milton barely ducked away from. The light blasted a set of three chairs on the next row, completely shattering them all.

Milton had positioned himself underneath the crocodile-spider, his body stretching and curling around the beast's crystal limbs in a bizarre and frankly disgusting manner. Then Milton's neck craned, his head twisting backward, making it seem as if what was previously his back was now his stomach. He wrapped his legs around the crocodile-spider's body from underneath, then hardened himself.

The crystal creature tried to shake him off, but its range of motion was severely limited by the rock-hard bear hanging onto it.

"C'mon," Balt said, edging up the steps toward the exit.

Alani followed, but kept her eyes on the crocodile-spider. It couldn't move much, but it started extending its legs up then slamming downward, smashing Milton's back (or was it still his belly?) onto the ground. Balt winced with every impact, but he continued his ascent. They had to stop a moment to let some pot-bellied Jekua with big horns cross the walkway, seeking out a crystal monster to batter and bruise.

Balt let out a yelp as the monster crushed Milton once more, and the bear unwrapped himself from its body.

The crocodile-spider skittered away from Milton, crawling over multiple rows of seats, headed straight for them.

"Go!" Balt yelled, shoving her toward the exit.

Alani raced up the stairs, trying not to focus on the bodies scattered around her.

But then a huge, flaming bird smashed into the

balcony above the exit doors. Stone crumbled and fell, blocking the exit. The bird collapsed onto the rock, breathing heavily, its flames sputtering out. A second later, it morphed back into soulclay and drifted away.

She thought she could climb over the debris, until another of the crystal monsters' blasts of energy exploded on the balcony above, sending even more stone and iron and plastic raining down. She dodged out of the way, slipping on a puddle of soda that had spilled on the floor. This time, she was able to break her fall, but she banged up her elbows pretty badly in the process.

Across the aisle, Milton was stretching out his arms to slap the crocodile-spider with hardened paws. The beast turned on its spindly limbs and opened its mouth wide, sending another blast of white energy his way.

The light struck Milton in the chest, but the bear was not bowled over or blown apart like Alani would have expected. Instead, his body glowed with energy of his own.

A moment later, Milton's mouth hung open and a blast of white light emerged. The beam hit the crocodile-spider in its long snout, instantly shattering the thing's face into hundreds of tiny pieces.

Balt looked momentarily pleased with himself, though he gripped his stomach as if it was bothering him. But then he made Milton headbutt the crystal beast, exploding the crocodile-spider's weakened body.

After that, the crystal shards littering the stands glowed bright and merged back into a ball of bright yellow before flying away to whichever member of the Facet they belonged to. Amongst the chaos, Alani could not see where the person was, nor did she particularly care at the moment.

Down in the arena, she saw everybody being swept up in a tidal wave created by the towering snail that had beaten Balt two days prior. She was glad that it was on their team now. It seemed to be highly annoying for the other Summoners down there who were trying to help, but at least it was inflicting some heavy damage to the Facet and their crystalline monsters.

Balt turned around and spotted her standing there, watching the snail. "Why are you still here?" he asked, his voice strained. His mouth dipped into a frown, his eyebrows furrowed.

It was a good question, although one that didn't require an answer. She just needed to move.

With the nearest exit blocked, she raced down the row of seats toward the next staircase leading up to another exit.

Across that staircase from her, though, standing on the same row, was a member of the Facet. They stood there, white-and-black suit clinging tight to their thin frame. Their face was completely obscured by the diamond mask, which Alani still didn't understand how they could see through. But there was no denying that they could see, because when they turned in her direction, their body visibly tensed at the sight of her.

The strange mask then started glowing, and that semi-translucent energy flowed out from it, curving onto the ground and taking shape.

To reach the exit, Alani would have to run right toward them.

She started moving.

Maybe she could get there before the person's crystal monster was fully summoned.

Go, go, she urged herself, but her legs were not carrying her as fast as she wanted to move. As fast as she *knew* she could move, in ideal circumstances, but her muscles ached. Her body was screaming at her to just stop, just take a rest for a while. Recharge.

The light shone bright, then faded quickly. What it left behind was a purple crystalline thing that was roughly the same size as Dipper, something like a cross between a rat and a cat. Most of its crystal was purple, while its feet were yellow and its whip-like tail was green.

Alani jumped over the chairs to her right as the creature lunged forward. She landed shakily, but then continued jumping down over the rows of seats. She was growing farther and farther from the exit, but she was also growing farther from the crystal beast that wanted to kill her.

Of course, Balt had noticed her fleeing down the stands, rocketing toward the arena. Milton barreled across rows and rows of seats, tangling himself up in the folded chairs while he raced to meet the crystal cat head-on.

The bear headbutted the Facet's crystalline feline, sending the smaller creature flying through the air. It knocked its head on one of the seats before bouncing off and crashing into the harder ground. There was a thin crack in its forehead as it stood, but it was able to shake off the damage pretty easily.

Where it landed was fairly close to Alani, though. She

started running back in the direction from which she'd first come, toward the staircase where Balt was standing. He was starting to jog over to where the action was, however. He stretched Milton's arms across the distance between him and the crystal monster, but the cat was too speedy. It ducked and dove out of the way of the bear's elongated limbs and pounced onto Alani's back.

The thing sent her sprawling onto the ground, smashing her chin on the floor yet again, making her bite her tongue. Another rush of blood flooded her mouth, filling it with the taste of iron.

Alani felt claws stabbing her back, ripping through her shirt and digging into the flesh beneath. She elbowed the feline off of her, shredding her own skin as it was flung from her back. Then she rolled over, wincing as her tender back hit the ground, and immediately had to fend the thing off again as it jumped on top of her.

Her vision was filled with purple crystal thrashing and snapping at her. She couldn't see anything else, had no clue where Milton was. She needed the bear's aid, and fast.

The cat came down hard on her again, biting the air repeatedly. Alain raised her arm to block her already-ravaged face, and the creature's teeth dug deep into her flesh.

There came the sharpness she anticipated, having been bitten by an animal before, but there was also something else. Something deeper, something unfamiliar. It felt like there was a hole inside her and air was being let out, as if she were an inflatable that had been popped.

The sensation was strange and uncomfortable, but she

couldn't focus on it for too long. The crystal cat was still scratching at her and trying to bite other parts of her body. When she paid closer attention, she saw that the creature's purple teeth were faintly glowing white. It licked its jagged lips, eyeing her hungrily. Whatever it had taken from her, it wanted another taste.

Suddenly the purple crystal vanished from her vision and was replaced with the blur of Milton's reflective arm.

Alani sat up to watch the cat smash into a seat on the next row, crumpling the plastic. Milton leapt onto the thing and started bashing it with his huge, flat paws. This thing was evidently not quite as durable as the crocodile-spider, because every slash of Milton's claws left deep etches on its face and body.

While Milton was distracting the crystal cat, Alani stood on unsteady legs and tried to balance herself. Her arm still felt weird, and there was an innate chill in the center of her chest now. For a second, she thought she was going to be sick, but she swallowed it down and got moving.

The cat and the bear danced their violent dance, and Alani bounded up the steps.

Standing at the top was the Facet member controlling the cat, seemingly fully concentrated on the battle. They didn't react at all to Alani's approach, and she could hear a muffled yelp of surprise when she tackled them to the ground.

She started pounding on the person's mask with her fists, which did not really do anything to the mask and instead bloodied her knuckles. By the end of this dreadful ordeal, she was going to be completely drenched in blood.

Although she wasn't damaging the mask in the least, it did start to glow and a few seconds later the beam of energy that comprised the person's crystalline cat floated back into it. Alani cast a look over her shoulder at Balt, who stood taking ragged breaths next to his Jekua.

Then the Facet member violently shoved her off of them, sending her tumbling down the staircase. She was able to shield her head as she rolled down, but she was going to be covered in bruises.

When she stood once more, she saw Balt had withdrawn Milton and was racing toward the Facet member himself.

She looked away from them and back out into the arena. The Tyrian Snail was inching across the battlefield while a ton of other Jekuas engaged in combat with crystal monsters. A few members of the Facet lay bleeding on the ground, possibly dead, shot by Chief Guapora's security team. Others were on their knees, being subdued, their hands cuffed behind their backs.

But she looked on with dread as two massive, winged crystal creatures were hoisting the Veptilo into the air.

They gripped either end of it with long, crooked claws. Dirt fell from one end of the Veptilo, dirtying the security guards underneath who were aiming their guns up at the monsters. Another figure—Chief Guapora, Alani assumed—was running over to them, shouting and flailing his arms.

There was nothing else to be done. They simply watched as the crystalline gargoyles flew up and up, cresting the arena's ceiling and disappearing out of sight. Where they were going, Alani had no idea. Nor did she understand how the Facet planned on escaping the city holding such a gigantic item without being apprehended.

With the Veptilo secured, the remaining members of the Facet began withdrawing their monsters and attempting to flee the scene. There were some who were able to make it out into the stadium's halls, but around half of them were caught by Guapora's security force.

Up near the top of the steps, Balt had pinned the cat Summoner to the ground and was awaiting assistance from a security guard. He looked over at Alani and yelled, "You should leave!"

Alani heard him, but didn't respond. And anyway, it seemed outdoors might be just as dangerous as inside, now that there were several members of the Facet out there. She decided to stay put, where Balt and the other Summoners could protect her, if necessary.

She gawked at the cloudless blue sky, staring at the spot where the Veptilo had dipped below the building's horizon and out of view. She couldn't quite believe that she'd actually seen it happen.

They had succeeded. The Facet had stolen a second Veptilo.

Alani was scared to discover what they intended to do with them.

48
CRUSHED

BALT SUNK INTO THE CUSHION OF AEIKO'S COUCH, STARING numbly ahead at the television screen. News outlets had been playing nothing else but coverage of the Facet's attack on Xatetu Field for several hours now. If not for him and Alani speaking to Chief Guapora, no one would even know the name of the group or that they should contact the local Church about what precisely was going on.

Right now, an attractive young reporter was interviewing Elder Neiata, who was absolutely furious with the stadium's security and dismayed at the thought of what the Church was going to do now that *two* of their Veptilos were stolen, which was news to the general public. Behind the Elder stood Eila, blinking rapidly and tittering about nervously.

Balt wasn't much paying attention to what they were saying, though. He was in a daze, his eyes lost in the fuzz of colors on the screen, the reporter and Neiata's words no more than a dull ringing in his ears.

After things settled down back at the stadium, they'd tracked down Niona and spoken to Chief Guapora. The man was red-cheeked, with purple veins popping out of his neck and head, as he rushed all over the arena trying to mitigate the huge amount of damage already done. More than half of the Facet had escaped—either by running through the halls to the exits or summoning a flying crystal beast to carry them out—though hopefully not unscathed. The Summoners present had delivered them a beating they would not soon forget.

An hour passed waiting for a medic to examine them all and deem them healthy enough to leave. They then found Aeiko waiting outside, anxiously pacing back and forth. Their face sagged into relief when they laid eyes on them, although Balt suspected it was mostly felt for Alani. They pulled Alani into a tight embrace, then apologized over and over for running away. Alani assured them they had done the right thing, with which Balt wholeheartedly agreed.

Now they were all sitting around Aeiko's apartment, no one particularly feeling up to talking, despite Holly's best efforts. Balt was sure he wasn't the only person who wanted to wring her neck just to get her to shut up, but he tried not to be too annoyed by her. He understood that she'd been freaking out here at the apartment, watching the chaos unfold on television, with Aeiko's condition unknown.

Plus, she had ordered a multitude of different pizzas for them to eat. They were all in desperate need of some comfort food, she'd said, and no one remotely disagreed with that. In an effort to calm himself down, Balt had eaten nearly an entire pizza's worth of slices on his own.

He flicked his eyes away from the TV and scanned Alani, who was sitting over at the dining room table with Aeiko. The two of them were talking softly with each other, absentmindedly dragging half-eaten pizza crusts across their plates. Brine was standing statuesque in the kitchen, completely blocking the fridge, never finding himself too far from Aeiko.

Looking at Alani hurt Balt. Made him feel like he'd failed all over again, just like on Qwi Island.

She was covered in scrapes and bruises, all further illuminated by the faint white glow of her shineink tattoos. The manastreams swirled and cut across her tan arms in tangles, intermingled with bright red cuts and purple splotches.

Regardless of his failure, he couldn't let the subject remain unspoken between them. They'd been scooting from one person and place to the next with such haste, this was the first time since the attack a couple hours ago they had any downtime to talk.

He stood with a groan and walked over to the table. Alani and Aeiko looked up from the food they were playing with. "Hey," Alani said to him, offering a light, pained smile. There was a big, nasty red mark on her chin where she'd hit it on the stadium floor.

"Hi," he muttered awkwardly. "Can we talk for a minute?"

Alani nodded and pushed her chair back from the table.

"You can use my room, if you want some privacy," said Aeiko.

"Thanks," Balt told them. He and Alani then whisked themselves away into Aeiko's room and shut the door behind them with a click.

Alani's arms were folded across her chest as she slowly paced into the center of the room. She was looking down at the floor when she asked, "What's up?"

He got right into it. "I'm sorry," he said.

She looked confused by his apology. "What for?"

Her reaction, in turn, confused him. He blinked and said, "For not protecting you."

Alani unfolded her arms and slipped her hands into her pockets. The shineink on her face pulsed soothingly. "What do you mean?"

Balt let out a hollow laugh. "I mean, look at you!"

"Rude."

"Sorry. Again. But you're covered in bruises and scratches! You look terrible!"

"Rude!" she repeated.

"Sorry! You know what I mean." He groaned and thwacked his head against the closed door, leaning against it. He could hear Alani continuing to pace behind him, but he shut his eyes and welcomed the black.

She said, "I really don't. You *did* protect me."

"You—"

"Look terrible, I know. You've made that crystal clear."

He was glad to detect some mirth in her tone. "Poor choice of words," he said, pushing himself off the door and turning to face her.

That made her chuckle. Then, "I don't know what

would've happened to me if you weren't there. I was knocked out for I don't even know how long. Without you and your Jekuas, things could have turned out a lot worse."

He absorbed her words, trying to formulate what to say next. "I should've done better," he said finally. His voice was low, and he had to avert his gaze when he spoke.

"Don't beat yourself up over it," Alani said, and even though he wasn't looking directly at her, he could practically hear her rolling her eyes. "You did exactly what I brought you along for. Unlike last time."

Balt glanced up at her and saw that she was smirking. He laughed faintly.

"I'm sorry," he apologized again.

"I know. It's okay. Really, I'm fine."

"You don't *look* fine."

"Soon, I'm going to stop taking that as a joke and actually get mad," she warned him, though she was smiling when she said it.

"Who said I'm joking?"

"Oh, shut up. Anyway—I'm a little banged up, and I'm sure I'll be sore for a week, but I'm alright. I promise. Thank you for doing what you did."

Even though it wasn't enough, Balt scolded himself, but refrained from saying it aloud.

She could tell just from the expression on his face that he didn't fully believe her. "I forgave you for everything that happened on Qwi. You and I are okay. You did good."

Balt nodded. He just hadn't totally forgiven himself yet.

"Have you talked to Wasaaru yet?" she asked, changing the subject before the conversation grew too cyclical.

He shook his head. As far as family went, at least he'd briefly spoken to his parents. They were both hysterical after he ignored their numerous phone calls, his mother absolutely convinced that he was dead in a ditch. In the end, he still hadn't called them back, being in no mood to exert such a huge amount of mental and emotional energy on the task. He'd texted them, though, assuring them that he and all of his friends were safe.

Balt said, "I saw him afterwards, when we were waiting for the medic. He looked fine."

"Maybe you should text him."

He shrugged. "Yeah, maybe."

Alani looked puzzled once more. "I thought you two were mending things," she said.

"We were. We are," Balt said. He still needed to forgive himself in that department too, if he wanted to continue making progress with his cousin. Not to mention they needed to have a larger discussion about their relationship—it was one thing to set aside their differences to spar Jekuas, but it was another to genuinely move on from their strained past and try to forge a new relationship.

That was a heavier topic than he wanted to discuss right now, after the day's gruesome events. So, he suggested they return to the living room, and they did.

Alani returned to the table where Aeiko and Holly were chatting, while Balt tossed himself back onto the couch. Niona was sitting nearby, glaring at the television.

Her broken kayet lay in her lap. She had spent the past hour fiddling with it, trying to crack it open to extract the four memory cards held within. They weren't ejecting normally, and it was causing her immense stress. Holly had suggested she just take it down to a Jekua shop and have them take a look at it, but Niona snapped at her and said she'd do it herself.

She was seemingly taking a break from her efforts to watch the news report on the stadium attack. Balt was about to ask her something when the reporter's words captured his attention.

"...of the members of the organization has been identified as well-known Summoner Rika Yonomi," the young woman said, staring intently into the camera.

Balt and Niona exchanged wide-eyed looks, then turned back to the screen.

There on the TV was Rika Yonomi's face, one that the both of them knew well. Rika was a popular Summoner, especially amongst younger fans. Before dropping out, Balt had been sure she would go on to become one of the tournament's finalists.

Her back was hunched over, and she was sitting on a piece of rubble next to several of her cohorts. They were all wearing those matching, skin-tight white outfits and authorities had removed their diamond masks so that there was no risk of them summoning their crystal monsters again.

The reporter went on. "Yonomi was originally set to compete in this year's Makanuele Rumble, taking place here at Xatetu Field, before dropping out of the tournament roughly six weeks ago. At the time, there was much speculation as to the reason she was removing herself from the competition, but Yonomi and her team only stated that there were conflicting circumstances."

"Yeah, I'd say there were some pretty big conflicting circumstances, alright," Niona grumbled.

"No kidding," said Balt, still in disbelief.

How in the hell had someone like Rika Yonomi become involved with the Facet? She was well on her way to becoming one of the most famous, highest paid Summoners in the circuit. What could they have possibly offered her that would make her want to throw away her career and her entire future?

"I'm sorry. I'm so sorry to all my fans," Rika said, tears welling in her eyes as she addressed the camera. "I can't apologize enough. It wasn't meant to happen like this. Nobody was supposed to get hurt, nothing was supposed to be destroyed, but…some people got out of hand."

"Oh, you don't say?" Niona said to the woman on the screen, as if Rika could respond.

"Again, I apologize sincerely for my actions and those of my colleagues," said Rika.

"*Colleagues*? Oh, shut the hell up," Niona groaned, beginning to tinker with her kayet again.

The rest of the unmasked Facet members did not look familiar to Balt, and he was admittedly relieved that there were no more recognizable Summoners in their ranks. None who had been arrested today, at the very least. That thought made him shudder.

A few more minutes were spent on the reporter talking to various members of the Facet, who varied in how ashamed and remorseful of their actions they looked.

Rika Yonomi was the most apologetic by far, no doubt due to the fact that she had a fanbase to cater to.

Balt wondered how many of them would stick by her side after this. It wouldn't be the first time crazed fans performed mental gymnastics to justify why a celebrity they were obsessed with had done something awful and it was okay for them to still be a fan. He hoped a line would be drawn at a full-blown terrorist attack, but he could not be so sure, which was depressing.

The reporter moved on to interviewing Chief Guapora again, grilling him about how his team had failed so spectacularly and allowed this attack to happen in the first place. That redness was returning to the man's face as he attempted to downplay his and the security team's undeniable screw-up.

Balt turned his attention to Niona, who was prying at the device in her lap with a screwdriver and some other assorted tools that Aeiko and Holly had laying around the apartment.

"Sorry about your kayet," he said.

She didn't do so much as glance up at him, her concentration entirely trained on the kayet. "It's fine," she sighed. "I can buy another one. It's not a big deal. I just need these cards."

Losing his kayet would be a crushing blow for someone like Balt, given how expensive they were, but purchasing a new one obviously wouldn't be an issue for Niona. Since the new device would be registered to her preexisting KIN, all of her memory cards would be compatible with it, as well. While this could have been the worst thing in the world for some Summoners, for her it was nothing more than a minor inconvenience. A hiccup.

"Ah-ha!" Niona cheered, popping the front plate of the kayet off. She set the piece of metal on the empty cushion beside her and reached her fingers into the device's innards.

Her look of elation quickly turned into one of uncertainty, and then despair.

From where he sat, Balt couldn't see what she saw. "What's wrong?" he asked.

Niona pulled out a memory card, placing it beside the cracked front plate. Then another.

But then her movements slowed. The next memory card she pulled out was completely crushed, nearly split in half by metal and other gears folding in on it. A spiderweb of cracks rippled out from the middle of the card, covering the entirety of it.

Balt's mouth hung open. He was at a loss.

"It's Garbo's card," she said.

They both stared silently at the crushed memory card. There was no doubt that the card was lost, its data unrecoverable. She wouldn't be able to summon her Nuri again.

"I'm so sorry," Balt said.

Niona gently placed the broken memory card next to the two intact ones, then pulled out the final card.

Like Garbo's card, this one was damaged, but not anywhere near so severely. There were a few cracks in it, and it appeared that the top left corner of it had snapped off, but it was in much better shape than the Nuri's.

"Who's that?" Balt asked.

She bit her lower lip, like she was trying to keep the Jekua's name inside. Like if she didn't say it out loud, she could wish it away. Change reality.

But she said at last, "Pops."

Now Balt was truly at a loss. After a few seconds processing what she'd said, all he could manage was, "...shit."

Niona held the memory card up to her face, rotating it, examining the small piece of technology from every available angle.

He didn't want to ask, but he had to. "Is it salvageable?"

It felt like hours passed before Niona finally answered his question.

"I don't know," she said. "Maybe. Maybe not."

Her voice was flat and even. No hint of emotion in it at all. But her eyes looked hollow, and her body sagged as she leaned back in her seat. Balt didn't know what to say, didn't know how anything he could say in that moment would possibly comfort her.

She placed Pops's broken card next to the others, then tossed the useless husk of her kayet onto the floor with a loud clatter.

49
SOULTEAR

EVERYONE WAS FEELING SHAKEN UP AFTER THE STADIUM attack, and no one wanted to spend the night alone. Niona stayed over at Aeiko's place, nuzzling up next to Alani in the pull-out sofa bed. Apparently Holly had cheekily offered her a spot in her own bed, which Niona declined. As they got settled in to sleep, Alani was amused by Niona's taunts to Balt over on the floor, nestled amongst his pillows and blankets.

Alani had felt exhausted the entire evening, which did not come as a shock to her. She'd been tossed around those stands like a ragdoll, and it was also a hugely taxing experience, emotionally speaking. It made sense that she would not be at her sharpest.

When she was trying to drift off to sleep, though, she was hit by waves of nausea. They were mild at first, but as the hours wore on, they got worse.

She'd jumped out of bed and scurried to the bathroom, dropping to her knees in front of the toilet bowl. She retched a few times, her throat burning, but nothing came out. Tears welled in her eyes that she blinked and wiped away.

There then came a light knock on the door. "You alright?" asked Niona. The door squeaked open, just a crack, and Niona's face filled the gap. "Can I come in?"

"Mhmm," Alani said, her throat too sore to speak real words.

Niona stepped inside, quietly closing the door behind her. She turned to face at Alani on the floor and gave her a curious look.

"You threw up?" she asked.

Alani shook her head.

"Nauseous, though."

A nod.

Niona peered closer, then said, "Your eyes are a little bloodshot."

That had been news to her. She'd tried to lean backward to catch a glimpse of herself in the mirror, but she couldn't at that angle.

It was then that an amused, yet befuddled, expression crossed Niona's face. She said, "These are, uh…classic symptoms of some super mild soulsickness."

Alani hadn't been sure what to say. Niona's diagnosis didn't make any sense whatsoever. How could she possibly be soulsick? Nothing she did expended mana, so how could her body be out of it? She didn't even know *how* to use mana.

As a test, Niona had then slipped out of the bathroom to retrieve something from her bag. When she returned a minute later, she was holding an unopened can of Thunderjolt.

"No," Alani managed to say.

Niona fought past her protestations and said, "If I'm right, which I think I am, then this should help. It'll get you back on track to refillin' your little baby reserves." She then extended her arm, wagging the drink in Alani's face.

It was a blueberry-flavored one, which was always the flavor that smelled the least vile when Balt cracked them open. That was something, at least.

Alani had then reluctantly popped the top of the Thunderjolt and slurped a bit of it down. While it might have smelled less acidic, it still tasted like poison to her. Poison with just a hint of sweetness. Too much sweetness, at that.

Weirdly, in spite of the carbonation and awful taste, it had indeed made her throat feel better.

"I don't know how you two can drink this stuff," she'd said, wiping some of the purple-blue liquid from her lips.

"Drink up," was Niona's reply.

As the hour progressed, Alani's condition steadily improved, and she realized that at least part of that fatigue she'd been feeling was due to this supposed soulsickness. When they crawled back into bed (with Balt seemingly undisturbed), she was well enough to fall asleep, but not convinced that she had been soulsick.

In the morning, she woke up feeling just as bad as before. The nausea had returned, as had her bleariness.

Aeiko wanted to take her to a clinic, and they weren't going to take no for an answer, so Alani didn't refuse. She could see the guilt creeping into Balt's features again, hidden behind his confusion at her symptoms. He too was unwilling to accept Niona's suggestion of soulsickness, but he also had nothing else to offer in its place.

Now the four of them were seated in a doctor's office, awaiting the results of some tests the man had done on her for the past half hour. She'd had blood drawn, taken an x-ray, and provided a urine sample. The doctor had also given her an injection of something that he claimed would be good for her mana, regardless of what her problem was. It was not the way she'd wanted to spend her morning.

Alani was seated on the long, uncomfortable chair covered in thin, crinkly paper, while Balt and Aeiko stood next to her. Niona was on the other side of the room, examining a medical poster hanging on the wall.

"I'm learnin' a lot about the digestive system over here," she told them.

The door swung open and in stepped Dr. Yunosté with a clipboard in hand. An expression of concern was on his face, which chilled Alani.

"Okay," the man started, taking a deep breath. "Just to clarify, you say you are not a Summoner?"

Alani thought that the manastreams covering her body would be enough for him to hazard a guess that no, she was not a Summoner, but she said, "Correct."

"And you say you've never actually used your internal mana before?"

"Not that I am aware of." She coughed.

Dr. Yunosté nodded, then said again, "Okay."

"What's goin' on?" asked Balt impatiently.

The doctor's brow furrowed as he spoke. "It's the

damnedest thing," he said, which was not what one ever wanted to hear from their doctor. "Based on your bloodwork and your other scans, it would appear that you were indeed soulsick. We took a sample, then gave you an injection to jumpstart the mana reabsorption process, and took a secondary sample. When comparing the two, it's clear that the injection helped, although…not as much as we would expect, given the dosage."

"So what does any of that mean?" Aeiko asked. They were beginning to grow impatient as well. "How could she have been soulsick? And why didn't the medicine help as much as it should've?"

"Those are good questions," said Dr. Yunosté unhelpfully. More ambiguities that a person would not want their doctor to say.

"Yeah, and what are the answers?" Balt asked. Niona still stood over by the digestive system poster, rife with detailed illustrations of intestines and stomachs and throats and the like. She had turned to face the others, though, and had her arms folded across her chest.

Dr. Yunosté said, "I shared this information with some of the other doctors, and the best conclusion we can come to is that your body is leaking mana faster than it can reabsorb it, so it is constantly draining away. This is exceptionally rare, but it *has* happened before. It typically only crops up in Summoners, as you can imagine, and only those who have suffered tremendous damage in battle. Something like the medicine we gave you—or like the Thunderjolt your friend had you drink last night—can help temporarily, but those are not long-term solutions."

Alani opened her mouth to speak, then closed it when

she couldn't find the proper words. But then she said, "So what *is* a long-term solution?" She was still trying to wrap her head around why her body was leaking mana suddenly.

"Well, I can recommend you to a specialist on Kou Tekkis who might be able to do more," said Dr. Yunosté, "but this is, I'm sad to say, a field that we still don't have a good handle on. Lakahlo Labs is always working with the medical community on new technologies related to mana, of course, but soulsickness is not something we've been able to fully tackle as of yet."

"So you can't do anything," said Balt flatly. "You know what's goin' on, but you can't do shit to fix it?"

"Balt," said Alani with an edge in her tone, urging him to quiet down.

"What?" he said. "That's what it sounds like to me. Right? You can't do anything?"

"The specialist I have in mind might be able to—"

"*Might*. That's the key word. Nothing certain."

"Well, no," said Dr. Yunosté.

"Great."

Alani ignored him and asked, "What will happen to me, if the specialist can't help?"

Dr. Yunosté went on to explain that, if left unchecked, her body would eventually get to the point where it ran out of mana and could not absorb more fast enough for her to recover. If that happened, her body would slowly deteriorate, as those with severe soulsickness did. His description brought to mind the old man she'd encountered in Mapa all those weeks ago. His eyes sunken, devoid of awareness. His arms and legs all shrunken and withered away, binding him to a wheelchair that he couldn't even push himself. The thought of that happening to her was enough to make her cry, but she held herself together in the doctor's presence.

They left the clinic with information about the specialist on Kou Tekkis, some pills for Alani to take daily in the meantime, and a bunch of dour moods. Balt's expression wavered between anger and guilt, while Aeiko looked determined. Niona, standing behind them, appeared more confused than anything else, trying to piece together how this could have happened. She had graciously paid for the visit, knowing that Alani's stipend from the Church was not particularly large.

While Niona had been handling the bill, Alani mulled over the past twenty-four hours and thought she might have landed on what had done this to her.

She turned to address the others. "Yesterday, during the attack, one of those crystal things pinned me down and bit my arm." She held up the arm in question, pointing at two white slashes on her skin. Hidden amongst her glowing white tattoos, they were somewhat hard to make out, but they were there. They were like scars, although they had not first been real cuts. "When it bit me, it felt like…I don't know how to explain. Like something was leaving my body."

"Your mana?" suggested Balt.

"I guess so. I don't know. I've never used my mana before."

"So you think that thing, like…"

"Ripped through your soul?" Niona interjected.

Balt said, “That’s kind of a dramatic way to put it, but yeah, I guess that’s what I was going for.”

“I dunno how else to put it,” said Niona. “It tore through your body, right through your soul, and now it’s leaking mana.”

Alani agreed that it was dramatic, but not entirely inaccurate.

Suddenly Niona grabbed her linkpad out of her pocket and her eyebrows shot up.

“Uh…sorry, y’all, I need to take this call real quick,” she said, then hurried out of earshot.

All this time, Aeiko had said nothing, acting as if they weren’t even listening to the discussion. But then they said, “I have an idea. Something that can maybe keep you steady until you see that specialist. You have to go to Yuluhu before Kou Tekkis, right?”

Alani shrugged. “I mean, I’m sure the Church wouldn’t want me to prioritize the pilgrimage over my health…” She trailed off, not even sure if the statement was true. “If you have something in mind, though, I’m all ears.”

“It sounds like that specialist might not even be able to do anything, anyway,” said Balt. “What’re you thinkin’?”

“It’s kind of…out there,” said Aeiko.

“*Out there* is fine,” Alani told them. To be honest, she would try anything if it meant preventing herself from withering away.

Aeiko braced themselves before speaking. They said, “So, you remember that conversation we had about the tech I’m experimenting with at work? The stuff I’m doing with Brine?”

Alani nodded, but Balt asked, “What is it, exactly?”

"Coral golems are all outfitted with devices that absorb mana from the atmosphere and give them life, right? But they only last so long. This new one I'm testing out on Brine is supposed to split the mana it absorbs, transferring some into the golem and using the rest to make the battery self-sufficient, basically."

"You want to treat me like a coral golem?" Alani asked tentatively.

"Uh...I mean, kind of?" said Aeiko. "Obviously, it can't work *exactly* the same, but maybe with the same principle in mind, I could make something work for you? Make it so that this thing can absorb mana, convert it into a form that would be compatible with your body, and inject you with it. I mean, you just got an injection of shit that was kind of like that anyway. I'm sure I could pull up some research at the office that could help."

It all sounded very dubious to Alani. Aeiko had warned her that the solution was out there, but this was even more than she'd been expecting.

Niona returned to the group looking visibly relieved, albeit somewhat shocked, too. She scanned the expressions on everyone's faces and said, "What's up? What's goin' on? Did I hear somethin' about experimenting on Alani or somethin'?"

"Yes," said Aeiko.

"Cool."

Aeiko turned back toward Alani and said, "Look, I know it sounds ridiculous. We haven't tried this on humans before. Well, I mean, maybe we have—again, I could pull up some research that could tell me if we have or not. Honestly, I'd be shocked if we hadn't. But I think maybe it's worth a shot, right?"

"Is it, though?" said Balt.

"I say go for it," said Niona. "I still don't know what you're talkin' about, but go for it. Aeiko's smart. They know what they're doin'. I'd let you do science experiments on me," she told them.

"How would it even work?" Alani asked. "It would latch onto me? Would it go on my head, or be embedded inside my body like the golems, or what?"

"I don't know," Aeiko confessed. "We'll have to figure that out."

Alani took a deep breath and let it out, trying not to let her anxiety overpower her.

"Why would this not be a common thing already if it works?" she then asked, poking holes in Aeiko's theory. "I would think that this could help prevent tons of people from suffering debilitating soulsickness."

Before Aeiko could answer, Balt stepped in. "Well, the thing is, soulsickness usually isn't, like…a *slow* process," he said. "It's gradual, yeah, but it's always instantaneous. I mean, your arm shriveling up isn't an instant thing, but the soulsickness hits you immediately when you deplete your mana. Whatever effects you get from it happen right then, not constantly over time. It's letting yourself get to that point over and over again that makes the arm wither away or whatever other example you can think of, but it's always due to suddenly losing the last of your mana. But then, with most people, your mana starts to recover. What that guy described happening to you isn't…it's not anything I've heard of."

"He said it's happened before, but yeah, I haven't heard of it either," said Niona. "It has to be pretty damn rare. Makes sense that they might not have figured out a solution for it yet."

"It might be too rare for most institutions to put a lot of money toward funding cures," said Aeiko with a frown. "I know that's grim to say, but…it might be the case. In the end, these businesses want to make money, so they're probably more focused on things that affect more people."

Alani breathed out again. She was feeling fine right now, but she wasn't looking forward to another bout of nausea. It was a good thing the doctor had given her a ton of those pills.

She said, "Fine. Let's try it. It can't hurt to try, right?"

Aeiko smiled. "Nope."

"Let's go right now," said Balt. "Can we go to Lakahlo? Are the offices open?"

"I can swipe my keycard and get in any time," Aeiko said.

"As much as I'd love to watch y'all poke and prod Alani, I've gotta run to a meeting real quick," said Niona, still gripping her linkpad in her hand.

"What was that call?" Balt asked.

"I'll explain later," she said. "Y'all go save Alani's life or whatever. I'll meet y'all back at the apartment, yeah? Text me."

The three of them said bye to Niona, who headed in an easterly direction, toward the epicenter of the city. Then Aeiko said, "Shall we go?"

Alani nodded and had to take one more deep breath to steady herself. Then they were off to Lakahlo Labs.

50
POUR ONE OUT

THE CALL NIONA HAD RECEIVED WAS FROM VANESSA REN.

In truth, Niona had expected to never hear from the woman again. She hadn't even given Vanessa her number, so she had no idea how the woman managed to contact her or why. In Niona's mind, she'd blown her big shot at being signed to Atoll Talent after that pathetic loss to Uil in round five. No self-respecting agent would want to work with her.

Luckily, it seemed that perhaps Atoll Talent was filled with agents who had no self-respect, because Vanessa wanted to meet with her as soon as she was free, over at Xatetu Field. The area surrounding the stadium, not inside of it—that was surely still off-limits to the public and would be for the foreseeable future while repairs were done.

Niona couldn't imagine Vanessa would want to meet with her just to say sorry, we don't want to work with you, see ya later. It had to be good news, right? Was this her moment?

A part of her felt undeniably guilty about being so giddy so soon after Alani's devastating diagnosis, but she couldn't help it. This was what she'd been striving for the past six years. She had to grasp the opportunity while it was here.

Assuming that's what this was, anyway.

The hopefulness she now felt helped bury the sadness and worry she held in regard to Pops's memory card. Losing Garbo was bad enough, but her connection with the Nuri had been nowhere near as deep as it was with Pops. If she couldn't get the data off of there and onto a new memory card, she didn't know what she was going to do.

For now, she didn't want to think about that potential outcome. Pops would be fine, she was sure. And she needed to be bright and cheery for her meeting with Vanessa.

When she reached the crater twenty minutes later, she leaned on the railing, scoping out the area below. She easily spotted Vanessa, sitting on a brightly colored bench with her legs crossed. She was wearing a slick black dress and her earrings glistened in the sunlight, even from this far away. Also, she was almost the only person present in the crater; most people did not feel comfortable hanging out around the ravaged stadium, apparently. The only other people there were two young men sharing a picnic, seemingly unperturbed by the destruction nearby.

Niona rushed down the steps and joined Vanessa at the bench. "Hi there," she said, smiling wide.

"Ah, hello, Ms. Daneo!" Vanessa beamed, standing up. She clapped her hands together and said, "Thanks for meeting me on such short notice."

"Oh, it's no problem at all," Niona assured her. "I thought I said you could just call me Niona, though," she grinned.

Vanessa chuckled and said, "Yes, you did. How are you feeling, by the way? I hope you weren't too hurt yesterday. I saw some footage of you fighting those awful people last night."

"I'm totally fine," Niona said, though the loss of Garbo and the damage to Pops's memory card still stung. "My kayet's busted, but I can grab a new one. How about you?"

"I made it out pretty quickly," Vanessa replied. "One of the perks of being a VIP at these things is that I didn't have to fight my way through a crowd. The halls that I and the other agents left through were pretty clear."

"That's good."

"Yes, I'm very lucky and grateful. That was just horrific, what happened yesterday. I commend you for standing up to those people."

Niona couldn't help but think about the fact that one of those people, Rika Yonomi, had fairly recently been signed to Vanessa's agency. She wondered if that was weighing on the woman's mind, but she was obviously not going to ask.

"Anyway," said Vanessa, "let's take a walk, shall we? Let's discuss lighter things."

"That sounds good to me."

They strolled around the crater as they talked. While the stadium itself may have suffered a great deal of damage the day before, the greenery surrounding it was still pristine and beautiful.

"I want to start by apologizing for my lateness. It took me a while to track down your contact information. Obviously, I would have simply found you at the stadium yesterday, but I couldn't find you after your match. So I was going to speak with you after the closing ceremony, but…"

"But," Niona said. They didn't need to elaborate.

"Yes. The point is, I would like to extend you an offer to join us over at Atoll Talent."

Niona's heart skipped a beat. Vanessa had really just jumped right into it. She appreciated that. No beating around the bush.

"You would?" Niona said, almost in a whisper.

"Of course," said Vanessa, taken aback. "How could I not? You displayed immense talent out on the field."

Niona said, "But I, uh…I didn't make it to the finals."

Vanessa laughed. "Are you trying to talk me out of signing you?"

"No, no," said Niona hastily. "I'm just surprised, is all."

"You didn't make it to the finals, but you made it to the semi-finals. That is no small feat," said Vanessa. "You should be proud of that. There were sixty other Summoners who failed to make it that far, after all."

"That's true. Sucks for them."

That garnered another light chuckle. "We can pour one out for them later," Vanessa said. "I also must say, I was highly impressed by the ingenuity you showed in all of your matches. You've got great control of your Jekuas, of course, but you're clever, too. I like that. That's something we value over at Atoll."

"Thank you," said Niona sincerely.

"You're welcome. So, are you interested in working with us?"

"I am. I definitely am."

"Excellent," said Vanessa, smiling. Once again, Niona was struck by the preposterous whiteness of the woman's teeth. There had to be magic involved there, somehow. "I can't tell you how happy I am to hear that. I'll get some paperwork drawn up, and I'll send it to you for you to look over along with your lawyer, if you need to. We can go back and forth if necessary, but once we agree upon terms, you'll need to travel to our headquarters on Kou Tekkis to officially sign the deal in person. Is that okay?"

"It is," Niona nodded.

"Great. I'll get that address to you as well when I send over the first draft of the contract. Our office is in Asanak, have you ever been there?"

"I have not."

"I think you'll like it. It has some great nightlife. It's also where people first came up with naio paupa, so you know we've got the best in the isles."

"Well, I love both those things," Niona said with a grin. Naio paupa was one of her favorite dishes that she did not get to eat very often, slow-roasted pork that was cooked underground. Her mouth was already watering just thinking about chowing down on a heaping bowl of it while signing her contract.

Vanessa stopped walking and turned to Niona. "Well, I don't want to take up any more of your time today. I'm sure you're extremely tired after everything you went through, both with the tournament and with…everything else."

Niona enjoyed the woman's company, but she was eager to link up with her friends and share the amazing news. "Alright," she said. "Thanks so much for this opportunity. I'm, like, honestly *super* excited to work with you guys. You have no idea."

"So are we," Vanessa said kindly.

"I only have one question, though."

"Oh?"

"Yeah. Is Brian Deerheart as big in person as he looks on TV?" Vanessa laughed, and Niona grinned, saying, "Dude is just muscles on muscles. He looks like he could eat me. I'm absolutely sure he's eaten full human beings before. If you say he hasn't, I'll just assume that's a PR cover-up."

"I can neither confirm nor deny," said Vanessa.

"I knew it."

Vanessa then said, "Unless you have any more questions, I suppose I'll let you go. I'll be sure to send all that info to you soon."

"Info about Brian's diet?"

"That, and also your contract, where to find our office, stuff like that."

"Oh! *Useful* stuff."

"Precisely."

"Got it. Sounds good. Talk to you soon," Niona said, then turned to climb upward out of the crater, leaving Vanessa to tend to her affairs.

As she navigated through Makanuele, heading back to

Corsseo Court, Niona could only hope that the others' errand was proving as fruitful as her own.

She then realized that they probably wouldn't be finished for a long while, and she would be sitting around the courtyard outside of Aeiko's apartment for a long time if she went there now. Not only would she be dreadfully bored, but she would also run the risk of Holly spying her through the window and coming down to join her.

Plus, if she was now in the process of signing to a talent agency, there was somewhere else she needed to go. The highest priority. She exited the navigation on her linkpad and instead input a search for the nearest Jekua shop.

She needed to get herself a new kayet.

51
TIMESTAMP

BALT'S MIND WHIRRED RESTLESSLY ALL THE WAY FROM THE clinic to Makanuele's branch of Lakahlo Labs. Aeiko ordered them a car to ride over there in, not wanting Alani to exert any more energy than was strictly necessary. All of them needed the break, really, they figured.

While they toyed with their security badge next to one window and Alani sat staring straight ahead in the middle seat, Balt sat by the other window, gazing out at the buildings and pedestrians whizzing past. He was trying to solve this new, seemingly insurmountable problem they had. Obviously he possessed no expertise on any of the subjects involved—medicine, mana, technology, none of it—but that didn't stop him from feeling obligated to fix everything.

As always, Alani's problems always came back to him. Balt Vana, the professional life screw-upper. His recklessness and obsessive nature had gotten her attacked at the Qwi shrine, and now it had happened all over again. If he hadn't insisted they attend this tournament, the damned Makanuele Rumble, she wouldn't be potentially crippled for life now.

I told her to bring another Summoner, I told her I wasn't experienced enough...

Even though he told himself this over and over in his head, it didn't help alleviate his guilt. If anything, it made him feel even worse, acting as a reminder of how much trust his friend had put in him.

If he had been better, he could have stopped her from getting hurt. If he'd learned more moves with all of his Jekuas, if he'd trained longer to deepen his mana reserves even more, if he'd—

The list could go on and on endlessly. There was no shortage of ways he could have prepared himself better for the situation they'd found themselves in. Not that he could have ever predicted a gang of thieves would parachute down into the stadium and attack a bunch of civilians, but still. He knew when embarking upon this pilgrimage that there was a hint of danger.

He drummed his fingers on his knees, his right leg bouncing up and down nervously. Next to him, Alani was completely stoic. Motionless.

Looking at her, he never would have guessed she'd just been handed a life-altering diagnosis. She sat in her seat, back straightened, looking out through the windshield at the city passing them by. The manastreams visible on her arms and face pulsed faintly, almost in rhythm with the sound of the tires rolling through the street.

Balt knew that she had a tendency to keep her true feelings bottled up, but this was ridiculous. If it were him, he'd be sobbing. He'd be breaking shit. He would probably puke his guts out with anxiety about the future.

But Alani was just sitting there, enjoying her little car ride, headed to her friend's workplace.

Maybe she just had too much misplaced trust in Aeiko on account of her feelings for them. Personally, Balt was not so sure their plan to alter the coral golem thing was going to yield any positive results. It hardly made any sense to him. But, again, he had no expertise in that field. What did he know, really? Maybe the math checked out in Aeiko's head. He couldn't refute them.

If it didn't work, he didn't know what they would do. Surely the pilgrimage would be called off, right? The Church couldn't possibly expect her to continue trekking across the Volukho Isles in her condition. There was too much risk now. Especially if their next stop was meant to be Yuluhu, which was practically brimming with poison.

That wasn't his call to make, he knew. He had told Alani countless times before: she was the leader. If she chose to press onward, he would back her up.

Maybe.

He dismissed the thought. That was an argument they could have later. No point in playing it out in his head right now, since it might not ever actually happen.

Lakahlo Labs was in the southeast district of Makanuele. It was a huge complex, and it took up the space of two entire city blocks on its own. Balt knew that most of the company's branches had their own campuses, and that sort of real estate was impossible to find in a city as densely packed as Makanuele, yet Lakahlo had prevailed. The office was comprised of several tall, gray buildings, with elegantly curved sides that were covered in windows. Only half of them had their blinds drawn, the others allowing bystanders to peer into the offices. There was a parking garage entrance attached to the side of one building that led underground, and Balt had to imagine that it burrowed several stories deep into the earth to accommodate parking for so many employees. On the front of the building, underneath a random row of windows, it said "lakahlo.labs" in all lowercase, white serif lettering. There was no personality to the complex whatsoever, which Balt did not find surprising.

The car dropped them off out front and Aeiko led them inside with a quick swipe of their badge. The interior was exactly as cold and uninteresting as its exterior. Nobody was inside except for a security guard manning the lobby, who they all waved to as they passed him. He waved back without looking up from his linkpad.

Aeiko gave them a brief tour as they traipsed through the empty facility, but there was not much about the Lakahlo office that was different from what Balt would expect at any other tech company. They might be the best in the business and one of the most successful companies in the world, but their offices were pretty mundane. He *was* intrigued by them having their own cafeteria with multiple different cuisines on offer, but it was currently closed outside of business hours.

The three of them rode an elevator up to the ninth floor in silence. The tension between them was palpable. While they dinged through the various floors, climbing their way upward, Balt let his mind wander to what it was Niona had left them to meet about. It had to be something to do with the agency, surely. He couldn't think of any other pressing business she had in town.

"Here we are," said Aeiko as the elevator doors slid open with a mechanical whir.

They led them over to their desk, which was cluttered with papers and knickknacks. The papers were covered with equations and bits of code and lots of other complicated stuff that Balt had no chance of ever understanding. There was also a tiny round vase by their computer monitor holding a bouquet of plastic lavender.

Aeiko plopped down in their black leather rolling chair and gestured toward the myriad empty desks surrounding them. "Grab yourselves a seat," they said, typing in their login information.

Balt and Alani both wandered to nearby desks and rolled chairs over to Aeiko's. When he sat down, Balt asked, "What are you looking for, exactly?"

"I need to pull up some research that my own team and one other has done in this field. I also need to grab some schematics. I know how to put these devices together, I've done it plenty of times, but I still need a guide to do it right. I've almost got the process locked down, but I might as well take any assistance I can get. What I'm planning to do is slightly different than what we're currently using for Brine, anyway, so I'll need to do some double-checking with those alterations."

"Let's do triple-checking," said Balt. "Maybe quadruple, even."

"Right," Aeiko nodded, clicking through folders on the screen. The speed with which they did so was dizzying. Balt didn't know how they were even reading and processing the information on the screen before moving on.

"Do you have all the supplies you'll need at home?" Alani asked, speaking for the first time since they left the clinic. Balt almost jumped at the sound of her voice.

Aeiko shrugged. "I doubt it, but anything I need should be here at the office."

"Will the company just…let you take shit?" asked Balt.

"I mean, it's common knowledge that I'm monitoring Brine at home," they replied. "It's not out of the question that I'd need to take supplies back there. Everything I need will be related to that project, so it shouldn't raise any flags with the higher-ups."

They continued clicking through folders and writing stuff down on a previously blank piece of paper. They had to scribble their pen at the top of the page a few times to get the ink to run.

After almost ten minutes of this (which also included printing out a few different blueprints for various Lakahlo devices which were absolutely inscrutable to Balt), Aeiko pushed their chair back a few inches from the desk.

"That should do it, I think," they said.

It was an exceedingly anticlimactic moment, considering it was meant to signify that they'd cracked the case on Alani's impending soulsickness. Perhaps if Balt had any idea what any of this shit was or meant, he'd feel much more confident and accomplished. Or if he'd done anything to contribute, as well.

"You're sure?" he said, not knowing how else to help

besides making sure the sole knowledgeable person had done their due diligence.

Aeiko nodded. "As sure as I can be," they said. "I quadruple-checked, just for you."

"Thanks," he said, his tone dry.

Alani chimed in. "And you think this will work to fix whatever that fake Jekua did to me?"

Aeiko swiveled in their chair to face Alani. "Fake Jekua?" they said. "The things that attacked the stadium were fake Jekuas?"

Alani nodded and said, "Oh, I guess you weren't around long enough to get a good look at them. I guess 'fake Jekua' isn't the best way to describe them…"

"I dunno what they *literally* are, but 'fake Jekua' seems accurate enough to me," said Balt. "People are summoning them—through masks instead of kayets, of course, but maybe the tech is the same—and they're monsters with magical abilities. One magical ability, mainly, but still."

"Hmm…" Aeiko murmured, rotating back around to face the computer. They said, "I think I might've seen something about that in here…"

"About fake Jekuas?" asked Balt, perplexed.

They nodded. "Years and years ago, before my time, I know they were working on creating Artificial Jekuas. They figured that if they had cracked Artificial Abilities, then they should be able to create fully-formed Jekuas too. Not preexisting ones, like they weren't going to sell you a memory card with a Bingst on it or anything, but Jekuas that were entirely made in-house. They'd even hired a bunch of designers for the project, who were all let go after the project fizzled out."

"Why'd it fizzle out?" Balt wanted to know.

"I'm not sure. Like I said, it was years before I got hired," said Aeiko. "All I've really heard about it are rumors. I've seen files for it on the server, but they're all password-protected, so I've never been able to read any of them. It was a top-secret project, one that they didn't want to leak until they were sure they could pull it off, which obviously never happened."

"As far as we know, anyway," said Alani.

"Mhmm," Aeiko nodded, clicking their cursor through more folders. "I just saw something about it a minute ago, but I glazed over it. I haven't thought about any of that stuff in a long time, it's ancient history as far as Lakahlo's concerned."

Balt looked between the two of them dubiously. "You think that might have something to do with the Facet's crystal monsters?"

"I have no idea," Aeiko confessed. "I wouldn't have given it a second thought if you hadn't just called those things fake Jekuas." They clicked around some more, then said, "Ahh, here we go. Artificial Jekuas."

"You said the files were password-protected, though," Alani said. "If you can't get into them, then what's the point of pulling them up?"

"My own curiosity, I guess. And also, maybe I can glean something from the file names, who knows? Any crumb of info might be useful. And also, if..."

They trailed off, letting the rest of their sentence dangle in the air. They cocked an eyebrow as they stared at the glowing screen.

"What?" asked Balt, leaning in closer.

He couldn't tell what had captured their attention. The folder they were in was named "AJ01 - 28952896," which was gibberish to him. Listed within the folder was an absurd number of files with names and extension types that all seemed nonsensical. They all appeared to follow a rigid naming scheme, which apparently meant something to Aeiko, even if Balt was too stupid to decode it.

"I, uh…well, hmm."

Their words were not especially illuminating. "What?" Balt prompted them again.

They found their words a moment later. "So, the way Lakahlo's server works is that—alright, let me back up. Lakahlo has a ton of offices, right? Locations all over not only the archipelago, but across the world. But not every team is fully comprised of people who work at the same branch, some of them work together remotely. Or, in other cases, some teams' research overlaps, so multiple teams are touching the same files. The server automatically backs up on a routine schedule, and the way we keep track of who's used each file is with the timestamps on each file. They're set up to not just show what date and time someone last saved the file, but also what branch accessed it. That way, people have an easier time knowing which team was looking at stuff."

"Okay," said Balt. That all tracked, he guessed. A big company like Lakahlo Labs needed to know who was altering files and when.

Without another word, Aeiko then pointed at the right-hand side of the screen, at a long list of all the timestamps associated with each file in the folder.

Balt squinted, reading the tiny electronic text. Once

more, it made no sense to him. All the timestamps varied, but they followed the same general scheme: "YL01 – 56/SP/2905 – 8:02 PM"

"I don't know what any of that means," said Balt.

"Have you never read a date on a computer before?" Aeiko asked incredulously.

He groaned. "Okay, yes, clearly someone looked at whatever this is on, uh…" He trailed off, just as Aeiko had. "The fifty-sixth of Spring," he then said. "This past year."

"Yes," said Aeiko.

"But you said this project's been dead for years."

"Correct."

"That's weird."

"Yes. But that's not the weirdest part." They tapped their finger on the screen again, emphasizing the "YL01" portion of the timestamp.

"I don't know what that is," Balt reiterated.

"Yuluhu Lab number one?" Alani ventured a guess.

"Bingo," said Aeiko. "You're clearly the brains of the operation."

Balt stared at the string of letters and numbers for a few seconds. "So that…means that someone accessed the files this past Spring, from the lab on Yuluhu?"

"Nice of you to join us. Yes," Aeiko confirmed.

"But that doesn't make any sense. That lab's been shut down for years, ever since the incident that got the whole island quarantined. Nobody works there anymore."

"Precisely why I'm confused," said Aeiko. "You're right, that lab location is completely shut down. The building is still there, of course, but it's been closed for ages. But the system doesn't make mistakes like this—yeah, it might mess up the *time* every once in a while if someone's clock is out of sync, but there's no way it could glitch and say someone used the server on Yuluhu when really they were on Kou Tekkis, or something."

"Would they really be so brazen if that were the case, though?" Alani asked. "It's not like they've hidden their tracks, here."

Aeiko shrugged. "These folders have been buried deep in the project archives. They aren't exactly sitting around in the main directory. Any relevant discoveries from them have already been ported over to other projects, and the rest was deemed unusable or even outright dangerous. I doubt many people ever lay their eyes on these throughout their entire tenure at the company."

Balt let out a deep breath, then said, "Where's this lab located, exactly?"

Aeiko pondered for a moment. "I would have to check, but I think it's somewhere on the northwest side of the island?"

He turned to Alani and asked, "Where's our next shrine destination?"

"Lopatowk," she answered.

"And where's that?" He really did not know a single thing about Yuluhu.

"Elder Neiata said it was on the northeastern coast."

"Well, hell. Alright, that's still, like, not too far, I guess. It's not like Yuluhu's very big." In fact, it was the smallest of the Volukho Isles. "Maybe we can hit both up."

Alani looked at him like he was crazed. "Why would we go to the lab?" she asked.

Now it was Balt's turn to look at her like she was

losing her mind. "Are you not curious about this at *all*?" he asked.

"I don't think it's any of our business."

"The Facet very much made it our business when they attacked us yesterday," said Balt. "If they didn't want us involved in their bullshit, then they shouldn't have gotten us involved in their bullshit."

"I don't think it's smart," said Alani.

"I don't either," Balt agreed. "But if we're bein' forced onto the island by the Church anyway, we might as well check it out while we're there, right? See if somethin' fishy's goin' on? I bet the Church would be very interested in knowing if that's where their Veptilos were hauled off to, and I'm sure Lakahlo would want to know if some insane group is using their resources. Right?" He was looking at Aeiko now.

They muttered, "Uh, I mean…probably?"

The last thing Balt wanted to do was put Alani or himself in any further danger, but another part of him had to know what was going on. Clearly something shady was happening at that lab, and he had a bone to pick with the Facet. If they hadn't invoked his wrath before on Qwi, they certainly had now.

He said, "If we want answers about all of this—what the Facet's doing with the Veptilos, who they even are, all of it—then we'll find the answers there." He jabbed a finger at the incriminating timestamps.

"But why us?" Alani asked him, growing exasperated. "Why do you feel like we have to be involved with this at all?"

"We're *already* involved!" he said, trying his best to

resist shouting. "They've attacked you multiple times! They stole from the Church! They attacked a Jekua tournament! We've already been dragged into this mess."

"We don't have to *stay* involved, though," she said. "We can let the authorities handle it from here. Just pass this info along to them and let them sort it out. Aren't the timestamps proof enough?"

Balt's blood was boiling. It had been simmering the whole afternoon, and he wanted nothing more than to explode on these Facet assholes.

Alani was right, though. This was just his reckless streak rearing its ugly head yet again. But he still couldn't understand how she was acting so calm and collected after what those people had done to her.

He said, "Aren't you mad?"

She blinked, then furrowed her brow. "What?"

"Aren't you mad at them? For what they did to you?" He indicated the strange scars on her arm. "For what they did to the Church? What they did to Niona? Not to mention all the other Summoners who were there yesterday, and all the innocent people who got hurt for the sake of whatever it is these selfish pricks are doing."

Alani looked away, staring at the floor as she spoke. "Of course I'm mad," she said. Her voice was shaky.

Finally, a little emotion out of her.

"I don't see what giving in to that anger does, though."

"It gets us answers," Balt said.

"What if I don't want answers?"

"I think that you do."

Alani looked up from the floor and back at the computer screen.

"Maybe I do," she finally said. "But this isn't our place."

"We're right at the center of this, Alani. You can't deny that. It's not *about* us, sure, but we've been involved for weeks now. Look, I..." He took a beat before continuing. He felt foolish admitting this next part, but it was the truth. A truth that he hadn't even fully realized until he started vocalizing it. "When I first saw those crystal creatures, the fake Jekuas, all I could think about was Pakree Island. They look like they're made out of the same exact crystals that swallowed up the island, don't you think?"

Alani and Aeiko both exchanged a look, but all Alani could do was shrug. "Maybe," she said, soft as a mouse.

"Well, I do," Balt said. "The crystals on Pakree are different from the random crystal spires we see on the islands, like the arch in Tanepke or those ones on the beach in Mapa. It's plain to see they're not the same. But these monsters, whatever the Facet's using...they look the same. They look the same as those crystals all over Pakree, and I have to know why. I've never known what really happened to my grandparents, and maybe I never will, and that's...it's not *fine,* but it is what it is. But this is the biggest clue I've ever stumbled upon. The *only* clue, honestly. Even if the chances are slim to none that this has anything to do with my grandparents, I know I'll regret it if I don't see it through."

Alani was silent, looking at him with a frown. She looked away momentarily, then locked her eyes on his again.

Finally, she said, "I can't believe you pulled the grandparent card on me."

Against all odds, that made him laugh. He said, "Sorry. Had to do it."

She pondered his argument for another few seconds. "You really think that the Facet might have something to do with what happened to your grandparents?"

"I don't know," he admitted. "All I know is that their creatures look like they're made out of the same sort of crystal."

Alani nodded, then said, "We don't even know that it's the Facet at that lab, though. The two things might be totally unrelated."

"It'd be an awfully big coincidence," said Balt.

"Sure, but coincidences *do* happen. That's why we have a word for it."

"Fair enough." He turned his attention back to Aeiko and said, "It's *gotta* be the Facet, though, right? Who the hell else would it be?"

They leaned back in their chair, sighing, and said, "I can't say for sure who it is, but it definitely seems like someone has been experimenting with Artificial Jekuas on Yuluhu. Tucked away in a lab that no one monitors, on an island that no one goes to."

"Yeah," said Balt, "and I think it's about time someone paid them a visit."

EXCERPTS FROM REMISTI VANA'S BESTIARY

V = FEMALE
X = MALE

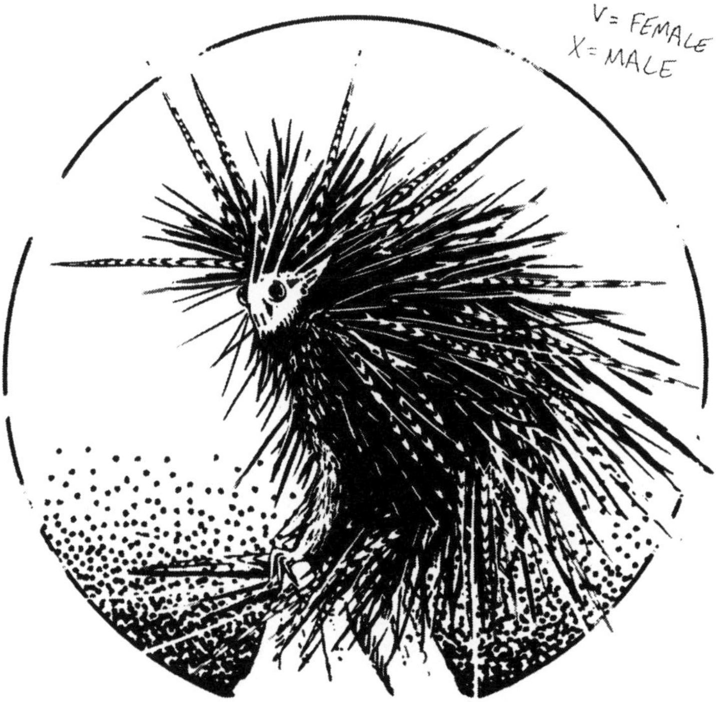

POKIBUVV

GRAVITY

KOU TEKKIS

Large, intelligent rodent with a coat of sharp quills that protect it from predators. They are typically found in forests, but on rare occasions have been found living in nearby mountains, using their Gravity magic to construct shelter out of rocks. When attacked, their bodies instinctively produce gravity fields that either repel or attract their attacker, at which point they use their quills to either fire upon or impale them, respectively. It has been found that males create attraction fields, while females create repulsion fields. Males are unable to fire their quills at predators, but it is a common technique amongst females.

Common abilities:

- Gravity attraction/repulsion fields (see above)

XAMANEKI

RADIANT/SONIC

NA TANA / PAKREE

No two Xamanekis look the same, although they all share a few distinct characteristics: mushroom growths, hollow eyes, and pig snouts. Some have horns or tusks as well. Groups of anywhere from thirty to eighty Xamanekis tend to live together, creating a community that sticks together through several generations. They are highly elusive Jekuas, tending to live in hiding for most of their lives. The most common time to spot a colony is during the rain, which attracts them and initiates a strange ritual. It is currently unknown why Xamanekis react this way to the rain.

Common abilities:

- Illuminating its body to stun and blind enemies
- Manipulating light to camouflage itself, rendering it invisible

BIG BUT SOFT. PIERCE BODY W/ HORNS OR TAKE A SPIKE FROM ITS SHELL

TYRIAN SNAIL

USUALLY HEADS TO SHORE DURING/AFTER STORMS

TIDAL

ALL ISLANDS

Megafauna murex snails that live in the ocean. They crawl along the ocean floor and release a purple pigment into the water, which gives the world's oceans their lavender color. They are as large as a typical Jenu, but not nearly as powerful or diverse in their skillset, although they possess many strong Tidal abilities. They are quite docile, so they are easy for a Summoner to capture, but given their location at the bottom of the ocean it's incredibly rare for someone to encounter one, though there are occasional sightings closer to shore. Tyrian Snails mate for life, and copulation typically lasts for 12 hours at a time.

Common abilities:

- Creating a massive, watery cyclone
- Retreating into its spiky shell, then rolling over its enemies

ACKNOWLEDGMENTS

Nothing seems to go very well for this group, huh? At least they've concluded their business on Na Tana and can hold their heads high on their way to the next island. Never mind that it's plague-ridden.

Writing this book was an extraordinary challenge, considering that my greatest insecurities as a writer come from trying to do action scenes. So why not write a 700-page book that takes place entirely during a tournament filled with countless battle chapters? Good idea!

I fell in and out of love with this book multiple times throughout the writing process, but as I sit here writing these acknowledgments, I find myself really proud of how the story turned out. I pushed myself in many ways, and I think it resulted in one of the coolest books I've written yet. And it's by far the longest, too, so that's kind of neat.

There are many people I have to thank for the book turning out as good as it did. As always, the first person I have to thank is John Bierce, who always reads the first (and worst) drafts of these books and lets me know where I can improve, while also bolstering my confidence by hyping up the parts he loved. His words of encouragement always manage to make me feel like perhaps I'm not a total failure after all, and that maybe this series actually *does* have something to offer. Imagine that!

Next, a huge amount of thanks to my crew of beta readers. Thank you to Emily Atwood, Tobias Begley, Tyler Gruenzner, and Tim Simmons for taking the time to read this enormous book and be brutally honest about what wasn't working. In all honesty, this book is the most I've ever needed to revise a book, but without my beta readers' critiques it wouldn't be nearly as strong as (I think) it turned out to be.

And many thanks to my fellow author pals, for always being there to share advice, show off cool stuff in advance, or complain to: Zamil Akhtar, Jon Auerbach, Steven McKinnon, Phil Williams, and Dave Woolliscroft. Each of them are brilliant storytellers, so please look up their books if you have yet to do so. Seriously, you're missing out!

Also, huge thanks to Podium for taking a chance on the audiobooks for this series. If you haven't checked them out, you're missing out on some amazing performances from Graham Halstead and Rebecca Woods, so I highly recommend you go give them a listen! Might as well experience the fun all over again in another format, right?

The Jekua series wouldn't be anywhere near as successful as it has been without the support of bloggers and the fantasy community at large. Thank you to Sakina from A Reader's Reflections, Calvin Park, Jordan from Forever Lost in Literature, Ezeekat on TikTok, and also to the folks on R/Fantasy and R/Progressionfantasy. Thank you all for taking a chance on these books and sharing them with other readers.

And unending thanks to everyone who subscribes to my Patreon, helping fund the incredible art I am blessed with for this series and my dog's medication/vet bills. And of course, an extra special shoutout to those in the Blighted tier: Anna, Candis, Colleen, Doug, Jacob, Liv, Madison, Mountain, Saffron, Sydney, Tim, and Tobias.

About a month before this book's release, we had to say goodbye to our dog. I co-adopted him with my best friend during college, and he'd been with us for almost 12 years. He had two sets of parents who loved him dearly, and I know everyone says this about their pet, but it's true when I say he was the sweetest guy you ever could've met (although he was the dumbest, too, but we liked that). He's been around for the writing of all my books, and he's been by my side through every up and down for the past decade. I miss him a lot, and this book is dedicated to that little fool.

Just so we don't end this on a complete downer, I of course need to thank you for reading this book. If you enjoyed it, I only ask that you tell all your friends and enemies about it. If you're able, I'd also request you leave a rating and/or review on Amazon or Goodreads. You have no idea how valuable those are to indie authors like me. I would truly appreciate it.

See you on Yuluhu!

ABOUT THE AUTHOR

Travis M. Riddle lives with his girlfriend in Austin, TX, where he earned his bachelor's degree in English Writing & Rhetoric at St. Edward's University. His work has been published in award-winning literary journal the Sorin Oak Review. His previous novels "Spit and Song" and "Flesh Eater" were semi-finalists in Mark Lawrence's SPFBO.

twitter.com/traviswanteat
instagram.com/traviswanteat
patreon.com/travismriddle

Made in the USA
Monee, IL
13 March 2023

29588957R10430